Writing Shame

Phaidra: 'Out of what is shameful I am contriving something good.'
(Euripides, *Hippolytos*, trans. Anne Carson, in *Grief Lessons*)

Writing Shame

Contemporary Literature, Gender
and Negative Affect

Kaye Mitchell

EDINBURGH
University Press

Edinburgh University Press is one of the leading university presses in the UK. We publish academic books and journals in our selected subject areas across the humanities and social sciences, combining cutting-edge scholarship with high editorial and production values to produce academic works of lasting importance. For more information visit our website: edinburghuniversitypress.com

Edinburgh University Press Ltd
The Tun – Holyrood Road
12(2f) Jackson's Entry
Edinburgh EH8 8PJ

First published in hardback by Edinburgh University Press 2020

Typeset in 11/14 Adobe Sabon by
IDSUK (DataConnection) Ltd, and
printed and bound by CPI Group (UK) Ltd,
Croydon, CR0 4YY

A CIP record for this book is available from the British Library

ISBN 978 1 4744 6184 9 (hardback)
ISBN 978 1 4744 6185 6 (paperback)
ISBN 978 1 4744 6186 3 (webready PDF)
ISBN 978 1 4744 6187 0 (epub)

Contents

Acknowledgements   vi

Introduction: Beginning with Stigma   1

1   Forgetting and Remembering Lesbian Pulp: Shame,
    Recuperation and Queer History   45

2   Cleaving to the Scene of Shame: Stigmatised Childhoods
    in *The End of Alice* and *Two Girls, Fat and Thin*   97

3   'The Dumb Cunt's Tale': Desire, Shame and Self-Narration
    in Contemporary Autofiction   149

4   The Shame of Being a Man: Humiliation and/as Heroism   199

Conclusion: The Shame is (Not) Over   245

Bibliography   255
Index   279

Acknowledgements

This book enjoyed a gestation period that some might deem to be shamefully extended, beginning as a diversionary interest in lesbian pulp fiction and a quite serious concern with the directions and possible futures of queer theory, and becoming, ultimately, a gradually coalescing desire to bring together questions of gender, shame and writing in ways that might have some political utility in the world beyond the text.

During its writing, I benefited enormously from two crucial sabbaticals: in 2011, as a Visiting Scholar at New York University's Center for the Study of Gender and Sexuality; and from January 2014 to August 2015 as a Humboldt Fellow in Berlin. Many thanks to Carolyn Dinshaw, Ann Pellegrini and Robert D. Campbell for making that NYU stay possible, and for inviting me back to present my work in progress in 2012; thanks also to Heather Love for being a really magnanimous and insightful respondent in 2012; the book first took shape during my time at NYU. Special thanks, too, to the Lesbian Herstory Archives in New York, where I spent many happy weeks pillaging their pulp collection, and to the fantastic archivist there, Desiree Yael Vester; thanks also to the staff of the Sallie Bingham Center for Women's History and Culture at Duke University, where I was able to read some out-of-print and otherwise hard to find 1950s pulp material.

The biggest thanks, though, must go to the Alexander von Humboldt Foundation, whose provision of an Experienced Researcher Fellowship allowed me to spend a luxurious amount of time concentrating solely on research, as a fellow in the Institut für Anglistik und Amerikanistik at Humboldt-Universität zu Berlin. I was fortunate enough to have a wonderful host there – Eveline Kilian – whose welcome and encouragement made me feel instantly at home; long may the connection and collaborations continue. Thanks also to my generous referees who supported that fellowship application: Ann Cvetkovich, Laura Doan and Patricia Waugh. The bulk of the research for the book and much of the writing of it happened during the period of the Humboldt Fellowship, and I am hugely grateful for the gift of that time for dedicated research and reflection.

At various points in the last few years I have also presented work from this project at Birkbeck, the University of Exeter, Freie Universität Berlin, Humboldt-Universität zu Berlin, King's College London, the University of Leicester, Liverpool John Moores University, Newcastle University, Queen Mary University of London and the University of Roehampton, as well as at the (sadly now defunct) Queer Up North festival in Manchester, Liverpool's Homotopia festival, and events for LGBT History Month at Lancashire Archives and in Nottingham. Thanks to all those who invited me to present my research, and to all who asked questions and made comments, helping me to refine and revise my thinking in crucial respects. Excerpts from and earlier versions of the material here – as well as corollary musings on shame and gender – have also been published in several collections or journals; thanks in particular to the editors of those publications for their feedback – Heike Bauer and Matt Cook, David Glover and Scott McCracken, Jodie Medd, Rebecca Pohl and Christopher Vardy, Katrin Röder and Christine Vogt-William, Suzanne Keen and Emma Parker, Barry Sheils and Julie Walsh.

I was immensely fortunate to work with Jackie Jones and Ersev Ersoy at Edinburgh University Press on *British Avant-Garde Fiction of the 1960s* (2019), so it is a real pleasure to be able to publish this book with EUP too. Thank you to them, and to the anonymous readers whose diligent, generous feedback helped me tune and tweak the manuscript of *Writing Shame* in the final stages. Thanks to Wendy Lee for her eagle-eyed copy-editing.

My colleagues at the University of Manchester have, as ever, been incredibly supportive, collegial, forgiving and stimulating; I feel very lucky to have stumbled into such a great department. Thanks, in particular, to David Alderson, Anke Bernau, Daniela Caselli, Emma Clarke, Laura Doan, Honor Gavin, Jerome de Groot, John McAuliffe, Monica Pearl, Alan Rawes, Jackie Stacey, Chris Vardy and Jeanette Winterson.

Looking beyond Manchester, I am grateful to Laura Salisbury for friendship and inspiration over many years, despite the distance; I owe extra-special thanks to Katherine Angel and Jennifer Cooke, for brilliant conversations and formative thinking about sex, shame and life-writing, and for invaluable feedback on Chapter 3; and I am immensely grateful to Maria Alexopoulos, who provided the generous, careful, kind feedback on the Introduction and Conclusion that helped nudge me over the finishing line. Thanks to Paul Fullbrook for the striking cover image. Thanks too to Pete Bennett for oining, nipping, word-of-the-day and other lovely distractions from writing.

I would like to dedicate this book, though, to the expanding constellation of Berlin friends, the people who have contrived to make that city such a joyful and transformative place for me, and who always have something to say about shame: Maria Alexopoulos (whose friendship is so important I have to thank her twice, for dinners on the balcony as well as editorial suggestions); Julia Bell (for a conversation begun one night in Neukölln, which I hope will continue indefinitely); Amélie Bonet (for bike rides and lake-swimming); Orlando Lovell (for book-browsing companionship and perfect postcards); Judith Schmitt (for the most welcoming Stammtisch); Philip Venables (for inspiration across art forms); and, above all, Mark Chadwick and Graeme Vaughan for love, late nights, sarcasm and the best holidays.

And finally: thanks and love to Mitch and Fiona Mitchell for never being *too* ashamed of me, no matter what I say or do.

Introduction: Beginning with

'What's the point of accentuating the negative, of beginning with stigma [. . .]?'[1]

Shame culture and contemporary subjectivity

Writing Shame takes as its subject the gender and sexual politics of shame in diverse texts – theoretical, literary, pulp and autofictional – published (or, in the case of the lesbian pulp novels, republished) since 1990. If shame is 'an inner torment, a sickness of the soul',[2] it is also an emotion of self-assessment, a peculiarly *social* experience and, I suggest, a culturally pervasive affect with particular pertinence for understanding contemporary constructions of gendered subjectivity, expressions and experiences of sexual desire, the complexities of embodiment, and social processes of 'othering'. Putting this literary material in conversation with a range of feminist, queer theoretical, psychoanalytic and philosophical accounts of shame, this book analyses the political uses, fraught eroticism and disjunctive narrative forms of this most intriguing of affects. In particular, the triangulation of gender, shame and writing lies at the heart of the project, and in what follows I seek to identify both the inextricability of shame and writing – contrary to analyses that figure the writing of shame as a redemptive act – and the structural, constitutive (not merely regulative) role that shame plays in the formation of femininity in particular.

First, though, I want to establish the significance of shame within contemporary culture and to map its definitional connections with selfhood. 'Today, shame (and shamelessness) has displaced guilt as a dominant emotional reference in the West,' writes Ruth Leys, and she describes this as a 'major paradigm shift'.[3] In *Writing Shame*, that paradigm shift – and the corollary suggestions that, more and more, we in the West inhabit a kind of 'shame culture', that (paradoxically) we organise our (increasingly fractured) sense of self around and through shame, that the popular cultural realm is marked both by displays of apparent shamelessness and by public acts of shaming – forms the context and premise to my arguments concerning shame, gender and writing in the contemporary period. According to Leys:

> Shame's rise to prominence in the United States is a relatively recent phenomenon. To be sure, the emotion of shame figures importantly in numerous philosophical, literary, critical and other writings extending all the way back to the ancient Greeks. But from the start of the twentieth century until the early 1960s, shame was rarely differentiated from guilt, appearing instead as a minor variant of the latter. The subordination of shame to guilt reflected the dominance of psychoanalysis and the significance Freud attached to guilt (or anxiety) as the decisive psychic affect.[4]

It is a shift evident, she claims, 'in the medical and psychiatric sciences, literary criticism, and even philosophy away from the "moral" concept of guilt in favour of the ethically different or "freer" concept of shame'.[5] This distinction between shame and guilt arises frequently in the theorisation of shame; the most straightforward way of understanding the distinction is that guilt concerns *something you have done*, while shame concerns (again, in Leys's words, but this is a common formulation) 'not your actions but *who you are*, that is, your deficiencies and inadequacies as a person as these are revealed to the shaming gaze of the other'.[6] Sandra Bartky offers a fuller analysis in her explanation that

> [s]hame is called forth by the apprehension of some serious flaw in the self, guilt by the consciousness that one has committed a transgression. The widely held notion that shame is a response to external and guilt to internal sanctions is incorrect: Shame and guilt are alike in that each involves a condemnation of the self by itself for some failure to measure up; it is the measures that differ.[7]

In other words, the question of shame is utterly imbricated with questions of identity and selfhood – particularly, but not only, *flawed* selfhood. Leys claims that the shift from a guilt culture to a shame culture constitutes 'a shift of focus from actions to the self that makes the question of personal identity of paramount importance'.[8] It is no surprise, then, that shame achieves a kind of prominence in a period when 'personal identity' is *already* viewed as being 'of paramount importance' – but also a period in which the stability of identity is severely tested: by poststructuralism and constructivist theories of identity formation; by intersectionality in the realm of identity politics; and by a neoliberal variant of late capitalism that refigures the self as possession, as a commodity in need of continual (re)construction or (re)fashioning. The contemporary preoccupation with shame is, on my reading, inextricable from – and perhaps even a product of – a longer-standing preoccupation with questions of selfhood and identity. Shame, like trauma before it, becomes a kind of 'key' to identity, its organising principle, its origin – as well as its undoing. In Eve Sedgwick's pithy formulation:

> Shame is a bad feeling attaching to what one is: one therefore *is* *something*, in experiencing shame. The place of identity, the structure 'identity', marked by shame's threshold between sociability and introversion, may be established and naturalized in the first instance *through shame*.[9]

In an era in which identity is felt to be imperilled, then, shame paradoxically offers a kind of ground – an affect around and through which selfhood might, temporarily, precariously, coalesce.

The philosophical exploration of shame's relationship to selfhood has an established history. In 1935, Emmanuel Levinas writes that shame has to do with 'the impossibility of fleeing oneself':

> What appears in shame is thus precisely the fact of being riveted to oneself, the unalterably binding presence of the I to itself. [. . .] It is [. . .] our intimacy, that is, our presence to ourselves, that is shameful. It reveals not our nothingness but rather the totality of our existence. [. . .] What shame discovers is the being who *uncovers* himself.[10]

Shame is therefore not simply about wrongdoing or about the self's flaws; it 'does not depend – as we might believe – on the limitation of our being, inasmuch as it is liable to sin, but rather on the very being of our being, on its incapacity to break with itself'.[11] Shame is built into the experience of selfhood – or rather, into the experience of selfhood as both necessary ground and necessary limitation. But shame – poised, as Sedgwick says, 'between sociability and intro-version' – is also centrally concerned with questions of self–other relations, self-awareness, self-consciousness, and visibility to others; the experience of shame is, at least partly, the experience of becoming an object for others, even if that 'other' is in some instances an internalised 'other'. Thus, one of the best-known philosophical accounts of shame – found in Jean-Paul Sartre's *Being and Nothingness* of 1943 – notes first the intentional' structure of shame (in the philosophical/phenomenological sense), the fact that it is 'a shameful apprehension *of* something and this something is *me*. I am ashamed of what I *am*. Shame therefore realizes an intimate relation of myself to myself. Through shame I have discovered an aspect of *my* being';[12] he then clarifies that, despite shame being apparently a 'phenomenon of reflection [. . .], it is in its primary structure shame *before somebody*. [. . .] I am ashamed of myself *as I appear* to the Other.'[13] As Sartre explains it, 'shame is shame *of oneself before the Other*; these two structures are inseparable';[14] and he proceeds to describe shame as 'the recognition of the fact that I am indeed that object which the Other is looking at and judging'.[15] While this may seem to be a peculiarly negative experience – even an experience of *subjection* (both becoming an 'object' for others and suffering 'the impossibility of fleeing oneself') – it is also a necessary one, arguably forming part of the process and experience of *subjectivation* (that is, the process of becoming a subject). As Gershen Kaufman tells us: 'no other affect is more disturbing to the self, none more central for the sense of identity', in the way that shame works, simultaneously, to shore up and to threaten a sense of self in relation to, and in contradistinction from, others.[16] Shame thus speaks to a tension that lies at the heart of the experience of being a subject, as the Italian philosopher Giorgio Agamben posits:

> We can therefore propose a first, provisional definition of shame. It is nothing less than the fundamental sentiment of being *a subject*, in the two apparently opposed senses of this phrase: to be subjected and to be sovereign. Shame is what is produced in the absolute concomitance of subjectification and desubjectification, self-loss and self-possession, servitude and sovereignty.[17]

Shame is fundamental to the constitution and maintenance of the self as a distinct, discrete entity, while also (at least potentially) threatening that self (its stability, its boundaries, its autonomy). As Agamben writes, 'In shame, the subject thus has no other content than its own desubjectification; it becomes witness to its own disorder, its own oblivion as a subject,' and he claims that 'This double movement, which is both subjectification and desubjectification, is shame.'[18] Shame speaks to this apparent paradox of subjectivation that Agamben identifies: we are 'subjects' only in relation to others, whose recognition grants us that status as subjects, to whose gaze we are *subjected*; we achieve what 'sovereignty' we have only through that relationality, recognition and subjection. Furthermore, the acute self-consciousness of shame announces a moment in which the self comes into being (through this consciousness, this viewing of oneself as object for one's own gaze) *and* is undone by the intensity, the intimacy of that self-scrutiny. For Agamben (as for Levinas and Sartre), shame is 'an ontological question concerning the subject's relation to its own being or non-being'.[19]

As I will argue in due course, however, this ontological grounding of shame does not mean that it is experienced in the same way by everyone, because one's 'relation to [one's] own being or non-being' is also a social and political question, relative to culture and context. Shame is fundamental to the operation of social relations: we cannot and should not do without shame (there is no particular advantage and certainly no virtue in being *shameless*) as it helps to regulate our social behaviour and interactions with others; however, an excess of shame can prove similarly disabling. Meanwhile the shaming of others can all too often be a way of asserting power over them. As Martha Nussbaum explains:

> Some people [. . .] are more marked out for shame than others. Indeed, with shame as with disgust, societies ubiquitously select certain groups and individuals for shaming, marking them off as 'abnormal' and demanding that they blush at what and who they are.[20]

Emphasising that social regulation function, Freud, in the *Five Lectures on Psychoanalysis*, suggests that shame and disgust are like 'watchmen', maintaining the 'repression' of certain instincts and directing the 'flow' of 'sexual demands' at puberty into 'what are called normal channels' (so shame is just one of the ways that so-called 'normality' is produced and policed);[21] shame's 'function' is 'as a dam against immoral, exhibitionistic excitement'.[22] One argument of *Writing Shame*, however, is that those identified and identifying as women are 'more marked out for shame' than others, despite not falling into a category that might present itself as 'abnormal', that they must 'blush at what and who they are' in a way that men are not required to do, and that the shaming of women is not merely a matter of social regulation, because to describe it as such would imply the existence of some 'proper' or compliant way of being a 'woman' that did not invite shame; I will discuss this gendering of shame further in the next section.

Freud actually has relatively little to say about shame, preferring to direct his attention to the subject of guilt, yet an interest in shame forms part of the popular Freudianism of the 1950s, and from the 1950s onwards psychoanalysis pays increasing attention to shame – one landmark publication being Helen Merrell Lynd's *On Shame and the Search for Identity* (1953). In recent years, the work of psychologist and personality theorist Silvan Tomkins – notably his *Affect, Imagery, Consciousness – Volume II: The Negative Affects* (1963) – has been hugely influential, particularly since the publication of the third volume of *Affect, Imagery, Consciousness* in 1991 and the rediscovery of his work by Eve Kosofsky Sedgwick.[23]

The late twentieth- and early twenty-first-century critical interest in shame has emerged in and across various fields and disciplines: in psychoanalysis;[24] in philosophical work which, contra Leys, does still tend to regard shame as a 'moral' emotion;[25] as part of Holocaust Studies;[26] in political theory;[27] within feminism;[28] in literary studies;[29] and within queer theory, as part of a wider interest in negative affect that seeks to complicate the pride discourse of earlier decades.[30] That growing cultural and critical preoccupation with shame that begins in the late 1980s can be distinguished from earlier psychoanalytical accounts in its various attempts to move away from a vision of shame as the 'guardian of morality' and the tool of normativity, as envisaged by Freud.[31] Queer theoretical accounts of shame, in particular, have tended to elide or sideline the arguments concerning moral agency that are integral to many philosophical accounts of shame – that is, the idea that shame functions to alert us to inappropriate behaviour or injustice, to make us aware of the needs of others, or to 'motivate an agent to seek a (re)considered moral identity and a closer approximation to an improved and improving moral ideal'.[32] Shame, in these more recent theorisations of it, does not necessarily function to make us better citizens or bring us into a more compassionate, unselfish relationship with the Other.

Furthermore, whilst psychoanalysis historically has aimed, at least in principle, at the reduction of shame in the individual (although not its eradication), recent cultural and critical investigations of shame have sought its positive potential, carefully sidestepping a psychoanalytical language of redemption, healing and recovery. As Leys explains, much of the recent theorising has offered 'a reevaluation that casts shame as at least potentially a positive, not a destructive emotion', and, she notes, 'for some theorists, indeed, shame serves at the limit as a site of resistance to cultural norms of identity'.[33] Some recent queer theoretical writing on shame, then – material that I will engage with in some depth in Chapter 1 – goes further than merely delineating the social causes and effects of shame or noting its pervasiveness: it embraces shame as a form of politics, gesturing towards its queer potential.

Leys's claim that the popularity of shame is due to the fact that it is 'a better affect than guilt to think with', 'a privileged operator [. . .] for diverse kinds of theoretical–interpretive undertakings', whether this is the theorisation of selfhood, morality, queer theory, 'survivor testimony', gender theory or trauma theory, helps to explain shame's popularity in scholarly contexts.[34] However, what Christopher Lasch has referred to as 'the current vogue of shame' (he is writing in 1992)[35] is evident also in the world beyond the academy: in the misery memoir boom of the 1990s (with its fixation on the shame of child abuse); in the wider trauma culture (a culture in which 'a trauma paradigm [. . .] has come to pervade the understanding of subjectivity and experience in the advanced industrial world' and in which 'extremity and survival' have become 'privileged markers of identity');[36] in what Mark Seltzer has termed, analogously, both a 'wound culture' and a 'pathological public sphere' (wherein shame and trauma often overlap);[37] in the rise of reality television (with its practices of exposure, humiliation and shameful spectacle); in the resurgence of confession (across multiple media);[38] and in an explosion of online communication, whose forms, ease of access, public nature, seeming unaccountability and apparent anonymity have dramatically multiplied the possibilities and manifestations of both self-exposure and the shaming of others.

In *So You've Been Publicly Shamed* (2015), Jon Ronson writes of his realisation, around 2012, that

> [s]omething of real consequence was happening. We were at the start of a great renaissance of public shaming. After a lull of 180 years (public punishments were phased out in 1837 in the United Kingdom and 1839 in the Unites States) it was back in a big way. When we deployed shame, we were utilizing an immensely powerful tool. It was coercive, borderless, and increasing in speed and influence.[39]

Although, initially, Ronson thinks that online shaming amounts to 'the silenced [. . .] getting a voice' and 'the democratization of justice', he swiftly realises 'how vicious the resurgence of public shaming had suddenly turned', and how 'when shamings are delivered like remotely administered drone strikes nobody needs to think about how ferocious our collective power might be. The snowflake never needs to feel responsible for the avalanche.'[40] Ronson's book sounds a warning note in its uncovering of the personal devastation resulting from incidents of online shaming. Countering claims that 'young people don't feel shame any more', or that we are inhabiting 'a shameless society',[41] Ronson in fact insists that 'shame hasn't died. Shame has just moved elsewhere, gathering tremendous strength along the way.'[42] The tacit implication here is that the internet not merely provides new outlets and arenas for manifestations of shame that already existed, it also serves to intensify, diversify, alter and proliferate those manifestations.

However, it is not only in the realms of mass and social media that the 'great renaissance of public shaming' can be found. Nussbaum notes how, in the contemporary period, 'shaming penalties are frequently defended as valuable expressions of social norms by political theorists whose general position might be described as communitarian', and this 'revival of shaming' is defended 'on the grounds that society has lost its communitarian moorings by losing a shared sense of shame at bad practices'; 'shame penalties' – that is, using shame as a form of punishment or using punishments that shame the perpetrator of a crime – are thus presented as '[promoting] a revival of our community's common moral sense'.[43] This is despite the existence of 'a wide range of legal practices that currently protect citizens from shame'.[44] Nussbaum argues, in fact, that 'a liberal society has particular reasons to inhibit shame and to protect its citizens from shaming',[45] and yet both Nussbaum and Ronson – in their very different works – consider examples of legal practices that seek to shame the wrongdoer as part of their punishment, so the law does not always work 'to protect its citizens from shaming'; sometimes it makes use of the power of shame to humiliate, penalise and correct. Thus Ronson interviews a Texan judge whose 'nationally famous trademark was to publicly shame defendants in the showiest ways he could dream up' – for example, by making them carry signs in public detailing their crimes,[46] while Nussbaum notes the endorsement of shame penalties by Dan M. Kahan of Yale law school:

> In a wide range of legal areas, ranging from sex offenses to drunken driving to public urination, Kahan, like [Amitai] Etzioni, favours bringing back the brand on the face: offenders should be forced to wear signs on their property, or car, or to perform some clearly humiliating ritual before the public gaze.[47]

Both Ronson and Nussbaum express disapproval of these shaming penalties.

Jill Locke, similarly, notes 'a resurgence of preoccupation with shaming punishments in the past twenty years',[48] and argues that

> the defense of shaming punishments – by legal scholars, judges, and legislators – turns on the idea that the experience of shame is not an affront to dignity, but essential to it. Self-respect in this view requires that one has the capacity to feel ashamed when one has failed to live up to some necessary and agreed-upon social standard.[49]

Locke is critical of this attitude – and these punishments – not least because, in such instances, '[t]he state or the shaming party within civil society can behave in ways that are as unchecked, immoderate, and "shameless" as they wish', but her objection turns also on her reading of the place of shame in modern political discourse.[50] For Locke – echoing the anecdotal evidence offered by Ronson – 'the modern and late-modern eras' are marked by 'lamentations about the death of shame, calls for "more shame" or a "return to shame," typologies of "good" and "bad" shame that will resolve our problems', as well as by these debates about the 'effectiveness' of 'shaming punishments'.[51] Such calls *can* be 'well-intentioned', as attempts 'to shame the polity back into a just moral and political order by identifying both individual practices and collective attitudes that have prioritized the self against the public good',[52] but they are more often conservative in character and are directed against 'Feminism, liberalism, identity politics, multiculturalism, gay liberation, and the "therapeutic turn" toward a culture of self-esteem'.[53] What she later refers to as '*The Lament That Shame Is Dead*' is, thus,

> a nostalgic story of an imagined past that represents a longing for a mythical place and time when shame secured and regulated social life. It operates as a narrative of civilizational decline that expresses a fear of untethered, autochthonous, self-fashioning and self-authenticating subjects who wreak havoc on the social order and status quo.[54]

On this reading, the emergence of a shame culture is both a product of perceived liberalisation and a reaction against this, and it harks back to an impossible golden age of moral certainties; moreover, it speaks also to an apparent shift in the understanding of identity from fixed to 'self-fashioning', and to the anxieties surrounding this shift. Arlene Stein, writing specifically on the topic of sexual shame (and shamelessness) in contemporary American culture, suggests that while 'progressive social movements have tried to sever the link between sexuality and shame, [. . .] conservatives, in contrast, use shame as a weapon against liberalization.'[55]

However, this is not the whole story: as Chapter 1 will document, many queer theorists have, in recent years, sought to explore the prevalence and persistence of shame in queer communities, rather than '[severing] the link'; meanwhile, activists of various persuasions (environmental, feminist) have come to recognise the positive power of shaming. Locke acknowledges that the return to shame appeals not only 'to conservatives who fear the death of moral standards' but also to 'liberals committed to individual responsibility; democratic theorists attuned to the emotions; and poststructuralist and perspectivist accounts of ethics and politics as antiuniversalist and always embedded in particular social locations'.[56] For Jennifer Jacquet, in *Is Shame Necessary?* (2015), the coercive power of shame is, at least potentially, a force for positive structural (social and political) change in the contemporary moment. Jacquet, unusually, finds guilt rather 'more widespread in the West' than shame and 'more prevalent today than it was in the past';[57] she also characterises guilt as individual and leading to self-regulation, and suggests that collectivist cultures favour shame, while individualistic cultures favour guilt – a reading at odds with most accounts of guilt and shame, and at odds with my own argument, here, that the current shame culture is inextricable from the dominance of individualistic and identitarian modes of thinking in the second half of the twentieth century.[58] Nevertheless, in the context of Jacquet's environmental arguments, making individual consumers feel *guilty* about purchasing environmentally unfriendly products is held to be much less effective than *shaming* the producers of those products or the wider forces (institutions, governments, corporations) that cause environmental damage. *Is Shame Necessary?*, then, makes a case for the strategic utility of shaming, setting out 'seven habits of highly effective shaming':

> The transgression should (1) concern the audience, (2) deviate widely from desired behaviour, and (3) not be expected to be formally punished. The transgressor should (4) be part of the group doing the shaming. And the shaming should (5) come from a respected source, (6) be directed where possible benefits are highest, and (7) be implemented conscientiously.[59]

While public shaming undeniably has significant uses for activists, there are plenty of possible faultlines here, should Jacquet's 'habits' be taken up by those whose motivations and goals are less worthy: what counts as 'deviating widely', who decides this, and is deviation necessarily a problem or a threat? What or who counts as a 'respected source' to do the shaming and what counts as 'conscientious' implementation? It is interesting to compare this to the enforcing of gender norms, as transgression of gender norms certainly '[concerns] the audience', can be seen as a deviation from what is desirable, the transgressor is part of the group in a broad sense, and such deviations do not usually receive formal punishment, but rather something more like social disapproval. Jacquet would surely agree that the shaming of gender non-normativity is unacceptable, but her 'seven habits of highly effective shaming', despite – or even because of – the fact that they concern methodology rather than motivation or content, unwittingly reveal the ways in which shaming might be used to contain and punish 'deviance' and perpetuate a conservative status quo.

The various cases of online shaming considered by Ronson expose precisely shame's tendency to curb perceived 'deviance', as well as showing the myriad ways in which public shaming might go awry. Ronson's examples also reveal key continuities between offline/ predigital and online shaming. One case concerns Adria Richards, who overheard a couple of men behind her at a tech conference making sexual innuendo-laden jokes and tweeted a picture of them. One of the men subsequently lost his job. Having shamed the men for what she felt were inappropriate remarks at the conference, Richards was then herself publicly shamed on the internet forum 4chan, where the comments took on a notably sexualised and violent flavour: 'Let's crucify this cunt,' 'Cut out her uterus with an xacto knife'; in addition, Ronson tells us, 'Someone sent Adria a photograph of a beheaded woman with tape over her mouth. Adria's face was superimposed on to the bodies of porn actors.'[60] Interviewing a young woman who is on trial for internet hacking and online shaming, Ronson asks her why these 'modern shamings' on the internet are 'so breathtakingly misogynistic', with female targets routinely being threatened with rape and sexual violence.[61] She tells him that

> 4chan aims to degrade the target [. . .] [a]nd one of the highest degradations for women in our culture is rape. We don't talk about rape of men, so I think it doesn't occur to most people as a male degradation. With men they talk about getting them fired. [. . .] With Donglegate [as the tech conference incident became known] she pointlessly robbed that man of his employment. She degraded his masculinity. And so the community responded by degrading her femininity.[62]

Ronson does not develop the point, but the Adria Richards case and the responses to it reveal not only the gendering of shame – the different things that men and women are shamed for or ashamed about, the different forms that those shamings take – but also the ways in which effective shaming seeks both to devalue the target and to identify already latent sources of shame (note Bartky's assertion that 'shame requires the recognition that I *am*, in some important sense, as I am seen to be').[63] If the 'value' of men is connected to employment status, income and achievement, the 'value' of women is connected instead to body, sexuality and desirability.[64] Yet, for women, these are things that exist already in a fraught relation to shame; they are sources of shame *and* sources of pleasure. Bartky (again) writes of 'the peculiar dialectic of shame and pride in embodiment' for women, 'consequent upon a narcissistic assumption of the body as spectacle'.[65] Importantly, they are sources of shame even *before* the individual is subjected to some particular incident of shaming for alleged 'deviation'. In the chapters that follow, I aim above all to bring into the foreground the peculiar, ineluctable, persistent entanglement of femininity and shame – the ways in which femininity is already a 'degraded' state. On my reading, shame is not something that sits outside femininity, working to police it and punish impropriety; it is integral to it from its inculcation.

Let us return to Leys's analysis of the shift from a guilt culture to a shame culture with which I began, and to her suggestion that shame is 'ethically different' to, and 'freer' than, guilt.[66] She claims that

> what is crucially at stake in the current tendency to replace guilt with shame is an impulse to displace questions about our moral responsibility for what we *do* in favour of more ethically neutral or different questions about our personal attributes. Normally we cannot be held responsible for who we are in the same way we can be held responsible for what we do.[67]

However, while these questions regarding 'personal attributes' may appear to be 'more ethically neutral' than questions about actions, I argue, by contrast, that we *are* 'held responsible for who we are' in an era of neoliberal self-fashioning, an era in which the self (viewed as performative, viewed as a possession and/or commodity) is precisely something that we are supposed to work on, adapt and improve. The shift from a guilt culture to a shame culture does not get us off the hook; it simply changes the nature of the hook. And I argue also that women in particular are continually made accountable to a model of femininity that encodes moral failure from its inception; that 'failure' (experienced as shameful) is, then, part of what it is to be a 'woman' in our culture. It is therefore no coincidence that this transition to a shame culture happens in the same (postwar–contemporary) period in which successive feminist movements have – especially, but not only, in the Western world – brought about unprecedented levels of emancipation, autonomy and public visibility for women. The emergence and development of shame culture are, then, coincident with (but, more importantly, *inextricable from*) the rise of feminism and the perceived feminisation of the public sphere, and with the concurrent backlash against that feminism/feminisation. As Locke's extensive historical overview (from the classical to the modern world) in *Democracy and the Death of Shame* shows, the lament that 'shame is dead' as a scourge of apparent shamelessness emerges, crucially, 'during periods of increased egalitarianism or democratic expansion'.[68] If shame is the paradigmatic self-focused affect of our age, this is, at least in part, because of the prominent advances made by (some) women, and the persistent anxieties about those advances. And if shame is – according to Leys's glossing of recent shame theory – 'an attribute of personhood before the subject has done anything, or because he is incapable of acting meaningfully', then how does shame attach to female personhood in particular, regardless of the actions of specific women in specific situations, if it is in fact the *defining, foundational attribute* of that personhood?[69]

Shame and gender

As Sally Munt represents it, 'Shame can become embedded in the self like a succubus.' A succubus is, notably, a demon who takes on female form, usually to seduce men, the term dating back to late Middle English and coming from the medieval Latin for 'prostitute' (from *sub-* 'under' and *cubare* 'to lie'); in fact, the association between shame and femininity goes even further back, for, Munt reminds us, 'in classical thought shame is a woman'.[70] *Aidōs* (the Greek transliteration) or *Aedos* (the Latin version) is the classical personification of shame, modesty, reverence and humility – a *personification* rather than a *goddess*, strictly speaking, but always feminine; she is also sometimes called Aiskhyne (the transliteration of the Greek), Aeschyne (the Latin name), Pudor (the Roman version of Aiskhyne) or Pudicitia (the Roman version of *Aidōs*). There are references to her in Aeschylus' *Prometheus Bound*, Euripides' *Iphigenia at Aulis* and Sophocles' *Oedipus Rex*. Glossing the term, Douglas Cairns explains that

> [a]idōs is not shame (the two are very far from coextensive, and *aidōs*-words in Greek will bear a set of connotations different from those of shame in English), but the two concepts share many features in their phenomenology and associations. The notion of the 'other' or the audience is common to both, both are associated with the eyes and visibility, they share the characteristic symptom of blushing, and both may be attended by typical behaviour patterns such as averting the gaze or seeking to hide oneself.[71]

The association – as with modern 'shame' – with visibility, blushing and the averting of the gaze might already imply an association with characteristically *feminine* behaviour. Cairns notes, in addition, that in the classical world, 'Women's *aidōs* differs from that of men in its reference, and women can also be accorded *aidōs* as a special category on their own.'[72] In particular, women's *aidōs* is bound up with questions of sexual purity and sexual propriety, for 'the main virtue required of women [is] faithfulness'.[73]

Thus, in Euripides' play, *Hippolytos*, Phaidra – who has fallen in love with her stepson – confesses to her Nurse:

> Woman, hide my head again.
> I am ashamed of my own words.
> Hide me.
> Tears fall
> and my eye turns back for shame.[74]

Determining that the only way to protect her honour – and that of her husband, Theseus – is to kill herself, Phaidra asserts: 'Out of what is shameful I am contriving something good.'[75] Yet the shame of which Phaidra must absolve herself is really the shame of being a woman – particularly a woman who feels desire. As she opines:

> That my deed and my disease were dishonorable
> I knew.
> Realized too
> that as a woman
> I would be hated. I curse that one
> who first shamed her bed with another man.
> [. . .]
> I hate those women who talk self-control
> but get hot inside.[76]

Meanwhile, the object of Phaidra's desire – Hippolytos – asserts his piety and purity via his excoriation of the shamefulness of women, angrily proclaiming:

> O Zeus! Why have you settled on men this evil in daylight,
> this counterfeit thing – woman?
> If you wanted a human race
> there was no need to get it from them [. . .]![77]

A woman is, to Hippolytos, 'an evil', 'a flower of ruin', a 'degradation', the hyperbole of his hatred born of a kind of moral panic.[78] Hippolytos, writes Anne Carson, whose translation of Euripides I am quoting here, 'personifies Shame as the goddess who guards his private meadow of virtue [. . .]. Shame is a system of exclusions and purity that subtends Hippolytos' religion.'[79] On this reading, *aidōs* is both goddess of purity and avatar of degradation; Hippolytos can maintain his own virtue only by denouncing – excluding – the shamefulness of Phaidra (and of 'woman' more generally).

Carson parses the term *aidōs* further in the Preface to her translation of *Hippolytos*:

> *Aidos* ('shame') is a vast word in Greek. Its lexical equivalents include 'awe, reverence, respect, self-respect, shamefastness [*sic*], sense of honour, sobriety, moderation, regard for others, regard for the helpless, compassion, shyness, coyness, scandal, dignity, majesty, Majesty.' Shame vibrates with honour and also with disgrace, with what is chaste and with what is erotic, with coldness and also with blushing. Shame is felt before the eyes of others and also in facing oneself.[80]

This doubleness of shame is, of course, part of what interests me here: the fact that it is both deeply personal and ineluctably social/relational; its oscillation between discipline and desire, morality and amorality; the potential pleasures of shame, despite its ostensible negativity. As Carson claims, for Phaidra 'shame is a split emotion', both a good and a bad 'pleasure', and 'it is clear she believes shame of the bad kind can ruin her and that she must nullify it at any cost'.[81] The association with the erotic might give us particular pause (most of the literary texts that I will analyse in the course of this book treat of sexual desire, one way or another): Carson notes that '*aidos* turns up in Greek lyric poetry as a component of sexual pleasure',[82] and 'in epic poetry the word *aidos* is used in the plural (*aidoia*) as a euphemism for the sexual organs'.[83] Agamben, in his own philosophical account of shame, also cites Kerényi's comments on *aidōs*: 'The phenomenon of *aidos*, a fundamental situation of the Greeks' religious experience, unites respectively active vision and passive vision, the man who sees and is seen, the seen world and the seeing world – where to see is also to penetrate.'[84] Notably, neither Agamben nor Kerényi comments on the obvious gendering of this, whereby woman is shame (or, at least, modesty), and is also what is looked at and penetrated. Agamben merely paraphrases that: 'whoever experiences shame is overcome by his own being subject to vision', but women are 'subject to vision' to a degree and in ways that both express and compound their inherent shamefulness, I would suggest.[85]

In fact, it seems that *aidōs* and 'shame' – in its English sense – align quite closely with regard to women and women's sexual propriety, as the case of Euripides' Phaidra illuminates. Moreover, the shame that is particular to women brings dishonour not only to them, but to their husbands and male relatives too, and can be obviated only via the annihilation of self. As Phaidra concludes: 'For me, ladies, death is the answer. / I must not shame my husband / or children.'[86] As Cairns explains, in his discussion of the gendering of shame and honour in the ancient world:

> Although differences in the role and status of women have been detected between Homeric society and classical Athens, the relationship of women to male honour [. . .] remains a constant. A respectable woman's *aidōs* should protect her own honour, but this honour is, in all normal circumstances, bound up with that of a man.[87]

As will become evident in my discussion of authors such as Martin Amis, Philip Roth and (briefly) Joseph Conrad in Chapter 4, this matter of women's dishonour is not confined to the ancient world. In modern and contemporary literature, men's shame is still frequently displaced on to female bodies, while women's shame is seen to dishonour the men with whom they are connected (whose property they are assumed to be). Furthermore, as I will discuss in Chapters 2 and 3, when women choose to write about supposedly shameful topics – whether that is the novels with a focus on child abuse considered in Chapter 2, or the 'confessional' autofiction under analysis in Chapter 3 – they are thereby open to forms of social and critical disapproval of a significantly gendered nature, which tacitly take them to task for their perceived sexual impropriety.

In the modern era, psychoanalysis – although paying more attention to guilt than shame – has tended to reinforce the association between femininity and shame. According to Malcolm Pines, 'Freud linked the sense of narcissistic vulnerability and a sense of narcissistic inferiority to femininity and to the experience of genital deficiency';

'female morality' was therefore felt to be 'deficient in guilt and over-compensated by shame. Thus the primary shame of genital deficiency led to a secondary shame with the character traits of vanity, jealousy, revengefulness, secretiveness, passivity and submissiveness'.[88] It is that 'primary shame' that compels me here – the shame that is somehow built into the understanding and experience of feminine embodiment, whether or not that is viewed in these particular, reductive terms as 'genital deficiency' – a shame that is, in fact, *isomorphic with*, integral to, the structure and functioning of femininity, and not merely *associated with* it. According to Jennifer C. Manion, 'Sigmund Freud proclaims shame a feminine characteristic *par excellence*.'[89] But what Freud actually writes – according to the *Standard Edition* translation – is as follows: 'Shame, which is considered to be a feminine characteristic *par excellence* but is far more a matter of convention than might be supposed, has as its purpose, we believe, concealment of genital deficiency.'[90] This reads more like a statement about cultural beliefs and practices – 'is considered to be', 'a matter of convention' – than a statement of fact or of Freud's own beliefs. The deliberate rhetorical tentativeness of 'we believe' also presents the 'genital deficiency' argument as a speculative reading of the cultural convention of women's apparent shamefulness, as Freud seeks to discover what the 'purpose' of shame might be, what work it might do, psychologically and socially (for Freud, I would hazard, shame is more symptomatic than structural). Post-Freudian psychoanalytical writing, moving away from the description of femininity as characterised by a shameful sense of lack ('genital deficiency'), has nevertheless continued to present womanhood as marked by shame. Helen Block Lewis's work in the 1970s and 1980s hypothesised that

> [t]wo primary components contribute to shame-proneness in women [. . .]; first, girls are socialized from a very early age to define themselves less in terms of autonomy and independence but rather primarily in terms of their relationships with and dependence upon others, and second, this defining sense of interdependence makes girls especially vulnerable to social pressures, especially those urging them to conform to traditional conceptions of femininity.[91]

Relationality is posited as the key factor, here: that is, the suggestion that women are more defined by – and tend to define themselves by and through – their relations with others. They are defined by *interdependence* rather than *independence* and are therefore more vulnerable to the judgements of others. To this we might add the double-edged nature of feminine embodiment (as both empowering and disempowering, as source of pleasure and root of objectification or site of spectacle) and the particular *visibility* – or, more accurately, aesthetic self-consciousness – that attaches to femininity. This is most pithily explained in John Berger's famous formulation that '*men act* and *women appear*',[92] his claim that

> [a] woman must continually watch herself. She is almost continually accompanied by her own image of herself. [. . .] And so she comes to consider the *surveyor* and the *surveyed* within her as the two constituent yet always distinct elements of her identity as a woman.[93]

If, as Leys posits, 'shame is identical to exposure' and 'the feeling of shame is one of *already having been exposed* to the gaze of some real or fantasized other',[94] then we can begin to see why and how shame is built into the construction and experience of femininity: because femininity is, to a significant degree, defined by *self-consciousness* and by *the feeling of already having been exposed*. Gabriele Taylor claims that 'a person feeling shame will exercise her capacity for self-awareness, and she will do so dramatically: from being just an actor absorbed in what she is doing she will suddenly become self-aware and self-critical'.[95] Yet this inability to be 'just an actor absorbed in what she is doing', without self-consciousness, without watching herself (in a critical fashion), is exactly what Berger presents as characteristic of femininity. We can see, then, that woman's primary status as object-for-others – the visibility aspect of that and the relational aspect of that – makes womanhood a shamed state: not only, or not even, because of some alleged 'genital deficiency'. Writing in 2003, Manion notes that 'Associations between femininity and shame persist, at least in the collective imagination of contemporary American culture', while 'both men and women tend to hold stereotypes placing shame more centrally in women's affective lives than in men's'.[96]

Neither Berger nor Leys nor Taylor addresses directly the question of femininity's imbrication with shame, but this is Sandra Bartky's main focus in the sixth chapter of *Femininity and Domination* (1990), titled 'Shame and Gender'. Bartky, defining shame as 'a species of psychic distress occasioned by a self or a state of the self apprehended as inferior, defective, or in some way diminished', argues that 'women typically are more shame-prone than men' and that this type of shame is 'a pervasive affective attunement to the social environment'.[97] This is, she claims, 'a perpetual attunement' and must be distinguished from the experience of shame as a 'discrete occurrence'; while the latter may be an occasion for 'moral reaffirmation' and may facilitate 'a recommitment to principles', the former is unequivocally negative and isolating.[98]

For women, writes Bartky, feelings of shame are 'manifest in a pervasive sense of personal inadequacy that, like the shame of embodiment, is profoundly disempowering'; in Bartky's view, 'both reveal the "generalized condition of dishonour" which is woman's lot in sexist society'.[99] Manion, glossing Bartky's argument, presents this as a 'vulnerability to and powerlessness in response to negative judgments others make of us' and as the key sign of a 'correlation between shame and gender'.[100] In fact, I think 'correlation' is too weak a word here. What Bartky's argument edges towards, in its description of this 'perpetual attunement', this 'generalized condition of dishonour', and what my own argument in *Writing Shame* seeks to establish, is the claim that shame has an originary role in the production and shaping of femininity and female subjectivity. When Bartky argues that 'women, more often than men, are made to feel shame in the major sites of social life',[101] this is a fairly uncontroversial, empirical claim, which can be substantiated by reference to the various studies employed by Manion, Michael Lewis and others.[102] Where she goes further is in her assertion that '*it is in the act of being shamed and in the feeling ashamed that there is disclosed to women who they are and how they are faring within the domains they inhabit*'.[103] In the act or moment of feeling shame, women understand the 'condition of dishonour' by which their selfhood is marked, and 'what gets grasped' – the passive formulation is notable here – 'in the having of such feelings is nothing less than women's subordinate status in a hierarchy of gender, their situation not in ideology but in the social formation as it is actually constituted'.[104]

Inhabiting and exploring the feeling of shame – and the experience of womanhood *as* a 'condition of dishonour' – rather than simply trying to overcome shame (which is, in any case, impossible, given how integral it is to the process of subjectivation) might, then, have some value for feminists keen to understand, better, the situation of women within a patriarchal society. Shame has, I am suggesting, a vital revelatory function in this respect: if the feeling of shame 'discloses' to women 'who they are and how they are faring', then it is an ontological matter, properly speaking, that reveals what 'woman' is and means in the Western cultures that are my main focus here. It is not something that can be overcome or mitigated, and knowledge of it does not prevent us from feeling it;[105] nevertheless, the examination of shame's relationship to femininity might hold some further epistemological value for us in revealing 'the social formation as it is actually constituted' under patriarchy and as such might be a useful tool of analysis. Bartky, however, finds little political potential in shame. In the first place, she claims that 'The experience of shame may tend to lend legitimacy to the structure of authority that occasions it, for the majesty of judgment is affirmed in its very capacity to injure' – in other words, that patriarchal authority is maintained and strengthened via the wielding of shame against those who might otherwise undermine it.[106] In addition, she suggests that the 'heightened self-consciousness' of shame can become, for those who suffer it, 'a stagnant self-obsession', or it can 'generate a rage whose expression is unconstructive, even self-destructive'; shame is thus 'profoundly disempowering' in the way that it inhibits meaningful, effective action.[107] Finally, she notes the way that shame 'isolates the oppressed from one another and in this way works against the emergence of a sense of solidarity'.[108] While I agree that shame is *personally* 'disempowering' in these ways, and while I question the queer embrace of shame as a basis for solidarity (as I will discuss further in Chapter 1), I maintain that shame's imbrication with femininity is such that it serves to reveal the *structural* ways in which femininity is constituted and controlled in patriarchal societies.

Bartky ends by calling for 'a political phenomenology of the emotions – an examination of the role of emotion, most particularly of the emotions of self-assessment both in the constitution of subjectivity and in the perpetuation of subjection'.[109] *Writing Shame* builds on her work and on that request, but it does so by attending (as the title indicates) to the *writing* of shame in the late twentieth and early twenty-first centuries. If shame's 'disclosure' to women of 'who they are and how they are faring' is, as Bartky cautions, 'ambiguous and oblique', then literature seems a particularly apt field for an exploration and analysis of shame's functioning, able as it is to approach this topic both ambiguously and obliquely.[110] Moreover, as Barry Sheils and Julie

Walsh aver, 'If it's true that shame adheres to all bodies that write' – as they argue it does – 'then even a cursory look at the record of *what* gets published and *how* tells us that shame does not adhere to all writing bodies in the same way.'[111]

Shame and writing

To date, scholarship on the writing of shame has been preoccupied with the treatment of shame as a *theme* in literature.[112] While such readings can be instructive, they pay relatively little attention either to questions of form or to the effects or affects of a text and its reading and reception, and instead often seek to diagnose and psycho-analyse fictional characters. Joseph Adamson and Hilary Clark, for example, in their Introduction to *Scenes of Shame* (1999), profess an interest in 'the psychodynamics of literary works' and imply that the primary function of literature in such discussions is to 'illustrate' psychoanalytic theories and/or illuminate 'affective reality'.[113] Literature, on their understanding of it, and in contrast to more traditional psychoanalytical discourse, provides 'a sphere of expression where emotional life can be explored and refined in ways that are discouraged elsewhere'.[114] Asserting that 'in art and literature, shame and repression are diminished, and the richness of emotional life, its stimulation and turbulence and nuance, is investigated in its complexity', Adamson and Clark reiterate a view of 'art' as mimetic, exploratory, redemptive and therapeutic – there is little sense, in what they write, of the ways that writing itself might involve or even provoke or perpetuate shame.[115] In the essays collected in *Scenes of Shame*, there is a recurrent tendency to analyse characters as examples of symptomatic personality types – for example, Gordon Hirsch's essay on *Middlemarch* in which he 'analyzes the egotistical and jealous Casaubon as an illustration of this type of character, whose need to ward off his own feelings of vulnerability and shame have [sic] atrophied his ability to care about others', and so on.[116] Fictional characters (that is to say, textual constructs) and fictional plots thereby become examples of typical behaviour, case studies with (apparently) comparable validity to psychoanalytical case studies.

This naïvely expressive and mimetic view of literature elides both the more intricate, reciprocal relations between shame and writing and the more 'constructive', formative – but also dissonant, unpredictable – roles that literature might play in our understand-ing, experience and enactment of shame. In *Writing Shame*, I move beyond a thematic and character-based study of shame in litera-ture and, moreover, aim to consider the shame of the writer and the shame involved in writing – hence my title, which uses 'writing' as both verb and noun, to indicate both the *writing of shame* (shame as subject matter) and the *shame of writing*. As Elspeth Probyn avers, in the closing chapter of *Blush*, 'There is a shame in being highly interested in something and unable to convey it to others, to evoke the same degree of interest in them and to convince them that it is warranted.'[117] She is building here on Tomkins's claim that shame 'operates ordinarily only after interest or enjoyment has been activated, and inhibits one or the other or both'.[118] Without that 'interest' (which might also be a species of desire), there can be no shame. Probyn is mainly concerned with academic writing and with her own anxieties about (not) being equal to her subject; but her claims have some resonance for writers of fiction too. According to Probyn, 'Shame forces us to reflect continually on the implications of our writing,' and 'writing shame' is thus 'a visceral reminder to be true to interest, to be honest about why or how certain things are of interest'.[119] Shame therefore has the useful function of gal-vanising an 'ethics of writing', she claims: 'The blush of having failed to connect with readers should compel any writer to return to the page with renewed desire to do better – to get better – at this task of communicating that some of us take on.'[120] The idea of shame as a moral emotion that motivates self-improvement has a long history, but – as this Introduction has intimated – this regulatory function is not without its problems; nor is shame always predictable in what and how and who it regulates. More significantly, in my view, the shame that attends writing is not simply a desire, on the part of the writer, to do better, to communicate better, though that desire may often be present. And indeed, when shame itself is the subject, 'communication' of it is rarely straightforward. Timothy Bewes argues that shame is 'an experience so closely connected to the activ-ity of writing that writing is all but disabled from saying anything about it', and thus

[i]nsofar as it appears in the text, shame is a gap, an absence, an expe-rience that is incongruous with its own acknowledgement. As a phe-nomenon of life, meanwhile, what shame signals, more than anything,

is condemnation to, or imprisonment within, the inadequacy of forms. The attempt to comprehend shame, to find a conceptualization adequate to it, is inevitably to grapple with specters, illusions.[121]

Shame, on this understanding of it, eludes both representation and comprehension, and cannot so easily be contained, communicated – or overcome. In Bewes's chosen works (by writers including Kafka, Coetzee and Caryl Phillips), 'shame seems to be a placeholder for a quality or a modality of thought that cannot adequately be accounted for by language, or reduced to what is expressible in language'.[122] There is a danger here that shame slips into the role previously occupied by trauma: as what recurs, endlessly, disruptively, but cannot be put into language; as what resists narrativisation. In fact, Bewes's distinctively reflexive account of the work of shame in postcolonial literature is much more sophisticated than that, claiming that shame 'does not exist in some buried state' in a literary text, waiting 'to be unearthed by the penetrating critic', but rather 'appears overtly, as the text's experience of its own inadequacy'.[123] Bewes theorises the development, in the twentieth century – after Empire, after the Holocaust – of 'a literature that begins to constitute itself formally out of a sense of its own inadequacy',[124] an 'inadequacy' that he figures as an incommensurability of the aesthetic and formal possibilities of writing and its 'ethical responsibilities', with shame functioning as 'the material embodiment of that tension' between the aesthetic and the ethical in literature.[125] He suggests nevertheless that this 'inadequacy of writing' – or, rather, the text's self-conscious, self-reflexive awareness of it – may be seen 'as precisely constitutive of [literature's] worth'.[126] The idea that shame *exceeds* representation – that it is not *only* a theme or topic that literary texts can deploy in their mimetic relation to the world (although it might also be this), but rather is something that motivates, infects and frequently distorts the literary endeavour itself – is central to what follows, and it means that any consideration of the writing of shame cannot be *merely* a discussion of what is or is not, can or cannot be represented. *Writing Shame* therefore considers more minutely the *formal* challenges and disruptions of presenting shame in literature and attends to the functions and effects of shame within and beyond particular texts. It reflects, more broadly, on the shame that attends – inhabits, is associated with, is provoked by and sometimes inhibits – writing itself.

I welcome, then, Sheils and Walsh's recent suggestion that 'the very act of writing' might 'inevitably leave on the page a residue or trace of shame', their conclusion that 'there is no such thing as a writing devoid of shame', and the case they make, in the Introduction to *Shame and Modern Writing*, for 'the intrinsic relation between shame and writing'.[127] Within that collection, Denise Riley posits that

> [t]here's a proximity of shame to exhibitionism. An 'exhibited' kind of writerly shame can be concealment tangled with unconcealment. You do need a confident immodesty to display your own shame. Yet that real confidence could be covering over an equally real humiliation. Some bold authorial show of shame needn't cancel out the emotion itself.[128]

Writing brings with it a particular anxiety of exposure – yet also a desire for this exposure; Riley's comments bring out both shame's ambivalence (wanting to be looked at and, simultaneously, not wanting to be looked at, to paraphrase Tomkins)[129] and the necessary duplicities of writing ('concealment tangled with unconcealment'). This 'residue' of shame that we might find in any 'act of writing', as I have suggested, goes beyond what is (or can be) represented, so I take up here Sheils and Walsh's interest in what they call 'an economy of affective transfer between writer, reader and text, operating in excess of representation'.[130] Writing autobiographically – as several of the writers that I consider here do – brings its own perverse admixture of shame and pride, self-denigration and self-aggrandisement. For the writer representing supposedly shameful topics, whether true or fictional, the struggle to convey shame might in itself be shameful, while the reception of that work might seek to shame the writer for some perceived impropriety. At the same time, the shamefulness of the topic (whether child abuse or masochism or promiscuity or simply self-exposure) might prove to be both a lure to the reader and an infectious affect that the reader too takes on.

In Bewes's work on Coetzee, he is adamant that the South African writer's late work 'does not represent an overcoming of shame' but rather 'shows us how to do justice to the shame, preserving it in all its opacity and integrity'.[131] For Bewes, as we have seen, the *thematic* preoccupation with shame in the work of someone like Coetzee – and in modern and contemporary literature more generally – is expressive of a more fundamental 'misgiving at the heart of literary activity in the modern period', and 'should be understood as an *intimation* that there is no positive ethical or political dimension to writing'.[132] Such an understanding works against a view of literary treatments of shame as redemptive; yet the existing analyses of literary treatments of shame – particularly in relation to gender – have precisely tended to privilege stories of overcoming and/or to see the writing of shame as necessarily, and positively, transformative. Implicitly, they figure the writing of shame as *testimony* or as *catharsis*. In *Scenes of Shame*, Clark's own contribution 'explores the reparative role of poetry for Anne Sexton', noting how, 'in *The Death Notebooks* in particular, poetic composition [. . .] is held up, if only briefly, as a means of overcoming toxic narcissistic shame'.[133] The work of J. Brooks Bouson, who has written extensively and illuminatingly about shame, gender and contemporary literature, is another case in point. In *Quiet As It's Kept* (2000), on Toni Morrison, Bouson finds in Morrison's writing 'evidence of the desire to bear witness to the shame and trauma that exist in the lives of African Americans', alongside a 'desire to cover up or repair the racial wounds she has exposed'; she reads Morrison's 'artistic rendering and narrative reconstruction of the shame and trauma story' as an attempt to '[effect] a cultural cure' – though she does concede the 'precariousness of that cure'.[134] In *Embodied Shame* (2009), Bouson sets out from the premise that 'shame about the body is a cultural inheritance of women and thus an issue that pervades literature' and argues that her chosen authors – including Alice Munro, Dorothy Allison, Edwidge Danticat and Naomi Wolf – 'through their very explicit public exposure of female shame, [. . .] do vital cultural work by providing a powerful critique of the cultural narratives that shame women. And in their works, they also seek a remedy to shame.'[135] As Bouson represents it:

> Refusing to be silent, the authors examined in *Embodied Shame* demand an ethics of response as they, evoking the viscerality of shame in their works, expose the continuing cultural manipulation of women apparent in troubling images of female bodies as defective or spoiled or damaged or dirtied.[136]

'Bear witness', 'repair', 'cure', 'exposure', 'critique', 'remedy', 'refusing to be silent': this critical terminology posits shame as a secret to be unearthed or revealed, something latent rather than (as I figure it) pervasive and structural. It suggests that the writing of shame does both the work of exposure and (automatically, necessarily) the work of critique – indeed, on this understanding, exposure *just is* critique, and the writing of shame *just is* an admirable ethical and political act, whether or not it is presented as such.

In her most recent scholarship on contemporary women's writing and shame, *Shame and the Aging Woman* (2016), Bouson again reads the authors under consideration (such as Doris Lessing, A. S. Byatt and Anita Brookner) as '[daring] to disclose' gendered age-ism, 'through their relentless exposure of the myriad ways that our culture shames older women'.[137] The language here is again a language of 'exposure', as if the act of writing or making visible is, first, straightforward and, second, transformative and redemptive. But can shame so easily be put into words? And are the effects of writing shame so predictable and so positive? Bouson declares:

> Refusing to be silent or to hide in shame, these authors show how sexageism wounds older women. As they put shame to work politically, they seek to raise awareness of the plight of the older woman in our graying society, which is a needed first step if we are to develop a new age consciousness and find ways to resist the shame that inhabits and inhibits the lives of so many older women in our contemporary culture of appearances.[138]

This making visible is, however, a fraught enterprise, given shame's own complex relation with exposure and spectacle (concealment tangled with unconcealment), given its unpredictable transmissibility, and given the qualities that make its total banishment undesirable – if not actually impossible. This is not to say, however, that the writing of shame in fiction might not have the practical effect of drawing our attention to the cultural structures that shame some kinds of bodies more than others.

Erica L. Johnson and Patricia Moran's *The Female Face of Shame* focuses, similarly, 'on the link between shame and femininity' and on shame as 'a marker of female humanity'.[139] The editors are interested, as I am, in 'how shame structures relationships and shapes women's identities across the three major aspects of subject formation [. . .]: the individual, the familial, and the cultural or national'.[140] However, their editorial line is, like Bouson's work, underpinned by the idea that '*representing* women's shame is an inherently pro-active endeavour'[141] – a defiant challenge to a patriarchal culture of woman-shaming, a countering of the 'silence' surrounding this 'issue' – and they express the hope that 'by bringing gendered shame out into the open, by representing it, this volume will help to counteract shame's mortifying influence in women's lives'.[142] Again, then, literature is figured as a counter and remedy to shame, rather than being in any way complicit in its circulation. Many of their contributors, unsurprisingly, echo these sentiments: Nicole Fayard insists that, for the French autobiographical writer Samira Bellil, 'Writing [. . .] is empowering and an act of rebellion. It is conducive to a freeing of the self [. . .], a catalyst to the breaking of the barriers of shame and alienation';[143] Suzette A. Henke's reading of *The Bloody Chamber* concludes that 'Carter's "shameless" protagonists successfully free themselves and those whom they love from the stultifying mortifications imposed by the arbitrary and humiliating judgments of a shame-based society';[144] Tamar Heller reads both Simone Weil and Jean Rhys as 'daring to share the shame of the afflicted',[145] while Karen Lindo argues that Ananda Devi's novel *Pagli* (2001) 'challenges the role that shame plays in determining female subjectivity in contemporary Mauritius'.[146] This language of overcoming, courage and defiance, this view of writing as (necessarily) liberating and insubordinate, runs through most of the essays in the collection.

My own view is that the representation of shame in literature is more complex than this (relative) optimism allows. Shame's slipperiness is such that it frequently eludes and foxes attempts to represent it; its contagious quality means that the reader cannot help but be affected/infected by it; its persistence, and the very important roles that it plays in subjectivation, socialisation, civilisation and individuation, mean that it is not so easily dispelled. The intersubjective, affect-laden, both public and private, porous experiences of writing and reading, I argue, provide the perfect arena for what Sheils and Walsh call 'shame's mobility', facilitating the transmission of a vicarious shame that is 'more spectacular than a voluntary identification with others, understood as sympathy or compassion', and that 'potentially rips through the contours of the subject, throwing into disarray the formal distinctions between inside and outside, background and foreground';[147] those distinctions (inside/outside, background/foreground) are, I argue, already threatened by writing and by the identifications that literary texts invite.

In short: writing shame – even writing *about* shame – frequently trails more shame in its wake. Why do it, then? As Natalie Edwards asks, of Annie Ernaux and Christine Angot's autofictional documenting of the shameful and shameless,

> [w]hy put this out there to be read? Why try to shock, embarrass or disturb one's reader, repeatedly and relentlessly? The shame becomes the negotiation between reader and writer [. . .]. Each implicates the reader as an other in their story of shame, as the reader is the other who makes the shame exist: the spectator who enables the shaming mechanism.[148]

The intersubjective character of shame here intersects with the intersubjective activities of writing and reading, and that intersection produces both delight and disgust, gratification and discomfort. Noting Tomkins's style of writing, Sheils and Walsh suggest that 'shame is not simply what Tomkins writes *about*; it is *in* his writing'; and they assert that 'The pleasures of reading and writing shame – pleasures forever adjoined to reluctance, repetition, frustration and block – are not merely incidental to the theme.'[149] *Writing Shame* therefore focuses on texts that sidestep or refuse narratives of redemption or overcoming, thereby facilitating a more nuanced understanding of the complex relations between shame and gendered subjectivity. It is alert to the *pleasures* as well as the pitfalls of writing shame, and to the way that shame might infect the writing itself, might be *in* the writing, rather than simply what the writing is *about*.

Writing Shame: Contemporary Literature, Gender and Negative Affect

David Halperin and Valerie Traub, in their introduction to *Gay Shame*, tentatively ask whether we might 'try to see what happens when we linger in untransformed experiences of [shame]'.[150] I ask: what might this 'lingering' entail and what might its effects be? The literary texts that I consider in this book perform such a lingering, rather than necessarily seeking some transformative use of shame, and I suppose my own book does likewise: it is an exercise in scholarly 'lingering', though resisting the urge to report, self-reflexively, on my own shame in doing so.[151] Starting from the premise that shame

cannot be overcome or abandoned, and that femininity and shame
are utterly and necessarily imbricated, this book examines writing
that explores and inhabits this state of shame, considering the dissonant effects of such explorations on and beyond the page. My
epigraph for this introduction comes from Eve Sedgwick: 'What's the
point of accentuating the negative, of beginning with stigma [. . .]?',
Sedgwick asks, while claiming that 'there's no way that any amount
of affirmative reclamation is going to succeed in detaching the word
[queer] from its associations with shame'; I will discuss this connection between shame and queerness in the first chapter.[152] My claim is
that femininity and shame are similarly inextricable – indeed, even
more closely 'associated' than 'queer' and shame, because the imbrication of femininity and shame goes beyond the linguistic and arguably reaches further back into history – and my chosen texts are
those that seek to occupy, explore and sometimes even 'accentuate'
the negative. The queer theoretical writing under consideration in
Chapter 1 seeks to reclaim the positive potential of shame, while the
pulp material that I discuss towards the end of that chapter mixes
passionate desire with pathologising self-hatred – its pleasures are
therefore always mixed. The novels by Mary Gaitskill and A. M.
Homes that I analyse in Chapter 2 wade into the mire of childhood
shame without ever offering a clear route out of this, while their narrative strategies undeniably both tantalise and discomfit the reader.
The autofictional writing of Chris Kraus, Marie Calloway and Katherine Angel discussed in Chapter 3 stages acts of self-shaming that
turn vulnerability into a perverse tool of empowerment. The texts
that I analyse in Chapter 4 appear to tackle challenging feelings
around failed masculinity (emasculation, ageing, impotence), but in
fact end up projecting this shame elsewhere in a troubling reassertion
of narratorial and patriarchal mastery. In 'accentuating' the negative,
all of these texts foreground it, drawing our attention to shame – its
structural, ideological operations, its formal qualities, its ambiva-
lences – without, however, seeking an obvious remedy to it.

In Chapter 1, I begin with Michael Warner's question, 'What will
we do with our shame?',[153] and proceed to consider the revisiting of
shame in much recent queer theory – a revisiting that generally seeks
to mine that affect for its positive political potential and to present it
as a viable alternative to a mainstream pride agenda. In this chapter,
via a dual focus on queer theory and pulp fiction, I assess the uses

and limitations of 'queer shame': its appeal to a solidarity based on the precarious foundations of a shared history of pathologisation and oppression; its tendency to elide the specificities of race and gender in the experience of shame and the deployment of shaming. My literary archive in this chapter is mid-century lesbian pulp fiction, but I am interested here less in the original context of its publication and more in the 'recuperation' of this formerly shameful sub-genre in the twenty-first century, a recuperation made possible in part because of the turn to negative affect in recent queer theory. The term 'recuperation' is, of course, a loaded one, given pulp's prior banishment from the lesbian canon, and given its own preoccupation with homosexuality as illness. In my readings of Ann Bannon's *Women in the Shadows* (1959/2002) and Della Martin's *Twilight Girl* (1961/2006), both of which have been republished by a lesbian press in the twenty-first century, I focus particularly on questions concerning the (in)visibility and (un)intelligibility of gender and race, and matters of performance and 'passing'. Unusually for pulp texts of that period, both *Twilight Girl* and *Women in the Shadows* feature characters of colour, and in both novels race becomes a site of both fascination and shame (their titles also, of course, adopt a familiar pulp trope of referencing darkness or blackness – 'twilight', 'shadows'). Race also, I suggest, functions as both an intensifier of queer shame and a mirror of/analogy for that shame, in what might be viewed as a troubling case of shame appropriation.

In Chapter 2, I discuss two American writers – A. M. Homes and Mary Gaitskill – whose literary engagements with shame, in relation to sexuality in particular, have been notably provocative and disturbing, making their writing less obviously recuperable for the conventional, reassuring narrative of 'exposure' and 'overcoming' discussed earlier in this Introduction. I analyse the unsettling, contradictory admixture of desire, disgust and shame to be found in Homes's *The End of Alice* (1996) and Gaitskill's *Two Girls, Fat and Thin* (1991), both of which present stories of child abuse, both of which resist any straightforwardly redemptive or consolatory conclusion. In these novels, the childhood scene of shame is something that cannot be definitively vanquished – hence the double meaning of 'cleave' (to cling to, to separate from) in this chapter's title. In Chapter 2 I also consider the movement of shame through and beyond the texts: the self-reflexive emphasis on deviant or unreliable narration; the displacement of shame upon the reader, whose disconcerting complicity is thereby invited; and the critical reception of these novels, which has tended to express unease about the de-feminising implications of female authors writing about apparently 'shameful' topics. In this way, I show how shame is more than a theme in these works – how it disturbs the form of the text, and infects its reading and reception.

Chapter 3 extends my arguments around the inseparability of femininity and shame, the non-redemptive literary treatment of shame, the formal disruptions produced in the writing of shame, and the ways in which shame might seep into the contexts and processes of writing, reading and critical reception. It does so via readings of three contemporary, female-authored autofictions with a central focus on (female, heterosexual) desire and with a leaning towards literary 'experimentalism': Chris Kraus's *I Love Dick* (1997), Marie Calloway's *what purpose did i serve in your life* (2013) and Katherine Angel's *Unmastered* (2012). All three texts perform and reflect upon acts of self-exposure and states of vulnerability; all three construct the autobiographical 'I' in highly self-conscious ways. Kraus and Calloway, in their musing on unrequited attachments, turn their humiliation against the men who reject them, thereby raising questions too about the ethics of 'confession'. All three texts nevertheless complicate the confessional mode via their generic mixing of fiction, memoir, essay and theoretical discourse; and all three authors have been subject to critical commentary that, even when admiring (by, for example, praising their 'bravery'), somehow subtly seeks to impugn them for their candid treatment of sexuality and/or for their 'narcissism'. In her Foreword to *I Love Dick*, Eileen Myles claims that Kraus is 'marching boldly into self-abasement and self-advertisement, not being uncannily drawn there',[154] and in this chapter I ask what kind of agency is implied by such a march, what the relationship might be between 'self-abasement' and 'self-advertisement', and how these texts, by seeking to 'handle vulnerability like philosophy' (as Kraus puts it), might work to reveal the *structural* – not merely *personal* – nature of shame, as far as women are concerned.[155]

The final chapter turns to recent fiction and autofiction by relatively canonical male authors: to consider, first, the relationship between masculinity and shame; and to highlight, second, the persistence of the association between shame and femininity in works by male authors. Although Steven Connor expresses the cautious wish that 'Writing might [. . .] be a way of meeting with shame, a coming in to male shamefulness',[156] the textual analyses central to Chapter 4 – of works by Martin Amis, Philip Roth and Karl Ove Knausgaard – suggest that, frequently, men's writing of and on shame seeks to disavow that shame, to project it on to female bodies and/or to make of its confession a kind of heroism. Roth's *The Dying Animal* (2001) and Amis's *The Pregnant Widow* (2010) are read as instances of novels that seek to displace male shamefulness (particularly, but not only, sexual shame) on to vulnerable female bodies – bodies that are sometimes also racially othered. My reading of Knausgaard's *My Struggle II: A Man in Love* then shows how that text (and the *My Struggle* series as a whole), despite evincing an unusual perspicacity on the subject of masculine shame, ultimately (perhaps unwittingly) transforms its 'struggle' with shame into a literary struggle for 'authenticity' and leaves intact the association of shamefulness and the feminine. As I do elsewhere in this book, in Chapter 4 I also discuss the critical reception of both book and author, noting the ways in which Knausgaard's positioning as (exceptional, paradigmatic, Proustian) Author works to counter his narrative of shame and failure with one of literary 'greatness', remasculinising him in the process.

In a recent interview, the Canadian writer Sheila Heti discusses with a female journalist (Emma Brockes) the question of whether or not to have children. Heti feels shame for not wanting children; Brockes, for wanting them too ardently. Heti muses:

> 'Maybe there's a basic shame women feel and it just attaches to anything [. . .] Maybe if we both feel shame it's because it's shameful to be a woman. Whatever you choose you feel shame. [. . .] I wonder if it's ever going to change, or if women will feel that way until there are no humans ever.'[157]

This might appear, at first glance, to be a pessimistic view, but the texts I read in *Writing Shame* are not pessimistic – or, at least, not straightforwardly so – and neither am I. Even in 2019, it remains 'shameful to be a woman', and my chosen texts acknowledge that. In making that acknowledgement, they draw attention to the origins, the structural underpinnings and the daily operations of femininity; they do so without assuming that that 'basic shame' can be thrown off. However, in exploring that situation (that affect, that social position, that state of mind and embodiment) from within, they consider the different ways in which it might be inhabited, understood – and perhaps even perverted.

Of all the writers I consider here, it is those discussed in Chapters 2 and 3 (Homes, Gaitskill, Kraus, Calloway) who grasp most acutely the ways in which the shame of being a woman might be taken up, manipulated and turned outwards – but, as my readings reveal, this endeavour can always go awry. Shame is a slippery customer, its effects unpredictable (though not always unpleasurable). In the Conclusion, I will gesture towards the way in which a younger generation of writers has begun, whether obliquely or overtly, to engage with some of these questions around femininity, female embodiment, desire and shame in very recent years; but, in many respects, the figure of female shame who haunts these pages is one of the earliest – Phaidra. In 'Why I Wrote Two Plays About Phaidra', Anne Carson, assuming the voice of Euripides, has him declare to some imagined audience:

> In general I like women. [. . .] But this one seized me like no other character ever had – that first Phaidra [in *Hippolytus Veiled*], the pure chainsmoking nihilism of her, pacing the cage of her own clarity. What rushed through her speech wasn't fuss about mirrors and chastity. Only a fool would have asked her for a *moral* position. Her people feared her. Her own spirit feared her. You feared her.[158]

Phaidra is a shamed woman – the original shamed woman – yet she is not unequivocally a victim; 'pacing the cage of her own clarity', eschewing entrapment in the 'moral' even while seemingly acting to preserve her own and her husband's honour, Phaidra strikes 'fear' into those around her. This Phaidra, Carson's canny, provocative Euripides tells us, 'is not gone, her disappearance in fact reverberates everywhere in this so-called second version [*Hippolytus*]. I wrote it to show how that feels. Phaidraless world.'[159] And yet, this is not a 'Phaidraless world', for 'there is a residue of her gone down into Aphrodite's anger. It is sexual anger. [. . .] Little matchless breeze of what is perpetually igniting in her *at the core*.'[160] Women's shame, I discover time and time again (in books and in life), springs from and brings with it the desire that is 'perpetually igniting [. . .] *at the core*', and that burns its bystanders, as Phaidra's did. Phaidra's desire is a blazon – a 'mute apostrophe'[161] – even into the twentieth and twenty-first centuries. If my subject is *aidōs*, in its modern manifestations, my poster girl is a revitalised Phaidra, who burns still: with anger and desire, as well as with shame.

Notes

1. Eve Kosofsky Sedgwick, 'Queer Performativity: Henry James's *The Art of the Novel*', *GLQ* 1: 1 (1993): 1–16 (4).
2. Silvan Tomkins, 'Shame-Humiliation and Contempt-Disgust', in Eve Kosofsky Sedgwick and Adam Frank (eds), *Shame and Its Sisters: A Silvan Tomkins Reader* (Durham, NC: Duke University Press, 1995), pp. 133–78 (p. 133).
3. Ruth Leys, *From Guilt to Shame: Auschwitz and After* (Princeton: Princeton University Press, 2007), p. 4.
4. Leys, p. 123. Leys notes, for example, that there is no discussion of shame in Jean Laplanche and Jean-Bertrand Pontalis's *The Language of Psychoanalysis* (1973) (p. 123 n. 1).
5. Leys, p. 7. However, most modern philosophers do still treat shame as a 'moral' matter – Martha Nussbaum, for example, asserts that 'shame is typically connected with ideals or serious norms, and thus is always moral in a broad sense of that term', and also that, even if viewed as a *social* rather than *moral* matter (the distinction is a fine one), shame is not 'freer' in the way that Leys alleges; more on this anon. By describing shame as a moral emotion, Nussbaum is saying it is not *merely* a matter of 'social approval or disapproval'. See Nussbaum, *Hiding from Humanity: Disgust, Shame and the Law* (Princeton: Princeton University Press, 2004), p. 207. I am less willing to separate the moral and the social.
6. Leys, p. 11. My emphasis.
7. Sandra Bartky, *Femininity and Domination: Studies in the Phenomenology of Domination* (London: Routledge, 1990), p. 87.
8. Leys, p. 11.
9. Sedgwick, 'Queer Performativity', p. 12.
10. Emmanuel Levinas, *On Escape* [1935], trans. Bettina Bergo (Stanford: Stanford University Press, 2003), pp. 64–5.
11. Levinas, p. 63.
12. Jean-Paul Sartre, *Being and Nothingness* [1943], trans. Hazel E. Barnes (New York: Washington Square Press, 1956), p. 301.
13. Sartre, p. 302.
14. Sartre, p. 303.
15. Sartre, p. 350.
16. Gershen Kaufman, *The Psychology of Shame* (New York: Springer, 1989), p. viii.
17. Giorgio Agamben, *Remnants of Auschwitz*, trans. Daniel Heller-Roazen (New York: Zone Books, 1999), p. 107.
18. Agamben, pp. 105–6.

19. Lisa Guenther, 'Resisting Agamben: The Biopolitics of Shame and Humiliation', *Philosophy and Social Criticism* 38: 1 (2012): 59–79 (59).
20. Nussbaum, p. 174.
21. Sigmund Freud, *Five Lectures on Psychoanalysis* [1909], trans. and ed. James Strachey (New York: W. W. Norton, 1961), p. 48.
22. Freud, *Five Lectures*, p. 45.
23. Sedgwick, along with Adam Frank, edited a volume entitled *Shame and Its Sisters: A Silvan Tomkins Reader*, which was published in 1995.
24. For example, Léon Wurmser, *The Mask of Shame* (Baltimore: Johns Hopkins University Press, 1981); Donald Nathanson (ed.), *The Many Faces of Shame* (New York: Guilford Press, 1987) and *Shame and Pride: Affect, Sex, and the Birth of the Self* (New York: W. W. Norton, 1992).
25. For example, Jennifer C. Manion, 'The Moral Relevance of Shame', *American Philosophical Quarterly* 39: 1 (2002): 73–90; Martha Nussbaum, *Hiding from Humanity*; Gabriele Taylor, *Pride, Shame, and Guilt* (Oxford: Clarendon Press, 1985); and Bernard Williams, *Shame and Necessity* (Berkeley: University of California Press, 1993).
26. For example, Giorgio Agamben, *Remnants of Auschwitz*; Primo Levi, *The Drowned and the Saved* [1986] (New York: Simon & Schuster, 1988) and *If This is a Man* [1947], trans. Stuart Wolf (London: Orion Press, 1959); Ruth Leys, *From Guilt to Shame*; and Michael L. Morgan, *On Shame* (New York: Routledge, 2008).
27. For example, Jill Locke, *Democracy and the Death of Shame: Political Equality and Social Disturbance* (Cambridge: Cambridge University Press, 2016); Myra Mendible (ed.), *American Shame: Stigma and the Body Politic* (Bloomington: Indiana University Press, 2016); Christina H. Tarnopolsky, *Prudes, Perverts, and Tyrants: Plato's Gorgias and the Politics of Shame* (Princeton: Princeton University Press, 2010).
28. Notably Sandra Bartky, *Femininity and Domination*; but see also the gendered accounts of shame offered by Ullaliina Lehtinen, 'How Does One Know What Shame Is? Epistemology, Emotions, and Forms of Life in Juxtaposition', *Hypatia* 13: 1 (1998): 56–77, and Jennifer C. Manion, 'Girls Blush, Sometimes: Gender, Moral Agency, and the Problem of Shame', *Hypatia* 18: 3 (2003): 21–41.
29. For example, Joseph Adamson and Hilary Clark (eds), *Scenes of Shame: Psychoanalysis, Shame and Writing* (Albany: SUNY Press, 1999); Timothy Bewes, *The Event of Postcolonial Shame* (Princeton: Princeton University Press, 2011); J. Brooks Bouson, *Quiet As It's Kept: Shame, Trauma and Race in the Novels of Toni Morrison* (Albany: SUNY Press, 2000), *Embodied Shame: Uncovering Female Shame in Contemporary Women's Writings* (Albany: SUNY Press, 2009) and *Shame and the Aging Woman: Confronting and Resisting Ageism in Contemporary*

Women's Writings (Basingstoke: Palgrave, 2016); Jenny Chamarette and Jennifer Higgins (eds), *Guilt and Shame: Essays in French Literature, Thought and Visual Culture* (Oxford: Peter Lang, 2010); Ewan Fernie, *Shame in Shakespeare* (London: Routledge, 2002); Erica L. Johnson and Patricia Moran (eds), *The Female Face of Shame* (Bloomington: Indiana University Press, 2013); and Barry Sheils and Julie Walsh (eds), *Shame and Modern Writing* (London: Routledge, 2018).

30. For example, David M. Halperin and Valerie Traub (eds), *Gay Shame* (Chicago: University of Chicago Press, 2009); Heather Love, *Feeling Backward: Loss and the Politics of Queer History* (Cambridge, MA: Harvard University Press, 2007); Sally Munt, *Queer Attachments: The Cultural Politics of Shame* (Aldershot: Ashgate, 2007); Elspeth Probyn, *Blush: Faces of Shame* (Minneapolis: University of Minnesota Press, 2005); Eve Kosofsky Sedgwick, 'Queer Performativity', pp. 1–16, *Touching Feeling* (Durham, NC: Duke University Press, 2003), and the Tomkins reader co-edited with Adam Frank, *Shame and Its Sisters*; and Michael Warner, *The Trouble with Normal: Sex, Politics, and the Ethics of Queer Life* (Cambridge, MA: Harvard University Press, 1999).

31. Malcolm Pines, 'Shame: What Psychoanalysis Does and Does Not Say' [1987], in Claire Pajaczkowska and Ivan Ward (eds), *Shame and Sexuality: Psychoanalysis and Visual Culture* (London: Routledge, 2008), pp. 93–106 (p. 93).

32. Manion, 'The Moral Relevance of Shame', p. 73.

33. Leys, p. 124.

34. Ibid.

35. Christopher Lasch, 'For Shame: Why Americans Should Be Wary of Self-Esteem', *New Republic*, 10 August 1992. Lasch asks, among other things, 'why [shame] gets so much attention in a shameless society'. Available at: <https://newrepublic.com/article/90898/shame-why-americans-should-be-wary-self-esteem> (last accessed 27 November 2018). For more on the place of shame in contemporary American culture, see: Arlene Stein, *Shameless: Sexual Dissidence in American Culture* (New York: New York University Press, 2006), who writes of the 'curious mix of the shameless and the shamers' in American culture (p. 1); and Myra Mendible's 'Introduction: American Shame and the Boundaries of Belonging', in *American Shame*, pp. 1–26, where she claims that, in the media and popular culture of the US, 'shame is a hot commodity', 'more entertaining than disciplinary, more akin to a system of sociality than morality' (p. 1).

36. Roger Luckhurst, *The Trauma Question* (London: Routledge, 2008), pp. 1, 2.

37. Mark Seltzer, *Serial Killers: Death and Life in America's Wound Culture* (London: Routledge, 1998), pp. 1, 22.

38. Jo Gill notes 'what seems to be the sudden resurgence or re-emergence of confessional writing in the West in the second half of the twentieth century'; see Jo Gill, 'Introduction', in Gill (ed.), *Modern Confessional Writing* (London: Routledge, 2006), pp. 1–10 (p. 6). Peter Brooks considers a longer timeline, suggesting that confession 'has become in Western culture a crucial mode of self-examination; from the time of the early Romantics to the present day, confession has become a dominant mode of self-expression' – although not necessarily one that produces truth; see Peter Brooks, *Troubling Confessions: Speaking Guilt in Law and Literature* (Chicago: University of Chicago Press, 2000), p. 9. See Chapter 3 of this book for a more extensive discussion of confession.

39. Jon Ronson, *So You've Been Publicly Shamed* (London: Picador, 2015), p. 9.

40. Ronson, pp. 9, 47, 52.

41. Ronson, pp. 178, 179.

42. Ronson, p. 179.

43. Nussbaum, p. 3.

44. Nussbaum, p. 4.

45. Nussbaum, p. 15.

46. Ronson, p. 77.

47. Nussbaum, p. 175.

48. Locke, p. 7 n. 19.

49. Locke, p. 8.

50. Ibid.

51. Locke, p. 5.

52. Ibid. Locke, then, is noting a tendency to figure shame as a much-needed *counter* to that prioritisation of the self – while I am arguing that the preoccupation with shame in contemporary culture is, to a significant extent, a *product* of that prioritisation.

53. Locke, p. 7.

54. Locke, p. 18.

55. Stein, p. 3.

56. Locke, p. 9.

57. Jennifer Jacquet, *Is Shame Necessary? New Uses for an Old Tool* (London: Allen Lane, 2015), p. 29.

58. Jacquet is not wrong to claim that shame is 'an inherently social phenomenon' but, as discussed earlier in this Introduction, its relation with selfhood, socialisation and forms of social belonging is much more complex than that statement allows; its effects often take the form of painful isolation/individuation and it is 'social' in ways that are not always positive.

59. Jacquet, p. 100.
60. Ronson, p. 113.
61. Ronson, p. 121.
62. Ibid.
63. Bartky, p. 86.
64. Jennifer C. Manion cites the work of Michael Lewis, which notes studies of 'college-aged students' showing that men feel shame for 'failure in some task deemed important' (work or sport) or failure of 'sexual potency', while women feel shame due to perceived 'physical unattractiveness' and 'failure in maintaining interpersonal relationships'. See Manion, 'Girls Blush', pp. 24, 25. See also Michael Lewis, *Shame: The Exposed Self* (New York: Free Press, 1992), p. 187.
65. Bartky, p. 84.
66. Leys, p. 7.
67. Leys, p. 131.
68. Locke, p. 14.
69. Leys, p. 131.
70. Munt, *Queer Attachments*, p. 2. Regarding the longer history of the association made between shame and femininity, Bartky wonders also 'whether there is any relationship between women's shame – both the shame that is directly linked to embodiment and the shame that is not – to the persistence of religious traditions that have historically associated female sexuality with pollution and contagion' (*Femininity and Domination*, p. 90).
71. Douglas L. Cairns, *Aidōs: The Psychology and Ethics of Honour and Shame in Ancient Greek Literature* (Oxford: Clarendon Press, 1993), pp. 14–15.
72. Cairns, p. 120.
73. Ibid.
74. Euripides, *Grief Lessons: Four Plays*, trans. Anne Carson (New York: New York Review Books, 2006), pp. 184–5 (ll. 279–82). The spellings 'Hippolytos' and 'Phaidra' are Carson's; these are more often written as 'Hippolytus' and 'Phaedra'. Carson also writes '*aidos*' rather than '*aidōs*', so I have replicated her spelling when quoting her translation directly.
75. Euripides/Carson, p. 189 (l. 368).
76. Euripides/Carson, p. 194 (ll. 452–62).
77. Euripides/Carson, p. 204 (ll. 684–7).
78. Euripides/Carson, pp. 204 (l. 692), 205 (ll. 695, 713).
79. Euripides/Carson, p. 164.
80. Euripides/Carson, pp. 163–4.
81. Euripides/Carson, p. 164.
82. Euripides/Carson, pp. 164–5.

83. Euripides/Carson, p. 165.
84. Karl Kerényi, *La religione antica nelle sue linee fondamentali*, trans. Delio Cantimori (Bologna: N. Zanchelli, 1940), p. 88. Qtd by Agamben, *Remnants of Auschwitz*, p. 107.
85. Agamben, p. 107.
86. Euripides/Carson, p. 194 (ll. 467–9).
87. Cairns, p. 186.
88. Pines, pp. 93–106 (p. 99).
89. Manion, 'Girls Blush', p. 22.
90. Sigmund Freud, 'Femininity', in *The Standard Edition of the Complete Psychological Works of Sigmund Freud, Volume XXII (1932–1936): New Introductory Lectures on Psychoanalysis and Other Works*, pp. 1–182 (p. 132). The original German reads: 'Der Scham, die als eine exquisit weibliche Eigenschaft gilt, aber weit mehr konventionell ist, als man denken sollte, schreiben wir die ursprüngliche Absicht zu, den Defekt des Genitales zu verdecken.' As Nicholas Courtman kindly explained to me, in a discussion of the translation of this passage, there is 'a problem with the translation of "exquisit" as "par excellence", which makes us lose sight of the fact that exquisit is here an adverb qualifying weiblich/feminine'. He pointed out that '"Defekt" – translated here as deficiency – [. . .] has a specific meaning within a medical context of a missing or damaged limb or body part', a clear indication of the penis envy argument. Nevertheless, he suggested that it 'would definitely be wrong to read Freud as saying that shame is a feminine characteristic par excellence here. He's presenting that idea as common opinion, and then undermining it' (written correspondence online, 5 May 2019).
91. Manion, 'Girls Blush', p. 24. See, for example, by Helen Block Lewis, *Shame and Guilt in Neurosis* (New York: International Universities Press, 1971); 'The Role of Shame in Depression in Women', in Ruth Formanek and Anita Gurian (eds), *Women and Depression* (New York: Springer, 1987); and (ed.), *The Role of Shame in Symptom Formation* (Hillsdale, NJ: L. Erlbaum, 1987).
92. John Berger, *Ways of Seeing* (London: Penguin, 1972), p. 47.
93. Berger, p. 46.
94. Leys, p. 128.
95. Taylor, p. 67.
96. Manion, 'Girls Blush', p. 22.
97. Bartky, p. 85.
98. Bartky, p. 96.
99. Bartky, p. 85. Bartky takes the phrase 'generalized condition of dishonor' from another context, from Husseen Abdilahi Bulhan, *Frantz Fanon and the Psychology of Oppression* (New York: Plenum, 1985), p. 122.

100. Manion, 'Girls Blush', p. 23.
101. Bartky, p. 93.
102. See Manion, 'Girls Blush', and Lewis, *Shame: The Exposed Self*.
103. Bartky, p. 93. My emphasis.
104. Bartky, p. 95.
105. I am grateful to the second peer reviewer of the manuscript for Edinburgh University Press for this particular insight, very pithily expressed: 'Knowledge does not prevent shame. Politics doesn't shift the emotional terrain.'
106. Bartky, p. 97.
107. Ibid.
108. Ibid.
109. Bartky, p. 98.
110. Bartky, p. 93.
111. Barry Sheils and Julie Walsh, 'Introduction: Shame and Modern Writing', in Sheils and Walsh (eds), *Shame and Modern Writing*, pp. 1–32 (p. 13).
112. See, for example: Adamson and Clark (eds), *Scenes of Shame*; Bouson, *Quiet As It's Kept*, *Embodied Shame* and *Shame and the Aging Woman*; Fernie, *Shame in Shakespeare*; Johnson and Moran (eds), *The Female Face of Shame*.
113. Joseph Adamson and Hilary Clark, 'Introduction: Shame, Affect, Writing', in Adamson and Clark (eds), *Scenes of Shame*, pp. 1–34 (p. 1).
114. Adamson and Clark, 'Introduction', p. 6.
115. Adamson and Clark, 'Introduction', p. 15.
116. Adamson and Clark, 'Introduction', p. 24.
117. Probyn, p. 130.
118. Tomkins, p. 134.
119. Probyn, pp. 131–2.
120. Probyn, p. 162.
121. Bewes, *The Event*, p. 2.
122. Bewes, *The Event*, p. 14.
123. Bewes, *The Event*, p. 3.
124. Bewes, *The Event*, p. 16.
125. Bewes, *The Event*, p. 1.
126. Bewes, *The Event*, p. 19.
127. Sheils and Walsh, 'Introduction', p. 1.
128. Denise Riley, 'Lyric Shame', in Sheils and Walsh, *Shame and Modern Writing*, pp. 68–72 (p. 68).
129. Tomkins, p. 137.
130. Sheils and Walsh, 'Introduction', pp. 1–2.

131. Bewes, *The Event*, p. 163.
132. Timothy Bewes, 'The Call to Intimacy and the Shame Effect', *differences: A Journal of Feminist Cultural Studies* 22: 1 (2011): 1–16 (9).
133. Adamson and Clark, 'Introduction', p. 25.
134. Bouson, *Quiet As It's Kept*, p. 5.
135. Bouson, *Embodied Shame*, pp. 1, 15.
136. Bouson, *Embodied Shame*, p. 183.
137. Bouson, *Shame and the Aging Woman*, p. v.
138. Bouson, *Shame and the Aging Woman*, p. 47.
139. Erica L. Johnson and Patricia Moran, 'Introduction', in Johnson and Moran (eds), *The Female Face of Shame*, pp. 1–19 (p. 2).
140. Johnson and Moran, 'Introduction', p. 3.
141. Johnson and Moran, 'Introduction', p. 10.
142. Johnson and Moran, 'Introduction', p. 19.
143. Nicole Fayard, 'Rape, Trauma, and Shame in Samira Bellil's *Dans l'enfer des tournantes*', in Johnson and Moran, *The Female Face*, pp. 34–47 (p. 45).
144. Suzette A. Henke, 'A Bloody Shame: Angela Carter's Shameless Postmodern Fairy Tales', in Johnson and Moran, *The Female Face*, pp. 48–60 (p. 59).
145. Tamar Heller, 'Affliction in Jean Rhys and Simone Weil', in Johnson and Moran, *The Female Face*, pp. 166–76 (p. 176).
146. Karen Lindo, 'Interrogating the Place of *Lajja* (Shame) in Contemporary Mauritius', in Johnson and Moran, *The Female Face*, pp. 212–28 (p. 212).
147. Sheils and Walsh, 'Introduction', p. 5.
148. Natalie Edwards, '"Ecrire pour ne plus avoir honte": Christine Angot's and Annie Ernaux's Shameless Bodies', in Johnson and Moran, *The Female Face*, pp. 61–73 (p. 70).
149. Sheils and Walsh, 'Introduction', p. 8.
150. David M. Halperin and Valerie Traub, 'Beyond Gay Pride', in Halperin and Traub (eds), *Gay Shame* (Chicago: University of Chicago Press, 2009), pp. 3–40 (p. 23).
151. That reflexivity has become something of a convention in scholarly writing on shame: in the final chapter of *Blush*, Probyn writes of the intense bodily symptoms she suffered while trying to write this book about shame (pp. 129–30); in her contribution to the *Gay Shame* collection, 'Emotional Rescue' (pp. 256–76), Heather Love begins by mentioning her own 'gay shame', saying that 'I felt bad things about myself and others: contempt and self-contempt; pity and self-pity; and a range of boomeranging feelings, including disappointment, anger, alienation, and embarrassment' – though she also claims to feel 'good

things' (p. 256); in *The Event of Postcolonial Shame*, Bewes laments the fact that a focus on the treatment of shame in a literary work tends to fall back on autobiographical readings, even when the text in question is fiction: 'Even narrative fiction [. . .] is inserted into an economy of revelation and confession, symptom and pathology, interpretation and symbolism, once our reading becomes organized by the category of authorship. Shame functions, within such an organization, as an index of the text's origins: of the writer and the writer's life that doubtless inform and explain every word' (p. 2) – and yet, his dismissal of auto-biographical approaches is problematised by the fact that he begins his own book with autobiographical reflections on ageing, physical inadequacy (including a reference to his 'small, rather feminine hands') and feelings of intellectual inferiority, before citing Deleuze's comment about 'the shame of being a man' as a spur to writing (p. 1).

152. Sedgwick, 'Queer Performativity', p. 4.
153. Warner, p. 3.
154. Eileen Myles, 'Foreword', in Chris Kraus, *I Love Dick* [1997] (Los Angeles: Semiotext(e), 2006), pp. 13–15 (p. 13)
155. Kraus, p. 208.
156. Steven Connor, 'The Shame of Being a Man' (2000), unpag. Through-out, references are to the longer version of this paper, available at <http://www.stevenconnor.com/shame/> (last accessed 13 June 2019), rather than to the shorter version that appeared in *Textual Practice* (Connor 2000, n.p.).
157. Emma Brockes, 'Sheila Heti: "There's a sadness in not wanting the things that give others their life's meaning"', *The Guardian*, 25 May 2018. Available at: <https://www.theguardian.com/books/2018/may/25/sheila-heti-motherhood-interview> (last accessed 13 June 2019).
158. Euripides/Carson, pp. 311–12. As the editors of Euripides' *Fragments* explain, 'The hypothesis of Aristophanes of Byzantium [. . .] states that the extant play [*Hippolytus*] was the second in time [. . .], and that what was "unseemly and reprehensible" in the earlier one was "put right" in it. Modern scholars have almost all believed that the "unseemly and reprehensible" was a direct approach to Hippolytus by Phaedra herself.' Euripides, *Fragments*, ed. and trans. by Christopher Collard and Martin Cropp (Cambridge, MA: Harvard University Press, 2008), p. 467. Hanna M. Roisman, however, challenges the accepted scholar-ship that suggests that, in the first play, *Hippolytus Veiled*, Phaedra made a direct sexual proposition to Hippolytus, and that this was what caused the play to be unfavourably received (and Euripides to rewrite it). See Hanna M. Roisman, 'The Veiled Hippolytus and Phaedra', *Hermes* 127: 4 (1999): 397–409.

159. Euripides/Carson, p. 312.
160. Anne Carson, 'Euripides to the Audience', *London Review of Books* 24: 17 (5 September 2002): 24. This is an earlier version of the essay that appears in *Grief Lessons*.
161. Writing of the blushing student from Bologna who appears in Robert Antelme's account of the moving of prisoners from Buchenwald to Dachau – who blushes when he is randomly singled out to be killed – Agamben notes 'the intimacy that one experiences before one's own unknown murderer', but reads that 'flush' as 'like a mute apostrophe flying through time to reach us, to bear witness to him' (Agamben, p. 104). Lisa Guenther claims that, 'For Agamben, the student's flush bears witness to the inhuman in the human, the impropriety of the proper, the desubjectification of every subject – to that which can neither be evaded nor assumed', but her own argument insists that the 'mute apostrophe' does not '[bear] witness on its own'. Robert Antelme does too: 'With his testimony, Antelme not only saves the student's blush from oblivion; he also bears witness to the multiple relations between the student and himself, himself and the reader, the reader and the student, and even between the student and the SS officer' (Guenther, pp. 66, 67). Her analysis hints at both the value of writing – though, as I have maintained, this goes beyond the testimonial – and the intersubjective, unpredictably transmissible functioning of shame.

Forgetting and Remembering Lesbian Pulp: Shame, Recuperation and Queer History

Introduction

'[W]hat will we do with our shame?', asks Michael Warner, writing in 1999 about the imbrication of sex and shame, and, more particularly, about gay culture's 'primal encounter with shame'.[1] Although, historically, shame has been a tool of oppression and regulation of the queer community, in the period since the 1990s the answer to Warner's question on the part of queer theorists has tended to be: we will revisit our shame, recuperate it, explore its positive and productive potential. Writing a decade after Warner, Michael D. Snediker notes that '[m]elancholy, self-shattering, shame, the death drive: these, within queer theory, are categories to conjure with', and what he calls 'this queer-pessimistic constellation' has 'dominated and organized much of queer-theoretical discourse'.[2] In this recent theory, shame functions to express a certain ambivalence about, for example: the pride agenda; varieties of social and cultural assimilation; forms of community more generally (which are both desired and rejected); capitalism; identity politics; and queerness itself. In this chapter, I want to work through the possibilities and limitations of such uses of queer shame, considering – among other matters – the elision of gender and race from those discussions, and the tensions between the individual and the social. I will do this in two ways: by engaging in some depth with recent queer theoretical accounts of shame, and by thinking through the instance of 1950s lesbian pulp fiction (its republication and renewed popularity, its critical recuperation) as a particularly illuminating case study in relation to a model of queerness and queer historiography deeply invested in negative affect. My focus in this chapter is, then, a dual one – both theoretical/academic discourse and popular fiction – and my interest is as much in the reception of the pulp texts, their symbolic value (as embodiments of queer shame), and what the recent attention to them might tell us about contemporary constructions/ conceptions of queerness as in the texts themselves (although I will offer closer readings of them later in the chapter).

The language of 'recuperation' is central, here. 'Recuperation' comes from the Latin *recuperat*, meaning 'regained', from the verb *recuperare*, from *re* 'back' and *capere* 'take'. It suggests regaining something lost or buried (an archaeological imperative); it involves an assertion of ownership, the taking back of something, the reclaiming of something that had been excluded and abjected – this is certainly the case with pulp, so long omitted from official histories of lesbianism and lesbian literature, and it is particularly resonant given the centrality of both loss and abjection to queer history. (Comparably, Christopher Nealon uses the word 'resuscitation' to describe the republication of, and renewed interest in, pulp novels in the late twentieth and early twenty-first centuries.)[3] Recuperation's concomitant meaning of 'recovery from illness' also plays interestingly in relation to homosexuality, which is so often figured as a sickness in pulp fiction and in fact was listed as a mental illness by the American Psychiatric Association until 1973; and of course Silvan Tomkins, memorably, notes how, '[a]t the moment when the self feels ashamed, it is felt as a sickness within the self'.[4]

Writing in 1981, the historian of lesbianism (and of romantic friendship), Lillian Faderman, asserted that, although the new paperback market of the 1950s 'provided abundant lesbian stories for the masses', such books were 'designed to titillate while upholding conventional values', and with few exceptions (she cites Patricia Highsmith's *The Price of Salt* – now republished under the title *Carol*):

> The paperbacks mirrored the familiar images: sadistic and inexplicably evil lesbians, often spouting feminist philosophy and corrupting the innocent; or confused and sick lesbians, torturing themselves and being tortured by others because of their terrible passions, made inescapable by nature or nurture.[5]

And she claims, 'almost invariably the characters end in violence or suicide if they are not rescued by some strong man'.[6] The lesbian is presented as 'twisted', even, writes Faderman, by 'the nonfiction paperbacks which pretended to sympathize with the lesbian and called for an end to the persecution against her', and she includes the lesbian writer of pulp fiction and non-fiction Ann Aldrich (one of Marijane Meaker's various pseudonyms) in this description.[7] Faderman subsequently suggests that writers like Aldrich and Paula Christian had 'internalized society's views of them' as sick; and she mentions Ann Bannon as one of those writers who had 'latched on to Radclyffe Hall's trick of presenting the lesbian as a poor suffering creature'.[8] Although Faderman would go on to title her later book *Odd Girls and Twilight Lovers* (1991) – a clear allusion to the titles and taglines of 1950s lesbian pulp novels – she remained critical of the genre, suggesting that 'the characters of the lesbian pulp novels almost always lived in shame' and '[s]elf-hatred was requisite in these novels'.[9] She was not alone in this viewpoint – a viewpoint that I would characterise as one of unease and ambivalence rather than unequivocal criticism (as Yvonne Keller has noted, Faderman 'names pulps as her personal starting point' in *Chloe Plus Olivia*, her anthology of lesbian literature, yet includes no pulp authors in that otherwise diverse collection).[10] In *Sexual Politics, Sexual Communities* (1983), John D'Emilio describes lesbian pulp in the following derogatory terms:

> Lurid covers with sensationalistic copy encased stories that were written most often by men to excite a male heterosexual audience. The plots frequently reflected stereotypical views of lesbianism, with characters plagued by self-hate and submerged in lives of alcoholism, violence, and despair.[11]

Yet he also concedes that there were some pulp novels 'written by lesbians, and though editors might tack on unhappy endings, the final versions still retained strong, brazen, rebellious women who embraced a lesbian identity'.[12] Susanna Benns, meanwhile, declares that

> [e]ven the best [lesbian pulp fiction] contains a high incidence of role-playing, despair, suicide [. . .], sentimentality, jealousy, heavy drinking, misogyny and heterosexual reinforcement. Some of this was the result

of writing to a formula; but some was not. Considering the atmosphere of repression under which these books were written, it is not surprising that they distort and exaggerate the lesbian lifestyle.[13]

On the whole, despite the huge commercial success of lesbian pulp fiction during the 1950s and early 1960s,[14] and despite some significant evidence of its popularity with lesbian readers at the time,[15] in the decades after its publication it tended to be excluded from anthologies of and critical texts on lesbian literature and derided for its pathologisation of lesbianism and its poor writing, alike. Lesbian pulp fiction bears an association with shame on various levels: the content of the novels is often concerned with experiences of shame and with the presentation of homosexuality as shameful; the novels are omitted from lesbian literary history on the grounds of their shamefulness (bad writing, homophobic messages); and even enthusiastic readers are infected by the shame of the novels' content and by their own shameful visibility as readers (of which, more anon).

Musing, then, in 2005, on the 'republication and rediscovery of a lesbian literary history', Stephanie Foote claims that

> [l]esbian pulps are now undergoing something of a revival. They have been the source of a great deal of fascinating literary and cultural criticism, but my interest in them focuses on their historical ability to initiate readers into a sense of the historicity of lesbianism, for the pulps are now beloved texts about which readers maintain a sense of irony and affection. Often cited, often parodied, lesbian pulps exist now as a touchstone for popular lesbian writing in a pre-Stonewall past.[16]

One question underlying my analysis of the phenomenon of pulp in the twenty-first century concerns what *kind* of 'historicity of lesbianism' the novels offer us, and how central shame is, to both the history that is being constructed/resurrected and the present affects guiding its construction and reception. We might also question how far the 'irony and affection' of pulp novels' (recent) reception work to defuse – but also to highlight – their historical association with shame: can that historical shame be neutralised, or must it inevitably seep into the present? And if so, what are the effects of that seepage?

In addition, it is worth noting that in fact the 'revival' of pulp began some time ago. There is, however, no smooth, teleological movement from rejection to recuperation; instead, pulp's reception has been characterised by fluctuation, disagreement and ambivalence; it remains shameful, yet the variety of shame that it models is now available to us in transformed and transformative ways, it seems. As early as 1983, Jeff Weinstein, writing in the *Village Voice*, suggests that, in Naiad Press's rebranding of Ann Bannon's pulp novels as 'lesbian classics', 'they have become something other than train-station propaganda' and 'the books have won another life'.[17] Nealon cites such views as evidence of 'the unstable nature of the [lesbian pulp] genre', asserting that 'changing historical conditions have altered it retroactively'.[18] Reading three pieces on Bannon published since 1980, he suggests that 'the novels have changed genre since their original publication', arguing 'that 'readership influences genre identity, not least because books like Bannon's can be claimed for different purposes in the 1980s and 1990s than in the 1950s and 1960s'.[19] This is at least partly what I am keen to analyse here: the ways in which the purportedly 'unstable nature' of lesbian pulp fiction makes it available for quite distinct – even incommensurable – readings and thus for diverse political appropriations. But I also wish to examine what those appropriations might tell us about the historical moment in which they are taking place, and the goals, preoccupations and conceptualisations of queer and feminist politics at that time. So, for example, in the 1970s to 1990s, the reading of pulp is held to be 'therapeutic' and necessary, if not always enjoyable.[20] Writing in 1980, Andrea Loewenstein avers that

> it is important to understand and to bear witness to the kind of pain which is behind the clichéd writing in these 'pulp' novels. This pain and self hatred is not our only past. But it is a part of it.[21]

And in Carol Ann Uszkurat's suggestion that pulp texts should 'be understood as forming part of the expansion of lesbian culture(s) in this century',[22] and Joan Nestle's description of pulp as 'survival literature', pulp fiction is positioned as, or appropriated for, a lesbian-feminist project of history-making.[23]

What is involved in this process of 'bearing witness'? Foote suggests that it is the 'feeling of revelatory identification [on the part of readers] that has driven the republication of some of the lesbian pulps' in recent years,[24] but arguably quite contradictory affects are involved in that 'revelatory identification' and, again, this is evident in earlier avowals of the combined shame and pleasure of reading pulp. In 1974, Kate Millett writes of her collection of pulp novels that she

> [k]ept them hidden in a drawer so visitors would never spy me out. Afraid the sublet might find them, I burned them [. . .]. Really I was ashamed of them as writing, the treacle of their fantasy, the cliché of their predicament, heartbroken butch murders her dog, etc. The only blooms in the desert, they were also books about grotesques.[25]

Lee Lynch, writing in 1990, proclaims that

> [t]heir ludicrous and blatantly sensational cover copy were both my signals and my shame. Valerie Taylor's *The Girls in 3B* and Randy Salem's *Man Among Women*: these books I would savor alone, heart pounding from both lust and terror of discovery, poised to plunge the tainted tome into hiding.[26]

Lynch and Millett's 'confessions' of their personal responses to pulp touch on the 'pain' and 'self hatred' of which Loewenstein speaks, but they also reveal more turbulent and unpredictable emotions – including pleasure. They root their experience of pulp in the physical (highlighting pulp's shameful connection with and appeal to the base and bodily), and in their respective responses they echo the hyperbole and lurid language of the books themselves: the invocation to 'burn' the novels, rather than just throw them away; the alliterative cadences of phrases such as 'poised to plunge the tainted tome into hiding'. Such confessions demonstrate Heather Love's point that

> [t]he experience of queer historical subjects is not at a safe distance from contemporary experience; rather, their social marginality and abjection mirror our own. The relation to the queer past is suffused not only by feelings of regret, despair, and loss but also by the shame of identification.[27]

And, indeed, pulp might seem to invite and intensify such identifications. In particular, Millett and Lynch's comments emphasise the dangerous *visibility* of pulp (the fear of being 'spied out', the 'signal' of the cover, the 'terror of discovery'); pulp's allure lies partly in its availability as spectacle but the transmissible nature of its shameful content and style ('I was ashamed of them as writing', 'the tainted tome') means that the reader too is exposed, their shameful desires – their shameful *self* – brought to light, made visible. As Nealon notes,

> [w]hat begins to emerge in reading these accounts [by lesbians who read pulps at the time, or a little later] is a sense of deep ambivalence about this 'survival literature' and the conditions it imposed on its readers, the tax, in a sense, it leveled for the right to read about lesbians at all.[28]

While pulps undeniably offered pleasure and passion, the 'tax' they levied comprised more difficult, discomfiting feelings and responses; 'revelatory identification' might be more exposing than consolatory.[29]

More recent scholarship on lesbian pulp fiction, while still emphasising pulp as a notable, neglected element of lesbian history and culture and a source of identification, has tended to treat it as camp or ironic, to claim it as queer or read it 'queerly', celebrating its 'productive contradictions',[30] and privileging 'undecidability'.[31] Yvonne Keller, then, for example, argues for pulp's 'importance as a readily available popular discourse that put the word *lesbian* in mass circulation as never before';[32] but she also notes pulp's facility for 'promoting danger and reassurance in the same gesture', describing her own critical methodology as 'queer' and arguing that, 'despite emphasizing a harshly pro-hegemonic voyeurism and surveillance, the [prototypical pulp] text also demonstrates the mutability of, and so the potential for subversion of, these powerful visual structures of voyeurism and surveillance'.[33] And while Amy Villarejo stresses questions of materiality, economics, labour, and racial and class politics in her reflection on pulp, she also counsels that 'to remember these things is not, however, to move out from "under cover" into what is right and true; it is simply to be more critically vigilant within contradiction and undecidability', emphasising thereby the queerness of her approach.[34] Writing on Ann Aldrich's non-fiction lesbian pulp text, *We Walk Alone* (1955), Stephanie Foote concludes that 'Aldrich is contradictory, and there is no way to reconcile some of those contradictions' – but for Foote this makes Aldrich an 'agent provocateur', and makes it possible 'to see the value in what she is doing'.[35] Martin Meeker, meanwhile, sets out an argument about the 1950s pulp paperback as 'a queer and contested medium':

> The paperback was a queer and contested medium for a variety of reasons, most basically because paperbacks contained information and stories about homosexuality to an extent and with a kind of detail that set them apart from movies, television, and newspapers of the era – as well as from the sensational dime novels and pulps that preceded them. Yet paperbacks also were queer and contested in ways familiar to queer theorists and scholars of deviance in general. Not only did they contain a great deal of content about prostitution, adultery, interracial sex, and transsexuality as well as homosexuality, but paperbacks also played a role in affirming deviant identities by spreading knowledge of those identities and by establishing a print culture which could sustain and nourish individuals who were beginning to organize their lives according to the logic of those identities.[36]

Meeker here invokes a (tacitly) Foucauldian logic to argue that pulp's attempts to regulate various kinds of sexual deviance instead end up – necessarily, if unwittingly – 'affirming deviant identities'; that the attempt to regulate *through* identification (often of the most taxonomic and pathologising kind) in fact enables a burgeoning queer community organised in relation to those 'identities'. Nealon, as part of his 'ambivalence' argument, suggests that, 'in most readings of lesbian pulp fiction today, two theories of US queer history are at work':

> In one reading, the melodrama of the pulps, their failure to depict long-term monogamous relationships, all the self-hatred they wallow in – all this has been transcended but must be respectfully memorialized. In the second reading, the pulps are worth calling heritage because they lead, pretty directly, to the door of a contemporary sex-positive queer politics.[37]

In fact, and bearing in mind that Nealon was writing this passage in 1999/2000, I think that recent readings of pulp have moved beyond the apparent two paths of respectful memorialisation and queer origins, developing the latter idea of anticipatory or originary queerness and thereby altering quite profoundly the way the novels are read. Such readings of pulp frequently attempt to locate the texts' subversive

potential in their very contradictoriness, in this way reclaiming them –
not for some 'therapeutic' purpose, and *not* for some compensatory lesbian history, founded on ideas of visibility, progress and solidarity, but rather for a variety of queer studies that privileges the
contradictory, the unintelligible, the incoherent, the indeterminate
and – increasingly – the shameful. The recuperation of pulp – despite,
or even because of, its association with shame – is made possible *and*
thus is inflected by a conception of 'queerness' that has a marked
investment in unintelligibility; on this reading, 'queer' amounts to a
refusal to signify in any straightforward or stable way. Pulp texts are
riven by internal contradictions of style, message and meaning, and
infused with emotional excess; they thus seem both to invite a queer
reading (that is, a reading that resists the urge to locate coherent
identities, histories and meanings, and which embraces the excessive, the unintelligible and the ex-centric) and to be categorisable as
'queer', as possessed of an anticipatory queerness, in their posited
self-reflexivity, their modes and methods of self-deconstruction. As
Heather Love has mused, in a discussion of other sad, queer literary
figures from the pre-Stonewall era:

> Contemporary critics approach these figures from the past with a
> sense of the inevitability of their progress toward us – of their place
> in the history of modern homosexuality. Their relation to this future
> remains utterly tenuous, however. If their trajectory to a queer future
> seems inevitable, this appearance is perhaps best explained by the
> fact that *we are that future*. Our existence in the present depends on
> being able to imagine these figures reaching out to us.[38]

Those accounts of lesbian pulp fiction that figure it as possessed of
a kind of anticipatory queerness assume (desire, establish) a certain
'trajectory to a queer future' and ignore *what might be* the 'utterly
tenuous' relation of pulp to this future.

Furthermore, pulp might function, nevertheless, as a kind of check
or limit case for the politics of queer shame for, as Nealon's comments about ambivalence show, the question remains of whether we
are – even in the twenty-first century – sufficiently recovered from the
view of homosexuality as sickness that we can displace pulp's more
pathologising effects. How might pulp speak back to – even resist –
our readings and deployments of it in the present? The recuperation of

pulp fiction amounts to *more* than simply its republication; rather, it welcomes what was once abjected back into the corpus of queer texts and histories, in a way that raises questions both about the meanings of 'queerness' in the present and about the structural, ideological interplay of memory and forgetting – and the role that shame might play in both. Roger Luckhurst claims that

> [t]o think through the intensity of memory-work in the contemporary moment, it is important to see it as inextricably intertwined with an anxiety concerning systems that induce structural forgetting. But memory and forgetting are not opposing things; rather, they are an interplay of the same process.[39]

In this chapter, I am less interested in the 'systems that induce structural forgetting' than in those systems that encourage the remembering of particular representations and particular histories at a particular moment. Why remember lesbian pulp fiction of the 1950s – with its politically dubious, self-hating content and connotations – now? The shame with which pulp is both infused and associated is not easily overcome; indeed, the reading of pulp in the present precisely reveals the persistence of shame, the ways in which it might live on, in the body, in a body of work. I want to address this remembering of pulp as part of a broader question about the uses and meanings of shame for us, whilst considering the affective power in the present of those lesbian pulp texts of the 1950s that have been republished in the last decade. Arguably, the very *same* reasons lie behind both the forgetting of pulp (its exclusion, until relatively recently, from histories of lesbianism and anthologies of lesbian literature) and its recuperation, notably its close association with shame, its investment in and stimulation of affective excess, and (what is perceived as) its wilful contradictoriness or unintelligibility.

My argument is motivated by several intuitions: that the recuperation of pulp *now* is neither incidental nor accidental; that its recuperation can, therefore, tell us something about the meanings, uses and political utility of queer (as a term, category and methodology) for us *now*; and that the peculiar temporalities of 'recuperation' make possible new forms of relationality between queer individuals across time, but also make the 'shame' of the past something that we cannot simply put behind us or forget; 'recuperation', then, is always double-edged.

I want to suggest, also, that pulp's recuperation is *made possible* by (at least) four late twentieth-/early twenty-first-century developments: by a fetishistic attachment to a 1950s aesthetic;[40] by an impulse towards cultural and historical memorialising, but one that operates with an increasing awareness of the fraught and unreliable workings of memory and which evolves alternative temporalities in tracking the relationship between past and present;[41] relatedly, by a burgeoning fascination with feeling within queer studies; and by that variant of queer theory most indebted to poststructuralism, which advocates a position of unintelligibility, a refusal of straightforward signification. These are the conditions that compel a kind of 'structural remembering' of lesbian pulp fiction.

The emphasis on feeling – and on negative affects in particular – has become central to the operations and practices of queer history; it forms part of a wider 'affective turn' in cultural and critical studies, and it is key to the recuperation of pulp. In *An Archive of Feeling*, Ann Cvetkovich aims to show 'how affective experience can provide the basis for new cultures' and she examines cultural texts as 'repositories of feelings and emotions'.[42] Cvetkovich argues that 'trauma challenges common understandings of what constitutes an archive. Because trauma can be unspeakable and unrepresentable and because it is marked by forgetting and dissociation, it often seems to leave behind no records at all.' It has an 'ephemerality' that demands an archive of similarly 'ephemeral' materials.[43] Pulp novels, in the divergent (even divisive) and hyperbolic affective responses that they provoke and document, in their preoccupation with traumatic feelings of longing, loss, self-loathing and repression, and in their 'ephemerality' (their disposability), can thus find a place in such a 'queer' archive. It is not surprising, then, that Cvetkovich notes the Lesbian Herstory Archive's inclusion of pulp fiction, and praises it for '[embracing] the archive of popular culture, even when it is homophobic, inventing an archival [. . .] aesthetic *more interested in preserving affect than in collecting positive images*'.[44] 'Preserving affect' in this way becomes a value, a political goal, in itself. Before offering readings of novels by Ann Bannon and Della Martin, then, I want to engage in a more sustained fashion with some of the recent queer theorisations of shame and negative affect, for within scholarly discourse it is queer theory that has led the way in the turn to shame of the last couple of decades.

Reading queer theory: accentuating the negative

Recall Giorgio Agamben's definition of shame, quoted in my Introduction:

> We can therefore propose a first, provisional definition of shame. It is nothing less than the fundamental sentiment of being *a subject*, in the two apparently opposed senses of this phrase: to be subjected and to be sovereign. Shame is what is produced in the absolute concomitance of subjectification and desubjectification, self-loss and self-possession, servitude and sovereignty.[45]

On this analysis, as I discussed in the Introduction, shame speaks to a tension that lies at the heart of the experience of being a subject: necessary to the establishment of our sense of bounded selfhood, but also posing a threat to that sense of self, revealing it as dangerously porous or precarious; necessary to the workings of civilisation and society, helping to regulate our behaviour (particularly in public), but also, in its more extreme forms, debilitating, isolating and functioning as a tool of oppression. In what Agamben says about subjection versus sovereignty, and in what numerous theorists of shame claim about its links to identity and to the social, we might begin to see its resonance for the queer community: a community with a history of subjection and oppression from which it is only recently (and only in some areas of the world) emerging; a socially abjected community (historically); and a community somewhat precariously founded upon questions of (sexual) identity. Indeed, the association between shame and queerness has a long history, arguably stemming from the emergence and subsequent pathologisation of homosexual identity in the late nineteenth century, when shame becomes a code word for homosexuality: as Alfred Douglas (Oscar Wilde's lover) writes, 'Of all sweet passions Shame is loveliest.'[46] Commenting on the recent turn to negative affect within queer theory, Heather Love notes that 'The feeling of shame – once understood as a poison that must be purged from the queer community – has proven to be particularly attractive as a basis for alternative models of politics';[47] and in the late twentieth and early twenty-first centuries, the centrality of shame to queer history and identity has been extensively investigated, as has what David Halperin and Valerie Traub call gay pride's 'ongoing struggle with shame'.[48]

Notably, this recent investigation of queer shame has been more interested in exploration than in overcoming or redemption; more interested in mining the positive potential of shame than lamenting its historical (and current) ill effects. In *Beautiful Bottom, Beautiful Shame* (2006), Kathryn Bond Stockton writes of shame's 'beautiful, generative, sorrowful debasements',[49] and asserts that 'I think it is time for a study devoted to valuable, generative, beautiful shame', positioning her own work within 'a line of thought' already evident within queer theory; she cites, in particular, the work of Eve Kosofsky Sedgwick, Leo Bersani, Lee Edelman, Joseph Litvak and José Muñoz.[50] Sedgwick is especially prescient and provocative in turning her attention to shame, in the first issue of *GLQ*, in 1993; her thinking on the subject – derived, in large part, from the work of Silvan Tomkins – has effectively inaugurated a whole sub-strand of queer theory. In choosing to organise her analysis of queer performativity around the utterance 'shame on you', Sedgwick asks:

> What's the point of accentuating the negative, of beginning with stigma, and for that matter a form of stigma – 'Shame on you' – so unsanitizably redolent of that long Babylonian exile known as queer childhood? But note that this is just what the word queer itself does, too: the main reason why the self-application of 'queer' by activists has proven so volatile is that there's no way that any amount of affirmative reclamation is going to succeed in detaching the word from its associations with shame [. . .]. If queer is a politically potent term, which it is, that's because, far from being capable of being detached from the childhood scene of shame, it cleaves to that scene as a near-inexhaustible source of transformational energy.[51]

Sedgwick '[begins] with stigma' because she situates stigma (in this case, queer shame) at the beginning of identity, in 'queer childhood' – the 'Babylonian exile' of which suggests both captivity and identity/community formation. I will engage further with this notion of 'queer childhood', and with shame's emergence in and association with childhood, in the next chapter, but it is worth emphasising here: (a) the way that Sedgwick situates shame as originary, both for the individual (rooted in childhood) and for her theoretical project ('beginning with stigma'); (b) her suggestion that queerness cannot be detached from shame, however much we might want to effect that detachment; (c) that 'queer' is 'a politically potent' term for Sedgwick *because* of its association with shame, not despite that association; (d) that shame itself is 'unsanitizable', and will thus always bear its negative connotations and associations, whatever more positive purposes it may be put to; and (e) that she organises her analysis of shame, in this original *GLQ* article, around a speech act ('shame on you'), thus revealing the performative power of shame and shaming (like other classic performatives – 'I name this ship . . . ', 'I hereby declare you man and wife' – this statement is an action that brings about what it states).[52] Sedgwick's comments mark a first move beyond 'affirmative reclamation', a moment at which queer studies (distinct from the Gay Liberation movement, which relied upon protestations of pride) begins to 'cleave' to the 'scene of shame'.[53]

For Sedgwick, as for Agamben, shame connects to identity in a manner both ineluctable and contradictory:

> Shame floods into being as a moment, a disruptive moment, in a circuit of identity-constituting identificatory communication. Blazons of shame, the 'fallen face' with eyes down and head averted [. . .] are semaphores of trouble and at the same time of a desire to reconstitute the interpersonal bridge.
>
> But in interrupting identification, shame, too, makes identity. In fact, shame and identity remain in very dynamic relation to one another, at once deconstituting and foundational, because shame is both peculiarly contagious and peculiarly individuating.[54]

Shame is both 'disruptive' and 'identity-constituting', both 'deconstituting' and 'foundational', precisely because of the forms of self-consciousness that it provokes: an acute, uncomfortable, over-awareness of one's self (as an object for others and a disgraced object at that); an awareness, again uncomfortable, of relationality (and thus, of the precariousness and porousness of selfhood, which relies upon a recognition that might be revoked). The 'contagious' nature of shame might be connected here with the perception of homosexuality as a disease and as (socially or culturally) infectious – one chapter of *The Troubled Sex* (1961), a pulp sexological work with a focus on female homosexuality, is titled 'The Infection Spreads',[55] while Ann Aldrich in *We Walk Alone* (1955) describes lesbianism as a 'cancer'[56] – and again it seems to threaten the stability and boundedness of selfhood in its positing of a relationality that is vulnerable to the viral. This 'dynamic relation' between shame and identity, in its ceaseless movement, might also be read as a source of anxiety and (perceived) instability. Considering the view (of Tomkins and others) that guilt concerns what you have done and shame what you *are*, Sedgwick comments, 'the implication remains that one *is something* in experiencing shame' – shame, then, bequeaths us selfhood as both gift and burden – and she notes that 'In the developmental process, shame is now often considered the affect that most defines the space wherein a sense of self will develop'; she interprets this as meaning that shame 'is the place where the *question* of identity arises most originarily and most relationally' – but this indicates, again, the way that identity is both instituted ('arises') and left *in question* or *open to question*, unresolved or under threat.[57]

In her discussion of shame's (formative, constitutive) relationship with identity, Sedgwick touches relatively briefly on the identity markers (such as race and gender) that will further inflect that identity's formation, claiming that

> the shame-delineated place of identity doesn't determine the consistency or meaning of that identity, and race, gender, class, sexuality, appearance and abledness are only a few of the defining social constructions that will crystallize there, developing from this originary affect their particular structure of expression, creativity, pleasure, and struggle.[58]

The order(s) of priority and causality is tricky to determine here. Identity is formed in, or emerges out of – or simply *is* – this 'shame-delineated place'; shame does not 'determine' that identity's 'meaning', yet the 'social constructions' of race, gender and so on that will flesh out that 'meaning' themselves derive from shame ('this originary affect') 'their particular structure of expression'. Shame, then, on Sedgwick's analysis, plays both an originary and a structuring role in the formation of gender (my key concern in this book), but not a determining one. Snediker asks, 'Why, in the midst of all these social constructions, is shame granted originary privilege?'[59] I, too, am tending to grant shame an 'originary privilege', positioning it as productive of certain identity formations; my critique of Sedgwick differs from Snediker's, then, in that I am arguing that shame has a *distinctive* originary force in the case of femininity, and that this distinctive connection between shame and femininity goes unrecognised in Sedgwick's analysis. Snediker suggests that Tomkins, by contrast, posits an 'originary positivity' out of which shame emerges, and he quotes Tomkins's claim that 'To the extent to which socialization involves a preponderance of positive affect the individual is made vulnerable to shame and unwilling to renounce either himself or others.'[60] In other words, we feel shame only because we first feel interest, and that interest is a kind of 'positive affect'. Snediker argues, therefore, that

> I don't disagree with Sedgwick on the point of shame's interlineation and coloring of queer experiences. I nonetheless challenge the insistence of shame's anteriority at the expense of elaborations of the sorts of positivity that might have preceded it [. . .].[61]

However, this is a different question from that of shame's originary role in identity formation: Tomkins is writing of the interest that arises from socialisation – that is, from a point when identity formation has already taken place (or is at least well under way). This is perhaps the difference between shame as event and shame as structure; while the event of shame may – indeed, on Tomkins's account, *must* – be preceded by 'interest', the structural work of shame in the process of subjectivation has already taken place. Sedgwick's concern, in the passage cited above, is very much with the latter, with shame as structure (and so, I think, is mine). As she asserts, quite clearly, 'The forms taken by shame are not distinct "toxic" parts of a group or individual identity that can be excised; they are instead integral to and residual in the processes by which identity itself is formed.'[62] That they are 'integral' and 'residual' signals Sedgwick's conception of shame as structure rather than event; she therefore dismisses the possibility that shame might be overcome or banished ('therapeutic or political strategies aimed directly at getting rid of individual or group shame, or undoing it, have something preposterous about them'),[63] and eschews any discussion of shame as a moral emotion. As she explains, 'at least for certain ("queer") people, shame is simply the first, and remains a permanent, structuring fact of identity: one that [. . .] has its own, powerfully productive and powerfully social metamorphic possibilities'.[64]

Those '[socially] metamorphic possibilities' are latent in Sedgwick's assertion that the 'blazons of shame [. . .] are semaphores of trouble and at the same time of a desire to reconstitute an interpersonal bridge' – a claim echoed in the work of subsequent theorists of shame, such as Elspeth Probyn, who avers that shame 'promises a return of interest, joy, and connection',[65] and Sally Munt, who claims that shame 'presages a desire for reconnection'.[66] Yet Snediker insists that '[s]hame (at its most felicitous) cedes to a desire to reconstitute interpersonality, but this desire seems neither synchronous with nor equivalent to shame's desire to hide'.[67] Munt's 'presages', with its emphasis on temporal *consecution* rather than logical or causal *consequence*, might best express the hazardous movement from the 'desire to hide' (the introversion of shame, an act of turning away from others) to the 'desire for reconnection' (a turning back towards others); what, though, might intervene in or prevent this movement from occurring? This is a crucial question for determining the political potentiality of shame: to what extent does it make available, and to what extent does it preclude, forms of community, collectivity and solidarity? For Sedgwick, 'the forms taken by shame' are 'available for the work of metamorphosis, reframing, refiguration, *trans*figuration, affective and symbolic loading and deformation', but are 'perhaps all too potent for the work of purgation and deontological closure'.[68] If this expresses caution about the political potential of shame, then the original version of Sedgwick's argument – in the 1993 issue of *GLQ* – displays an even keener awareness of the possible limitations of a politics of queer shame in its concession that shame is '*unavailable* for effecting the work of purgation', rather than 'perhaps all too potent' as she writes in *Touching Feeling*.[69] In addition, it is precisely the contagion/individuation aspect of shame – the way that someone else's shame 'can so readily flood me [. . .] with this sensation whose very suffusiveness seems to delineate my precise, individual outlines in the most isolating way imaginable' – 'that offers the most conceptual leverage for political projects'.[70] (Again, in the original *GLQ* essay, Sedgwick writes 'the most theoretically significant', rather than 'offers the most conceptual leverage for political projects'; the former seems like a weaker claim.[71]) Shame, then, makes 'a double movement [. . .] toward painful individuation, toward uncontrollable relationality'.[72] 'Uncontrollable' may be the key word here: the unpredictability of the operations of shame, its doubleness (subjectification and desubjectification, isolation and contagion/connection, individuation and relationality), the dynamic (ever-shifting) relation between shame and identity – all of these might be seen as limiting shame's potential as a basis for a more sustained queer relationality and a more agential and effective queer politics.

Nevertheless, subsequent queer theorists have enthusiastically taken up Sedgwick's points concerning the connection between queerness and shame, and the conceptual potentiality of shame for 'political projects' and sociality.[73] Michael Warner understands shame as 'the premise of a special kind of sociability that holds queer culture together', claiming that 'a relation to others, in these contexts, begins in an acknowledgement of all that is most abject and least reputable in oneself', and '[t]his understanding of a shared abjection cuts through hierarchies'.[74] Douglas Crimp considers that the feeling of shame, in its very persistence and isolationism, has 'the capacity for articulating collectivities of the shamed'.[75] Cvetkovich argues that 'trauma can be a foundation for creating counterpublic spheres rather than evacuating them',[76] praising Sedgwick's work on 'the reclamation of shame' ('traumatic experiences of rejection and humiliation') as 'an alternative to the model of gay pride', and suggesting that work within queer theory on melancholy and mourning has 'produced understandings of collective affective formations that *break through the presumptively privatized nature of affective experience*'.[77] While Cvetkovich's interest lies in public cultures and manifestations of 'affective experience' more generally, Jennifer Moon spells out the particular, prospective relationship between shame, sexual 'deviance' and radical politics, in her claim that

> [s]hame distinguishes the queer from the normal, not because there is anything inherently shameful about having deviant desires or engaging in deviant acts, but because shame adheres to (or is supposed to adhere to) any position of social alienation or nonconformity. Shame thus seems especially useful to a radical queer politics for three main reasons: (1) it has the potential to organize a discourse of queer counterpublicity, as opposed to the mainstream discourse of pride; (2) it provides the basis for a collective queer identity, spanning differences in age, race, class, gender, ability, and sexual practice; and (3) it redirects attention away from internal antagonisms within the gay community to a more relevant divide – that is, between heteronormatic and queer sectors of society.[78]

Love is more cautious, in her invocation to us to 'pursue a fuller engagement with negative affects and with the intransigent difficulties of making feeling the basis for politics'.[79] Those difficulties – bearing in mind Moon's three points, cited above – might include: (1) the work that shame already does to regulate, maintain and perpetuate the (mainstream) public sphere and the operation of norms *against* more 'deviant' practices and 'counterpublics'; (2) shame's unreliability as a 'basis for a collective queer identity', given its isolating and individuating properties and given its dynamic/contradictory relationship with identity (of all kinds, not only queerness); (3) shame's pervasiveness and (if we follow Sedgwick) its originary function in the formation of queer identity, which means that it cannot straightforwardly be located either 'outside' or exclusively 'inside' the queer community. More generally, Moon's argument suggests that the only kind of politics shame facilitates is a 'deviant', oppositional (antinormative) and marginal politics. This may, of course, be precisely what is desired. However, in the introduction to a recent special issue of *differences* entitled 'Queer Theory without Antinormativity', Robyn Wiegman asserts that 'nearly every queer theoretical itinerary of analysis that now matters is informed by the prevailing assumption that a critique of normativity marks the spot where *queer* and *theory* meet', and she asks (as does the issue as a whole), 'what might queer theory do if its allegiance to antinormativity was rendered less secure?'[80] One casualty of any failure or abandonment of the anti-normative impulse within queer theory might be, I suggest, a move away from the privileging of negative affects such as shame as a basis of queer politics and a focus of queer history.

The turn to shame in queer theory that has occurred in the late twentieth and early twenty-first centuries is most starkly evidenced by the *Gay Shame* (2009) collection of essays. In the introduction, editors David Halperin and Valerie Traub proclaim that

> [g]ay pride has never been able to separate itself entirely from shame, or to transcend shame. Gay pride does not even make sense without some reference to the shame of being gay and its very successes (to say nothing of its failures) testify to the intensity of its ongoing struggle with shame.[81]

They aim 'to identify topics that the imperative of gay pride had tended to place off-limits to legitimate inquiry, or had simply repressed – shameful topics, that is, or topics gay pride itself might make us ashamed to investigate', in addition to attempting 'to imagine a queer community founded not only in collective affirmations of pride but also in residual experiences of shame'.[82] As well as investigating 'the residual effects of shame on lesbian and gay subjectivity in the era of gay pride', Halperin and Traub ask:

> What affirmative uses can be made of shame and related affects, now that not all queers are condemned to live in shame? Are there important, nonhomophobic values related to the experience of shame that gay pride does not or cannot offer us? Can we do things with shame that we cannot do with pride?[83]

In what they are claiming here we can note: a continuing desire for 'community' and for shared experience (even if that is an experience of shame); a desire to own, remember and memorialise a difficult and contentious history (not just a history *of* shame, but also a history of which we may *be* ashamed); and an injunction to recognise and investigate all aspects of that experience and history, even those that might seem less than productive, progressive or positive. The Pride agenda, it is suggested, has been counter-productive in its repression of certain histories – even of certain types of queerness. And yet, Halperin and Traub contend that they do not want shame 'to displace or replace gay pride', and their aims are basically in support of 'an affirmative queer future unrestricted by the increasingly exhausted and restrictive ethos of gay pride'.[84] In their continuing desire for some 'affirmative queer future', gay shame, as they construe it, is not necessarily at odds with gay pride:

> Gay shame confers potential legitimacy and acceptability on the discussion of issues that don't make gay people feel proud, that even proud gay people aren't always proud of. In this sense, gay shame is continuous with gay pride, insofar as the success of gay pride now makes it possible to address realities that may not present a 'positive image' of gay people. Because of gay pride, we have become proud enough that we don't need to stand on our pride.[85]

What is posited instead of pride, then, is simply an 'exemption from the imperative to affirmation', rather than an injunction to pride's seeming opposite ('at once its emotional antithesis and its political antagonist'),[86] and indeed they maintain that this 'exemption from the imperative to affirmation might itself turn out [. . .] to be bracingly affirmative'.[87] Again, then, there is a reassuring nod here towards the possible *affirmative*, positive outcomes of an apparent reclaiming of shame.

In fact, I would suggest that where Halperin and Traub err is not in their equivocation over gay shame and its relationship to gay pride, but rather in their failure to contextualise queer studies' 'turn to shame' within some wider expansion and popularisation of shame culture. One tacit argument of this chapter is that the turn to shame within queer culture represents, potentially, a kind of conformism/ assimilation into mainstream culture (which is, as the Introduction to this book set out, increasingly a shame culture), even while (often) presenting itself as an anti-assimilationist and anti-normative move. There are further problems with Halperin and Traub's stance, how- ever: in one of their more succinct statements of their position, Halperin and Traub aver that 'We have become proud enough that we are now unashamed of our shame.'[88] The 'we' of this statement – in its implied universality and self-evidence – is troubling and warrants fur- ther examination. Who is this 'we' – who qualifies? – and what does it mean to be 'proud enough' that one can safely and productively approach more shameful and shaming experiences and histories? Has gay pride really been a 'success' for everyone, everywhere? The *Gay Shame* book emerged from a conference at the University of Michigan in 2003, and the conference was, from the outset, controversial in its themes, its programme and its selection of speakers. Writing in the pages of *Social Text* a couple of years after the conference, J. Halberstam recalls their initial response to the conference invitation, which was that 'the idea of gay shame felt anachronistic'; Halberstam proceeds to argue that the notion of 'gay shame', when 'used in an uncritical way', can end up being 'for, by, and about the white gay men who had rejected feminism and a queer of color critique and for whom, therefore, shame was still an active rubric of identification'.[89] Much of Halberstam's argument is (rightly, usefully) concerned with pointing out how shame is experienced differently by different groups (that is, how it is racialised and gendered), and how it is projected on to others (that is, on to those in less powerful groups, such as queers of colour and women). As Halberstam explains:

> The subject who emerges as the subject of gay shame is often a white and male self whose shame in part emerges from the experience of being denied access to privilege. [. . .] Shame for women and shame

for people of color plays out in different ways and creates different modes of abjection, marginalization, and self-abnegation; it also leads to very different political strategies.[90]

If one has never had 'access to privilege', how does that change one's experience of shame? In the next section, in my reading of two pulp novels, I will look in particular at their treatment of the (perceived, lived) experience of shame when this is added to, and inextricable from, the forms of shame already attending femininity and blackness. Such representations, even (or especially) when derived from mass-market literature with an investment in sensationalism, might help us think through the possibilities and limitations of an embrace of 'gay shame' (the sensationalism, in fact, reveals one further element here, which is the dangerous susceptibility of shame to spectacularisation, in a way that might be politically unproductive). Halberstam therefore warns against a 'romanticization of gay shame, a romanticization that [. . .] glosses over both the particularity of this formation and the damage of its myopic range', even while acknowledging, first, that 'we cannot completely do without shame' and, second, that 'shame can be a powerful tactic in the struggle to make privilege (whiteness, masculinity, wealth) visible'.[91] Pulp novels may well make privilege visible – and open to critique – even without meaning to; this is one of their values for us in the twenty-first century.

Ultimately, Halberstam critiques the gay shame project (such as it is) on three counts: for 'glorifying the pre-Stonewall past'; for 'idealizing youth' as the scene of shame; and for 'focusing perhaps too much on interiority', that is: privileging the '"inside of the subject"' (quoting Lauren Berlant).[92] As Halberstam asserts:

> The notion that social change can come about through adjustments to the self, through a focus on interiority without a concomitant attention to social, political, and economic relations, can be a disastrous tactic for queer studies and queer activism.[93]

There are flaws in this critique – for example, the focus on gay shame is not straightforwardly celebratory in its treatment of the 'bad old days', pre-Stonewall – but the exhortation to shift our focus from 'interiority' (the self) to structural inequalities is a useful one, and I will return to it at intervals throughout the course of this book.

Reading pulp: Bannon and Martin

In this section, I offer analyses of Ann Bannon's *Women in the Shadows* (1959) and Della Martin's *Twilight Girl* (1961), two relatively late examples of the lesbian pulp fiction genre, both of which have been republished by a specialist lesbian publisher – the San Francisco-based Cleis Press – in recent years. Both authors have received renewed attention and acclaim in the twenty-first century, with Bannon in particular frequently, and gleefully, heralded as the 'Queen of Pulp'.[94] Both novels fall into the category that Yvonne Keller has termed 'pro-lesbian pulps' (female-authored, 'without obviously extraneous sex scenes, and with well-developed characters', displaying some sympathy for those characters and for lesbianism more generally), as distinct from 'virile adventures' (male-authored, more obviously salacious, more obviously pathologising in their treatment of lesbianism).[95] I have discussed the limitations of this 'good versus bad' pulp model elsewhere,[96] but for my purposes here it is useful to consider two texts/authors that form part of the recent recuperation of pulp, and that had some recognition also in their period of original publication.[97] In my readings of these two novels, I focus particularly on the (in)visibility and (un)intelligibility of gender and race – including questions of performance and 'passing'. As Sinéad Moynihan explains it:

> Broadly defined, to 'pass' is to appear to belong to one or more social subgroups other than the one(s) to which one is normally assigned by prevailing legal, medical and/or socio-cultural discourses. To pass as white, if one is 'black', or male, if one is 'female', is to challenge assumptions that the evidence of one's race and/or gender is always visually available.[98]

Passing's relation to shame is a complex one: shame might cause one to try to pass; one might feel shame at a failure to pass, an unwitting (self-)disclosure; one might feel shame at the act of passing itself; and shame itself is so much a matter of visibility and concealment, of becoming-visible in ways that might be painful or difficult, of being too self-conscious, of wanting to hide something that is felt – by you or by others – to be a flaw.

In her work on the figure of the tomboy in literature and in history, Michelle Ann Abate claims that pulp fiction of the 1950s 'provided a new cultural home for tomboyism', and that 'the figures in lesbian pulp novels reflected postwar beliefs that a boyish type of childhood tomboyism would lead to a mannish form of adult lesbianism'.[99] Like much lesbian pulp fiction, Bannon and Martin's novels present what now seem like stereotypes of 'butch' and 'femme' identity, tending to run together questions of sexual and gendered 'deviance', and stressing 'oddness' – the word 'odd' appears frequently in the titles and taglines of pulp novels – in relation to gender as well as sexuality. Thus, the protagonist of *Twilight Girl*, Lon (Lorraine) Harris, is described, early on, as 'the gangling odd-ball with the hazel eyes', and her apparent refusal to conform to feminine standards of dress and behaviour – she wears t-shirts and jeans, and loves cars and dogs – is presented both as a major source of her oddness and unhappiness, and as a key indicator of her incipient homosexuality.[100] When she meets the super-femme Violet, a 'curved and compact doll' in clinging clothes, with lavender hair, a face 'buried somewhere beneath layers of pinkish pancake',[101] and a girlish lisp, Violet instructs Lon:

> 'It's kinda mixed-up at first, but you get the hang of it. Like there's girls that're butch. I mean, they wish they could be a guy and they treat you the same as they were a guy, on'y better. And there's fems [sic], like me. See, like one is the guy and one is the girl [. . .]. You're butch, Lon. You mean you didn' know it?'[102]

The butch is here defined by the desire to 'be a guy', but also by being 'better' than – and therefore distinct from – a 'guy'. With the advent of this information, Lon's innocent (literally *unknowing*) and yet visible tomboy behaviour shades into something more adult, self-conscious – and threatening to social norms; her behaviour becomes an identity. As Abate elaborates:

> In inexpensive paperback novels, tomboyism moved out of the realm of heteronormativity and was firmly yoked with homosexuality. In addition, it shifted from being linked with boyishness to being associated with a new form of female masculinity known as butchness. Also, in a radical break from its origins, it abandoned its previous aim of improving female health and instead was associated with more antisocial elements and even self-destructive behaviors.

Finally, in a characteristic that was perhaps the most controversial, it went from signaling a transgressive code of conduct to a potential index of something that would come to be known in the wake of Christine Jorgensen's much-publicized sex-change operation in 1952 as transsexualism.[103]

Identification as butch or femme is, in *Twilight Girl*, a source of consolation – offering a sense of belonging, a ready-made identity to inhabit, complete with its own patterns of speech, appearance and behaviour – but also, potentially, a source of shame, particularly as far as butchness is concerned. Thus the troubled character Sassy Gregg, with whom Lon later crosses paths (and fists), denies her butchness, even as her lover Mavis taunts her: 'don't you ever admit to Sassy Gregg that she's butch – butch all the way!' and, we are told, '[t]he agony of that truth twisted itself in Sassy's gut'.[104] What is shameful here is not lesbianism *per se*, but the apparent gender deviance of butchness.

In the description of butches in the lesbian bar, the novel leans toward a sexological explanation of the 'third sex' variety, without ever quite employing those terms. The butches are:

> [r]egular guys, remembering a girl and laughing it up. Regular guys, flicking kitchen matches with their thumbnails for a light, burrowing hands in the front-zipped pants for a crushed cigarette pack and belting each other in the back to punctuate a bellylaugh. Regular guys, and less than twenty years before, unknowing nurses had checked the wrong box on the hospital form that offered only *Male* and *Female*. For perhaps the choice was incomplete.[105]

Butchness, here, becomes a set of learned behavioural tropes, utterly performative in this instance – the thumbnail flicking of matches, the bellylaughs – and yet also both recuperated and pathologised (as congenital) through the pathos of 'the wrong box on the hospital form'. The stereotypically masculine behaviour is an attempt to pass as 'regular guys', which is just what these butches can never be; the repetition of 'regular guys' underlines their effort and mocks their failure to be what they perform; it emphasises the precarious citationality of the performance of masculinity.[106] This 'failure' would later be taken up by gender theorists such as Judith Roof and Judith

Butler as a sign of the challenges that butch–femme role-playing could pose to gender and sexual norms:

> Butch/Femme [. . .] is internally self-contradictory from the beginning: inconceivability is nonetheless conceivable; a woman is nonetheless a man. What is important in the case of Butch/Femme is that the two processes – inconceivability and recuperation – and their internal contradictions coexist in a tension that never quite resolves itself, producing a systemic challenge to the necessary connection between gender and sexuality while appearing to reaffirm heterosexuality and forcing a consciousness of the artificiality and constructedness of gender positions.[107]

But in *Twilight Girl*, as befits the period in which it was written, there is an unease, in this passage and elsewhere, about the extent to which such identities are constructed or innate (again, without using this kind of language, which the novels predate). In the bar, one butch asks another, about a recent date, 'Just tell me one thing. Was she butch or fem? Christ, I couldn't tell!' And her interlocutor replies: 'Smorgasbord. By the time she went home I wasn't sure which I was!'[108] Despite the humorous tone in which this anecdote is related, the anxiety of not being able to 'tell' – what someone else is, what you are – is not liberating in this 1950s context; it is, instead, an anxiety about visibility and about passing, about how others will read you and what the consequences of that reading might be; it is an anxiety in the mode of shame, of wanting and not wanting to be looked at, of wanting and not wanting to be 'known' as a particular kind of 'object' for others.

For Abate, Beebo Brinker, who appears in several of Ann Bannon's pulp novels of the 1950s and 1960s, is 'the epitome of pulp tomboyism'.[109] In *Women in the Shadows*, Beebo (who routinely dresses in trousers, and also an outfit of jodhpurs and boots – to the 'dismay' of her girlfriend, Laura) says of herself: 'I'm no man. Okay. But I'm sure as hell no woman, either.'[110] And we are told: 'She did not look mannish like some Lesbians. She simply looked like a boy. But she was thirty-three years old, and there were very faint lines around her eyes and mouth.'[111] She is misread, by her manager at work, as 'a *male* homosexual'.[112] While Beebo's tomboyism might have been acceptable when she was younger, its adult implications, and the visible marks of age/adulthood upon her (the 'faint lines') make it newly/additionally shameful; in her failure to grow out of it she reveals a more deviant disposition. It is also, for Beebo herself, never enough, this masquerade of masculinity, for she wishes she could be 'an honest-to-God male', so that she could marry Laura and 'give her kids'.[113] She is shamed for her masculinity, but is also ashamed at the *limitations* of that masculinity, which does not extend to maleness.

In Nealon's view, it is 'Bannon's understanding of lesbian sexuality as gender-inverted' that 'makes the novels compelling to contemporary readers', and he argues that:

> [a]ll Bannon's protagonists are depicted as beautifully mis-embodied, women in boy-men's bodies, or boys in women's bodies; and the anguish of this mis-embodied position serves as the emotional crux for all five of Bannon's novels, as well as the place where she foregrounds the question of what an authentic lesbian is.[114]

However, there are actually plenty of Bannon characters for whom this is *not* the case – characters such as Laura or Tris in *Women in the Shadows*, or Venus Bogardus in *Beebo Brinker* (1962), whose femininity is stressed,[115] and/or whose lesbianism is explained via other means (Laura's difficult relationship with her father, for example).[116] Indeed, Diane Hamer has argued that the value of Bannon's novels lies in her 'ultimate refusal to settle on *any* definitive cause of lesbianism', and in the fact that 'the roles of masculinity and femininity, activity and passivity are not allocated in any clear-cut or fixed way'.[117] (We might, however, view these characteristics as a product of the novels' incoherence/inconsistency, rather than a political gesture to thwart 'dominant explanations' – to which, as Hamer concedes, Bannon does sometimes subscribe.) And while Beebo does indeed fit the inversion model of a boy trapped in a woman's body, Bannon presents the issue as less to do with gender inversion *per se* and more a matter of the *visibility* of her queerness. As Beebo says to Laura, 'I embarrass you. You don't like to be seen in the nice stores with me. I look so damn queer [. . .]' And the narrator informs us: 'It was true that Laura was ashamed to go anywhere out of Greenwich Village with her . . . Beebo, nearly six feet of her, with her hair cropped short and her strange clothes and her gruff voice.'[118] Looking 'queer' is shameful – a shame that Laura seems to feel more than Beebo herself – yet Beebo cannot look (or sound) anything other than queer. She might sometimes 'pass' as a 'male homosexual' but she cannot pass as 'normal'. In the novel's apogee of misery, Beebo kills her beloved dog, Nix, with a knife, and beats herself up; she then claims to have been attacked, beaten and raped by four men, but refuses to go to the doctor, saying she has not gone 'in twenty years [. . .] Because they might find out I'm a woman.'[119] There are limits to passing, then – and also, for Beebo, there is a particular shame attached to being 'a woman'.

Beebo is not the only character in *Women in the Shadows* to worry about the visibility of her 'queerness'. Jack is closeted from his workmates; he is, we are told, 'a past master at deception', and thinks this is necessary in order to 'survive in the world'. So he tells Laura, who thinks:

> [h]er own vagrant sensuality had dominated her ever since the fatal day she first recognized it, and her efforts to hide it or deny it had always backfired sooner or later. Jack filled her with determination to make herself a part of what he called 'the real world,' the *straight* world. He made it seem very desirable to her for the first time.[120]

The novel frequently advances such arguments for repression and/or denial and for assimilating or 'passing' within the 'straight world'; it also 'begins and ends on an unhappy note for almost everyone concerned', as *The Ladder*'s review of the original edition opined.[121] At the end, after a brief return to Beebo, Laura goes back to Jack, vowing to be his wife and also – it is implied – discovering new (potentially sexual, or at least sensual) feelings for him. This is quite different in tone from Bannon's other novels, which tend to hold out more positive possibilities for their characters,[122] but it is much more in keeping with the traditional 'recuperative' pulp ending (such as we see in *Twilight Girl* and Vin Packer's *Spring Fire* (1952), both of which feature protagonists who end up in some kind of asylum and/ or who renounce their homosexuality). Indeed, in its portrayal of the ultimate marriage of Jack and Laura, who can then 'pass' as a 'normal' heterosexual couple, *Women in the Shadows* appears to endorse the desirability of this assimilation.

In her Afterword – which is written in a notably apologetic mode – Bannon lays at least some of the blame for her characters' problems at the door of societal intolerance. This, however, is a retrospective rationalisation and is not evident in the novel itself: 'Such was the atmosphere of the time. It pushed some gay people over the edge. For a brief moment in her life, Beebo was one of them.'[123] Yet she concedes:

> I was saddened when I found bias within the community itself: confusion and shame over one's own sexuality, alcoholism, partner abuse, broken relationships. [. . .] It would not be accurate to say that I became embittered. But I did feel the need to explore some of these newly discovered imperfections in a place and a population I had always admired without reservation.[124]

Women in the Shadows is, throughout, much more introspective – and pessimistic – than the other novels in Bannon's 'Beebo Brinker' series; it is much more focused on arguments, unhappiness, break-ups, alcoholism and violence; in that sense, the unhappy ending is not out of place. As Nealon comments, 'Reading this book is extremely painful: characters that retained hints of good humor in the two earlier books seem to have lost everything in their repertoires except cutting sarcasm, and most of them are bitterly, exuberantly alcoholic.'[125] Thus, the novel begins with Laura's diary entry lamenting that she will 'go crazy' if she stays with Beebo – describing Beebo as 'not rational' and the party as 'more like a wake', saying of Jack that 'if he doesn't crack up it won't be because he hasn't tried'. She asks, 'What's wrong with us all, anyway? What's the use of living when things are like this all the time?'[126]

This 'wrongness' is precisely a kind of shame – not just about the lives they are living and the choices they are making but, more profoundly, a shame about *who they are*. *Twilight Girl* similarly teases the reader with the moralising tagline: 'Lon was "different" – but was she bad?' Both novels, then – in quite different ways – express anxieties about the revelation of self, the revelation of some inner wrongness or badness; this plays out in recurrent concerns with the visibility (or not) of certain identity markers, the pleasures and perils of passing (as straight, as female or male, as white), and the dangers of social abjection or stigmatisation arising from the wrong kind of visibility. In the novels' preoccupation with the wrong kind of visibility, we can see a thematic and structural concern with shame that extends beyond the 1950s pathologisation of homosexuality. As an

affect centrally concerned with visibility, with structures of looking and being looked at, with objectification and self-consciousness,
with the double-edged nature of spectacle (as visually alluring but
also superficial and ridiculous), with the face and the blush, shame
is arguably the dominant affect of pulp – to be found not only in
the genre's subject matter, but also in the garish covers of the books,
the sensationalistic plotting, the melodramatic description and the
(embarrassed, implicated) responses of readers. When *Twilight Girl*
and *Women in the Shadows* present instances of passing and failing
to pass, they tap into a contemporaneous anxiety about being able
to identify a person's sexuality, gender and race by sight, and they
tend to oscillate between a concern that lesbianism is all too visible
and a suggestion that appearances may be deceptive – and thus, more
subversively, that lesbianism might be anywhere and everywhere.[127]

Stephen J. Belluscio distinguishes between passing as the attempt 'to
conceal a unitary, essential, and ineffaceable racial identity and substitute it with a purportedly artificial one, as in the oft-discussed case of a
light-skinned black person passing for white', and as something that is

> linked to performativity and that refers not to an assumption of a
> fraudulent identity but more broadly to 'the condition of subjectivity
> in postmodernity', in which our Lyotardian distrust of totalizing
> metanarratives, when applied to identity, has caused us to focus not
> so much upon identity as a unitary, essentialized entity, but rather as
> a process-oriented performance drawing upon a seemingly infinite
> number of cultural texts, 'ethnic' or otherwise.[128]

The two different conceptions of passing, and of identity more generally, could be historicised as belonging to the two contexts of pulp's
original publication (1950s to 1960s) and its most recent republication and recuperation (2000s), though the texts themselves seem to
waver between a view of identity – particularly sexual identity – as
'unitary' and 'essential', and a view of it as contingent, unstable,
and thus alterable by certain treatments or under certain conditions.
Arguably, the shift from one conception (of passing, of identity) to
another is one of the factors that facilitates the recuperation of pulp:
we are to some degree protected from the more negative, pathologising and shameful/shame-ridden aspects of the novels because we
read the identities that they showcase as performative rather than
essential. Belluscio warns that,

while the latter notion of passing carries more critical currency in the postmodern era, we as critics cannot forget that many passing narratives written in the late nineteenth and early twentieth centuries [or, we might add, from the 1950s] are governed by the logic of the first cultural notion, and our readings must be ever aware of this.[129]

Discussions of passing have, of course, most often concerned themselves with race. Elaine K. Ginsberg claims that

[a]s the term ['passing'] metaphorically implies, such an individual crossed or passed through a racial line or boundary – indeed *trespassed* – to assume a new identity, escaping the subordination and oppression accompanying one identity and accessing the privileges and status of the other.[130]

In the case of the butch characters of lesbian pulp novels, then, such 'trespassing' might conceivably allow them to access the 'privileges and status' afforded to masculinity, though in fact this rarely, if ever, occurs; in availing themselves of the notion of passing, however, Martin and Bannon might be read as making analogies between the experiences of homosexuals and the experiences of black people in 1950s America. Abate has remarked that 'Few pulp narratives feature characters who hail from racial or ethnic minority groups, and even fewer are written by authors who are nonwhite.'[131] How, then, should we read, now, the forms of cultural appropriation involved in such a move? Unusually for lesbian pulp fiction, both *Twilight Girl* and *Women in the Shadows* do feature characters of colour, and in both novels race becomes a site of both fascination and shame;[132] race also, I want to suggest, functions as both an intensifier of queer shame and a mirror of, or analogy for, that shame, in a troubling case of shame appropriation.

In *Twilight Girl*, the first description of the character Mavis – the object of Lon's burgeoning desire – emphasises her blackness as both lure and otherness:

Lon had never exchanged words with a Negro before – nor gazed at enigma that surpassed mere physical beauty. Mavis was slight, loose-limbed, the *café-au-lait* flesh pulled tightly over bone structure well defined. Yet it was not the effortless grace with which she moved the languid wrists, floated the slender fingers when she talked. And not the uninterrupted sweep of features, from broad, intelligent forehead past high-rising cheekbones, downward below

the cherry-tinted mouth to the defiant little chin. It was in the line
of blue-black hair drawn rigid to the coiled bun from which black
wisps played with the back of her neck. And in the fierce pride of
distended nostrils, the negroid nose. There, and in the regal tilt of
her head, the impassable curtain of velvet black eyes. Eyes almond-
shaped and weary from too much seen. If she rose, Lon knew, she
would walk with a haughty bearing [. . .].[133]

Mavis's racial identity here is written into her very movements
('effortless', 'languid', 'floated'), while her character is written into
her (racialised) physical appearance ('grace', 'intelligent', 'defiant',
'pride', 'regal', 'weary', 'haughty'). The repetition of colour words
('café-au-lait', 'blue-black', 'black', 'velvet black') reinforces her
blackness, making it impossible to ignore, determining every aspect
of her; and yet, even in the minutiae of this description, Mavis
remains unknowable ('the impassable curtain'), enigmatic, irredeem-
ably other, even if she is here being cast in the role of idol (or rather
queen, with the 'regal tilt of her head'). She both invites Lon's interested, desiring gaze and repels it.

As if in defiance of this 'regal' quality, Mavis also chooses to speak –
at least some of the time – in what Sassy calls 'plantation' speak: a
parody of poor 'negro' intonation and dialect ('Poor chillum!' and so
on).[134] If she does this in order to shame *others* – it undeniably creates
a certain social discomfort – she nevertheless achieves this discomfort
by wilfully placing *herself* in a shamed position on the basis of her
blackness. She speaks like this to goad Sassy, and the latter responds
'Stop that! I don't need that slut talk to tell me what you are,' labelling her a 'black bitch'.[135] Later Mavis says to Sassy (again, using her
own blackness to emphasise the extent of Sassy's debasement as a
self-denying, butch, queer, neurotic drug addict): 'Must be a grind to
be big, queer, butchy Sass, getting your jolts from a colored gal. What
can you do but run and run?'[136] The text thus oscillates between Lon's
near-fetishistic worship of Mavis's enigmatic blackness (the very quality that allows Lon so readily to incorporate Mavis into her childish,
utopian fantasy of a far-away, implicitly Sapphic, 'island'), Mavis's
own shameful and shaming denigration of her racial identity, and
her denigration by others in racist terms – whether Sassy, or Sassy's
mother, who refers to Mavis as 'that jig', as she abuses her daughter for
'foisting that – that thing on us!'[137] While both Sassy and her mother
are portrayed in a distinctly unsympathetic (and strongly neurotic)

manner, it is nevertheless the case that Mavis's blackness functions in the text to compound the shame that Sassy feels and the shamefulness (to others) of her actions/desires – indeed, to compound that negative portrayal of her. Thus, Sassy's desire for Mavis (who tolerates her caresses but does not reciprocate) is described as a 'degrading agony' and a kind of addiction, which is directly compared with her drug addiction: 'the need for this distant body was like that other painful hunger; unsatisfied, it would destroy her completely. [. . .] The desire consumed Sassy, gutting her insides. *"Mave, love me. Love me, love me! You rotten bitch – love* me!"'[138] That Sassy might genuinely desire this 'black bitch' / 'rotten bitch' (these monikers rendering Mavis bestial, abject) is the ultimate source and signifier of her debasement; and, indeed, both characters who love Mavis are severely punished for that particular sin in the end.

In *Women in the Shadows*, when the character of Tris is introduced, the narrative – focalised through Laura's admiring perspective – returns repeatedly to her skin:

> She was black-haired and her skin was the color of three parts cream and one part coffee. In such a setting her green eyes were amazing. [. . .] Her skin was incredibly pure and her color luminous. [. . .] She touched her sleeve and that lovely beige face swiveled toward her [. . .]. Laura had a brief vision of all that creamy tan skin unveiled and undulating to the rhythm of muffled gongs and bells and wailing reeds.[139]

Again, what is represented as Tris's brownness ('coffee', 'beige', 'tan') is here fetishised as edible (or, at least, imbibable), and when Laura learns that Tris is a dancer, the image this brings to mind partakes of a lexicon and imaginary of the exotic and sensuous ('unveiled and undulating'). Subsequently, when Laura visits Tris at her dance studio, she finds the young dancer wearing a bandeau top and tights: 'She was the same luscious tan from waist to bosom, and Laura, sitting there watching her, was helplessly fascinated by it; almost more by what she could see than by what she couldn't.'[140] The use of 'it' is ambiguous here, but clearly it is Tris's skin that fascinates Laura. What she can 'see' is 'fascinating' because it is still other/unfamiliar – and therefore, in its own way, hidden; as we will later discover, it is Tris's 'true' racial identity that is hidden. In the remainder of the novel, there are repeated desiring, eroticising and exoticising references to Tris's 'sweet skin redolent of jasmine',[141] her 'slim smooth body' and 'warm brown body',[142] and 'that marvelous fragrant tan skin'.[143] She is also described in terms of *ripeness*: in the lamplight 'Tris looked even riper and lovelier than she did in bright daylight' and, on another occasion, 'Her smile was as warm and luscious as ripe fruit in the sun.'[144]

It is revealed, ultimately, that Tris is 'a Negro' called 'Patsy Robinson', and has a black husband (despite being only seventeen); she pretends to be 'Indian' (Asian-Indian rather than American-Indian) because she thinks to be black would hurt her career (though it is clear that it is more than this – and that she has a good deal of internalised shame at her blackness). Abate asserts that 'Tris's racial masquerade is interconnected with her sexual one',[145] but does not mine the nature of that 'interconnection'. We might ask: to what extent does one form of passing reinforce or undermine the other? To what extent does one manifestation of shame compound or mitigate or disguise the other? To what extent is racial passing used by Bannon – problematically – as a metaphor for the denials and disidentifications of lesbianism? Increasingly, sexuality and race are aligned in *Women in the Shadows*, with homosexuality and blackness figured as equivalent and/or analogous (and, it is suggested, mutually reinforcing) sources of shame. When Laura asks Tris if she is gay, she says 'not really'; when pressed, she replies, '"Then I'm not [. . .]. If you force me to choose between black and white, I'm white," [. . .] and Laura thought she heard a double emphasis on the word "white."'[146] Tris hates and denies her queerness as well as her blackness: 'I do not like to become involved with women,' she insists to Laura. 'It has always been unpleasant for me.'[147]

Later in *Women in the Shadows*, when talking about her homosexuality to Milo (Tris's husband), Laura asks, 'Do you think I live this way because I like it? Would you live like you do if you could live like a white man?', and he shakes his head.[148] Again, some kind of equivalence is being suggested between homosexuality and blackness, blurring the boundaries between how one is *born* and how one might *choose* to live (the aspects of one's identity that might be chosen), and presenting both states (gayness, blackness) as implicitly undesirable, not just socially abjected. As Abate has conceded:

> In an act that ignored the presence of racial and ethnic minorities within their community, as well as collapsed the vast differences

between race and sexuality, the homophile movement [in the 1950s] frequently argued that being a (white) homosexual was parallel to being a member of a racial minority group. [. . .] [A]dvocates often asserted that gay men and lesbians faced similar types of personal prejudice, societal stigma and social exclusion.[149]

Neither *Twilight Girl* nor *Women in the Shadows* does this explicitly, but both novels avail themselves of the language and imagery of blackness in order to make new points about shame, visibility and homosexuality.

In addition to concealing her own blackness, Tris comments frequently on Laura's blonde hair and 'fair skin': 'If mine were that light I would never expose it like you do. I'd do everything to keep it as light as I could. Even bleach it [. . .].'[150] At one point the two women have this notable – and notably peculiar – exchange about their respective skin colours:

'Me so white and you so brown. It looks like poetry, Tris. Like music, if you could see music. Your body looks so warm and mine looks so cool. And inside, we're just the other way around. Isn't it funny? I'm the one who's always on fire. And you're the iceberg. [. . .] Maybe I can melt you [. . .].'

'Better not. The brown comes off,' Tris said cynically, but her strange thought excited Laura.

'God, what a queer idea!' Laura said. 'You'd have to touch me everywhere then, every corner of me, till we were both the same color. Then you'd be almost white and I'd be almost tan – and yet we'd be the same.'[151]

The references to 'music' and 'poetry' evoke the beauty and harmony of this claimed racial complementarity, while the oppositions of brown/white, cool/warm, fire/iceberg reintroduce otherness into a same-sex encounter (much in the way that butch/femme relationships are sometimes held to do). Nealon argues that 'this conciliatory "poetry" of racial difference is arguably a way of depoliticizing it, of whitening the black', yet he asserts that

[i]f the bodies of Laura and Tris are implicitly in the service of a discourse of 'opposites' that formalizes the politics out of racial difference, [. . .] they are also enmeshed in Bannon's poetics of gender

inversion: Laura and Tris's interiors are both 'just the other way around' from their exteriors [. . .]. Race, in other words, is not only formalized in the service of sexual aesthetics; it is also made a metaphor for the opposition between inside and outside that govern[s] Bannon's sense of what a lesbian is.[152]

This 'formalization' of race 'in the service of sexual aesthetics' is certainly problematically depoliticising, but it returns us again to questions of visibility and identity: the visibility of sexuality, of gender, of race; the extent to which identity of any kind is a matter of 'inside' or 'outside'; it returns us to the skin, the body's surface, as both site of and barrier to intimacy, and as the screen upon which shame is so often displayed or projected. Furthermore, what begins as an idealistic vision of stark difference/otherness ('me so white and you so brown') metamorphoses into a much more discomfiting fantasy of merging and swapping, and yet being 'the same'. Bannon delivers a conception of brownness (in this instance) as something transferable, something that 'comes off'; the ambivalence of that phrase – 'comes off' – is such that it can be read as a forced analogy with homosexuality, suggesting that brownness/homosexuality is something that could be cured *or* that could be contagious. The novel boldly, curiously and confusedly eroticises a scene of miscegenation.

In the US (including in the state of New York, where both these novels are set), anti-miscegenation laws prohibiting interracial marriage (and, in some states, cohabitation and/or sex between people of different races) were not repealed until 1967. Earlier in the century, the language surrounding the attempted introduction of *federal* anti-miscegenation laws had emphasised shame and debasement in particular:

Intermarriage between whites and blacks is repulsive and averse to every sentiment of pure American spirit. It is abhorrent and repugnant to the very principles of Saxon government. It is subversive of social peace. It is destructive of moral supremacy, and ultimately this slavery of white women to black beasts will bring this nation a conflict as fatal as ever reddened the soil of Virginia or crimsoned the mountain paths of Pennsylvania. [. . .] Let us uproot and exterminate now this debasing, ultra-demoralizing, un-American and inhuman leprosy.[153]

This language – 'abhorrent', 'repugnant', 'subversive', 'leprosy' – reveals both personal disgust and social anxiety; its connotations of shame and sickness are echoed in some of the language used in the public discussion of homosexuality in the early to mid-twentieth century in the US, and in the language of the most sensationalising pulp novels of the 1950s and 1960s. As late as 1958, a Gallup survey suggested that 94 per cent of Americans disapproved of interracial marriage.[154] While an interracial relationship between two women does not threaten so-called racial purity in the way that an interracial heterosexual relationship does (because of its capacity for reproduction), the backdrop of anti-miscegenation feeling should still be taken into account when reading *Twilight Girl* and *Women in the Shadows*; it adds an additional level of perceived 'unnaturalness' to the relationships depicted, and another possible source of shame.

It is perhaps wrong, however, to read this relationship between queerness and blackness purely in terms of one compounding the shame of the other. How else might that relationship work? In her reading of Nella Larsen's *Passing*, Judith Butler asks:

> What would it mean, [. . .] to consider the assumption of sexual positions, the disjunctive ordering of the human as 'masculine' or 'feminine' as taking place not only through a heterosexualizing symbolic with its taboo on homosexuality, but through a complex set of racial injunctions which operate in part through the taboo on miscegenation. Further, how might we understand homosexuality and miscegenation to converge at and as the constitutive outside of a normative heterosexuality that is at once the regulation of a racially pure reproduction?[155]

If this suggests the parallel and mutually reinforcing functioning of the 'heterosexualizing symbolic' and the 'taboo on miscegenation', it nevertheless raises further questions about whether, as part of the 'constitutive outside of a normative heterosexuality', homosexuality and miscegenation occupy the same territory, with both functioning according to – or rather in tension with – a reproductive imperative or whether they occupy it differently. What form does this 'convergence' take? What other apparently deviant identities and practices might form part of this 'constitutive outside'? Bond Stockton has argued that:

> there is much to learn about 'black' and 'queer' by asking how these signs even outside of black gay people – maybe especially outside of gay blacks – have congress with each other. Debasement, I claim,

supremely informs us of this conjunction. And fictions help us to theorize both the social communion of shameful states and the social communion of crossing signs.[156]

In reading the 'congress' of 'black' and 'queer' in these two novels, I want, appropriately, to *invert* Bond Stockton's question: if 'debasement [. . .] supremely informs us of this conjunction', then might it not also be the case that, in these two pulp novels, this conjunction supremely informs us of debasement – telling us something about the forms and functions and feelings of shame – and revealing shame as the pre-eminent affect of lesbian pulp fiction?

Conclusion

Reflecting, from the perspective of the early twenty-first century, on our relationship with lesbian pulp fiction, Nealon asks: 'are the novels to be remembered primarily as "self-hating," because of the violent instability of the relationships they depict, or are they to be canonized as camp melodrama, whose erotic rondelé reflects the proud sexual autonomy of women?'[157] The novels I have looked at in this chapter contain both violently unstable relationships – which lead to acts of significant physical violence, even murder – and scenes and descriptions of 'camp melodrama'. Is it, in fact, possible to separate the two? As Nealon himself seems to realise – in his recognition of the novels' own 'ambivalence' and the ambivalence that readers then and now might have felt or might feel towards them, in his understanding that pulp offers us 'histories of both celebration and shame' – this is too polarising a question.[158] The 'self-hating' and 'camp melodrama' elements of pulp are impossibly entwined; the melodrama is directly related to, derived from and sustaining of – not at odds with – the moral panic that fuels the genre in the first place. Yet, as he notes, 'both feelings (camp pleasure and intense sadness) are crucial to the project of trying to understand why the novels interest contemporary readers, why they are becoming "heritage"'.[159] Shame, I suggest, might be the bridge between these two 'feelings', and might express their ambivalent relation, as found in lesbian pulp fiction. It might speak also to Love's suggestion that

[q]ueerness is structured by this central turn; it is both abject and exalted [. . .]. This contradiction is lived out on the level of individual subjectivity; homosexuality is experienced as a stigmatizing mark as well as a form of romantic exceptionalism.[160]

Pulp, then, might be seen as encapsulating both stigma and exceptionalism, in its oscillations between passion and despair, desire and torment, melodrama and moralising. It might be read also as mimicking the work of shame in the business of both subjectivation and subjection, self-formation and the unravelling of self.

Moe Meyer, after claiming – contra Sontag – that camp is both 'political' and 'solely a queer (and/or sometimes gay and lesbian) discourse', argues that 'the function of Camp [. . .] is the production of queer social visibility'; he asserts, in fact, 'that *all* queer identity performative expressions are circulated within the signifying system that is Camp. In other words, queer identity is inseparable and indistinguishable from its processual enactment, or Camp.'[161] Such readings of queerness through camp and performativity arguably facilitate the recuperation of pulp, allowing new understandings and appropriations of the genre, whatever its apparently shameful content and aesthetic. As Love notes:

Many negative representations from the past have been reappropriated through the mode of camp. [. . .] [The] images that have been reclaimed tend to be those that reflect, in an excessive or ambivalent way, values that are acceptable or even desirable within the contemporary context. [. . .] Through the mode of camp or hero worship, these once-debased figures are transformed into icons by subjects who recognize them as incomplete, premature, or distorted images of themselves.[162]

We might want to ask, however, what 'values [. . .] within the contemporary context' the recuperation of pulp might be reflecting and what remains of shame in the metamorphic movement from debasement to iconicity. What do we elide, what do we forfeit, when we describe (celebrate, dismiss) pulp as 'camp'? Love herself notes that 'certain images' – she includes Stephen Gordon 'in front of the mirror in *The Well of Loneliness*' – 'remain resistant to appropriation', a point that might give us pause in considering those elements of pulp fiction (its racism; its desiring/disgusted relationship with

female masculinity) that might similarly 'remain resistant to appropriation'.[163] How far can camp – how far *should* camp – neutralise
pulp's more toxic aspects and angles?

Meyer's particular point about camp as centrally concerned with
the production of queer social visibility does, however, return us to
questions of positive and negative visibility, to passing, to spectacle,
to the structure of shame itself – when the right kind of 'social visibility' becomes the wrong kind – and these have been my subject here,
as a means of thinking through pulp's relation to shame as more than
its partial or predominant subject matter. Pulp trades on sensationalism and spectacularisation; it has a way 'of rendering the clandestine
spectacular', writes Amy Villarejo.[164] Shame operates at the axis of
the clandestine/spectacular, being about both secrecy and revelation;
shame is what must be hidden, forgotten, and yet what keeps resurfac-
ing, declaring itself in the painful visibility of the blush. This is what
pulp does – it exploits the hidden (twilight, shadows) and transforms
the deviant and shameful into something lurid and saleable. Whatever our *feelings* about pulp, it raises difficult questions for us: about
the relationship between queerness and shame; about the relationship
between memory and forgetting; about the significance of *how* (rather
than *what*) we remember, the material forms that our memories take
and the uses to which they are put; about the economic imperatives
underlying both the 'systems that induce structural forgetting' and the
processes of remembering and recuperation; and, finally, about the
increasing imbrication of queer culture and the market, the seeds of
which may have been sown as early as the 1950s.

Indeed, it is worth itemising some differences between pulp then
and now, between the old editions and the new. No longer published
on cheap wood grain paper, but rather glossy and desirable, meant to
be kept and displayed, not hidden, the very materiality of the book
has altered. No longer disposable (Ann Bannon once commented
that the pulp novel is the one that you bought on the way home to
read on the bus, and then left on the bus at the end of the journey).
No longer, in Bannon's words, 'ephemeral literature for a casual
audience',[165] rarely reprinted (so authors got a one-off payment,
instead of royalties); now reissued, reprinted, rediscovered, the originals archived and protected, and so given a kind of historical and
material permanence.[166] No longer cheap: titles that once cost 25c,
approximately one-tenth of the cost of a hardback in the 1950s, now
retail for around $12.99 or as much as £12.99. No longer sold at

newsstands, bus depots and drugstores, but rather found in specialist sections of bookshops. No longer aimed at a heterosexual male readership, but rather marketed directly to gay and lesbian readers and found in gay bookshops or gay sections in bookshops. Contemplating the covers of republished titles, we can note as well the ways in which they cite or quote images and motifs from the originals, clearly placing the books, their themes and images, within inverted commas, reframing them, resituating them (de-historicising them), radically de- and recontextualising them, redeploying them in the service of an increasingly commodified homosexuality, ironising them, determining the manner in which we might read them, fetishising them, rendering them as 'kitsch' or 'camp' in a way that might seem to deaden or disguise the novels' production of shame. And despite this shiny surface, this lure of the camply shameful/shameless, there is less of an 'ironic distance' between past and present than we might imagine.[167] As Love argues – even while instructing us to look to the moments of melancholy, backwardness and shame in the queer past – 'the history of queer damage retains its capacity to do harm in the present'.[168]

To this critique I would add the need to distinguish with more precision between the *productive* and the *generative* potentialities of shame. I began this chapter with Michael Warner's question: 'what will we do with our shame?' Halperin and Traub ask a related question: 'can we do things with shame that we cannot do with pride?' Both questions assume a conception of shame as something that you can *do something with*; alternatively, they imply a moral imperative to do something with or about shame. Both questions emerge from an intuition that shame is, or might be, *productive* – that it might serve various desirable (as well as undesirable) functions (queer solidarity, perhaps, or the puncturing of the pride bubble). Compare Probyn's claim that shame is productive because it 'always produces effects – small and large, individual and collective' (a rather self-evident assertion), and her assurance that it can be 'positive in its self-evaluative role' (that is, if we continue to read shame as a moral emotion).[169] She argues that we should not be ashamed 'to admit to shame' because

[s]hame [. . .] can entail self-evaluation and transformation. To consider shame is not to wallow in self-pity or in the resentment that accompanies guilt. It is to recognize that the reduction of interest that prompts shame is always incomplete. As such, shame promises a return of interest, joy, and connection.[170]

There is a familiar slippage here from *productive* to *positive* – though Probyn subsequently disputes this, claiming that her argument 'should not be understood as yet another celebratory account of transgression. Shame is not subversive. Shame just *is*. [. . .] It is productive in how it makes us think again about bodies, societies, and human interaction.'[171] As a precursor to the following two chapters – on women's writing of shame in fiction and autofiction – I want to test out a slightly different hypothesis, however, which is that shame is not necessarily something that we can marshal, or *do something with*; that shame's productivity is not something that can be appropriated and used; rather, that shame is something that we inhabit, it is structural; and finally, that shame is *generative* rather than *productive* – that it generates both effects and identities, and that one of the things it generates is femininity. Much of the apparent 'embrace of shame' within queer theory relies on this uneasy conflation of the positive and the generative. Bond Stockton is on the right track here when she writes of shame's 'beautiful, generative, sorrowful debasements'.[172] We might then look at what is generative about pulp, or what it is being asked to generate (what kinds of affects, what kinds of histories, and what kinds of possibilities in the present), rather than simply falling into a tired argument concerning how positive or negative its depictions of lesbianism are.

In her reading of Ann Aldrich's non-fiction pulp, Foote remarks on moments when Aldrich moves 'from a social critique to a psychological diagnosis, not pausing to connect the two'.[173] If this failure to 'connect' the social and the psychological – and, indeed, the tendency to privilege the latter over the former – is a common flaw of pulp, it might also be seen as pointing up the limitations of a queer politics organised around feeling, rather than social structures. But shame, as I am conceptualising it (uncontroversially, I think), is *both* feeling and structure, both individual/personal and social; and, as I want to suggest, following Berlant, there are obstacles to the building of collectivity 'through channels of affective identification and empathy'.[174] The answer is then to develop a more nuanced understanding of the *structural* and *generative* operations of shame as a means of understanding better its formative – not merely regulative – role in the construction and functioning of femininity. In the chapters that follow, I pursue these questions through readings of diverse contemporary texts, turning next to that original scene of shame: childhood.

Notes

1. Michael Warner, *The Trouble with Normal: Sex, Politics, and the Ethics of Queer Life* (Cambridge, MA: Harvard University Press, 1999), pp. 3, 8.
2. Michael D. Snediker, *Queer Optimism: Lyric Personhood and Other Felicitous Persuasions* (Minneapolis: University of Minnesota Press, 2009), p. 4.
3. Christopher Nealon, *Foundlings* (Durham, NC: Duke University Press, 2001), p. 141.
4. Silvan Tomkins, 'Shame-Humiliation and Contempt-Disgust', in Eve Kosofsky Sedgwick and Adam Frank (eds), *Shame and Its Sisters: A Silvan Tomkins Reader* (Durham, NC: Duke University Press, 1995), pp. 133–78 (p. 136).
5. Lillian Faderman, *Surpassing the Love of Men* (New York: William Morrow, 1981), p. 355.
6. Ibid.
7. Ibid.
8. Faderman, *Surpassing*, p. 392.
9. Lillian Faderman, *Odd Girls and Twilight Lovers* (New York: Columbia University Press, 1991), p. 147.
10. Yvonne Keller, '"Was It Right to Love Her Brother's Wife So Passionately?": Lesbian Pulp Novels and U.S. Lesbian Identity, 1950–1965', *American Quarterly* 57: 2 (2005): 385–410 (387).
11. John D'Emilio, *Sexual Politics, Sexual Communities* (Chicago: Chicago University Press, 1983), p. 135.
12. D'Emilio, p. 135. He mentions, in particular, Valerie Taylor, Ann Bannon, Paula Christian and Dallas Mayo as examples of the latter category.
13. Susanna Benns, 'Sappho in Soft Cover: Notes on Lesbian Pulp', in Makeda Silvera (ed.), *Fireworks: The Best of Fireweed* (Toronto: Women's Press, 1986), pp. 60–8 (p. 68).
14. For example: Tereska Torres's *Women's Barracks* (1950), which is often heralded as the first lesbian pulp novel, sold one million copies in the first year of publication and ultimately more than three million copies before going out of print; it has been back in print since 2005 as part of the '*femmes fatales*' pulp series published by CUNY's Feminist Press.
15. This evidence might include, for example, the fact that pulp novels were routinely (and often positively) reviewed in Gene Damon's (Barbara Grier) 'Lesbiana' column in *The Ladder*, the newsletter of the lesbian organisation, the Daughters of Bilitis. Pulp novels were listed here alongside lesbian literary classics by the likes of Gertrude Stein, Radclyffe Hall and Colette, and *The Ladder*'s letters page included numerous letters from readers discussing pulp titles and making recommendations.

Nevertheless, Grier comments in one issue: 'Now that paperbacks have flooded the market, the "penny-dreadful" Lesbian novel has become unduly prevalent, giving as warped and one-sided a portrayal as any works of the "saint and monster" schools of the past' (*The Ladder* 2: 7 (April 1958): 18).

16. Stephanie Foote, 'Deviant Classics: Pulps and the Making of Lesbian Print Culture', *Signs* 31: 1 (2005): 169–90 (177).
17. Jeff Weinstein, 'In Praise of Pulp: Bannon's Lusty Lesbians', *Village Voice Literary Supplement* (October 1983): 8–9.
18. Nealon, *Foundlings*, p. 146.
19. Nealon, *Foundlings*, p. 152.
20. Nealon, *Foundlings*, p. 154. Nealon is commenting here on Andrea Loewenstein's 1980 piece on Ann Bannon: 'Sad Stories: A Reflection on the Fiction of Ann Bannon', *Gay Community News* 7: 43 (24 May 1980).
21. Loewenstein, p. 12. Quoted in Nealon, *Foundlings*, p. 154.
22. Carol Ann Uszkurat, 'Mid Twentieth Century Romance: Reception and Redress', in Gabriele Griffin (ed.), *Outwrite: Lesbianism and Popular Culture* (London: Pluto Press, 1993), pp. 26–47 (p. 26).
23. Nealon cites the introduction to a 1993 exhibition of lesbian pulp fiction at the Lesbian Herstory Archives in Brooklyn, which notes that 'Joan Nestle, one of the Archives' founders, called these works "survival literature"', suggesting that, despite the anxiety that many women felt at buying and reading the novels at the time, 'they helped form many a fledgling lesbian's idea of what life might be for her' ('Invert-History', p. 748).
24. Foote, p. 178.
25. Kate Millett, *Flying* (New York: Ballantine Books, 1974), p. 202. The 'heartbroken butch murders her dog' comment is a reference to Ann Bannon's *Women in the Shadows* (1959), which I will discuss later in this chapter.
26. Lee Lynch, 'Cruising the Libraries', in Karla Jay and Joanne Glasgow (eds), *Lesbian Texts and Contexts* (New York: New York University Press, 1990), pp. 39–48 (p. 43).
27. Heather Love, *Feeling Backward: Loss and the Politics of Queer History* (Cambridge, MA: Harvard University Press, 2007), p. 32.
28. Nealon, *Foundlings*, p. 149.
29. Note, for example, the various excerpts from readers' letters that Ann Aldrich includes in *We, Too, Must Love*, many of which express a keen identification with what she has written in her previous book, *We Walk Alone*, but also a great unhappiness at that identification. One writes, 'I am a girl who is a Lesbian. I am trying to stop being one'; another describes herself, unhappily, as 'one of those transvestites you write

about' (Ann Aldrich, *We, Too, Must Love* [1958] (New York: Feminist Press, 2006), pp. 148, 151).

30. Stephanie Foote, 'Afterword: Productive Contradictions', in Aldrich, *We, Too, Must Love*, pp. 159–85 (p. 182).

31. Amy Villarejo, *Lesbian Rule: Cultural Criticism and the Value of Desire* (Durham, NC: Duke University Press, 2003), p. 188.

32. Keller, '"Was It Right"', p. 387.

33. Yvonne Keller, 'Ab/normal Looking: Voyeurism and Surveillance in Lesbian Pulp Novels and US Cold War Culture', *Feminist Media Studies* 5: 2 (2005): 177–95 (177).

34. Villarejo, p. 188.

35. Stephanie Foote, 'Afterword: Ann Aldrich and Lesbian Writing in the Fifties', in Ann Aldrich, *We Walk Alone* [1955] (New York: Feminist Press, 2006), pp. 157–83 (p. 177).

36. Martin Meeker, 'A Queer and Contested Medium: The Emergence of Representational Politics in the "Golden Age" of Lesbian Paperbacks, 1955–1963', *Journal of Women's History* 17: 1 (2005): 165–88 (167–8).

37. Nealon, 'Invert-History', p. 745.

38. Love, p. 40.

39. Roger Luckhurst, 'Memory Recovered/Recovered Memory', in Roger Luckhurst and Peter Marks (eds), *Literature and the Contemporary* (Harlow: Longman, 1999), pp. 80–93 (p. 83).

40. Michelle Abate distinguishes between this recent return to the 1950s and that which occurred in the 1970s (evinced in such cultural phenomena as *Happy Days*), claiming that 'The final decade of the twentieth century did not experience a nostalgic longing for the 1950s but rather a retro revival of it [. . .]. Whereas nostalgia is characterised by a melancholic yearning for a lost era, retro is known for its ironic, camp nature. Retro resurrects facets of a bygone historical period only to drench them in irony, [and] subject them to sharp cultural critique.' However, the 'critique' is not as sharp as Abate avers and I want to stress that we should be wary of a politically neutered rendering of the 1950s as kitsch. See Michelle Ann Abate, 'From Cold War Lesbian Pulp to Contemporary Young Adult Novels: Vin Packer's *Spring Fire*, M. E. Kerr's *Deliver us from Evie*, and Marijane Meaker's Fight against Fifties Homophobia', *Children's Literature Association Quarterly* 32: 3 (2007): 231–51 (246).

41. See, for example, Laura Doan and Sarah Waters's suggestion that 'retrospection is a condition of homosexual agency', but see also Annamarie Jagose's comments in *Inconsequence* (2002), where she asserts that 'retrospection can function as a further regulatory effect of the logics of sequence', and warns against 'misperceiving retrospection

as the critical solution to lesbian derivation' (Laura Doan and Sarah Waters, 'Making Up Lost Time: Contemporary Lesbian Writing and the Invention of History', in David Alderson and Linda Anderson (eds), *Territories of Desire in Queer Culture* (Manchester: Manchester University Press, 2000), pp. 12–28 (p. 12). Annamarie Jagose, *Inconsequence: Lesbian Representation and the Logic of Sexual Sequence* (Ithaca NY: Cornell University Press, 2002), p. xi).

42. Ann Cvetkovich, *An Archive of Feelings* (Durham, NC: Duke University Press, 2003), p. 7.
43. Cvetkovich, p. 7.
44. Ann Cvetkovich, 'In the Archives of Lesbian Feelings: Documentary and Popular Culture', *Camera Obscura* 49, 17: 1 (2002): 106–47 (pp. 115, 116). My emphasis.
45. Giorgio Agamben, *Remnants of Auschwitz*, trans. Daniel Heller-Roazen (New York: Zone Books, 1999), p. 107.
46. Qtd in Sally Munt, *Queer Attachments: The Cultural Politics of Shame* (Aldershot: Ashgate, 2007), p. 86. This phrase comes from Douglas's poem, 'In Praise of Shame', published 1894 in *The Chameleon*, alongside another – 'Two Loves' – in which the speaker encounters two figures 'walking on a shining plain / of golden light', one of whom is 'Love', the other 'Shame' or 'the Love that dare not speak its name'.
47. Love, p. 13.
48. David M. Halperin and Valerie Traub, 'Beyond Gay Pride', in Halperin and Traub (eds), *Gay Shame* (Chicago: University of Chicago Press, 2009), pp. 3–40 (p. 4). We might note, in addition, the emergence of 'gay shame' activism as a riposte to the increasingly commercial, depoliticised, mainstream 'Pride' festivities – initially via an event in Brooklyn, New York, in 1998, and subsequently through the spread of this radical anti-assimilationist activism to San Francisco and beyond. The Gay Shame San Francisco webpage describes their mission in the following terms: 'GAY SHAME is a Virus in the System. [. . .] We will not be satisfied with a commercialized gay identity that denies the intrinsic links between queer struggle and challenging power. We seek nothing less than a new queer activism that foregrounds race, class, gender and sexuality, to counter the self-serving "values" of gay consumerism and the increasingly hypocritical left. We are dedicated to fighting the rabid assimilationist monster with a devastating mobilization of queer brilliance' (<http://gayshamesf.org/> (last accessed 28 August 2015); <https://gayshame.net> (last accessed 5 July 2019)). For more on gay shame activism, see Mattilda Bernstein Sycamore, 'Gay Shame: From Queer Autonomous Space to Direct Action Extravaganza', in Sycamore (ed.), *That's Revolting! Queer Strategies for Resisting Assimilation* (Brooklyn: Soft Skull Press, 2004), pp. 268–95.

49. Kathryn Bond Stockton, *Beautiful Bottom, Beautiful Shame: Where 'Black' Meets 'Queer'* (Durham, NC: Duke University Press, 2006), p. 8.

50. Bond Stockton, p. 22. Bond Stockton clarifies, however, that the 'embracing' of shame 'in cultural criticism and social commentary does not begin with queer theory', but rather is evident in earlier cultural output – she asserts that 'Genet, Tarantino, and Morrison, among other writers discussed in this book, are intensely engaged in embracing certain aspects of shame' (pp. 9, 10).

51. Eve Kosofsky Sedgwick, 'Queer Performativity: Henry James's *The Art of the Novel*', *GLQ* 1: 1 (1993): 1–16 (4).

52. See J. L. Austin's *How to Do Things with Words* (1962) for the classic account of speech acts and the idea of the 'performative' – an account reworked by numerous subsequent theorists, including Jacques Derrida and Judith Butler, to their own ends.

53. In Chapter 2, I will say more about the interesting resonances of 'cleave', with its double meaning of adhering to and separating from or splitting asunder.

54. Eve Kosofsky Sedgwick, *Touching Feeling* (Durham, NC: Duke University Press, 2003), p. 36.

55. Carlson Wade, *The Troubled Sex* (New York: Beacon Envoy, 1961), p. 33.

56. Aldrich, *We Walk Alone*, p. 24.

57. Sedgwick, *Touching Feeling*, p. 37.

58. Sedgwick, *Touching Feeling*, p. 63.

59. Snediker, p. 20.

60. Tomkins, pp. 138–9.

61. Snediker, p. 21.

62. Sedgwick, *Touching Feeling*, p. 63.

63. Sedgwick, *Touching Feeling*, p. 62.

64. Sedgwick, *Touching Feeling*, pp. 64–5.

65. Elspeth Probyn, *Blush: Faces of Shame* (Minneapolis: University of Minnesota Press, 2005), p. xiii.

66. Munt, p. 103.

67. Snediker, p. 20.

68. Sedgwick, *Touching Feeling*, p. 63.

69. Sedgwick, 'Queer Performativity', p. 13. My emphasis.

70. Sedgwick, *Touching Feeling*, p. 37.

71. Sedgwick, 'Queer Performativity', p. 14.

72. Sedgwick, *Touching Feeling*, p. 37.

73. N.B. This suggests that the investment in/appeal to shame within queer theory needs to be distinguished from what is sometimes called the 'anti-social turn', as found in the work of Lee Edelman, most notably. The critics I cite here proclaim the value of shame as a shared

experience and a basis of the social (which, by extension and implication, they also see as valuable); Edelman, by contrast, endorses a 'queer negativity' – the negativity of queerness itself – that poses a 'radical challenge to the very value of the social itself' (Lee Edelman, *No Future: Queer Theory and the Death Drive* (Durham, NC: Duke University Press, 2004), p. 6).

74. Warner, p. 35.
75. Douglas Crimp, 'Mario Montez, For Shame', in Stephen M. Barber and David L. Clark (eds), *Regarding Sedgwick: Essays on Queer Culture and Critical Theory* (London: Routledge, 2002), pp. 57–70 (p. 66).
76. Cvetkovich, *An Archive*, p. 15.
77. Cvetkovich, *An Archive*, p. 47. My emphasis.
78. Jennifer Moon, 'Gay Shame and the Politics of Identity', in David Halperin and Valerie Traub (eds), *Gay Shame* (Chicago: Chicago University Press, 2009), pp. 357–68 (p. 359).
79. Love, p. 14.
80. Robyn Wiegman, 'Introduction: Antinormativity's Queer Conventions', *differences* 26: 1 (2015): 1–25 (1).
81. Halperin and Traub, pp. 3–40 (pp. 3–4).
82. Halperin and Traub, p. 4.
83. Ibid.
84. Halperin and Traub, p. 5.
85. Halperin and Traub, p. 10.
86. Halperin and Traub, p. 3.
87. Halperin and Traub, pp. 11–12.
88. Halperin and Traub, p. 11.
89. J. Halberstam, 'Shame and White Gay Masculinity', *Social Text* 84–5 (2005): 219–33 (219).
90. Halberstam, p. 223.
91. Halberstam, pp. 221, 220.
92. Halberstam, pp. 221–2.
93. Halberstam, p. 224.
94. Cleis Press uses this description of Bannon on the back covers of the republished Beebo Brinker series.
95. Keller, '"Was it Right"', pp. 390–1.
96. See: Kaye Mitchell, 'Gender and Sexuality in Popular Fiction', in David Glover and Scott McCracken (eds), *Cambridge Companion to Popular Fiction* (Cambridge: Cambridge University Press, 2012), pp. 122–40 (p. 130).
97. In 5: 11 of *The Ladder* (August 1961), Martin's *Twilight Girl* appears in Barbara Grier/Gene Damon's 'Lesbiana' column, where it is described as 'an unusual, intuitive book' (p. 23). Quotation taken from the 1975 Arno Press reprint edition of *The Ladder* (New York).

98. Sinéad Moynihan, *Passing into the Present: Contemporary American Fiction of Racial and Gender Passing* (Manchester: Manchester University Press, 2010).

99. Michelle Ann Abate, *Tomboys: A Literary and Cultural History* (Philadelphia: Temple University Press, 2008), pp. 173–4.

100. Della Martin, *Twilight Girl* [1961] (San Francisco: Cleis Press, 2006), p. 12.

101. Martin, p. 20.

102. Martin, p. 44.

103. Abate, *Tomboys*, p. 176.

104. Martin, p. 85.

105. Martin, pp. 30–1.

106. It is not only the butches who are presented as performing their identities. The first description of Violet makes it clear how constructed her femme identity is – through make-up, hair and clothes; even her voice displays 'a practiced attempt at sexy intonation', which Lon, as it happens, finds distinctly unattractive (Martin, p. 21).

107. Judith Roof, *A Lure of Knowledge: Lesbian Sexuality and Theory* (New York: Columbia University Press, 1991), p. 245.

108. Martin, p. 30.

109. Abate, *Tomboys*, p. 174.

110. Ann Bannon, *Women in the Shadows* [1959] (San Francisco: Cleis Press, 2002), p. 9.

111. Ibid.

112. Ibid.

113. Bannon, *Women in the Shadows*, p. 27.

114. Nealon, 'Invert-History', p. 755.

115. There is also Beth, who, as Nealon explains, 'starts out playing butch to Laura's femme [in *Odd Girl Out*], and ends up playing femme to Beebo's butch' (Nealon, 'Invert-History', p. 760). Again, this character trajectory seems to me to fall outside the 'inversion'/'mis-embodiment' model that Nealon is otherwise proffering.

116. In *I Am a Woman* (1959), Laura strongly suggests that her father is the main cause of her lesbianism – the novel opens by detailing her difficult relationship with him (see pp. 1–4), and towards the end of the book he makes a pass at her; when she tells him she is a lesbian, she says that he is responsible (see pp. 206–8). In *Women in the Shadows*, when talking with Milo, Laura suggests that she was 'made' a lesbian by 'A lot of people. My father. A girl named Beth. Myself. Fate', so the blame is rather more evenly distributed (p. 159).

117. Diane Hamer, 'I Am a Woman', in Mark Lilly (ed.), *Lesbian & Gay Writing* (Basingstoke: Macmillan, 1990), pp. 47–75 (pp. 54, 66).

118. Bannon, *Women in the Shadows*, p. 28.

119. Bannon, *Women in the Shadows*, p. 57.
120. Bannon, *Women in the Shadows*, p. 114.
121. Barbara Grier/Gene Damon, 'Lesbiana', *The Ladder* 4: 7 (April 1960): 18. Quotation taken from the 1975 Arno Press reprint edition of *The Ladder* (New York).
122. At the end of Bannon's *Beebo Brinker* (1962), for example, one character asserts confidently that 'women have a special knack for loving . . . There's a tenderness, an instinctive sympathy, between two women when their love is right . . . it's very rare in any kind of love. But it comes near perfection between women' (Ann Bannon, *Beebo Brinker* [1962] (San Francisco: Cleis Press, 2001), p. 232. Ellipses in original). The review of Bannon's *I Am a Woman* (1959) in *The Ladder* 3: 5 (February 1959; quotation taken from the 1975 Arno Press reprint edition of *The Ladder*, New York) notes that 'the ending is so very happy that it sets the book almost in a class by itself' (p. 17). However, as Diane Hamer notes, 'in Bannon's novels, momentary happiness is *always* followed by further conflict' (Hamer, 'I Am A Woman', in Lilly, pp. 47–75 (p. 69)).
123. Ann Bannon, 'Afterword', in *Women in the Shadows* (San Francisco: Cleis Press, 2002), pp. 197–202 (p. 198).
124. Bannon, 'Afterword', pp. 198–9.
125. Nealon, *Foundlings*, p. 163.
126. Bannon, *Women in the Shadows*, p. 1.
127. For other examples of this in lesbian pulp, see Ann Aldrich's response to the question 'Who is the lesbian?': 'She is many women. Look at her and she cannot be distinguished from her more normal sisters' (*We Walk Alone*, p. 3). See also the scene in *Odd Girl Out*, Bannon's first novel, in which Laura looks at herself in the mirror and tries to understand how she can both *look* like a woman ('She had breasts and full hips like other girls') and *be* a lesbian ('if I'm a girl, why do I love a girl?') (*Odd Girl Out* [1957] (San Francisco: Cleis Press, 2001), pp. 68, 69).
128. Stephen J. Belluscio, *To Be Suddenly White: Literary Realism and Racial Passing* (Columbia: University of Missouri Press, 2006), p. 9.
129. Belluscio, pp. 9–10.
130. Elaine K. Ginsberg, 'Introduction: The Politics of Passing', in Ginsberg (ed.), *Passing and the Fictions of Identity* (Durham, NC: Duke University Press, 1996), pp. 1–19 (p. 3).
131. Abate, *Tomboys*, p. 182.
132. Their titles also, of course, adopt a familiar pulp trope of referencing darkness or blackness – 'twilight', 'shadows'.
133. Martin, pp. 33–4.

134. Martin, p. 39.
135. Martin, pp. 72, 73.
136. Martin, p. 84.
137. Martin, p. 94.
138. Martin, pp. 88–9.
139. Bannon, *Women in the Shadows*, p. 31.
140. Bannon, *Women in the Shadows*, p. 40.
141. Bannon, *Women in the Shadows*, p. 43.
142. Bannon, *Women in the Shadows*, p. 81.
143. Bannon, *Women in the Shadows*, p. 128.
144. Bannon, *Women in the Shadows*, pp. 48, 69.
145. Abate, *Tomboys*, p. 186.
146. Bannon, *Women in the Shadows*, p. 46.
147. Bannon, *Women in the Shadows*, p. 74.
148. Bannon, *Women in the Shadows*, p. 176.
149. Abate, *Tomboys*, p. 183.
150. Bannon, *Women in the Shadows*, p. 102.
151. Bannon, *Women in the Shadows*, pp. 102–3.
152. Nealon, *Foundlings*, p. 165.
153. Speech by Seaborn Roddenbery, *Congressional Record, 62d. Congr., 3d. Sess., December 11, 1912*, pp. 502–3.
154. This figure comes from a more recent Gallup report on interracial marriage, which is available at: <https://news.gallup.com/poll/163697/approve-marriage-blacks-whites.aspx> (last accessed 13 June 2019).
155. Judith Butler, *Bodies That Matter* (London: Routledge, 1993), p. 167.
156. Bond Stockton, p. 23.
157. Nealon, *Foundlings*, p. 16.
158. Ibid.
159. Nealon, *Foundlings*, p. 144.
160. Love, pp. 2–3.
161. Moe Meyer, 'Introduction: Reclaiming the Discourse of Camp', in Meyer (ed.), *The Politics and Poetics of Camp* (New York: Routledge, 1994), pp. 1–22 (pp. 1, 4).
162. Love, p. 170 n. 26.
163. Ibid.
164. Villarejo, p. 139.
165. Ann Bannon, 'Introduction', in *Journey to a Woman* [1960] (San Francisco: Cleis Press, 2003), pp. v–xii (p. v).
166. Pulp novels are archived at the Lesbian Herstory Archive in Brooklyn, in Duke University's Sallie Bingham Center for Women's History and Culture, and at Mount Saint Vincent University in Canada.
167. Nealon, 'Invert-History', p. 745.

168. Love, pp. 8–9.
169. Probyn, p. xii.
170. Probyn, p. xiii.
171. Probyn, p. xviii.
172. Bond Stockton, p. 8.
173. Stephanie Foote, 'Afterword: Ann Aldrich and Lesbian Writing', p. 176.
174. Lauren Berlant, 'The Subject of True Feeling', in Austin Sarat and Thomas R. Kearns (eds), *Cultural Pluralism, Identity Politics, and the Law* (Ann Arbor: University of Michigan Press, 1999), pp. 49–84 (p. 53).

Chapter 2

Cleaving to the Scene of Shame: Stigmatised Childhoods in *The End of Alice* and *Two Girls, Fat and Thin*

Introduction

In *Embodied Shame* (2009), J. Brooks Bouson details contemporary women writers' engagements with shame, showing how writers such as Alice Munro, Toni Morrison and Jenefer Shute expose and lament women's feelings of 'embodied shame'; Bouson seeks an 'ethics of response' and a 'remedy to shame'.[1] In each instance, the implication is that the shame is *unwarranted* and undeserved, and therefore that the rendering visible of the feeling of shame is a way of contesting certain norms or cultural imperatives (such as the imperative to be thin or the idealising of whiteness). Her chosen authors, Bouson claims, 'through their very explicit public exposure of female shame, [. . .] do vital cultural work by providing a powerful critique of the cultural narratives that shame women.'[2] In her earlier work on Toni Morrison, Bouson similarly stresses the 'important cultural function' of Morrison's fiction, which '[r]epeatedly [. . .] stages scenes of shame', 'dramatizes' the pain of the shame experience, and '[bears] witness to the shame and trauma that exist in the lives of African Americans'.[3] In a recent collection entitled *The Female Face of Shame*, editors Erica L. Johnson and Patricia Moran similarly present shame as 'a marker of female humanity', and proceed to argue for the benefits of representing and exposing female shame, claiming that '*representing* women's shame is an inherently proactive endeavour even if the content of such representations reveals how women have been condemned to a shame status'.[4] Writing shame constitutes, for Johnson and Moran, a courageous refusal to be silenced – to be shamed, in fact – and is, by implication, 'a therapeutic act' that can work 'not only to reveal but to alter women's shame', and to challenge the culture of women-shaming.[5] They conclude their introduction with the (somewhat hyperbolic) warning that '*shame kills*' and the hope 'that by bringing gendered shame out into the open, by representing it, this volume will help to counteract shame's mortifying influence in women's lives'.[6]

As set out in my Introduction, my aim in this book is not to present the writing of shame as, necessarily, a redemptive or cathartic act (though in certain instances it could be, of course), but rather to explore the more complex relations between shame, gender and writing, to consider the shame involved in and invoked by the acts of writing and reading too – the ways that shame becomes more than subject matter – and to be alert to shame's persistence, but also its pleasures. In this chapter, then, I focus on two writers whose engagement with shame, in relation to sexuality in particular, has been decidedly provocative and ambivalent, and is, therefore, less obviously recuperable for the conventional, consolatory narrative of 'exposure' and 'overcoming'. I also seek to suggest the more constructive (not merely reflective, mimetic, dramatic or testimonial) role of literature in its engagements with shame and to consider the movement of shame through and beyond the text (its unpredictable contagiousness or transmissibility). In the work of A. M. Homes and Mary Gaitskill, romantic feeling is supplanted or undermined by more contrary, contradictory feelings of desire, disgust and shame; feelings of shame are not straightforwardly critiqued, nor do they necessarily lead to a positive outcome. Frequently, shame is displaced on to the reader, whose discomfiting complicity is invited. Topics such as paedophilia, sado-masochism, abject bodily practices and promiscuity are treated both graphically and with a startling equivocality amounting, in some instances, to an eroticisation of shame and disgust. Homes and Gaitskill, I suggest, explore what Sally Munt has described as the 'radical unpredictability' of shame for the subject, while resisting obviously transformative or affirmative readings of the work of shame.[7] Their work, therefore, poses some exacting questions for a contemporary readership. Can shame simply be made visible and then exorcised? Is it ever taken on willingly? Might there be pleasure in shame, or erotic potential? What are the cultural functions – but also the cultural effects – of literary deployments of shame, particularly deployments that are not straightforwardly redemptive? Is shame not both *structural* and socially and personally *necessary*, and – given this – is it not the case that it is never really vitiated, simply displaced on to something or someone else?

Reading Homes's *The End of Alice* (1996) and Gaitskill's *Two Girls, Fat and Thin* (1991) in the context of debates about child abuse, and in relation to theorisations of childhood and theorisations of shame, this chapter explores the links between childhood and affectivity, the 'queerness' of shame and the strange allure of the childhood 'scene of shame'. Building on the discussion of lesbian pulp in Chapter 1, my analysis of these works by Homes and Gaitskill unpacks further the political work that shame does in the wider world, the aesthetic forms that it adopts and the complexity of shame's eroticism. Reading the fiction in tandem with the theory may help us to uncover the motivations underlying the cultural and critical preoccupation with shame that has developed in the last few decades and to assess the ramifications – political, aesthetic, erotic – of such a preoccupation. Such fictional engagements might prove to be test cases for the political utility of shame at the same time as they allow us to mine the formal and libidinal complexity of this most challenging of affects. *The End of Alice*, for example, illustrates with startling perspicacity the transmissibility of shame from character to character and from text to reader, and – in its self-reflexive emphasis upon (deviant) narration – gestures towards the perverse pleasures to be found in telling and reading shameful stories. *Two Girls, Fat and Thin*, meanwhile, through its exploration of questions of fantasy, recognition, identification and affect in the lives of two rather damaged young women, offers insights into how shame might both foster and threaten interpersonal relationships.

If the accounts of shame in literature proffered by Bouson and by Johnson and Moran, with which I began, have their limitations, they nevertheless do vital work in drawing attention to the extent to which shame is gendered – a factor that the recent queer theorisations of shame discussed in the preceding chapter have tended to sidestep; Munt, for example, notes that 'in classical thought shame is a woman', but does not develop the point.[8] On one reading, Gaitskill's *Two Girls* neatly dramatises Bouson's assertion that 'the female socialization process can be viewed as a prolonged immersion in shame' – both protagonists experience such an 'immersion' in their formative years, and this continues into adulthood.[9] The novel does this, however, without explicitly condoning or condemning that 'process', and any movement toward redemption or overcoming is undercut by suggestions of the girls' complicity in (and occasional enjoyment of) their shamed status, and by the formal (that is, textual) refutation of the idea that narrativisation can, in itself, provide a cure to the pain of shame and abuse.[10] *The End of Alice*, in a different manner, complicates Bouson's point, in its pervasive dissemination of blame and, again, complicity, and in its knowing presentation of shame as titillating and alluring.

As the concluding section of this chapter discusses, critical responses to both novels have tended to express unease about the *defeminising* effects of writing shame, for women writers: if a particular kind of (sexual, bodily) shame is held to be a peculiarly feminine and/or *feminising* experience, then the conventional suggestion is that it should be spoken of only in certain accepted, regulated, implicitly redemptive ways. Both Homes and Gaitskill can be read as drawing attention to the gendering of shame, yet neither offers anything as constructive or optimistic as a critique of it. What such texts may do, however, is illuminate the extent to which the continuing association of sexual shame with the *female* (and/or feminised) body tends to be elided or overlooked in recent critical and popular accounts of shame. In their focus on childhood, these novels also highlight the relationships of reciprocity and mutual constitution between cultural conceptions of childhood and of affect (and also, to some degree, femininity). Daniela Caselli argues that 'childhood [. . .] has never escaped affectivity as its defining component',[11] while Karín Lesnik-Oberstein notes how 'the child is the guarantee for a transcendent human emotion'.[12] To this I would add: first, that it is shame that is the negative affect most closely associated with childhood and most often attributed an agential role in the allegedly awkward transition from childhood to adulthood; and second, that it is in narratives of child abuse that this association between childhood and affectivity is most starkly illustrated.

Childhood shame

As Johnson and Moran record, '[f]or theorists such as [Silvan] Tomkins, [Léon] Wurmser, and [Andrew P.] Morrison, shame begins in the earliest stages of development'.[13] Psychoanalytical accounts of shame tend to focus upon the emergence of the capacity for shame in early infancy, suggesting that shame is intricately tied up with the relationship between childhood and adulthood, and with processes of socialisation and subjectivation. Indeed, Freud even figures this emergence of the shame response as an expulsion from the 'paradise' of childhood, writing, in *The Interpretation of Dreams*, that

> [t]his age of childhood, in which the sense of shame is unknown, seems a paradise when we look back upon it later, and paradise itself is nothing but the mass-fantasy of the childhood of the individual. This is why in paradise men are naked and unashamed, until the moment arrives when shame and anxiety awaken; expulsion follows, and sexual life and cultural development begins.[14]

There are various points of interest here: the implied association between the development of a sense of shame and the inauguration of 'sexual life' (although shame is not *only* associated with sexual feelings, experiences and memories, paradigmatic examples of shame and shaming frequently have a sexual aspect to them); the emphases on self-consciousness and on the body (emphases that are common to diverse disciplinary accounts of shame, not only those found in psychoanalytical literature); the particular figuring of childhood as a 'paradise', and as a paradise precisely because of this absence of shame and shameful self-consciousness; the suggestion of childhood innocence (that is, of innocence as a key, constitutive characteristic of 'childhood'); and the nostalgic, desiring relation that is implied between adulthood and childhood, such that childhood structures our adult understanding of the ideal and the desirable, while remaining, by definition and of necessity, irrevocable, out of reach.

Malcolm Pines explains this 'expulsion' from the paradise of early infancy as the dawning of a 'painful' self-consciousness 'between the ages of 18 and 24 months', a move from the 'pleasurable state of "subjective self-consciousness"' to the unpleasurable 'sense of "objective self-consciousness"'; and thus

> the child begins to recognize that he or she is now an object in a world of other objects, visible in a world of other visible persons, and that he or she can therefore be the object of the scrutiny of others in a disappointing or critical manner.[15]

Both Wurmser and Morrison cite the role of family members in delivering this critical 'scrutiny' in a way that fosters the shame response: for Wurmser, it is the lyrically monikered 'soul blindness', a 'systematic, chronic disregard for the emotional needs and expressions of the child, a peculiar blindness to its individuality and hostility to its autonomy', that helps to produce this feeling of shame in the child;[16] for Morrison, it is similarly 'empathic failure' on the part of a parent or carer that is to blame, and he also suggests that 'a narcissistic, ashamed parent usually produces a narcissistically vulnerable child'.[17] (This failure of empathy, recognition, and the granting of autonomy is notably evident in the parent–child relationships in Gaitskill's *Two Girls*.) The child, as a consequence, 'becomes acutely aware of its smallness, weakness and relative incompetence in the larger scheme of things', which 'destroys' any 'fantasies of grandiosity' and causes a 'deflation of self' that is 'extremely painful'.[18] If the emphasis is often on the 'painful' nature of the dawning of shame, the suggestion is nevertheless that such an 'awakening' is necessary in order for shame to fulfil its remit as one of the 'watchmen' that work to 'maintain repressions' and guard against 'immoral, exhibitionistic excitement', in Freud's summation.[19]

These accounts of childhood shame imply a particular trajectory (from childhood to adulthood, from innocence to experience, from unashamed to shame-prone), a particular, progressive process (of socialisation). However, Jacqueline Rose warns against any 'reductive' reading of psychoanalysis in this matter, noting its 'insistence that childhood is something in which we continue to be implicated [as adults] and which is *never simply left behind*', and arguing that '[c]hildhood persists [. . .] as something which we endlessly rework in our attempt to build an image of our own history'.[20] Any suggestion of a linear, progressive trajectory of development is complicated, moreover, by a more critical, interrogative understanding of the relationship between childhood and adulthood – of the *functions* of the former, the functions of the *figure* of the child, *for* the latter, one of which functions might be precisely to deliver us some comforting notion of (personal and societal) progress. As Erica Burman and Jackie Stacey assert, the child as the 'embodiment of projected adult fantasies' works to '[cement] together history and biology', and is thus 'pivotal in the determining relationalities between past, present and future which constitute these linear temporalities of conventionalized narratives of progressive becoming'.[21] Given these 'adult fantasies', given the 'persistence' of childhood and its susceptibility to 'reworking', the move from childhood into adulthood cannot be viewed as a move in one direction, and nor – by implication – can the movement into or out of shame.

Furthermore, as Karín Lesnik-Oberstein and Stephen Thomson aver,

> [t]he child is made to wander around within the discourses of many disciplines, accruing and fulfilling many and varied functions. It is the principal character only in educational studies, but is the carrier of meanings and ideologies wherever it is encountered.[22]

These 'meanings' have been scrutinised in much recent research into childhood, which has sought 'to examine [the] cultural and political positioning of the child and to ask how and why childhood has become a magic mirror for culturally mediated adult desires'.[23] The child – as a figure, a trope – is most often presented as authentic, natural, or instinctive in some way, thereby offering us some (ostensible) ground outside or before the social and the rational. The child functions, variously, as 'the guarantee for a transcendent human emotion';[24] as 'the fantasmatic beneficiary of every political intervention';[25] as 'a particularly privileged window to the world-as-it-is, liberated from the indeterminacies and pluralities of interpretation';[26] as 'an occasion of pathos and of, moreover – and therefore? – an *anti-theoretical* moment';[27] and as 'a pure point of origin in relation to language, sexuality and the state'.[28] Childhood remains 'a repository of hope yet a site of instrumentalisation for the future, but with an equal and opposite nostalgia for the past'.[29] Childhood is, however, an unstable signifier, the very 'mutability' and 'incompleteness' of the idea/category of the child precisely making it, in Claudia Castañeda's estimation, 'so apparently available: it is not yet fully formed, and so open to re-formation. The child is not only in the making, but is also malleable – and so can be made.'[30]

Writing about childhood then, as Homes and Gaitskill do in these novels, addresses – implicitly or explicitly – questions of origin and subject formation, intersects with complex ideological narratives about family and society, and partakes of the complex affects associated with children and childhood. Their novels might also be read, more productively, as helping to 're-form' childhood in unexpected ways. Significantly, the affects aligned with childhood are frequently negative affects, due to its status as always already 'spoiled' and 'over'.[31] In the last few decades, that more fundamental/ abstract view of childhood as 'spoiled' has been exacerbated by what Steven Angelides describes as 'a veritable explosion of cultural panic and alarming media reportage regarding an apparent "crisis" of pedophilia',[32] and what Erica Burman calls 'an unprecedented level of concern over child sexual abuse'.[33] Whether or not there has been a rise in levels of child abuse, there has certainly been, in the preceding decades, a rise in critical and cultural *interest* in child abuse. Ian Hacking records that 'child abuse' was first listed as a medical category in the US in 1965, and he claims that, 'while there were no books on the topic in 1965, there were 9 in 1975. A bibliography for 1975–1980 lists 105 books in print'; Hacking, writing in 1991 – the year in which Gaitskill's novel was published – claims that 'There are now over 600 books in English devoted to child abuse.'[34] Notably, the definition of 'child abuse' during this period increasingly came to mean 'sexual abuse'.[35] In the late 1970s and early 1980s – in publications such as Louise Armstrong's *Kiss Daddy Goodnight* (1978), Florence Rush's *The Best Kept Secret* (1980) and Judith Herman's *Father–Daughter Incest* (1981) – feminist analyses also began to figure child sexual abuse as 'one part of a spectrum of male violence against women and children':[36] that is, as a problem of patriarchy, as structural rather than incidental, and as pervasive.[37] By the time Gaitskill and Homes's novels are published, the backlash against this feminist work had begun, alleging 'a "moral panic" promoted by a sensation-hungry media', and suggesting that this was 'one of a series of 1980s public panics about different types of predator targeting women and children, stirred up by an alliance of moral entrepreneurs including feminists, the moral Right and children's charities'.[38] In this way, 'concern over child sexual abuse in any particular instance began to be characterized as being the likely result, not of particular acts of male violence, but of discursively generated female "hysteria"'.[39] It is against this background – of 'moral panic' and 'hysteria', of claim and counter-claim, that Homes and Gaitskill are writing. The decade in which these novels were published, the 1990s, also witnesses the emergence of the new (sub-)genre of the 'misery memoir', epitomised by Dave Pelzer's best-selling *A Child Called 'It'* (1995), which spawned numerous imitators and fed an apparently burgeoning public appetite for childhood abuse, sexual or otherwise – a veritable 'market for misery'.[40] If these popular 'trauma memoirs', as Roger Luckhurst calls them, 'often [work] to *guarantee* subjectivity', presenting 'sequences of catastrophe, survival, and supersession as trajectories that recompense the felt depredations to identity' and thus 'help to narratively reconvene the self', Homes and Gaitskill offer, I argue, much less in the way of consolation and much more disruptive accounts of selfhood.[41]

Queer children

As the last chapter documented, in recent years the centrality of shame to queer history and identity has been extensively investigated, as has gay pride's 'ongoing struggle with shame'.[42] While neither Homes's nor Gaitskill's novel is about homosexuality, both treat of forms of being, expressions of desire, types of relationship and, most importantly, experiences of 'stigmatized childhood' and 'spoiled identity' that are arguably queer. The idea of 'spoiled identity' is first used in the subtitle of Erving Goffman's 1963 book, *Stigma: Notes on the Management of Spoiled Identity*. Goffman builds on the (Greek) etymological origins of 'stigma' as 'bodily signs designed to expose something unusual and bad about the moral status of the signifier' in order to develop an account of 'the situation of the individual who is disqualified from full social acceptance'.[43] It is this link between the body and morality – the suggestion that immorality or deviance is manifested in and through the body – and this emphasis on 'social acceptance' (that is, forms of social regulation and othering) that connect stigma to shame, which is similarly concerned with both bodies and morality (and the regulation of both – remember Freud's comments on shame as a kind of 'watchman' and tool of repression). For Goffman, the stigmatised individual is a 'person with a shameful differentness',[44] who might yet find comfort in collectivity, in the company of 'sympathetic others', including 'those who share his stigma'.[45] The notion of 'spoiled identity' is taken up more recently by Heather Love, in her work on loss and negative affect in queer history and queer fiction, to describe, in particular, 'the ambivalence that '[stigmatized individuals] feel when confronted with their "own kind"'.[46] This is an ambivalence – which Love calls a 'dynamic of identification and disidentification', a kind of 'identity ambivalence' – that arguably militates against more productive or long-lasting forms of affective solidarity on the basis of shared shame.[47]

Returning to Sedgwick's account of the relationship between shame and queerness, as cited in the previous chapter, might help us to parse further this particular dynamic:

> There's no *way* that any amount of affirmative reclamation is going to succeed in detaching the word [queer] from its associations with shame and with the terrifying powerlessness of gender-dissonant or otherwise stigmatized childhood. If queer is a politically potent term, which it is, that's because, far from being capable of being detached from the childhood scene of shame, it cleaves to that scene as a near-inexhaustible source of transformational energy.[48]

Notice the ambivalence of the term 'cleave' here, which can mean both *to adhere to* and *to separate from or split asunder*.[49] (Love likewise repeats this in her assertion that 'political change can happen not only through disavowing loss but also through cleaving to it'.)[50] The idea of 'cleaving to the scene of shame' in this chapter's title embodies this peculiar ambivalence, this process of simultaneous 'identification and disidentification' that is, I argue, both subject and effect of my chosen novels and that indicates, crucially, both the particular queerness of shame and its double-edged relationship with femininity (of which it is both constitutive and disruptive). It might also prove to be a useful way of thinking through Rose's comments on the 'persistence' of childhood – which is 'never simply left behind'.

Importantly, the 'scene of shame' for both Homes and Gaitskill is childhood – and it is childhood shame that the protagonists of the two novels both disavow and cleave to, in their awkward attempts at identity formation. Weaving together queerness, childhood and shame, Sedgwick writes that

> [s]ome of the infants, children, and adults in whom shame remains the most available mediator of identity are the ones called (a related word) shy. [. . .] *Queer*, I'd suggest, might usefully be thought of as referring in the first place to this group or an overlapping group of infants and children, those whose sense of identity is for some reason tuned most durably to the note of shame.[51]

Both Homes and Gaitskill, in their respective novels, present portraits of individuals whose identities are (in Sedgwick's terms) 'tuned most durably to the note of shame', but both go further in suggesting that any infantile paradise of unselfconsciousness is fleeting, even non-existent, and that, subsequently, the inner child is not so easily vanquished, the painful first shame of childhood not so easily overcome. In this way they also bear out Sedgwick's claim that

> [o]ne needn't be invested (as pop psychology is) in a normalizing, hygienic teleology of *healing* this relationship [between inner child and adult], [. . .] or in a totalizing ambition to get the two selves permanently merged into one, in order to find that this figuration opens out a rich landscape of relational possibilities – perhaps especially around issues of shame.[52]

The very action of cleaving precisely precludes such a 'healing' or 'merging', while the 'relational possibilities' facilitated by shame remain as ambiguous, indeterminate and precarious as Sedgwick implies here.

What is more, both Homes and Gaitskill present us with children who are arguably 'queer' – not in the sense of being proto-gay children, but rather in the way that they are 'just plain strange' and serve to illustrate, in Kathryn Bond Stockton's terms, 'how every child is queer' and how some children in particular are defined by their 'sideways relations, motions, and futures'.[53] If we accept the distinction offered by Steven Bruhm and Natasha Hurley between the 'normal child' who is part of 'a simple story' and the 'queer child' who is part of 'stories that often appear beyond the narrative pale', then the children in *The End of Alice* and *Two Girls, Fat and Thin* (as well as the adults they become) live out the latter kind of story and, in so doing, test the limits of narrative in the representation of childhood shame and deviant sexuality.[54] This is because Homes and Gaitskill refuse to '[edit] out or [avoid] the kinds of sexuality children aren't supposed to have – all in an effort to simplify what is, in fact, not at all a simple story'.[55] While complicating that 'story' of childhood and childish sexuality, they also trouble the adult stories of child abuse (the manufactured outrage, the moral panic, the journey to redemption, the covert titillation), failing to grant us the 'pleasure' that such stories usually offer as they '[channel] [. . .] our concern into self-gratification' – although arguably they offer us other, equally disconcerting, forms of pleasure.[56] In *The End of Alice*, then, I will argue, the queer ambivalence of the shame response is evident in the (deviant) development of the characters and in narratorial unreliability, but also in the techniques by which readerly complicity is invited; the pleasure of reading partakes of the ambivalent pleasure of shame. This illustrates the contagiousness, the transmissibility, of shame, but also its troubling imbrication with desire. In *Two Girls, Fat and Thin*, meanwhile, shame facilitates a fragile relationship, an affective connection, between the two protagonists, while its self-conscious, individuating, isolating properties dictate that this connection will be as much fantasised as real: although the two girls' stories are eloquently and extensively narrated to the reader, they are never fully narrated to each other.

James R. Kincaid claims that 'we are all implicated in a contemporary discourse on children, sexuality, and assault so mighty that it comes close to defining our moment', and he proceeds to argue that 'the subject of the child's sexuality and erotic appeal, along with our evasion of what we have done by bestowing those gifts, now structures our culture'.[57] Neither novel is straightforwardly a critique of the culture of 'erotic innocence', as Kincaid labels it. Homes delivers a titillating narrative of child abuse, while drawing the reader's attention to the hypocrisy of the 'outrage' about child abuse and, simultaneously, presenting a view of children's sexuality as more complex and knowing than we might want to concede. Gaitskill, in her emphasis on pain and trauma, and in the glacial quality of her narration, resists the presentation of a titillating narrative, yet also complicates both the understanding of children's sexuality and the relationship between childhood and adulthood. Both texts therefore operate as products of the culture that Kincaid outlines and potentially as critiques of that culture *from within*.

'This is the story you've been waiting for': shameful narration in *The End of Alice*

A. M. Homes's 1996 novel, *The End of Alice*, engages with the topic of shame in numerous ways: by giving voice to an imprisoned paedophile and murderer; by representing his relationship with a teenaged female correspondent, who herself has paedophilic desires for a local twelve-year-old boy; by documenting 'deviant' desires and acts in graphic and unsettling detail, including the sexual abuse of children and male-on-male rape in prison; by focusing on bodily abjection and disgust; and by continually reinforcing the reader's complicity in what is being represented. In its reception, the novel had its own brush with shamefulness, with the National Society for the Prevention of Cruelty to Children (NSPCC) seeking to prevent its sale in UK bookshops, and the noted *New York Times* book critic Michiko Kakutani damning it as 'a lubricious and single-minded pursuit of sensationalism and sensation' and 'a doggedly repellent piece of pornography, devoid of authentic emotion and filled with gratuitous and calculatedly disgusting scenes'.[58] It is notable that her review, in focusing on the novel's strategic stimulation of 'sensation' and bodily affect, reveals its effectiveness in this endeavour (that is, Kakutani's own disgust at the novel's 'calculated' production of disgust) and suggests the availability of shame (and related affects) for spectacle and sensationalism.

Shame, in *The End of Alice*, is something viciously personal, but also something shared, infectious. As the first line of the novel proclaims:

> Who is she that she should have this afflicted addiction, this oddly acquired taste for the freshest of flesh, to tell a story that will start some of you smirking and smiling, but that will leave others set afire determined this nightmare, this horror, must stop. Who is she? What will frighten you most is knowing she is either you or I, one of us.[59]

This opening communicates not only the transmissibility of shame, but also the difficulty of locating the child abuser, who might be outside us or within us, who is everywhere and nowhere, and who – resisting our controlling, taxonomising gaze – might not be recognisable as such. It hints, also, at the ordinariness of the abuser, who is, precisely, 'one of us', a human being, no beast or monster (however monstrous his or her behaviour). Stylistically, the novel also announces, from its first page, a fraught indebtedness to Nabokov's Ur-text of child abuse, *Lolita* (1955): in its use of alliteration, assonance and looping syntax; in its nicknaming of the nymphet (Lolita is 'light of my life, fire of my loins', 'Lo', 'Lola', 'Dolly', 'Dolores' and even, once, 'Dorothy Humbird',[60] while Homes's victim is 'Ruby Diamond Pearl. Call her Jewel; ruby of my heart, Alice', her name of course also recalling her *Wonderland* predecessor);[61] in its direct address to the reader; and in its self-conscious awareness of the presence of some audience and of the provocative, tantalising nature of the tale being told ('ladies and gentlemen of the jury', appeals Humbert Humbert, but Homes's narrator addresses a much more indeterminate and dubious audience, imagining himself a contestant on *What's My Line* – this is trial by game show/popular culture).[62] As Humbert famously attests, 'You can always count on a murderer for a fancy prose style',[63] and in Homes's novel that style is deliberately exaggerated and parodied – made cruder, less winning, more obviously deluded.[64] The narrator is, from the outset, defined by his voice, by the eloquence that falters, crucially, as the narrative proceeds and he is compelled to remember and narrate the details of his murder of the 'Alice' of the title. In this way he both recalls his sophisticated, sophistic predecessor, Humbert Humbert, and deconstructs the class-bound association of articulacy and morality upon which Nabokov's *Lolita* relies.[65]

We might also note how, from its opening lines, the novel draws attention to the fact that it is *telling a story* (later, the narrator even refers to 'my characters', as if conceding their fictionality), and that this is a story that will produce both titillation and pleasure ('smirking and smiling') and repulsion or anger ('this nightmare, this horror').[66] Indeed, as it develops, the text seems to suggest a closer and closer relationship between titillation and repulsion, to imply that the 'nightmare' of child abuse holds a particular kind of (shameful) fascination for us, which might lead us to revisit it over and over. This is a revisiting that reveals a preoccupation with the identity of the abuser – 'who is she?' – and a perverse desire to revel in our feelings of fear and horror, in ways that both threaten and shore up our own identity (that is, our identity as innocent, as non-abusers), our own security, our morality.

As Kincaid argues, our 'storytelling' about child abuse may appear to be an attempt to control or contain the problem (an act of mastery, Freud's *fort da* game continued into adulthood), but in fact such an attempt must necessarily fail, must indeed have the opposite effect of continuing the story, perpetuating the problem:

> [W]e do not pretend that we are getting the problem [of child sexual abuse] under control; quite the contrary. We know we are dramatizing the issue, making it into a spectacle. We might even know that what we are doing isn't pointing to an ending but to a continuation. But these are forms of knowing that haven't yet found themselves a story to tell, at least not one we want to hear.[67]

Homes's novel is most challenging in its presentation of these 'forms of knowing' without accompanying moral commentary, and in its self-conscious emphasis on drama and spectacle in a way that appeals to our desire for these kinds of stories (a desire that actually propels their production), without offering reassurances of our own goodness or innocence. Kincaid suggests, of our cultural fascination with child abuse, that '[w]e are instructed by our cultural heritage to crave that which is forbidden, a crisis we face by not facing it, by writing self-righteous doublespeak that demands both lavish public spectacle and constant guilt-denying projections onto scapegoats'.[68] Arguably, Homes both makes use of and offers a critique of this situation of spectacle, scapegoating and guilt denial. Thus, at the outset, the narrator instructs his readers to

> know, [. . .] that as I tell you this, I feel like a contestant on *What's My Line*; before me is my tribunal, the three members of the panel, blindfolded – that detail should cause some excitement in a few of you. They ask me questions about my profession. The audience looks directly at me and recognizing my visage from its halftone reproductions is entirely atitter.[69]

Later, arriving before the 'committee' in prison, he laments that there are 'no spotlights, no proscenium, no bleachers or orchestra pit, none of the stuff of an extravaganza'.[70] This emphasis on visibility, on performance and exhibitionism, on looking and being looked at, recurs at intervals throughout the text, drawing our attention to child sexual abuse as salacious scandal, shameful/shameless titillation and public spectacle – but also to the spectacular nature of shame itself. Does this explain the novel's decidedly mixed reception?[71] Our relation to the story is evidently a conflicted one: we demand it, reiterate it, replay it and yet profess ourselves disgusted – a fact that *Alice*'s narrator plays on, asserting, of a particularly graphic scene of male rape that he has just narrated, 'I probably wouldn't have even mentioned the scene with Clayton except that I knew you were waiting for it, wanting it, had been wanting it all along.'[72] Any shame the reader feels (is made to feel) in response is in direct proportion to that reader's interest or investment (acknowledged or otherwise) in what is being narrated, for this tale of child abuse is undeniably a 'story' that is desired by the reader. When the narrator finally progresses to telling the story of 'the end of Alice' (for, like a story, she has an 'ending' rather than a death), he announces: 'This is the story you've been waiting for.'[73]

Even before the revelation of the story of Alice, the story proffered by the paedophile narrator of his correspondence with the teenaged girl with apparently paedophilic inclinations of her own is deviant and digressive in various respects: 'it is best if we stick to the story at hand, that being hers not mine',[74] he writes, before wandering off into the story of himself, his own desires, his own queasily erotic interest in her story. Later he concedes that, '[a]gain, as is my habit, my nervous tic, I have gotten away from the story at hand.'[75] And how reliable is this story, anyway? Early on, he admits that '[t]he minutiae of her ablutions [are] not so much described as deduced by my own inter-pretation, my more personal understanding of her'.[76] His view is, he concedes, 'obstructed': he claims to be able to see what she describes (and even what she does not) 'as though in the full light of day', but this is a light shed by (constituted by) his imagination, merely.[77] The line between fantasy and reality here is always blurred, but so too is the distinction between desire (his desire *for* her) and identification (his desire *to be* her): for example, when he imagines sending her a letter smeared with his own semen and fantasises her enthusiastic reciprocity;[78] or when he pictures her invading the boy's camp and is led off into an extended fantasy about the girl in her younger years, at a camp full of other girls.[79] Later he speculates that 'it is as though I am her, she is me, and we are in this together, doing this twisted tant-ric tango',[80] the boundary between them elided by the fantasy of their shared stigma. Is it merely that he lives vicariously through her or that she is to some degree his invention, a mere projection or cipher? Does he simply conflate her with his adored (but no less invented) Alice? Certainly, in his initial description of their relationship-by-correspon-dence, they are dependent on each other: 'She is there, waiting for me, waiting with something to tell me, needing me. Without me she is nothing'[81] (even if he will later complain, bitterly, that 'we are quite different, she and I. She is not who I thought she was, who I presented her to be').[82] In this way, their relationship of mutual reinforcement and mutual desire/repulsion echoes that between 'the paedophile' (as cultural scapegoat, figurative bogeyman) and the audience, the moral majority pronouncing judgement, whose fantasies precisely keep him alive in the popular imagination, thereby continuing to '[figure] the crisis of sexual child abuse as a demonic trap, a tale of terror from which there is no escape [. . .] an untreatable disease', in Kincaid's summation.[83] The narrator of *The End of Alice* constructs his corre-spondent and his victim(s) in a manner that fits his fantasies and grati-fies his errant desires, but on Kincaid's reading our own construction of the 'stark moral drama' of child-molesting is similarly distortive and self-serving, 'camouflaging needs so dark and urgent we want neither to face them nor to give them up'.[84]

Shame and desire are intricately linked in *The End of Alice*. The narrator's teenaged correspondent pursues the twelve-year-old object of her affections and expresses her predatory and yet shame-laden intentions via an urgent desire to ingest the body of her boy lover and via an eroticisation of his own self-cannibalising propensities. His reaction when she says to him, 'I bet you taste great" is one of shame (he blushes),[85] yet she proceeds, in a notably eroticised episode, to eat the boy's scab from one of his knees:

> She drops to her knees and crawls across the floor toward him, kicking the door closed along the way. He scoots to the edge of the bed. His legs are hanging over. She licks the knee, the scab, to soften it, to wash and ready it. The flavour is a wondrous mix of dirt, sweat, and blood. She licks slowly and then, with the long nail of her index finger, pries, peeling the scab up. It comes away slowly, painfully, leaving a pink well that quickly fills with blood. She presses her tongue to the coming blood and draws it away. [. . .] She slips the scab into her mouth. He shudders. She is eating him.[86]

The scene plays out like a parody of a pornographic encounter: the woman on her knees, seductively crawling towards the man, taking him in her mouth, his 'shudder' a kind of orgasm as she 'eats' him, the 'coming blood' a precursor of this erotic climax. Yet here the partici-pants are a teenage girl and a much younger boy, the power dynamics between them perilously confused and unstable, the ingestion of his body/scab a kind of violation and her apparently submissive position an act of domination and exploitation. Furthermore, the whole epi-sode forms part of the duplicitous narrative of the ageing paedophile: at the very least he is the leering spectator who compels and confirms its erotic tenor; and it may indeed be his own fantasy and fabrication.

The fascination with bodily shame evident in this scene of the scab recurs throughout the course of the novel. In a reading of *Lolita* and

Death in Venice, Margaret Morganroth Gullette notes the prevalence of 'distasteful physical images of mature, aging bodies' in narratives of paedophilia, and she claims that 'Pedophilia, in [Humbert's] version of it, exaggerates the normal dislike of aging, the normal anxiety over the passage of time.'[87] For Gullette, paedophilia – as subject matter for fiction – is 'an indirect but powerful way of dealing with anxieties about the life course', and she tracks its trajectory within what she calls the 'midlife novel' in particular.[88] If *The End of Alice* is not a 'decline story' of the kind identified by Gullette (or a 'midlife novel', for that matter – Homes was only thirty-four when it was published), it nevertheless uses images of the ageing body as indications of both the narrator's pathology and the corporeal nature of his shame, as he reflects on his 'genitalia [which] hang thick, puckered, and nearly nude', his skin with its 'turkey toughness', his breasts like 'fatty tumors', a nipple 'like a baboon's red butt'.[89] The combined images of vulnerability (even infantilism), animality and disease point to the dehumanising properties of shame, but in connecting this shame to the (necessarily) ageing body, the narrator hints at its universality – so shame is also what makes us human, sickeningly so.

A different kind of bodily disgust apparently provokes his murder of the twelve-year-old Alice. In the paedophile's story, he and Alice are in love and she is the precocious child–seductress; in the official version, he is a kidnapper, child abuser and murderer, a monster. In his story, his killing of her 'saves' her from her impending, awful womanhood (rescuing her from the shame of becoming a woman) – he kills her after she has her first period: 'In a way I saved her, I hope you can understand that. I spared her a situation that would only get worse. She was a girl, unfit to become a woman.'[90] In justifying himself thus, and in his actions towards her, he reveals a fear and hatred of the mature female body, which must be punished for its shameful leakages and licentiousness (the coroner's report itemises sixty-four stab wounds, the '[v]ictim decapitated, her head positioned between her legs, weapon recovered at the scene – jammed in victim's vagina').[91] If this is presented, here, as a personal pathology, the product of a sick and damaged mind, it nevertheless speaks to a prevalent cultural shaming of female bodies that is not unrelated to the widespread eroticisation of children and the prepubescent. As Burman and Stacey note, 'The infantilization of women has long been close to the feminization of childhood, as a state of dependency.'[92]

When the narrator first meets Alice, he has been swimming in a cold lake and is naked and 'shriveled'; she points and laughs at him, and 'her amusement I find humiliating, arousing. I instantly want to do something – to silence that stupid giggling.'[93] Sexual desire is, here, irrevocably tied to feelings of shame, disgust and experiences of abuse, whether as victim or perpetrator. Thus, in a pivotal scene in the novel – the remembrance of which prefigures the narrator's ultimate remembrance and admission of his final act of murder – he recollects his sexual assault by his mother, when he was a young boy. In the bath together, she forces him to fist her: 'My fist is inside her. My fist, like I'm angry. I turn it around, screwdriver, drill. I feel the walls, the meat she's made of, dark and thick.'[94] It is he who feels guilt and shame after this episode, not her, despite this dehumanising description of her body as 'meat', despite the violent, mechanical nature of his actions ('screwdriver, drill'), which expresses his resistance even as he gives in to her demands. His own confused desire for her – he '[begins] to rub her, to poke at her with my skinny stub' – elicits only mockery: 'she laughs and pushes me away', and '[s]hriveled, I climb out of the water', a direct foreshadowing of his later encounter with Alice.[95] After suffering this abuse from his beloved mother, he scrubs his hand with water and soap until it is sore:

> Were it not for my hand, my sore hand, I would think it had not happened at all. I would think it was something that had leapt out of me, a bit of my imagination. Me. It must be me. My stomach turns. It is I who's slipped through God's graces and done such a terrible thing. My hand beats, pulses, throbs with the terrible reminder, and yet she seems without these after-effects.[96]

The repetition of 'me', 'my', 'I' does more than signal the boy's (distorted, erroneous) sense of his own agency and culpability; it bespeaks a self-consciousness so intense that it amounts almost to a disintegration of self, while 'she' (the real culprit here) recedes into the background. The boy bears his shame as a mark on his body, a physical memory, and experiences it as sickness and horror. The following morning, his mother wipes a streak of her own menstrual blood across his mouth, like lipstick, another emasculating brand upon his body, and this is echoed elsewhere in the narrative when she kisses him and, he says, 'I go outside stained, the impression of her mouth everywhere,'[97] as well as later when he smears the blood of Alice's first period across the hotel notepad, shortly before murdering her.[98] That his relationship with his mother occasions shame, rather than merely guilt, is evident in the way he carries it as some flaw in *who he is* ('Me. It must be me'), not just a result of what he has done (what she, in fact, made him do). Her actions (her abuse of him) have merely revealed his nature, some 'weakness of my person', some unacknowledged and despicable 'desire' ('one often gets what one wants') that then lies at the root of his later crimes:

> *I know who I am.* I dance around it, use my words, my refraction, to obscure what is excruciatingly clear. Were I not to hide, to cloak and clothe myself, it would be unbearable for all – and I include you in this. The reptilian repulsive; even I don't like the look of me.[99]

This structure – of not wanting to be looked at, yet being excessively visible, exposed, and even taking some perverse pleasure in this exposure – expresses the double structure of shame. Similarly, in narrating the story of the teenaged girl and her twelve-year-old victim, the paedophile confesses that 'I am watching with my hands over my eyes. I want to know and yet I don't want to know'[100] – the reader of *The End of Alice* may feel correspondingly torn[101] – while his words simultaneously reveal and conceal his monstrousness. His shame, in addition, makes him something less than human ('reptilian' connoting both some other, notably cold-blooded, species and something or someone distasteful and untrustworthy).

The figure of the paedophile occupies centre-stage in the novel, dominating the worldview of the text, and at first glance the vision that Homes offers us is a familiar one of the paedophile as monster, as inhuman other. As Kincaid explains:

> The 'pedophile' is the place where a host of current revulsions are relieved; it is perhaps our most frequented cultural and linguistic toilet. The central figure in our drama of child molesting has been pried free from medical and psychological explanations and is now subject only to moral ones.[102]

The paedophile is a 'cultural demon' and 'our Iago',[103] and thus

> is something more than a scapegoat for us; it does more than siphon off and bottle dark desires and fears the culture cannot otherwise contain. Our pedophile handles those chores, certainly, but not so

well that these desires and fears are expelled. We need to torture
pedophiles as if they were scapegoats, but we need always to make
sure the torture isn't fatal – not to the breed, anyhow.[104]

While *The End of Alice* might appear to replicate this vision of the
paedophile as 'cultural demon' and to contribute to the public drama
of child abuse as spectacle by delivering us so monstrous and deluded
a narrator, it also asks us continually to remember that the narrator
is 'A boy, a man, a person quite like yourself [. . .] no better or worse
than you.'[105] When he asserts, in obvious self-justification, that 'A
conspiracy, a social construct supported by judge, jury, and tattle-
tales, has put me away because I threaten them,'[106] the accusation –
that child abuse is 'a social construct' that 'threatens', not because it
endangers our children, but because it endangers our sense of ourselves as (moral) adults – cannot be wholly dismissed. The novel thus
asks us to reflect on the problematic nature of our own desires and
the pleasure we might take in the protagonist's seductive narration.
Highlighting the reciprocity of the relationship between the incarcer-
ated criminal and the 'innocent' public outside the prison, the protagonist challenges:

> I am here. The criminal element is contained – held under lock and
> key – and still [crime] happens. How could it go on without me (us)
> [. . .]? [. . .] [W]ith so many of us locked up, you'd think it would
> stop. That it continues means that it is you and not me.[107]

And he adds:

> [W]hile you might think I'd find it heartening [. . .] that in all this
> random senselessness we are all of us caught in a kind of forced
> criminality – you are in error. You are breaking your promise, the
> very terms of our agreement – the one that puts me in here and lets
> you stay out there – if I commit the crimes for you, you must be
> good for me. You and I, we're in this together, best not to forget.[108]

What is the nature of this 'agreement' – a kind of forced division
between guilt and innocence in order to cover over how blurred the
line between them might be? The (monstrous) paedophile, then, carries
the shame of a society that cannot rationalise its contradictory desires
for childhood and children. The paedophile – this 'central figure in
our drama of child molesting', this more-than-scapegoat – commits

the crimes for us but, as Homes's protagonist reminds us, the shame is shared, not exorcised.

If shame is shared, even contagious, here, then it also infects the imagination (and even, perhaps, the body) of the reader. The narrator of *The End of Alice* repeatedly seeks to invoke the shame of the reader, to stimulate a physical response – blushing, even arousal, the suggestion being that these are closely connected – and to make the reading of the novel an uncomfortably embodied experience. No one is innocent here: 'Are you all so lily-white?', the narrator demands, later musing, 'I wonder what you are doing here, playing these pages.'[109] As the novel progresses, the attack on the reader becomes more graphic and explicit:

> I am fully aware of what you've been doing while you've been reading this – these are my pages you're staining with your spunky splash. Your arousal, the woody in your woods, tickle in your twitty-twat, the fact that as you've read my mental monologue you fished out the familiar friend, rubbed it raw, stroked yourself, hello, pussy, sweet kitty cat – let the tiny tongue between your legs lick your fingers, giving them a sticky bath – and despite the depths to which it disturbed, you were released.[110]

The effect is compounded by the emphasis on the body and its excretions, and by the use of infantile language ('twitty-twat', 'woody', 'sweet kitty cat'), which itself produces an almost inevitable readerly blush of shame (the shame of unwanted identification, unwanted visibility) and summons the inaugural, infantile scene of shame. If the obvious intent here is to shock (an avowedly puerile intent), then the narrator counters by asking 'what is shock if not some ancient identification, meaning that I have touched a sore spot, hit a nerve – think on it, will you'.[111] The narrative therefore plays with and provokes the dual movement of identification and disidentification – of isolating individuation and compromised intersubjectivity – that is typical of the shame response. As Homes has claimed (in a kind of banal understatement), 'For many people this book is erotically arousing. [. . .] Attraction and desire are deeply, deeply complicated. They're not always healthy, they're conflicted. I think we have to acknowledge that.'[112] Shame, then, in addition to being thematically central to *The End of Alice*, is part of the narrative technique of the novel and part of its desired effect: it invokes our interest, precisely as a way of stimulating our feelings of shame.

If *The End of Alice* succeeds in its evocation of the transmissibility and the spectacular nature of shame, also offering a challenging account of the cultural function of the child abuse *story*, its own tendency to reproduce shame *as spectacle*, in terms that are necessarily hyperbolic, militates against a more nuanced analysis of the intricacies of shame's role in identity formation. I want, therefore, to turn now to a novel that offers – and invites – a more sustained investigation of the ambivalent constitutive/disruptive role of shame in the formation of both individual identity and intersubjective relationships: Mary Gaitskill's *Two Girls, Fat and Thin*.

The 'evil universe' of childhood in *Two Girls, Fat and Thin*

Two Girls, Fat and Thin details the meeting of overweight loner Dorothy and thin, brittle, self-shielding Justine, as the latter – a jobbing but largely unsuccessful journalist – researches an article on a Randian cult ('Definitism'), of which Dorothy was previously a member.[113] As atomised individuals with a shared history of sexual abuse, their stories alternate – Dorothy's narrated in the first person, Justine's in the third person; in fact, they meet only three times (all brief encounters) during the course of the narrative and generally fail in their attempts to connect with and understand each other. Yet their stories intersect imaginatively in the mind of the reader, hinting at the possibility of communication and understanding, even while effectively refusing to provide so neat and affirmative a conclusion.

Both girls in *Two Girls, Fat and Thin* have early sexual experiences associated with feelings of shame and their subsequent lives are dominated by these feelings. Both are arguably 'queer children', aloof from their peers, stigmatised and self-stigmatising, caught in families that foster both an abiding sense of loneliness and a near-incestuous feeling of closeness and control. Dorothy remembers 'the evil universe of my childhood', and reflects:

> Whenever I think of the house I grew up in, in Painesville, Pennsylvania, I think of the entire structure enveloped by, oppressed by, and

exuding a dark, dank purple. Even when I don't think of it, it lurks in miniature form, a malignant doll house, tumbling weightless through the horror movie of my subconscious, waiting to tumble into conscious thought and sit there exuding darkness.[114]

This uncanny rendering of the family home (the house standing in, synecdochically, for the lives and relationships it contained) reveals not only its 'malignancy', but also its dogged persistence into the present, figuring childhood as a dark fantasy that is never wholly exorcised or shaken off. Justine, meanwhile, uses family photos – 'these proofs of family happiness and genetic beauty' – as 'talismans against her fear that there had been something unusually nasty about her childhood'.[115] While the early photos appear to confirm the vision of a stereotypically contented childhood in the company of her 'eager, rosy, smiling young parents', Justine's pictures from adolescence have, for her, 'the queasy, urgent, side-tilted quality of a dream that is rapidly becoming a nightmare'.[116] Thus, behind the most innocuous images of suburban American girlhood lurk more threatening portents of misery and cruelty.

For both girls, the shame of sexual abuse is located and stored in the body. The repetition of animalistic imagery signals the complex mesh of desire and repulsion that characterises Justine's sexual feelings, memories and experiences. When she is molested by a family friend, Dr Norris, in a local park, we are told that 'Her abdomen contracted like a crouching insect. [. . .] A strange and horribly powerful sensation flexed its claws in her body'; later, she reflects that 'this uncomprehended attack of invasive sensation had not felt like pleasure at all but rather like the long claws of some unknown aggression that had gripped her organs and her bones and never quite let go'.[117] This 'sensation' is not specified (is it pain or pleasure, or a mixture of the two? The very term 'sensation' links the body and other forms of awareness, mental and emotional), but it is 'horrible' in its 'power', overwhelming her, amounting to a lack of control; although 'invasive', and an 'attack' – that is, something that comes from without – it is nevertheless internal, bodily, deeply personal, and therefore, by implication, a source of shame.

Dorothy's shame at her abuse at the hands of her father produces similarly violent and contradictory feelings:

Sometimes I would gloat over this fact in a perverted way, feeling weirdly vindicated and special, enormous and corporeally real [. . .].

> But most of the time I felt as if my body had been turned inside out, that I was a walking deformity hung with visible blood-purple organs, lungs, heart, bladder, kidneys, spleen, the full ugliness of a human stripped of its skin.[118]

This image of 'walking deformity' signals her self-consciousness, the painful visibility of shame as expressed through a body turned inside out (her true 'ugliness' exposed, a moral failing expressed aesthetically), and suggests the violation of the boundary between inner and outer indicative of trauma. As Pines explains, glossing the psychoanalytical take on shame:

> Shame, a highly affective state, brings about a great awareness of bodily experiences and of autonomic reactions and involves some cognitive recognition of a sense of deficiency of the self. As this happens the sense of self moves suddenly from background to foreground awareness and self-consciousness, experienced as a painful intrusion into a previously quiet, smoothly operating sense of self as background, as a context or framework for experience.[119]

The invocation of a flayed body underlines the psychological and physical violence of the abuse Dorothy has suffered, expressing this sense of a 'deficiency' of the self; yet her secret knowledge of what has happened also gives her a bodily 'reality' that she feels her fellow students lack. Shame, then, provides her with an identity, of sorts – a realness and specialness about which she can 'gloat', or in which she can find some 'perverse' comfort. Even as her father berates and bullies her,

> I felt, in addition to the inevitable dislocated shame, a strange kind of pride; I was almost grateful to my father for hating me. I was accepting the discharge of an aggression that was an essential part of the life force.[120]

Both girls, then, experience this feeling of an unknown, essential, abstract and/or unlocatable aggression directed against them, and directed in particular against their bodies. Away at college, Dorothy even misses 'the dark, rank security of [home], the reliability of having it to crouch in, feeling the huge violent energies of my parents encircling me like a fortress of thorns',[121] her dysfunctional family seeming to offer protection from the world beyond the home, a world of 'sickening boundlessness' in which the self might be lost, subsumed.[122]

As the girls progress to adulthood, Dorothy's shame is further displaced on to her body as she develops an increasingly unhealthy relationship with food.[123] She pursues a highly idealised, largely intellectual and mostly chaste affair with an older man she meets through the Definitist movement; yet even this comes to seem shameful to her and, after discussing the relationship with Justine, she wonders 'why [. . .] the affair which I had always cherished as the most beautiful thing in my emotional life suddenly [seemed] like a rape'.[124] Meanwhile, Justine develops a vivid and violent fantasy life as an adolescent, getting a neighbourhood boy to whip her, masturbating often (and joylessly), and subsequently leading a sexual life marked by brutality in which arousal coincides with disgust. Two particular examples that I will discuss below illustrate the difficulty of characterising Justine straightforwardly as a victim or as a masochist, and the impossibility of separating her shame and her arousal. They recall Bond Stockton's claim that '*we are scared of the child we would protect*', and her suggestion that 'perhaps we stay focused on safeguarding children because we fear them. Perhaps we are threatened by the specter of their longings that are maddeningly, palpably opaque.'[125] But who are they 'opaque' to, exactly, and why is this a source of anxiety? Commenting on the otherness and unknowability of childhood, Allison James, Chris Jenks and Alan Prout submit 'that childhood presents a repository of the great unexplained in a manner that exceeds most phenomena. There is a wilfulness, even an anarchy, that the agency of childhood emits which resists containment and control through intelligibility.'[126] Whether this 'anarchy' is a characteristic displayed by actual children, or something implicit in the (adult) conception of childhood, is left rather ambiguous here, but what both Bond Stockton's and James's points reveal is an adult cultural unease about children, an adult anxiety to understand – and, through understanding, 'contain' – childhood.

This unease, which implies a fundamental awareness of our ambivalent and disingenuous relationship towards/with children, runs through both the novels under discussion in this chapter. Both Homes and Gaitskill play on the fact that children inspire in us feelings of love and protection, but also – more unsettlingly – darker feelings of fear, revulsion, arousal and shame. If Homes emphasises in particular our salacious and prurient interest in children (and the hypocrisy of our gestures of protection and denial), Gaitskill captures all too acutely the sadism and amorality of children, the self-interest that makes them more animal than human. Thus, when Justine arrives at a new school, she finds the classroom

> filled with murderously aggressive boys and rigid girls with animal eyes who threw spitballs, punched each other, snarled, whispered, and stared one another down. And shadowing all these gestures and movements were declarations of dominance, of territory, the swift, blind play of power and weakness.
>
> Justine saw right away that she'd be at home here.[127]

Dorothy, by contrast, is terrified of the threatening world of school, where she is repeatedly bullied and taunted; yet even as she notices 'the snake of cruelty coiling under the banal weave of words' in the conversations around her, she thinks:

> I knew that these were nice girls. I sensed that if their mundane words covered cruelty and aggression, the cruelty and aggression covered other qualities. Vulnerability, tenderness, curiosity, kindness – I sensed these qualities in the child harridans around me, yet I could not experience them.[128]

Justine's longings are 'opaque', even to herself, as the following examples demonstrate. One: aged eleven, she forces a 'mousy pretty thing', Rose – 'a girl she didn't even like much' – to enact pornographic scenes with her in a bathroom.[129] She ties 'her victim' up,[130] removes her underwear and penetrates her with the handle of a toothbrush (an action she will subsequently describe as 'rape', though in doing so it is unclear, even to Justine, whether this is a confession or a boast).[131] While the episode with Rose excites and empowers her, she also feels 'disgust' at the girl's body, which is really a kind of self-disgust. Justine threatens to tell everyone what they have done but, 'out of a muddled combination of shame and barely acknowledged pity, she kept it to herself, for her own frenzied, crotch-rubbing nocturnal contemplation'.[132] Two: aged thirteen, Justine flirts with older men at her parents' country club: the scene evinces a complex mixture of pleasure and disgust, with the men described as 'fat creatures mostly, baked pink and bearded', 'lotion-oily', with 'saggy-bottomed hips' and 'thick pink lips'.[133] Again, disgust at the bodies of others becomes a way of negotiating her own complex, half-understood feelings of shame at her burgeoning sexuality. Once more, Justine's complicity and knowingness are emphasised: 'She looked at them with dumb, shielded eyes, an imitation of wide-eyed young girlhood she had seen in magazines.'[134] Her feelings of disgust towards these 'hideous', 'sweaty' men both conceal and are an emanation of her own sexual shame and she can only imitate the innocence that itself constitutes her particular erotic appeal to these older men.[135]

Jenny Kitzinger notes 'the child protection movement's emphasis on two particular qualities of "real" childhood – innocence and vulnerability'; in particular, this emphasis on innocence 'has become a fetishistic focus in itself' and 'is itself a source of titillation for abusers'.[136] It also, claims Kitzinger, 'stigmatizes the "knowing" child': 'Innocence, then, is a problematic concept because it is itself a sexual commodity and because a child who is anything less than "an angel" may be seen as "fair game".'[137] Homes and Gaitskill present us with children who are sexual, if not, yet, fully self-aware; they are vulnerable but seemingly knowing, both hard (self-shielding) and sensitive; they are not 'innocent' but neither are they 'fair game'; as 'child harridans' (a notably gendered description), they inhabit some liminal land between childhood and adulthood, and raise questions about our own, adult, investment in preserving the border between the two (an investment both protective and self-interested). The adolescent world that Gaitskill depicts Justine moving through is tough and frequently seedy; the 'skinny and sharp-boned' little girls of Gaitskill's suburbia are 'made beautiful by the erotic ferocity that suffused their limbs and eyes and lips'.[138] Even when ignorant and inexperienced, the girls exude a kind of sexual charge: they boast of their sexual experience and desires, bully each other and swagger with assumed confidence, yet shame, fear and sexual abasement are never far away; the bullying taunts of 'retard' and 'queer' always conceal a fear that the bully might herself be one or both of those things – conceal, that is, a shame at some perceived or feared 'deficiency of self'. Justine's emotional and sexual life is characterised always by a painful ambivalence: her bullying of weaker children produces both 'excruciating enjoyment' and 'deep discomfort'; she is 'monstrously alive' and yet 'unable to bear being in the world, turning in on herself like an insect run through with a needle' (echoing the 'crouching insect' of her abdomen when Dr Norris molests her, the 'claws of some unknown aggression' in her body);[139] when boys in the mall leer at her and make comments, this is both 'exciting' and 'horrible'.[140] The particular shame, here, is the shame of exposure, of sickening visibility:

> It was horrible to be in front of people having the same feeling that she had while masturbating and thinking about torture. [. . .] The world of Justine alone under the covers with her own smells, her fingers at her wet crotch, was now the world of the mall filled with fat, ugly people walking around eating and staring. It was a huge world without boundaries [. . .].[141]

When the adult Justine becomes embroiled in a sado-masochistic relationship with Bryan, a man she meets in a bar, the escalating violence takes her back to this childhood world of contradictory and shameful feelings, tinged with arousal ('Oh Christ, she thought. Not this again').[142] When Bryan says to Justine, 'You're like a little girl. [. . .] Not a nice little girl though. You're like one of those little monsters who tortures other kids on the playground,' she feels:

> [s]hocked, flattered, and slightly frightened. She felt him looking through the layers of her adulthood, peeling away the surface until he found hot little Justine Shade of Action, Illinois, posing on the playground – he was right! – she had never really left. The child Justine pouted flirtatiously as he eyed her.[143]

Justine's erotic allure is located in childhood and she can access her adult desires only by revisiting this original (childhood) scene of desire – which is also the scene of shame. At first glance, this accords with an orthodox Freudian account of masochism: for Freud, 'perverse masochism in adults represented the pathological fixation or developmental arrest at this early [that is, pre-Oedipal] stage, a drive that was not sufficiently repressed or modified by later genital sexual aims'.[144] Stuck in childhood, the masochist is caught in the infantile sadistic anal phase, but this sadism is now turned against the self.[145] However, this is complicated by Justine's mixed reaction – she is both 'flattered' and 'frightened' – and by the suggestion that 'adulthood' is a kind of facade that can be 'peeled away', a veneer of civilisation, self-knowledge and self-control that is all too easily removed. As she feels 'the teeth of his ferocity cut open her body', she sees herself

> as a child, alone in the apartment after school, running through the rooms, smashing windows and destroying furniture like she had never been able to do, jumping up and down with delight to see big Justine doing the nasty with this dirty boy.[146]

Is this liberation or regression – or merely self-preservation? Barbara Schapiro claims that 'The paradox of masochism as a form of self-preservation distinguishes much of Gaitskill's fiction', noting not only Justine's masochistic sexuality but also Dorothy's obsession with Anna Granite, who tends to represent women as essentially masochistic in her books (a point that Dorothy and Justine disagree on).[147] In *Two Girls*, then, the focus on masochism is just one debt that Gaitskill owes to Ayn Rand – the model for her 'Anna Granite'. As Melissa Hardie writes:

> The 'sadomasochism' of Rand's representation of sexuality has been, for feminism, the most problematic aspect of her writing. Rand's predilection for highly choreographed scenarios of sexual violence has been read against her representation of women of integrity and intelligence, forgers of their own destinies.[148]

Hardie argues, however, that, despite Rand's 'apparent authorization of a discursive structure of subordinated femininity, almost inevitably described as masochistic', such scenarios as they occur in her fiction can be read as '[demonstrating] the asymmetry of that apparently symmetrical pair of pairs: masochist/sadist; man/woman'.[149] Masochism in Gaitskill's fiction – here and elsewhere, for example in the stories of *Bad Behaviour* (1988) – similarly has a more critical, ambivalent function. Rita Felski has written of the historico-political trajectory, the 'changing connotations', of (the idea of) masochism,[150] which moves from relative invisibility, to visibility as something 'perverse and shameful'[151] (specifically as 'shamefully anachronistic' in a period when 'human beings are viewed as rational creatures bent on maximizing their own happiness'),[152] to a reclamation of sorts as 'a transgressive practice'.[153] Gaitskill is most often read as a transgressive author – particularly in her staging of scenes of erotic domination, abuse and (mild) perversity – but the changing meanings and effects (and affects) of female masochism are both more imbricated and more in flux than Felski's narrative suggests (not least because the labelling of masochism as 'transgressive' precisely relies upon – that is, cannot obviate – its earlier labelling as 'shameful'). Gaitskill's work arguably participates in, and benefits from, this semantic and political indeterminacy – and from the (al)lure of the shameful.

For Jessica Benjamin, '[t]he fantasy of erotic domination embodies both the desire for independence and the desire for recognition', and she argues that 'the root of domination lies in the breakdown of tension between self and other', where extreme submission brings about a kind of 'renunciation of self' – a renunciation that is still, paradoxically, expressive of the desires for recognition and autonomy, which now come into conflict.[154] (This tension or conflict is also evident, I am arguing, in the work of shame, which strives simultaneously to establish a sense of discrete selfhood and to render that selfhood precarious – to imperil it, even – by revealing its dependence on some recognising or watching 'other'.) As Schapiro explains, glossing Benjamin, this constitutes a 'breakdown of the tension between self-assertion and mutual recognition that characterizes psychic and relational life from infancy onwards';[155] if this tension is established in childhood, then its 'breakdown' implies a reversion to childhood. On Schapiro's reading of Gaitskill, '[t]he longing for recognition is especially evident' in *Two Girls*[156] – notably in Dorothy's fantasies about Anna Granite: 'She would look at me and know everything I'd endured,' thinks Dorothy, 'I could allow her to penetrate that part of myself I'd held away from everyone, the tiny but vibrant internal Never-Never Land I'd lived in when there was no other place for me.'[157] When it eventually occurs, this scene of recognition is represented as transformative and healing for Dorothy:

> She looked at me and, as in my fantasy, *she saw me*, saw my pain – which no one had ever acknowledged or even allowed me to acknowledge. However, unlike my fantasy, to be seen and acknowledged by her wasn't to be penetrated and ripped apart by an obscene burst of energy. I did not feel her gaze boring through my pores to envelop my swooning spirit; I felt her at the perimeters of myself, attentive,

very close, but respectful, waiting for me to reveal myself. So I didn't swoon. I stood and met her gaze and felt my self, habitually held in so deep and tight, come out to meet her with the quavering steps of someone whose feet have been asleep for a long, long time.[158]

This longing for recognition is ultimately projected on to Justine, and it is a longing evident immediately after their first meeting, when Dorothy realises wistfully: 'I had wanted to tell Justine about my childhood.'[159]

Justine, in turn, seeks her recognition through her sado-masochistic relationship with Bryan. Once Bryan has compared Justine to a nasty child and she has taken on the role of nymphet, their sex life becomes even more marked by violence and her humiliation more complete. The further she retreats to this original scene of shame, the more dangerous the relationship becomes; nevertheless, the relationship with Bryan is *not* portrayed as wholly unpleasurable. Even as he beats her, 'her body opened more deeply until she felt herself split and revealed all the way into the pit of her guts, a place of heat and light that shone with tenderness for the lover who had come at last'.[160] She is 'caught in the steel trap that had closed on her when she was five years old', yet she clings to her 'humiliation', 'as if it were her only chance to feel'.[161] Dorothy, similarly, finds herself drawn back to the pain of childhood, even years later: after speaking to her father on the phone, she feels 'disgust and pain and covetousness – covetousness because part of me held onto the pain like it was a precious pet, the favourite stuffed animal I had clutched as a child'.[162] If the 'original trauma' of abuse, for both Dorothy and Justine, ostensibly 'induces dissociation and numbness', as Schapiro argues,

> the experience is also felt to be at the 'foundation' of one's being or experience of self. Simulations of that humiliating experience thus paradoxically represent the only path back to the recovery of feeling or authentic self-experience.[163]

Shame, here, marks the entry into feeling, even the beginnings of intimacy, and Gaitskill – like Homes – is always alert to its ambivalence, even its pleasurable potential. This double movement of cleaving to and cleaving from childhood that both Dorothy and Justine exhibit expresses a desire for authentic selfhood and true feeling, even when that feeling is of the most negative, painful variety. The sado-masochistic impulses of the adult Justine are represented as originating deep in her childhood and, while she moves between the (apparent) poles of sadistic and masochistic desire, the initiatory event and point of comparison is always the scene of public molestation with Dr Norris. Thus:

> She wanted to be tied up and whipped after watching cartoon characters being beaten and tortured for the viewer's amusement. She watched the animated violence with queasy fascination, feeling frightened and exposed. It was the same feeling she had had when Dr. Norris touched her [. . .].[164]

Again, the emphasis here is on the tension between fascination and fear (desire and repulsion), and on this sense of herself as 'exposed' (that is, of shame as excessive or inappropriate visibility); her 'queasiness', meanwhile, roots this feeling in her body. After watching a particularly brutal cartoon representing a dog's nightmare about hell,

> [s]he sat with the now familiar sensation of violation coursing through her body as if it could split her apart. [. . .]
>
> She didn't have the vocabulary to express, even to herself, the feeling these images evoked in her; it was too overpowering for her even to see clearly what it was. It seemed to occupy the place that all her daily activities and expressions came from, the same place Dr. Norris had touched. *It felt like the foundation that all the other events of her life played upon.*[165]

Again, we are offered a view of a body overwhelmed by feeling and a self threatened with disintegration or dissolution; the primal nature of these feelings (as 'foundation') renders them both 'familiar' and beyond words (prelinguistic). If the sensation is one of 'violation' – suggesting some outside aggression – it also seems to originate within the self (hence its connection with shame), being triggered by the abuse rather than caused by it, strictly speaking.

The connection between Dorothy and Justine is not easily achieved; their conversations are plagued by misunderstanding and miscommunication, and each girl betrays the other in some way. The physical embodiment of the two girls (one definitively 'thin', the other definitively 'fat') emphasises their difference, and even the structure of the novel and its mode of narration (Dorothy in first person, Justine in third) keep their stories apart – parallel but distinct. Hardie claims that 'personal and cultural history both inhibits and generates the eventual contact and intimacy between the two';[166] I would suggest that, if shame is both 'contagious' and 'individuating',[167] then the contagion of shame allows for the affective coming together of these two characters, but it also magnifies their isolation, their separation from everyone around them, and from each other. As they begin to forge a connection, towards the close of the novel, Gaitskill makes it clear that this connection is to a large extent a *fantasy* or *projection* of each girl – although its being so does not render it less nurturing and effective an attachment, ultimately. Notably, the relationship between them is generally conveyed to us from Dorothy's perspective (for example, when she figures Justine as 'breaking down doors I couldn't bring myself to open and storming in),[168] but the unreliability of this perspective – or rather, the unpredictable oscillations of feeling that she is subject to[169] – reveals the precariousness of this apparently burgeoning intimacy and its basis in a certain contrivance. When Dorothy observes, of their first meeting, how 'All my eagerness to like Justine frolicked in the air between us', she reveals the desire that both motivates and sustains this fantasy of intimacy.[170]

The habit of fantasy is long entrenched, for Dorothy. As a bullied child, she retreats from the world outside and the threats posed by school and other children, taking refuge in lurid fictions and romantic fantasies, drawings of Never-Never Land and heaven, musicals and movies. Her parents collude in this, thereby unwittingly exacerbating her isolation and powerlessness:

> Part of me accepted my mother's comfort, shutting out, with a huge effort, the rest of the world. But another part of me saw that the world created by my parents and me was useless. It was not translatable into the language of the tough, gum-popping kids around me, and it failed to protect me from them.[171]

In doing this, her parents seek to keep her in childhood – to maintain the stability of their own fragile fantasy of family by freezing her in her role of little girl. In time, Dorothy herself develops what she calls her 'mythology':

[T]he pattern I made of the people around me, a mythology for their incomprehensible activity, a mythology that brought me a cramped delight, which I protected by putting all possible space between myself and other people. The boundaries of my inner world did not extend out, but in, so that there was a large area of blank whiteness starting at my most external self and expanding inward until it reached the tiny inner province of dazzling colour and activity that it safeguarded, like the force field of clouds and limitless night sky that surrounded the island of Never-Never Land.[172]

If her 'inner world' is 'Never-Never Land', then it is not only a place of safety and isolation, but also – by implication – a place of *perpetual childhood* that Dorothy clings to in a bid to achieve her aim (unwisely communicated to a friend during the sixth grade) of never growing up.[173] Later she will change her name to 'Dorothy Never', an action that distances her from her past through the abandonment of the family surname, but forever connects her to that childish fantasy of withdrawal from the world and from adulthood. In the mean time, in forming 'beautiful and elaborate fantasies' about her classmates, 'bright phantasms' that she attaches to them, and 'in creating the imaginary world inside me', she finds that she has 'abandoned the world that had existed between my parents and me'.[174] Her father's subsequent anger towards her, his verbal and sexual abuse of her, she interprets as him punishing her for abandoning them – though in fact this abandonment, as my argument suggests, is really always a kind of bi-directional cleaving.

Given the role of fantasy in the lives of both girls, given their respective retreat from the world, it is not surprising that the tentative connection between them operates not through what they say to each other, but through more indeterminate communications of tone and feeling – affective communications that underlie (and sometimes contradict) their verbal communications. Indeed, the connection is figured most often as voice or vibration: after seeing Justine's card looking for interviewees – which gives no name and describes her simply as 'Writer' – Dorothy confesses that '"Writer" had sent a current quivering through my quotidian existence, and now everything was significant';[175] after their first meeting, she reflects that, 'While she had sat before me, a foreign vibration had quivered through the air, handling and examining everything it brushed against.'[176] If Dorothy, with her susceptibility to philosophical cults and new age healing, seems more prone to 'vibrations' than Justine, then the latter feels, nevertheless, that her potential interviewee has 'a voice that, although riddled with peculiarity and tension, stroked Justine along the inside of her skull in a way that both repelled and attracted her'.[177] And, for Justine, their first meeting has a similarly – if more cautiously received – vibratory effect:

> It would be an exaggeration to say that Justine's meeting with Dorothy disturbed the years-old insulation of her cloak of loneliness. But something about the encounter had sent an invisible ray under the cloak, a ray that subtly vibrated against everything it touched before it finally faded days later.[178]

However, the isolating 'cloak of loneliness' that Justine puts on in childhood, the world of fantasy that Dorothy builds around herself – these parallel forms of isolation cannot be utterly vanquished; nor, Gaitskill's novel seems to suggest, should they be. Indeed, when Justine experiences, in her teenage years, the 'loneliness and humiliation' of betrayal by a best friend, this is 'coupled with the sensation that she was, at this moment, absolutely herself';[179] the continuation of some sense of selfhood relies precisely upon this often alienating sense of distinctness or separation. These acutely personal questions – as they play out in the lives of Dorothy and Justine – are explored in *Two Girls* in an echo of larger questions of autonomy and recognition, but also in relation to the Randian arguments conducted within the novel's pages about individualism versus collectivism and/or community. 'To stand apart from the collective is the only choice a rational human can make,' one (rather slavish) Definitist tells Justine, when she expresses her interest in 'The concept of the beauty of loneliness', but she counters that 'People stand apart for irrational reasons, too. Sometimes it just happens.'[180] That awareness of the inevitability of 'standing apart' is always, in *Two Girls*, posited in quivering tension with a yearning for the 'matching components' that might, however transiently, bring people together.[181]

Vibrations, however seductive, are anyway apt to go awry: faced with Justine's own betrayal of her (the damning article on Definitism), Dorothy agonises over whether she has 'misinterpreted the message of her eyes', even while persisting in her belief that Justine 'had silently transmitted promises to me, promises of respect and allegiance'.[182] Their very 'silence', however, suggests that they may be figments of Dorothy's own imagination, emanations of her desire. Dorothy's reaction neatly encapsulates the tension between desire and repulsion, intimacy and misunderstanding, in their relationship, and so highlights Gaitskill's refusal to provide an utterly affirmative conclusion, a decisive step away from the scene of shame: 'I felt much as I had on first meeting Justine; insulted and yet seduced,' Dorothy tells us. In the article she finds 'condescension', but also 'respect' and 'a desire to understand me'; she is disturbed by the way Justine compares her 'to a traumatized child', while beginning to entertain 'the possibility that she was right'.[183] 'If I had been seduced, I had also been abandoned,' thinks Dorothy, comparing Justine to a 'flippant ex-lover', but also hinting at a parent–child relationship, in which Justine is the parent and she the (traumatised) child.[184] In Dorothy's outrage is contained the suggestion of a greater intimacy than appears actually to have taken place. She is furious, not because Justine has trashed Definitism, but because she has used and ruined 'the memory of our shared closeness' – that is, the 'closeness' of Justine and Dorothy, which arguably existed only in Dorothy's fantasy of it.[185]

At the conclusion of the novel, Dorothy bursts furiously into Justine's apartment and finds her tied up, with 'marks on her breasts and thighs, and dried blood on her lips', 'desolate and ashamed'.[186] In order for the two women to come together, finally, it is vital that Justine's shame (her shamed, beaten body) is made visible, and that Dorothy bears witness to it; shame as a particular mode of *becoming visible* (even *becoming an object for the other*) is what forges the connection between them (presumably we are meant to 'see' Dorothy's shame in her fatness, in the more mundane sartorial shame of her 'Sears clothing').[187] After Bryan has been ejected from the apartment, the two women sit on the bed drinking tea and talking. 'I sat with my heart opened to her,' thinks Dorothy, 'feeling her heart mournfully opening to me, sending me the messages that can be received only by another heart, that which the intellect can never apprehend.'[188] Each girl confesses to the other that she has thought about her, from time to time; but, as Justine explains it, 'They weren't really thoughts. Just images, feelings. I could tell you were very strong, and I wondered how you got to be that way.'[189] The 'relationship' between Justine and Dorothy is an affective, bodily connection – with affect understood as those 'visceral forces beneath, alongside, or generally *other than* conscious knowing' and located in 'those intensities that pass body to body [. . .], those resonances that circulate about, between, and sometimes stick to bodies and worlds'.[190] The 'intensities' or vibrations that pass between Dorothy and Justine do so despite and even because of their frequent miscommunication, their dogged, suspicious isolation, and the persistence of shame and disgust as formative framing narratives in their parallel lives.[191]

The novel closes with the two women going to sleep, their arms around each other, in a scene of tenderness and resolution that emphasises this affective (non-cognitive, pretheoretical, extra-linguistic) connection, without thereby precluding a future return of shame and struggle: 'Her body against me was like a phrase of music. My muscles were calmed, white flowers bloomed on my heart.'[192] In Dorothy's narrative, this metaphor of blooming flowers repeatedly signals moments of recognition in her fleeting intimacies with Anna Granite, Knight Ludlow (who is briefly Dorothy's lover) and now Justine: (of Granite) 'I imagined myself in a psychic swoon, lush flowers of surrender popping out about my head as I was upheld by the mighty current of Granite's intellectual embrace' and, later, 'I felt yellow flowers blooming on my internal organs'; (of Knight) 'I felt something open in my body, something like a rare flower that absorbs molecules, pheromones, and oxygen' and, later, 'A glimmering flower of blood and fire bloomed between my legs.'[193] In each case, this is a feeling located in the body; in each case, the metaphor of blooming suggests something flourishing, natural and organic (but also, by implication, extra-linguistic, non-cognitive). Hardie reads this 'intimacy' between the women as 'a scene that neither precludes nor specifically signals sexual contact',[194] suggesting that

> Dorothy offers Justine a horizon of possibility, to reanimate questions of dominance and submission outside the arena of sadistic heterosexuality – the novel finishes as Dorothy literally interrupts a potentially fatal sadistic scenario in which Justine finds herself. The 'gift' of this coincidence forms her reply to the insult of the article.[195]

For Schapiro, this coming together of Dorothy and Justine represents 'a scene of mutual recognition', but one that occurs 'only after each has witnessed the other's deeply painful humiliation. The shameful exposure that both characters had so dreaded in fact becomes their salvation.'[196] My own reading finds more ambivalence in this ending than Schapiro allows: because of the purely affective and largely fantasised nature of this recognition (which may be all that is possible); because of the dissonant effects of both the experience of shame and of this mutual witnessing of humiliation (which might, in turn, produce further feelings and memories of shame); because of the implied association of childhood and affectivity, the ways in which, in our culture, 'the figure of the child typically stands in for, and so apparently offers unmediated or interrogated access to, the realm of feeling'[197] (a phenomenon that the novel critiques, but on which it also relies for its pathos); and because of the double-edged nature of the relationship of 'cleaving' that each girl has to the childhood that has shaped them and that continues to reverberate in the adult present.

Conclusion: the shame of being a (woman) writer

Critical responses to Homes's and Gaitskill's work – when not dismissing or damning that work out of hand (as was largely the case with *The End of Alice*) – have tended to attempt a recuperation of it as 'moral' or redemptive, while struggling with its essential ambivalence.[198] Thus, despite describing her stories as 'open systems, with [. . .] no moral in tow', Matthew Sharpe concludes his interview with Mary Gaitskill by asking her about the 'healing' power of stories; she rejects the descriptions 'healing' and 'helping', before conceding that stories can be 'nourishing' when they succeed in giving 'full expression to whatever it is – I mean expression to the point of being able to glimpse those things that are always going to be outside our range of vision'.[199] This giving of 'full expression' is not, however, recuperated by Gaitskill herself as moral in either its ends or its means.

Similarly, Gregory Crewdson claims that, 'Despite its unrelenting tone of manic sexual transgression and perversity, *The End of Alice* is at its center a romantic, and even moral, tale,'[200] a statement eerily reminiscent of *Vanity Fair*'s description of *Lolita* as 'the only convincing love story of our century'.[201] While Homes proceeds to confess, in this same interview, that the novel 'is not particularly a critique [of sexual politics]', she nevertheless attempts a political recuperation of *The End of Alice* by comparing herself to Angela

Carter's notion of a 'moral pornographer', who 'might begin to penetrate to the heart of the contempt for women that distorts our culture
even as he entered the realms of true obscenity as he describes it'.[202]
Homes, then, excuses her lapse into 'obscenity' as a moral investigation of patriarchal contempt; yet, in the same passage just quoted,
Carter also describes the 'moral pornographer' as 'an artist who uses
pornographic material as part of the *acceptance of the logic of a
world of absolute sexual licence for all the genders*, and projects a
model of the way such a world might work'.[203] Is Homes likewise
interested in exploring such a 'world of absolute sexual licence', one
that would then include the paedophilic desires and actions of the
imprisoned man and his teenaged correspondent? *The End of Alice*
does more than simply make visible 'contempt for women' en route
to a facile or consolatory overcoming of sexual shame, violence and
degradation; it also seeks both to represent and to produce the experience of shame, and it presents us with three female characters (the
teenaged correspondent, the paedophile's ultimate victim, Alice, and
the paedophile's abusive mother), each of whom models a decidedly
disturbing expression of 'deviant' female sexuality. While all three
characters come to us via the distorting, unreliable consciousness
and voice of a deluded paedophile, the vision of female shamefulness
is not so easily erased.

Kincaid asserts that 'few stories in our culture right now [he is
writing in 1998] are as popular as those of child molesting', and
he asks: 'Why do we generate these stories and not others? What
rewards do they offer? Who profits from their circulation, and who
pays the price?'[204] Kincaid's claim is that we *do* 'profit' from, or take
pleasure in, these stories ('we wouldn't be telling this tale of the
exploitation of the child's body if we didn't wish to have it told'),
and our reiterations of these narratives of abuse 'keep the subject
hot so we can disown it while welcoming it in the back door'.[205] My
own claim is that the popularity of these child-molesting stories is
symptomatic of the cultural preoccupation with shame in general
and with the childhood scene of shame in particular. Homes and
Gaitskill exhibit this cultural preoccupation, but they might also
be read as drawing attention to the story of childhood sexual abuse
as a story – to its *narrative* complications and contradictions, as
well as its narrative *pleasures* – in ways that highlight the political
and aesthetic complexity of the turn to shame, illuminating both

the limitations and the possibilities of shame as a model of identity, community or femininity.

Shame's role in the constitution and disruption of identity may help to explain its appeal to the novelist in a post-psychoanalytic age. As Sedgwick explains, in a line that I have cited already:

> shame is a bad feeling attaching to what one is: one therefore *is something*, in experiencing shame. The place of identity, the struc-ture 'identity', marked by shame's threshold between sociability and introversion, may be established and naturalized in the first instance *through shame*.[206]

Shame, then, can be viewed as an originary experience and fram-ing narrative in the development of identity, and in this way the *Bildungsroman* becomes the narrative of shame where this 'structure, "identity"', can be tested out via the representation of an individual produced and undone by shame. Yet this lure of shame for the novel-ist is complicated by the possibility that, as Elspeth Probyn avers, 'a form of shame always attends the writer. Primarily it is the shame of not being equal to the interest of one's subject.'[207] Writing is always shameful, and this may be particularly the case for the woman writer. If we accept Sandra Bartky's description of shame as 'a pervasive affective attunement to the social environment', and one that is char-acteristically feminine, what are the ramifications of this for women's writing?[208] If, on one reading, shame is 'natural' for women, preserv-ing, problematically, the link between the female body and writing, writing about 'shameful' topics like paedophilia or sado-masochism remains contentious for women authors: the excoriating *New York Times* review of *The End of Alice* notably claims it as 'a novel that proves that a woman can write as badly, violently and misogynisti-cally as a man';[209] Margot Livesey, in the *TLS*, notes 'that it was written by a woman only added fuel to the fire' of its vexed recep-tion;[210] Daphne Merkin, also in the *New York Times*, claims that 'the fact that Ms. Homes is a female has only added to the feeling of violation that her book has elicited'.[211] It is unsurprising, then, that Homes has attempted to distance herself from women's writing' in order to be able to engage with such subjects: in interviews she has claimed that 'most of my models of writers are male. [. . .] When I was growing up, women wrote "women's fiction" – fiction about women's lives. And I couldn't have been less interested'.[212] As she elaborates, 'People read *Alice* and say, "How can a woman write this stuff?"'[213] Similarly, on the front cover of Homes's 1999 novel, *Music for Torching*, Zadie Smith is quoted: 'There have been very few women writers like Homes'.[214] Homes's attunement to shame is what unsexes her, here. Gaitskill, meanwhile, is frequently asked about her own sexual history and proclivities in interviews,[215] as if her willingness to depict deviant or debased expressions of female sexuality in her novels must have some autobiographical root or justification.

Shame retains, then, an ambivalent and yet vital relationship to both literature and femininity, a relationship at once constitutive and disruptive – and one that I will explore further in the next chapter. The lure of shame – in the contemporary moment – is undeniable. It is the point where crucial anxieties about childhood, about female bodies, about queer histories coalesce. Our interest in shame bespeaks both a desire for connection and a suspicion of solidarity. Shame has an explanatory force in relation to the crisis of identity politics and the complexity of desire; its very ambivalence satisfies our scepticism. Yet, in the attention to shame and to the (a)shamed individual, what gets lost, sometimes, is an attention to power, to the social, to those supra-personal structures that serve to decree *what counts as shameful*. This does not have to be the case – see, for example, Sara Ahmed's discussion of national shame in *The Cultural Politics of Emotion* (2004) or Kathleen Woodward's insistence, in her reading of Sedgwick, that 'it isn't the affect itself – or by itself – that carries the potential for transformation. It is, rather, the very context of a politicized movement.'[216] In continuing to assess the fraught politics of shame, as they appear in the literature and theory of recent decades, the insistence on *context* and *coalition* – the 'crucial alliances' made possible through 'shared stigma' – remains vital.[217] We might, in addition, want to include in this assessment some acknowledgement: first, of the continued *gendering* of shame (its displacement on to female bodies); second, of the limitations of a solidarity founded on affective connections that might be as much *fantasised* as real; third, of the problematics of figuring affective experience as beyond 'linguistic determinability',[218] beyond intelligibility, and associating affectivity with *childhood*; fourth, of the troubling *pleasures* available to us in the narration and/or witnessing of shame. My reading of Homes and Gaitskill has, I hope, gestured towards all four, and in the next chapter I will continue to pursue the questions raised here about shame's relationship to femininity, about the personal and the structural, and about the non-redemptive writing of shame via analyses of three autofictional works by women authors.

Notes

1. J. Brooks Bouson, *Embodied Shame: Uncovering Female Shame in Contemporary Women's Writings* (Albany: SUNY Press, 2009), p. 183.
2. Bouson, p. 15.
3. J. Brooks Bouson, *Quiet As It's Kept: Shame, Trauma and Race in the Novels of Toni Morrison* (Albany: SUNY Press, 2000), pp. 3, 4, 5.
4. Erica L. Johnson and Patricia Moran, 'Introduction', in Johnson and Moran (eds), *The Female Face of Shame* (Bloomington: Indiana University Press, 2013), pp. 1–19 (pp. 2, 10).
5. Johnson and Moran, pp. 14, 18.
6. Johnson and Moran, p. 19.
7. Sally Munt, *Queer Attachments: The Cultural Politics of Shame* (Aldershot: Ashgate, 2007), p. 103.
8. Munt, p. 2.
9. Bouson, *Embodied Shame*, p. 2.
10. Ibid.
11. Daniela Caselli, 'Kindergarten Theory: Childhood, Affect, Critical Thought', *Feminist Theory* 11: 3 (2010): 241–54 (250).
12. Karín Lesnik-Oberstein, 'Introduction: Voice, Agency and the Child', in Lesnik-Oberstein (ed.), *Children in Culture, Revisited* (Basingstoke: Palgrave, 2011), pp. 1–17 (p. 3).
13. Johnson and Moran, p. 6.
14. Sigmund Freud, *Five Lectures on Psychoanalysis* [1909], trans. and ed. James Strachey (New York: W. W. Norton, 1961), pp. 139–40.
15. Malcolm Pines, 'Shame: What Psychoanalysis Does and Does Not Say' [1987], in Claire Pajaczkowska and Ivan Ward (eds), *Shame and Sexuality: Psychoanalysis and Visual Culture* (London: Routledge, 2008), pp. 93–106 (pp. 98–9).
16. Léon Wurmser, *The Power of the Inner Judge: Psychodynamic Treatment of the Severe Neuroses* (Northvale, NJ: Jason Aronson, 2000), p. 191.
17. Andrew P. Morrison, 'The Eye Turned Inward: Shame and the Self', in Donald Nathanson (ed.), *The Many Faces of Shame* (New York: Guilford, 1987), pp. 271–91 (p. 283).
18. Pines, p. 99.
19. Freud, *Five Lectures*, p. 45.

20. Jacqueline Rose, *The Case of Peter Pan or The Impossibility of Children's Fiction* (Basingstoke: Macmillan, 1984), p. 12. My emphasis.
21. Erica Burman and Jackie Stacey, 'The Child and Childhood in Feminist Theory', *Feminist Theory* 11: 3 (2010): 227–40 (231).
22. Karín Lesnik-Oberstein and Stephen Thomson, 'What is Queer Theory Doing With the Child?', *Parallax* 8: 1 (2002): 35–46 (35–6).
23. Veronica Barnsley, 'The Child/The Future', *Feminist Theory* 11: 3 (2010): 323–30 (323). See, for example, the work of Erica Burman, Allison James, Chris Jenks, Karín Lesnik-Oberstein, Alan Prout and Jacqueline Rose.
24. Lesnik-Oberstein, 'Introduction', pp. 1–17 (p. 3).
25. Lee Edelman, *No Future: Queer Theory and the Death Drive* (Durham, NC: Duke University Press, 2004), p. 3.
26. Lesnik-Oberstein and Thomson, 'What is Queer Theory', p. 36.
27. Ibid.
28. Rose, p. 8.
29. Erica Burman, *Developments: Child, Image, Nation* (London: Routledge, 2008), p. 13.
30. Claudia Castañeda, *Figurations: Child, Bodies, Worlds* (Durham, NC: Duke University Press, 2002), pp. 2–3.
31. Burman, *Developments*, p. 131.
32. Steven Angelides, 'Historicizing Affect, Psychoanalyzing History: Pedophilia and the Discourse of Child Sexuality', *Journal of Homosexuality* 46: 1–2 (2003): 79–109 (80).
33. Burman, *Developments*, p. 132.
34. Ian Hacking, 'The Making and Molding of Child Abuse', *Critical Inquiry* 17: 2 (1991): 253–88 (269).
35. Hacking, p. 274.
36. Mary MacLeod and Esther Saraga, 'Challenging the Orthodoxy: Towards a Feminist Theory and Practice', *Feminist Review* 28 (1988): 16–55 (40).
37. See: Sara Scott, 'Surviving Selves: Feminism and Contemporary Discourses of Child Sexual Abuse', *Feminist Theory* 2: 3 (2001): 349–61.
38. Scott, p. 353.
39. Ibid.
40. Victoria Bates, '"Misery Loves Company": Sexual Trauma, Psychoanalysis and the Market for Misery', *Journal of Medical Humanities* 33 (2012): 61–81.
41. Roger Luckhurst, *The Trauma Question* (London: Routledge, 2008), p. 119.
42. David M. Halperin and Valerie Traub, 'Beyond Gay Pride', in Halperin and Traub (eds), *Gay Shame* (Chicago: University of Chicago Press, 2009), pp. 3–40 (p. 4).

43. Erving Goffman, *Stigma: Notes on the Management of Spoiled Identity* (London: Penguin, 1963), pp. 11, 9.
44. Goffman, p. 21.
45. Goffman, p. 31.
46. Heather Love, '"Spoiled Identity": Stephen Gordon's Loneliness and the Difficulties of Queer History', *GLQ* 7: 4 (2001): 487–519 (488). See also *Feeling Backward: Loss and the Politics of Queer History* (Cambridge, MA: Harvard University Press, 2007) and a more recent paper, 'Underdogs: On the Minor in Queer Theory', delivered at the Queer Theory Workshop, Columbia University, 8 February 2011.
47. Love, '"Spoiled Identity"', p. 489.
48. Eve Kosofsky Sedgwick, 'Queer Performativity: Henry James's *The Art of the Novel*', *GLQ* 1: 1 (1993): 1–16 (4).
49. The *Oxford English Dictionary* offers two distinct meanings/uses of the verb 'cleave'. For the first, it suggests the sub-meanings 'to part or divide by a cutting blow; to hew asunder; to split' and 'to separate or sever by dividing or splitting'. For the second, it posits 'to stick fast or adhere', 'to cling or hold fast to', and so on. See: 'cleave, v.1', OED Online, March 2019, Oxford University Press. Available at: <http://www.oed.com/view/Entry/34105?rskey=RNj5ZE&result=3> (last accessed 13 June 2019); and 'cleave, v.2', OED Online, March 2019, Oxford University Press. Available at: <http://www.oed.com/view/Entry/34106?rskey=RNj5ZE&result=4> (last accessed 13 June 2019).
50. Love, '"Spoiled Identity"', p. 515.
51. Sedgwick, 'Queer Performativity', p. 13.
52. Sedgwick, 'Queer Performativity', p. 8.
53. Kathryn Bond Stockton, *The Queer Child* (Durham, NC: Duke University Press, 2009), pp. 1, 3, 52.
54. Steven Bruhm and Natasha Hurley, 'Introduction', in Bruhm and Hurley (eds), *Curiouser: On the Queerness of Children* (Minneapolis: University of Minnesota Press, 2004), pp. ix–xxxviii (pp. ix, x).
55. Bruhm and Hurley, p. xi.
56. James R. Kincaid, *Erotic Innocence: The Culture of Child Molesting* (Durham, NC: Duke University Press, 1998), p. 7.
57. Kincaid, pp. 5–6, 13–14.
58. Michiko Kakutani, 'Like Humbert Humbert, Full of Lust and Lies', *The New York Times*, 23 February 1996. Available at: <http://www.nytimes.com/1996/02/23/books/books-of-the-times-like-humbert-humbert-full-of-lust-and-lies.html> (last accessed 13 June 2019).
59. A. M. Homes, *The End of Alice* [1996] (New York: Scribner, 2006), p. 11.
60. Vladimir Nabokov, *Lolita* [1955] (London: Penguin, 1980), pp. 9, 175.

61. Homes, *The End of Alice*, p. 192.
62. Nabokov, *Lolita*, p. 9.
63. Ibid.
64. Later, the text gives another sly nod to Nabokov's influence, with the reference to Alice's 'Schmitt boxes' for preserving butterflies: Nabokov was, famously, a lepidopterist.
65. Whether Homes's novel offers an explicit critique of the gender and sexual politics of *Lolita* is harder to say. Elizabeth Patnoe argues that 'readers come to *Lolita* inundated with a hegemonic reading of evil Lolita and bad female sexuality', and that critical commentary on the novel is largely 'complicit in the aestheticization of child molestation perpetrated by individual people and by the culture at large' (Elizabeth Patnoe, 'Lolita Misrepresented, Lolita Reclaimed: Disclosing the Doubles', *College Literature* 22: 2 (1995): 81–104 (84, 87)). While Patnoe opts to see 'the raped child' rather than 'a seductive little girl' (p. 96), Homes arguably gives us both.
66. Homes, p. 96.
67. Kincaid, p. 13.
68. Kincaid, pp. 20–1.
69. Homes, p. 12.
70. Homes, p. 207.
71. Writing in the *TLS*, Margot Livesey claimed that the novel 'was both widely reviled and widely admired' ('Surprise, Surprise', *TLS*, 31 October 1997). While Elizabeth Young found *The End of Alice* to be 'the best novel I have read this year' and 'the most literary of books' ('Books: Hell in Wonderland', *The Independent*, 1 November 1997), Kakutani's *New York Times* review dismissed it as 'revolting trash' ('Like Humbert Humbert, Full of Lust and Lies'). In a later *New York Times* review, Daphne Merkin manages to express the equivocal reception of the novel in a single sentence, describing it as 'a splashy, not particularly likable book whose best moments are quietly observed and whose underlying themes are more serious than prurient' ('Random Objects of Desire', *New York Times*, 24 March 1996).
72. Homes, p. 183.
73. Homes, p. 192.
74. Homes, p. 15.
75. Homes, p. 30.
76. Homes, p. 19.
77. Homes, p. 25.
78. Homes, pp. 68–9.
79. Homes, pp. 24–5.
80. Homes, p. 107.

81. Homes, p. 113.
82. Homes, p. 180.
83. Kincaid, p. 9.
84. Kincaid, p. 11.
85. Homes, p. 101.
86. Homes, pp. 101–2.
87. Margaret Morganroth Gullette, 'The Exile of Adulthood: Pedophilia in the Midlife Novel', *NOVEL: A Forum on Fiction*, 17: 3 (1984): 215–32 (221, 225).
88. Gullette, p. 215.
89. Homes, p. 111.
90. Homes, p. 265.
91. Homes, p. 269.
92. Burman and Stacey, 'The Child and Childhood', p. 228.
93. Homes, p. 203.
94. Homes, p. 124.
95. Homes, p. 126.
96. Homes, p. 152.
97. Homes, p. 202.
98. Homes, p. 264.
99. Homes, pp. 157–8. My emphasis.
100. Homes, p. 99.
101. In her *TLS* review, Margot Livesey confessed that 'I didn't want to see what the novel was showing me, but finally [. . .] I succumbed' ('Surprise, Surprise').
102. Kincaid, p. 88.
103. Ibid.
104. Kincaid, p. 94.
105. Homes, p. 188.
106. Ibid.
107. Homes, p. 74.
108. Homes, p. 75.
109. Homes, pp. 75, 99.
110. Homes, pp. 186–7.
111. Homes, p. 187.
112. Gregory Crewdson, 'Interview with A. M. Homes', *Bomb Magazine* 55 (1996): 38–42 (40).
113. The cult/movement of 'Definitism' in *Two Girls* is commonly acknowledged to be based on 'Objectivism', and the character of 'Anna Granite' on Ayn Rand. Objectivism is a philosophical system – centring on ideas of objective reality, rational self-interest and individualism – explored through Rand's fiction (such as *The Fountainhead*, 1943,

and *Atlas Shrugged*, 1957) and non-fiction, and enjoying some significant popularity in the US from the 1950s onwards. Gaitskill has discussed her interest in Rand and her research for the novel in interview
with Gary Percesepe ('Ayn Rand and the American Psyche: An Interview with Mary Gaitskill', 14 June 2011. Available at: <http://www.
thenervousbreakdown.com/gpercesepe/2011/06/ayn-rand-and-the-
american-psyche-an-interview-with-mary-gaitskill/> (last accessed 13
June 2019)). Melissa Jane Hardie discusses both Rand and Gaitskill
in 'Fluff and Granite: Rereading Ayn Rand's Camp Feminist Aesthetics',
in Mimi Reisel Gladstein and Chris Matthew Sciabarra (eds),
Feminist Interpretations of Ayn Rand (University Park: Pennsylvania
University Press, 1999), pp. 363–89.

114. Mary Gaitskill, *Two Girls, Fat and Thin* (New York: Simon & Schuster,
1991), pp. 30, 43.
115. Gaitskill, p. 54.
116. Gaitskill, pp. 54, 55.
117. Gaitskill, p. 59.
118. Gaitskill, p. 161.
119. Pines, p. 98.
120. Gaitskill, p. 133.
121. Gaitskill, p. 160.
122. Ibid.
123. In fact, as Lauren Berlant notes in some detail, both girls snack almost
constantly throughout the novel. See Lauren Berlant, 'Two Girls, Fat
and Thin', in Stephen M. Barber and David L. Clark (eds), *Regarding
Sedgwick* (New York: Routledge, 2002), pp. 71–108. See pp. 82ff. for
a discussion of food in the novel.
124. Gaitskill, p. 276.
125. Bond Stockton, pp. 37, 122.
126. Allison James, Chris Jenks and Alan Prout, *Theorizing Childhood*
(Cambridge: Polity Press, 1998), p. 9. In a very different context –
his book about the murder of James Bulger by two children – Blake
Morrison writes of the 'strange and unknowable' character of childhood: 'As you get older, as you recede from it, childhood becomes
strange and unknowable. Once left behind, it's a country you can't
visit in person, a place of exile, mourned and misremembered by the
adults at its gates.' What Morrison communicates particularly effectively is his sense of unease – not only with the crime and the reaction it provoked, but also the more fundamental unease provoked by
childhood itself: its *otherness*, its unintelligibility, its apparent amorality, its contradictory desires and feelings (Blake Morrison, *As If*
(London: Granta, 1997), p. 119).

127. Gaitskill, p. 95.

128. Gaitskill, pp. 114–15.

129. Gaitskill, p. 108.

130. Gaitskill, p. 109.

131. Gaitskill, p. 251.

132. Gaitskill, p. 110.

133. Gaitskill, p. 138.

134. Ibid.

135. Ibid.

136. Jenny Kitzinger, 'Defending Innocence: Ideologies of Childhood', *Feminist Review* 28 (1988): 77–87 (79).

137. Kitzinger, p. 80.

138. Gaitskill, p. 91.

139. Gaitskill, p. 100.

140. Gaitskill, p. 93.

141. Ibid.

142. Gaitskill, p. 201.

143. Gaitskill, pp. 250–1.

144. Robert A. Glick and Donald I. Meyers, 'Introduction', in Glick and Meyers (eds), *Masochism: Current Psychoanalytic Perspectives* (Hillsdale, NJ: Analytic Press, 1988), pp. 1–25 (p. 4).

145. For more on this idea of the masochist as stuck in childhood, see Sigmund Freud, 'A Child is Being Beaten' [1919], in *On Psychopathology*, trans. James Strachey (London: Penguin, 1979), pp. 159–93.

146. Gaitskill, p. 255.

147. Barbara Schapiro, 'Trauma and Sadomasochistic Narrative: Mary Gaitskill's "The Dentist"', *Mosaic* 38: 2 (2005): 37–52 (43).

148. Hardie, p. 379.

149. Hardie, p. 367.

150. Rita Felski, 'Redescriptions of Female Masochism', *Minnesota Review* 63/4 (2005): 127–39 (127).

151. Felski, p. 128.

152. Felski, p. 130.

153. Felski, p. 128.

154. Jessica Benjamin, *The Bonds of Love: Psychoanalysis, Feminism and the Problem of Domination* (London: Virago, 1988), pp. 52, 55.

155. Schapiro, p. 46.

156. Ibid.

157. Gaitskill, p. 167. The reference to 'Never-Never Land' suggests that Dorothy too is unable to move beyond childhood. As a child she is obsessed with Peter Pan; the 'very name' of Never-Never Land 'made me feel a sadness like a big beautiful blanket I could wrap around

myself. I tried to believe that Peter Pan might really come one night and fly me away; I was too old to believe this and I knew it, but I forced the bright polka-dotted canopy of this belief over my unhappy knowledge' (p. 81).

158. Gaitskill, p. 187. My emphasis.
159. Gaitskill, p. 39.
160. Gaitskill, p. 256.
161. Gaitskill, pp. 279, 281.
162. Gaitskill, pp. 241–2.
163. Schapiro, p. 43.
164. Gaitskill, p. 66.
165. Gaitskill, p. 67. My emphasis.
166. Hardie, p. 384.
167. Sedgwick, 'Queer Performativity', p. 5.
168. Gaitskill, p. 266.
169. For example, in the course of their first meeting, Dorothy veers from feeling 'a tendril of empathy appear between us' (p. 27), to thinking of Justine as 'this unresponsive creature' (p. 30), to feeling once again 'a sensation of personal contact and intimacy' and feeling sure that 'we could be friends' (p. 32), to regarding Justine 'with dislike' (p. 32). As she surmises: the 'world [that] had been created between this girl and me' was 'a subtle, turbulent, exhausting world' (p. 33).
170. Gaitskill, p. 36.
171. Gaitskill, p. 86. It also, of course, fails to protect Dorothy from her father, whose abusive behaviour her mother always refuses to acknowledge.
172. Gaitskill, p. 114.
173. Gaitskill, p. 86.
174. Gaitskill, pp. 117, 118.
175. Gaitskill, p. 15.
176. Gaitskill, p. 38.
177. Gaitskill, p. 23.
178. Gaitskill, p. 173.
179. Gaitskill, p. 156.
180. Gaitskill, p. 175.
181. Gaitskill, p. 32.
182. Gaitskill, p. 296.
183. Gaitskill, p. 294.
184. Gaitskill, p. 295.
185. Ibid.
186. Gaitskill, pp. 306–7.
187. Gaitskill, p. 267.
188. Gaitskill, p. 311.

189. Ibid.

190. Gregory J. Seigworth and Melissa Gregg, 'An Inventory of Shimmers', in Seigworth and Gregg (eds), *The Affect Theory Reader* (Durham, NC: Duke University Press, 2010), pp. 1–25 (p. 1). Seigworth and Gregg's definition of 'affect', such as it is, owes much to a particular strand of thinking on/of affect as preconscious, pretheoretical and pre-linguistic; this strand is perhaps best summed up in Simon O'Sullivan's claim that 'Affects can be described as extra-discursive and extra-textual. Affects are moments of *intensity*, a reaction in/on the body at the level of matter. We might even say that affects are *immanent* to matter. They are certainly immanent to experience [. . .] As such, affects are not to do with knowledge or meaning; indeed, they occur on a different, *asignifying* register' (Simon O'Sullivan, 'The Aesthetics of Affect', *Angelaki* 6: 3 (2001): 125–35 (126)).

191. Bryan's role in this coming together of Dorothy and Justine consti-tutes, interestingly, a subversion of the more conventional triangular relationship in which a female body (as commodity, as desired object) serves as a conduit for desire between two men. See Eve Kosofsky Sedgwick's take on this in *Between Men* [1985] (New York: Columbia University Press, 2015).

192. Gaitskill, p. 313.

193. Gaitskill, pp. 167, 189, 218, 222.

194. Hardie, p. 384.

195. Hardie, p. 385.

196. Schapiro, p. 46.

197. Burman and Stacey, 'The Child and Childhood', p. 234.

198. Note, for example, the review excerpts selected for the preliminary pages of the US edition of *Two Girls*, where the novel is described as 'ingenious and disturbing' (*Interview*), 'fine and disturbing' (*Kirkus Reviews*), 'lyrical' and 'harrowing' (*The Detroit News*), and the author as 'a dismayingly strong writer' (*The Boston Globe*) with 'a voice at once tender but unsentimental, lyrical and unfettered' (*San Jose Mercury News*). In each case, the highest praise is juxtaposed with some sense of the dark, disturbing or unsettling nature of her work.

199. Matthew Sharpe, 'Interview with Mary Gaitskill', *Bomb Magazine* 107 (2009), unpag. Available at: <http://bombmagazine.org/article/3265/> (last accessed 13 June 2019).

200. Crewdson, p. 39.

201. Quoted in Bond Stockton, p. 119. To be clear: I do not want to claim that *The End of Alice cannot* be read as 'moral', merely to question the *insistence* on that particular reading and to point up how this insistence forms part of the way that women authors are read when they touch upon so-called 'shameful' topics.

202. Crewdson, p. 41, quoting Angela Carter, *The Sadeian Woman* (London: Virago, 1979), pp. 19–20.

203. Carter, p. 19. My emphasis.

204. Kincaid, p. 3.

205. Kincaid, p. 6.

206. Sedgwick, 'Queer Performativity', p. 12.

207. Elspeth Probyn, *Blush: Faces of Shame* (Minneapolis: University of Minnesota Press, 2005), p. xvii.

208. Sandra Bartky, *Femininity and Domination: Studies in the Phenomenology of Domination* (London: Routledge, 1990), p. 85.

209. Kakutani, 'Like Humbert Humbert'.

210. Livesey, 'Surprise, Surprise'.

211. Merkin, 'Random Objects of Desire'.

212. Crewdson, p. 39.

213. Crewdson, p. 41.

214. A. M. Homes, *Music for Torching* (London: Granta, 1999), front cover.

215. See, for example, the *New York Magazine* interview by Emily Nussbaum, 'Mary, Mary, Less Contrary' (2005), which marvels at Gaitskill's apparent metamorphosis from 'downtown princess of darkness', someone who has 'worked as a stripper and a call girl', to someone who is 'happily married and lives on a country lane' (<http://nymag.com/nymetro/arts/books/14988/> (last accessed 13 June 2019)).

216. Kathleen Woodward, *Statistical Panic: Cultural Politics and Poetics of Emotions* (Durham, NC: Duke University Press, 2009), p. 87.

217. Love, 'Underdogs'.

218. Munt, p. 103.

Chapter 3

'The Dumb Cunt's Tale': Desire, Shame and Self-Narration in Contemporary Autofiction

'There was shame in her but not the kind you wanted to see, not woman's modesty.'[1]

Prelude: Famewhores

Remember Phaidra, she of the unruly desire, she with the core of shame? Anne Carson takes this fragment from the lost Euripides play, *Hippolytus Veiled*, spoken by the Chorus: 'In place of fire we women were born, a different fire, greater and much harder to fight.'[2] She revisions it thus, as Phaidra speaking to her husband, Theseus:

> Instead of fire – another fire,
> *not just a drop of cunt sweat!* is what we women are –
> you cannot fight it![3]

And Carson's Euripides challenges the audience: 'Are you safe from her now? Yes you are safe from her now. The sun is sinking fast, the evening sacrifice has just begun. You will hear a laugh in the night. Then nothing.'[4] In this chapter I return – at least obliquely – to the figure of Phaidra, the desiring woman whose desire constitutes a kind of challenge to a patriarchal world that figures her as the property of some man or other; whose desire might dishonour not only herself, but those men to whom she belongs, the contagion of (women's) shame threatening a civilisation. In her modern incarnation, what might Phaidra look like and how might she wear – or shrug off – her shame? After the laugh, is there really nothing?

As a prelude to my chapter proper, I want to begin by glossing this quotation from Emily Gould, herself the author of a confessional memoir,[5] quoted here in the *New York Observer* on the work of Marie Calloway and other young female authors who write (online and in print) in great detail about their personal lives and sexual experiences. Gould is quoted as saying:

> Why do women who aren't afraid to humiliate themselves appal us so much, and why do we rush to find superficial reasons to dismiss them ('she's crazy' 'she's a narcissist' 'she's young' 'she's a famewhore')?
>
> I think in part because they pose a threat to the social order, which relies on women's embarrassment to keep them either silent or writing in socially accepted modes.[6]

While there are various problematic assumptions and elisions in what Gould is saying, her statements raise some useful questions concerning female shame as spectacle: a kind of excessive visibility, for which the shamed woman is then held accountable. The use of terms such as 'famewhore' implies shameful or inappropriate sexualisation, as well as suggesting that a desire for celebrity or attention is shameful (despite the fact that this is a role that young women are encouraged to aspire to or inhabit). Indeed, the accusation of 'narcissism' suggests that too close a focus upon oneself is both shameful and pleasurable (does the narcissist not enjoy their narcissism?): is it this pleasure, then, that is the true source of shame? Either way, both terms imply shamelessness and both are used to shame the person they are applied to.

Gould's comments also position *self-humiliation* as a 'brave' act ('women who aren't afraid . . .'). Why? In this chapter I will be asking what is at stake in such a strategy, and what (positive) possibilities inhere in the claiming of postures and attitudes of 'humiliation' (erotic or otherwise) by women writers; but I also want to ask what negative consequences may follow both the claiming of such attitudes and the description of this as 'brave'. Does this assume greater agency in the act of narrating shame than is actually the case? Does it assume that the narration of shame allows shame to be overcome? One of the central threads of *Writing Shame* is, of course, the critique of that logic of writing-as-redemption.

In turn, self-humiliation and shame-as-spectacle are p(
as a 'threat to the social order'. Again: why? What exact
threatened and how? While not disputing this suggestion c
cal, transformative potential of autobiographical expres
representations of shame, I will later hint at the problems incurred
when an unwavering focus on the self, and on shame as a peculiarly
personal experience, comes at the expense of a more critical attention
to the 'social order' – that is, to the ways in which gendered shame
(in particular) is not merely personal, but *structural* and *systemic*.

Conversely, shame is also revealed, in Gould's comments, as one
of the ways the 'social order' is maintained (and therefore a ballast as
well as a 'threat' – which speaks to the peculiarly paradoxical operations of shame), but particularly one of the ways in which gender
norms are maintained and perpetuated; so, in fact, Gould's statement
here does reveal precisely the structural relations between shame,
femininity and the 'social order'. As discussed in the Introduction,
this argument – concerning shame as a structural feature of the way
women experience the world and themselves – is made most persua-
sively by Sandra Bartky, in *Femininity and Domination* (1990). To
reprise this: Bartky asserts that shame is 'gender-related' in the sense
that 'women are more prone to experience' shame than men, and
because 'the feeling itself has a different meaning in relation to their
total psychic situation and general social location than has a similar
emotion when experienced by men'.[7] Shame, then, experienced as or
through 'a pervasive sense of personal inadequacy' and as or through
'the shame of embodiment', reveals 'the "generalized condition of
dishonour" which is women's lot in sexist society'.[8] For women,
feelings of shame 'are profoundly disclosive of [their] "Being-in-the-
world"'.[9] The question that inaugurates this chapter is what is altered
in this experience of shame – and disclosure of self – when the 'act
of being shamed' is instead an act of self-shaming or an embrace of
a shamed position, and thus a route to more productive, challenging
or disruptive forms of self-disclosure – or even self-transformation.

Interestingly, Gould's comments position shame as integral to
both gender and writing, both of which are governed by notions of
social acceptability ('socially accepted modes'). My own suggestion
throughout this book has been that an analysis of shame, of its social
and literary operations, might provide a crucial way of understanding
the intersection of gender and writing, and in this chapter I discuss

texts that explore feelings of shame, embarrassment, vulnerability and rejection in ways – and through literary modes, vernacular languages and genre violations – that challenge such notions of 'acceptability'.

And yet, as I have already conceded, there are also problems and contradictions in Gould's statement: the elision of subtle differences (differences of both nature and degree) between shame, humiliation and embarrassment; the failure to acknowledge the *pleasures* implicit in both the act of (shameful, sexual) confession and the reception of confession; the complex forms of self-aggrandisement available, paradoxically, via an act of self-humiliation; and the performative potentiality of shame, in these instances. On the other hand, we need to be more alert than Gould is to the complex forms of complicity with the (coercive) shame culture on the part of the narrators/confessants themselves, a shame culture that requires confession as much as (if not more than) it requires silence (that old Foucauldian argument); to the fact that humiliated or, more specifically, self-humiliating female authors and artists (if that is what they are) are not 'dismissed' – they are either lauded or denigrated, but either way they are afforded a great deal of attention. One question here might be how we account for the undoubted cultural preoccupation with autobiographical narratives of shame, including what Peter Brooks calls 'our contemporary fascination with – though perhaps simultaneously revulsion from – the public, televised confession [which] demonstrates the banalization of confessional practices',[10] and also shows our conflicted attitudes to shame: simultaneous fascination and revulsion. Finally, despite elsewhere (in her blog, *Emily Magazine*) locating Calloway's work in a 'tradition' that includes Chris Kraus (another author who I will be discussing in this chapter),[11] Gould neglects to address fully the way that both authors, despite apparently being engaged in acts of 'self-humiliation', focus their writing on a pseudonymous male character who is both object of desire and target of shame, thus complicating the presentation of self-humiliation and illustrating the troubling intersubjectivity and transmissibility of shame.

Building on the discussion of A. M. Homes and Mary Gaitskill in Chapter 2, I here develop my argument around the gendered and sexual politics of shame, further exploring deployments of shame that might resist narratives of redemption while testing out the dissonant effects of such a deployment. In this chapter I also entertain the idea that the writing of shame might produce various formal challenges and disruptions, arising from what Timothy Bewes has identified as the 'tension between the ethical and aesthetic dimensions of literature',[12] an awareness of 'a certain inadequacy of all available forms with respect to representing experience' – and the experience of shame in particular.[13] In what follows, I pursue these intuitions about the non-redemptive, fundamentally ambivalent, formally disruptive writing of shame via an examination of three contemporary, female-authored autofictions with a central focus on (female, heterosexual) desire and with a leaning towards literary 'experimentalism': Chris Kraus's *I Love Dick* (1997), Marie Calloway's *what purpose did i serve in your life* (2013) and Katherine Angel's *Unmastered: A Book on Desire, Most Difficult to Tell* (2012).

A comparative reading of Kraus and Calloway facilitates a consideration of questions around life-writing, confession and the construction of a precarious narrating subject, a subject both constituted and undone by a shame that, according to Bewes, 'cannot adequately be accounted for by language',[14] through narrative forms that therefore refuse the consolations of coherence and linearity. In addition, I discuss the fraught erotics of shame and vulnerability in the narration of a female desire that is too often viewed as 'grotesque' and 'unspeakable', in Kraus's own words, but which also sometimes *elects* to occupy that position of (self-)humiliation.[15] The chapter's coda uses Angel's impressionistic – yet precisely polemical – text to raise further questions concerning the shame-producing tensions between apparently discordant desires: the desire to be a 'good' girl (reassuring The Man of his potency), the desire to be a good feminist (resisting objectification, remaining 'unmastered'), and the desire, sometimes, to be mastered, to be 'fucked' ('I long to be weighed down by the man's body').[16] If, as Sally Munt remarks, 'shame is a woman',[17] and if, as Elspeth Probyn suggests, 'a form of shame always attends the writer', what (more) is at stake in the autofictional fashioning of female sexual subjectivity?[18] For Jennifer Cooke, who writes about these same texts in *Contemporary Feminist Life-Writing: The New Audacity* (2020), these are 'audacious' works, and she argues that 'the opprobrium that frequently attaches to audacity has long cast its shadow over women who [. . .] are deemed shameless' and who flout 'the sexual norms of heteropatriarchy';[19] yet she notes also that audacity can be a kind of 'future-facing boldness', that is 'progressive and productive'. My focus here is on the shame (and shamelessness) rather than the audacity, and I remain somewhat sceptical about the degree of progressiveness in this focus on the (vulnerable and/or humiliated) self; nevertheless, shame and shaming, as they are deployed here (particularly by Kraus and Calloway), *do* constitute forms of audacity (shame's availability as spectacle makes it so), and the political potential of these texts does undoubtedly lie with their ability to point up – audaciously – the structures and systems that produce both the vulnerabilities of which these texts speak and the forms of 'opprobrium' attendant upon that act of speaking.

Autofiction: confession, coercion – and shame

Chris Kraus's 1997 book, *I Love Dick*, narrates the experience of film-maker 'Chris', her academic husband, 'Sylvère', and the cultural critic, 'Dick', with whom Chris develops a kind of romantic and sexual obsession. In Kraus's own succinct summation, it is 'the story of 250 letters, my "debasement," jumping headlong off a cliff'.[20] The book comprises numerous letters addressed to 'Dick' (some by Chris, some by Sylvère, some jointly authored), along with third-person commentary (by an unidentified but omniscient narrator) and first-person passages by Chris (some highly personal, some more critical–essayistic in style, ranging across various topics, artistic and political). *I Love Dick* is not straightforwardly classifiable as a memoir: read according to the terms that Kraus establishes, it is part case study, part art project, and in interview she has referred to her method as 'transcription' rather than 'memoir', suggesting that the former does not '[privilege] the emotional transformation of the narrator above other kinds of experience'.[21] And yet, while certain elements of the book are undoubtedly fictional (including some of the cited publications attributed to 'Dick'), the autobiographical elements are to the fore and have been confirmed by various extra-textual pronouncements by Kraus herself.[22] *I Love Dick* established a method – of mixing the fictional, essayistic, critical and confessional in highly self-conscious ways – that Kraus has used to good effect in subsequent publications. In *Aliens and Anorexia* (2000), Kraus intersperses the narration of her (failed) attempts to obtain distribution for her film *Gravity and Grace* and the development and later disintegration of a phone sex affair with musings on philosopher Simone Weil, the artist Paul Thek and Ulrike Meinhof of the Red Army Faction, among others; her novels *Torpor* (2006) and *Summer of Hate* (2012), meanwhile, borrow heavily from reality (referencing real-life artists and writers) and from Kraus's own life and her marriage to Sylvère Lotringer.

Several of the 'stories' in Marie Calloway's 2013 book, *what purpose did i serve in your life*, appeared initially in online publications such as Thought Catalog and MuuMuu House, as part of what has come to be known as the 'alt lit' scene in the US. The stories, which narrate (almost exclusively in the first person) the sexual experiences of one 'Marie Calloway', are arranged chronologically, beginning with the loss of her virginity at the age of eighteen and taking in various relationships and sexual encounters, including three instances of paid sex work, along the way; at the time of the final story, the narrator is twenty-two years old. This determinedly multimodal book also includes excerpts from critical responses to her writing, screengrabs of social media exchanges and numerous photographs of 'Marie' herself (selfies) that foreground the personality, face and body of the author and act – at least in part – as authenticating devices, despite Calloway's use of a pseudonym.

The generic indeterminacy of all three texts under consideration here makes them, in the first instance, difficult to categorise. I describe them as 'autofictions', tentatively, as all three sit somewhere on the boundaries between life-writing, fiction, essay and theory, thereby resisting assimilation into any one genre or mode of writing. The term 'autofiction' is generally held to originate in the work of Serge Doubrovsky, who defines it, on the cover of his 1977 novel *Fils*, as 'fiction of strictly real events or facts'.[23] As Arnaud Schmitt explains, of Doubrovsky's coining of the term:

> To be called autofictional, a text had to meet three requirements: a literary style, a perfect onomastic correspondence between author, narrator and main character, and finally a strong psychoanalytic angle [. . .]. Because his concept aimed at conveying the intricacies of the self, it was more an autobiographical mode of expression than a fictional one. But for the same reason, the autofictional author was allowed some flights of imagination, because [. . .] this is also what the real self is about. Depicting oneself in a referential textual environment doesn't mean that you can't stray from facts.[24]

This mixing of 'autobiographical [modes] of expression' and 'flights of imagination' has proved popular in the French context, where autofiction is now a recognised and established genre – as Armine Kotin Mortimer noted in 2009, 'Autofiction [in France] is front and centre right now and shows no signs of giving up its ostentatious primacy, both among creative writers and critical and interpretive theorists.'[25] In an English-speaking context, autofiction (both the term and the genre it is held to denote) has a shorter history, but the success in the twenty-first century of writers such as Ben Lerner, Rachel Cusk, Maggie Nelson, Chris Kraus, Sheila Heti, Olivia Laing and Karl Ove Knausgaard,[26] among others, has created a burgeoning interest in a genre understood – by one recent account – as 'a form of autobiographical writing that permits a degree of experimentation with the definition and limits of the self, rather than the slavish recapitulation of known biographical facts', as, indeed, 'a project of self-exploration and self-experimentation on the part of the author', and as 'concerned with the potential overlaps as well as the spaces that fall between such categories as truth and imagination'.[27] On this question of 'truth' in autofiction, Camille Laurens comments that 'What I respect is an intimate truth, a mental landscape, what got engraved in my memory [. . .] and not factual or referential accuracy', while Catherine Cusset claims that, 'in the context of autofiction', truth is 'the capacity to go back inside an emotion', insisting that 'the "I" of the autofiction writer is anything but egocentric. It is not centered on the self, but erasing the self so as to make the truth of past emotion emerge.'[28] That communication of an emotional 'truth' might be what distinguishes my chosen texts here, regardless of the extent to which they are or are not referentially correct; the question of the writing 'I' is one that I will return to in due course.

I Love Dick, *what purpose* and *Unmastered* also form part of a nexus of recent, female-authored autobiographical or semi-autobiographical works with a significant focus on erotic, romantic and personal life, which range from the popular and bestselling (Belle de Jour's *The Intimate Adventures of a London Call Girl* (2005) and *The Further Adventures of a London Call Girl* (2006); Toni Bentley's *The Surrender* (2004); Abby Lee's *Girl with a One-Track Mind* (2006)) to the self-consciously philosophical (Catherine Millet's *Sexual Life of Catherine M* (2001)) and formally innovative (Maggie Nelson's *Bluets* (2009) and *The Argonauts* (2015); Joanna Walsh's *break.up* (2018)). Some originate as blogs (the Belle de Jour books; Dodie Bellamy's *the buddhist* (2011)) and some as newspaper columns (Catherine Townsend's *Sleeping Around* (2007)). Some present themselves relatively straightforwardly as memoir/essay (Gould's *And the Heart Says Whatever* (2010); Emilie Pine's *Notes to Self* (2018)) and others as largely fictionalised (Sheila Heti's *How Should a Person Be?* (2012); *Crudo* (2018) by Olivia Laing). Some put the personal in the service of what is billed as an investigation of erotic life in the twenty-first century (Emily Witt's *Future Sex* (2017)). All, however, display characteristics of what might be termed 'confessional writing' – if we adopt Rita Felski's use of the term 'confession' 'simply to specify a type of autobiographical writing that signals its intention to foreground the most personal and intimate details of the author's life' – and it is these confessional qualities that might be seen as marking them out as shame narratives, in some sense.[29] Brooks argues that 'confessions activate inextricable layers of shame, guilt, contempt, self-loathing, attempted propitiation, and expiation',[30] and the majority of these texts engage with, explore or represent feelings and experiences of shame, as well as, in their reception, forming part of a wider discussion of femininity, female sexuality and female sexual narration – a discussion in which shame is often present, invoked or deployed (to different ends).

Kraus, Calloway and Angel's texts are not obviously apologetic or expiatory, yet they are 'confessions' in the sense of public revelations of emotional and sexual feelings (and behaviour) that are often held to be shameful (particularly as far as women are concerned). Indeed, Elizabeth Gregory notes 'the long-operative Western view of femininity as a kind of sin in itself, calling forth shame', and, in a discussion of confessional poetry by authors including Sylvia Plath, Anne Sexton and Robert Lowell, she asserts that:

> Principal among the transgressions at issue in confessional work, I suggest, is its exploration of shifting gender scripts. Gender roles (and the intimately linked issue of sexual orientation) are among the few behaviours subject to discipline in all three of confession's pre-poetic domains: the church, the clinic and the court.[31]

If such texts as I am considering in this chapter are, in some sense, *about* femininity (and about gender roles and sexuality, more generally), then they are concerned with disciplinary regimes and with 'the exploration of shifting gender scripts' – while often finding themselves trapped within scripts over and within which they have little agency. Although frequently read (in ideally neoliberal terms) as expressions of choice and freedom (amounting even to a kind of *shamelessness*), facilitated by successive waves of feminism, they can also be seen as, frequently, coercive in their forms and in their unwitting co-option into a public scene of spectacle, titillation and sensationalism. As Brooks notes, 'confession rarely appears to occur without some form of constraint "propelling" its utterance' – and then, we might add, shaping the form and reception of that utterance.[32] In the scholarship on confession, Foucault is a frequent reference point, notably his reminder that confession is:

> [a] ritual that unfolds within a power relationship, for one does not confess without the presence (or virtual presence) of a partner who is not simply the interlocutor but the authority who requires the confession, prescribes and appreciates it, and intervenes in order to judge, punish, forgive, console, and reconcile; a ritual in which the truth is corroborated by the obstacles and resistances it has had to surmount in order to be formulated; and finally, a ritual in which the expression alone, independently of its external consequences, produces intrinsic modifications in the person who articulates it: it exonerates, redeems, and purifies him; it unburdens him of his wrongs, liberates him, and promises him salvation.[33]

If confession is a 'ritual', then what form(s) does this ritual take? Within which systems or structures is the ritual inscribed? What (and whose) ends does it serve? And in the power relationships put into play by confessional autofictions, what position is the speaker in: empowered or disempowered, or an awkward combination of the two? The performance of abasement in some of these public 'confessions' of romantic injury, sexual disappointment – and worse – is not straightforwardly liberatory or redemptive, nor is it necessarily transgressive. Such 'confessions' may only appear shameful or shameless, when they are in fact invited, required, in a culture in which confession has 'become [. . .] a crucial mode of self-examination',[34] producing what Jo Gill identifies as the 'sudden resurgence or re-emergence of confessional writing in the West in the second half of the twentieth century'.[35]

We might also ask here who the listener/interlocutor/authority (fantasised or real) is in the case of these sexual memoirs by women, and what form their 'intervention' might take. This is most pertinent in the case of Calloway, who includes in *what purpose* the (largely hostile) words of interlocutors, but Kraus also appears to include material written by her husband and by 'Dick' himself. I will say more about the (mixed) critical response to these texts in due course, but it is worth noting Leigh Gilmore's argument that, following the 'surge in life narratives published in the late twentieth century' and the 'new prominence' of 'women's life stories' as part of this 'boom', there has been, more recently, 'a full-blown backlash against memoir itself and women's memoir in particular' – a phenomenon that she describes as 'a form of witness tainting'.[36] It is, in Gilmore's formulation, a 'boom/lash', so she asks: 'What accounts for the simultaneous popularity and denunciation of this form of testimony? How does the act of publishing a memoir provide material for further judgment that can stick to women witnesses?'[37] This demonstrates, again, a simultaneous fascination and revulsion in relation to the (shameful) confession of the intimate and personal. But the issue here may be not only the apparent shamefulness of the material (shameful either because of its low-brow nature – romance, relationships, femininity – or because of its sexual explicitness); it may also be, as Gilmore implies, the perceived unreliability of women as witnesses to their own lives.[38]

The potential constraints of confession are, then, manifold. Glossing and responding to Foucault's argument in *History of Sexuality, Vol. 1*, Gill argues that confession

> is not the free expression of the self but an effect of an ordered regime by which the self begins to conceive of itself as individual, responsible, culpable and thereby confessional. Most importantly, confession takes place in a context of power, and prohibition, and surveillance.[39]

This context has always to be kept in mind when reading these texts. However, while authors such as Kraus, Calloway and Angel may be driven by what Brooks describes as 'the [subtle] coercion of the need to stage a scene of exposure as the only propitiation of accusation, including self-accusation for being in a scene of exposure',[40] they also take undeniable pleasure (and, in Kraus's case, some notable polemical advantage) in that staging of a 'scene of exposure'. Such 'confessions', then, epitomise what Brooks refers to, succinctly, as 'the shame and the shamelessness of confession as an act of self-exposure'.[41]

Marching boldly into self-abasement

In her Foreword to *I Love Dick* (1997), Eileen Myles describes Kraus as 'marching boldly into self-abasement and self-advertisement, not being uncannily drawn there'.[42] What kind of agency is implied by such a march, and how does that affect the experience and presentation of 'abasement' (which the dictionary parses as 'humiliation or degradation')? And what is the relationship, in these texts, between 'self-abasement' and 'self-advertisement'? I suggest, first, that self-abasement and self-advertisement are, here, inextricable, despite being apparently contradictory; second, that this expresses a tension fundamental to shame itself – understood, in Agamben's phrase, cited in my Introduction, as 'the absolute concomitance of subjectification and desubjectification, self-loss and self-possession, servitude and sovereignty',[43] or as an experience in which 'I wish to continue to look and be looked at, but I also do not wish to do so' (in Tomkins's formulation);[44] and third, I argue that this tension (between self-abasement and self-advertisement) is explored to significantly different ends by the authors under consideration in this chapter. Taken together, these texts might be read as an illustration of Eve Kosofsky Sedgwick's claim that, 'shame and pride, shame and self-display, shame and exhibitionism are different interlinings of the same glove'.[45]

Meanwhile, shame operates on several levels in these texts. The act of confession – the revelation of intimate details of Kraus and Calloway's personal lives – is itself 'shameful', if read as 'oversharing' or narcissistic. The staging of vulnerability and a kind of excessive, inappropriate (because unrequited) emotional attachment (in Kraus), and of various forms of physical and sexual degradation (in Calloway) – these things might also provoke shame. But shame is also a topic to be reflected on in all three texts – though most overtly and polemically in *I Love Dick*, where it shadows Kraus's presentation of her sexual history and sexual present:

> Shame is what you feel after being fucked on quaaludes by some artworld cohort who'll pretend it never happened, shame is what you feel after giving blowjobs in the bathroom at Max's Kansas City

because Liza Martin wants free coke. Shame is what you feel after letting someone take you someplace past control – then feeling torn up three days later between desire, paranoia, etiquette wondering if they'll call.[46]

Indeed, reflecting further on her sexual past, Kraus concludes that 'all acts of sex were forms of degradation': 'The Serious Young Woman' – as she characterises her younger self – 'looked everywhere for sex but when she got it it became an exercise in disintegration.'[47] Yet being taken 'someplace past control' also holds an undoubted allure for Kraus, and it is the apparently uncontrolled (and ultimately unreciprocated) nature of her feelings for Dick that allows her, paradoxically, to reclaim control of her means of self-expression and artistic production, even as these feelings appear to force a 'disintegration' of her life and personality. As she embraces failure and rejection – indeed, parades her 'debasement' publicly – she gradually begins to find a voice and to turn her humiliation to her advantage.[48] As Chris opines in her notebook, '*My entire state of being's changed because I've become my sexuality: female, straight, wanting to love men, be fucked. Is there a way of living with this like a gay person, proudly?*'[49] To wish to 'become' her sexuality functions both as a defiant statement of desire and, more perilously, as a reduction of her personhood, her 'state of being'; in 'wanting to love men, be fucked', she signals a compliance with a heteropatriarchal culture that reduces her to sex object and/or wife, yet her very assertion of this troubles such a culture with its boldness.

If Kraus wants to live her (vulnerable, voracious, unreciprocated, shameful) sexual desires 'proudly' and productively, 'Marie', in *what purpose did i serve in your life*, seems to show little prospect of doing so. In the first (loss of virginity) story, she describes herself repeatedly as 'uneasy', 'embarrassed', 'like a hurt kitten', 'awkward', in pain and 'overcome by shame', and this sets the tone for the pieces that follow.[50] As the book progresses, the sexual encounters narrated become more obviously masochistic in nature. In 'the irish photographer', there is a growing emphasis on humiliation:

'Good girl.' It was like I was his dog. He was humiliating me but I felt safe and warm and completely turned on. Nothing could be more enjoyable than this. To be dominated and degraded was what I wanted. Sex is just a way to get those things. I felt valued, even though I actually wasn't. It didn't matter. Someone really wanted me and I didn't have to worry about anything besides making him feel good through a blowjob or whatever it was he wanted. Then he pushed my head down. I started to have flashbacks of being raped, having my head forced down, gagging. I tried to resist but couldn't. I gagged three times. He moaned the third time I gagged. He let go of my head. I looked up at him, shaking. He looked at me and gasped. He turned his head to look for his camera, but he didn't grab it. I got up and lay down on the bed and turned towards the wall. We went to sleep.[51]

The flatness of the prose, its staccato rhythm as it alternates between the actions of 'I' and 'he', belies the claim that 'nothing could be more enjoyable than this'; no modulation of tone or syntactical variation announces the shift from enjoyment to (apparently) traumatic experience (the rape flashback); the absence of reflection or commentary means that, despite the repetition of the word 'I' in Marie's narrative (indeed, even because of that repetition), we have little sense of her interiority here; the overall impression is of a kind of affectless monotony, as we are presented with encounter after encounter in which Marie occupies a position of near-mute passivity. And yet there are contradictory elements in the passage above that reveal a more complex narrating self at work: we might note her statement (more assertion than admission) that she does 'want' to be 'dominated and degraded' – the signalling of consent is unequivocal; and there is a keen awareness of the difference between being 'wanted' (which is easy to attain) and being 'valued' (which is not) – this might function as a kind of commentary on the social and sexual status of women; moreover, Marie is able to entertain, simultaneously, the *feeling* of being valued even as she *knows* this is not the case – she can be the person who feels *and* the person who knows, and can be the latter observing the former. Also evident here is the fact that sex is being used as a route to something else – it is not the sex she desires so much as the complex experience of recognition-of-self (in being wanted) and abnegation-of-self (in not actually being valued, in not having any responsibility beyond 'making him feel good') that comes from being 'dominated and degraded'. What this reveals is actually a relatively subtle understanding of the paradoxically powerful/powerless status of the masochist, and of the simultaneous sovereignty/subjection of this willed shamed state. In addition, as Jennifer Cooke notes, the self-conscious, neutral, apparently distanced tone of Calloway's writing grants her some unlikely agency in the *narration* of these encounters:

> Despite the sex she participates in often being physically demanding and overwhelming, Calloway's descriptions stress that sex does not stop her self-observing: the mind is not separate or subordinate to the body in these encounters. In other words, her writing of sex, with its interspersed observations, even while it shows her vulnerability in a patriarchal culture, does not depict her as a victim but as a sexual participant with agency.[52]

For Cooke, then, the 'potential pathos' of Calloway's accounts of being sexually humiliated in various ways is 'disrupted [. . .] by her forensic fascination with how men respond to her' – 'disrupted', however, not actually vitiated, so that taint of victimhood, I would suggest, remains.[53]

In addition, that 'forensic fascination with how men respond to her' produces a distinctly pessimistic view of sexual relations between men and women. In her third experience of sex work – a more embattled, humiliating experience than the previous two, Marie briefly asserts: '*I can't show any weakness, I can't let him humiliate me. I can't let him win.*'[54] Yet shortly thereafter she concedes:

> *I'm so tired of lying to myself and keeping up the illusion that I'm not a worthless sex object when I am, I am, I so obviously am. I am a stupid worthless whore and I like being treated like one. [. . .] He is going to cum in my mouth because he wants to degrade me, he sees me as less than human. He is honest and it's a relief. I am so tired of men pretending that they see me as something other than a whore, that they see any woman as anything other than that.*[55]

The 'honesty' here is in fact a significantly cynical view of sexual degradation as revelatory of entrenched patriarchal dominance more generally, of gender relations as inescapably combative ('*I can't let him win*'), and of the inability of men – on Calloway's reading – to see women as anything other than 'worthless whore[s]'. Perhaps it is not surprising, despite the ostensible incongruity, that Calloway takes her om Kate Millett's *Sexual Politics* (1970): 'Because of our mstances, male and female are really two different cultures fe experiences are utterly different.'[56] This is an odd quota-)ose because, taken out of context, it appears to advocate a form oi gender separatism that now seems decidedly out of date (and that is not borne out by the contents of *what purpose*). Millett is also an interesting choice for Calloway, as her argument in *Sexual Politics* is so centred on a particular view of heterosexual intercourse as both symptom and perpetuation of patriarchal dominance. Are Marie's sexual confessions meant to confirm or challenge that view?[57]

Later stories relate tales of both extreme emotional neediness ('insufferable') and sexual masochism and humiliation ('bdsm' – meaning bondage and discipline/dominance and submission/sadism and masochism, 'thank you for touching me'). The seeming lack of purpose and agency in her narration, the submerged nature of what self-knowledge there is here, the absence of pleasure in this trajec- tory of humiliation, and the deterministic sense of the inevitability of female victimhood render Calloway's narrative less a bold march into self-abasement and more an ambivalent, troubling acquiescence to a patriarchal narrative of female sexual shame. In the penultimate paragraph of the last story she wonders, 'when I would stop abusing myself for the sake of new experiences, new sensations'.[58]

The transmissibility of shame: subjects, readers, critics

Both Kraus and Calloway make use of a tension between self- abasement and self-advertisement – of the availability of shame as spectacle – though they do so to notably divergent ends. Yet *self- abasement* is not the only story here. The transmissibility of shame is commonly acknowledged – remember Sedgwick's suggestion that 'shame is both contagious and individuating'[59] – and that transmis- sion seems more deliberate act than accidental infection in the case of Kraus and Calloway. *I Love Dick* and Calloway's longest, best- known story, 'adrien brody', are each focused upon a pseudonymous (but only minimally concealed) real person, and at least some of the response to these texts has involved speculation about the identities of the men in question (both of whom have been 'outed', as it were). Who, exactly, is being shamed here?

Both texts, then, raise questions about the transmissibility of shame – its displacement from one person or body to another – and questions about the power dynamics of such a transmission/displacement when the object of shame is a relatively powerful, established, privileged man (as 'Dick' and 'adrien brody' appear to be), rather than a less powerful woman or a relatively anonymous female body. Moreover, it is not the case that Kraus and Calloway succeed in expunging their shame through these acts of narration, so the shame is shared rather than displaced, properly speaking.

Halberstam's injunction (cited in my first chapter) that 'shame can be a powerful tactic in the struggle to make privilege [. . .] visible',[60] accompanies their warning that shame is experienced differently by different groups and tends to be projected on to those in less powerful groups; in these texts, that tactic of shame projection takes on a new, more fraught and definitively political resonance. Thus, in one of the few generous readings of Calloway's work, Lisa Carver in *Vice Magazine* suggests that Calloway succeeds in 'exploiting (in print) her exploiters, by laying bare how she had offered up to these predators her own debasement, anxiety, needs, and wishes – some of them secretly malicious'.[61] On this reading, by '[offering] up [. . .] her own debasement' Calloway employs a strategy of (apparent) self-humiliation to shame 'her exploiters'. Yet the 'adrien brody' story – initially published on Calloway's blog using its subject's real name and a photograph of him, and only later given the 'adrien brody' title and published as 'fiction' at MuuMuu House – became (in the words of one commentator) 'an internet sensation', causing a 'firestorm' of publicity (much of it negative) and much 'debate over the story's ethics'.[62] On Carver's reading, however, Calloway should be excused both for her 'hateful' actions and for the fact that she has 'sought out her own debasement', for 'to say it plainly like this, to tell the truth about all the lies, is dissent – is an explosion, personal and political'.[63]

Similarly, Myles (in her Foreword to *I Love Dick*) concludes that Kraus's 'ultimate achievement' is that she has 'turned female abjection inside out and aimed it at a man'.[64] Anna Watkins Fisher, in an article on Kraus and Sophie Calle, argues that both artists have succeeded in making 'surrogate victims out of "actual" male subjectivities': that is, in displacing their own apparent shame/victimhood on to the male objects of their desire – and on to their writing.[65]

This Fisher describes as a kind of 'parasitism' as 'experimental art practice', as Kraus and Calle '[perform] the figure of the parasite as a figure of overidentification', insisting on 'loving men who reject them'.[66] While Kraus, on Fisher's reading, 'graphically recounts her humiliations' – Dick's indifference, her inferior status as the partner of an internationally renowned academic, her professional failures as a film-maker – she also employs that parasitism as a strategy for inverting the gendered relationship of parasitism and, thus, the associated humiliation.[67]

Yet, in Kraus's case, this is arguably a sharing of shame rather than shame's displacement, and that sharing brings its own feelings of shame, in turn. At one point, Chris acknowledges that this case study has become 'a persecution game' for which she feels 'some remorse',[68] and later she muses, in one of her letters to 'Dick':

> [S]ometimes I feel ashamed of this whole episode, how it must look to you or anyone outside. But just by doing it I'm giving myself the freedom of seeing from the inside out. I'm not driven anymore by other people's voices. From now on it's the world according to me.[69]

The justification, then, for this 'persecution' is her right to deliver 'the world according to me', to tell a story that cannot be only of her own abasement but must necessarily draw others' lives and stories into that shameful orbit. What Fisher calls 'the strategic supplementarity of the parasite' (here: Chris) 'to her host' (here: Dick) models a promising though conflicted version of agency (that *bold march into self-abasement*). What Fisher does not consider are the possible problems with this strategy: the performance of victimhood as itself victimising; the unwitting reinforcement of heterosexual romance narratives (and women's supposed obsession with them); the narcissism implicit in both projects (and the cultural connections made between narcissism and femininity). Fisher ends her article by suggesting that the model of 'parasitical feminism' that she has outlined 'does not guarantee survival or even successful escape. Casualties are inevitable',[70] and towards the end of *I Love Dick* Chris reluctantly concedes that 'I was ashamed. My will had ridden over all your wishes, your fragility. By loving you this way I'd violated all your boundaries, hurt you.'[71] Kraus's shame is, then, the complex shame of someone who is simultaneously victim and persecutor.

Nevertheless, both Kraus and Calloway benefit creatively from their strategies of shame embracement and shame displacement. 'Dick' and 'adrien brody', in addition to functioning as objects of desire (and, occasionally, enmity), emerge as projections: fantasy constructions whose narrative existence *as ciphers* facilitates the creative emergence, renaissance or reflection of the female writer. In interview, Kraus has claimed of the letters to Dick: 'I started to realize the obsession was really with writing, not him' and 'I saw him as the most perfect *repository* of comprehension.'[72] Despite (or even because of) his refusal to engage with Chris – her project and her feelings – Dick becomes a stimulator of her creative energies, her writerly verbosity directly proportionate to his dogged silence. It is as passive 'repository' rather than active interlocutor that he is most useful to her. As Rachel Carroll writes, of Kraus and Calle's artistic appropriation of real relationships and real people:

> Where orthodox art history erases the lives and works of female artists, these artworks bring into the public arena the intimate lives of actual men to serve as exemplum in the documentation of heterosexual politics. Fictionalized or anonymized, these men are not the target of this art but rather its vehicle, unwitting performers in an artwork that exposes the role playing that shapes the experience of intimate lives.[73]

As 'vehicles' and 'repositories', 'Dick' and 'adrien brody' occupy the notably gendered position of muse, the shamefulness of this status deriving not only from the revelation of their dubious romantic and sexual behaviour, but also from the traditionally 'feminine' nature of that position (the blank screen, the empty vessel, the object rather than the subject of desire).

If Kraus and Calloway open themselves up to allegations of unethical practices in their 'use' of these men, then it is nevertheless the accusation of narcissism that is more obviously to the fore in the critical commentary surrounding the recent wave of women's confessional, sexually explicit writing and art. It speaks to what Bartky has described as a characteristically feminine experience – 'the peculiar dialectic of shame and pride in embodiment consequent upon a narcissistic assumption of the body as spectacle'[74] – and to what I have conceptualised more broadly as the inextricability of self-abasement and self-advertisement, an inextricability that expresses the paradox of the shame experience (wanting to be looked at; wanting not to be looked at).[75] The critical commentary on these texts itself comprises an additional layer in the complex, endlessly proliferating process of shame production or projection and shame as spectacle.

Again, rather than seeking to shirk or overcome the experience of humiliation, these authors seem to embrace it, with Calloway, notably, including a section in *what purpose* entitled 'criticism'. This comprises a series of selfies (some explicit, though pixelated), over-laid with text from feedback and commentary on her work; all but one excerpt is unremittingly negative (even abusive). In the course of these excerpts (which all read like online comments), she is described as: 'desperate for attention and validation'; 'a female train-wreck' with 'fucking ugly' and 'pathetic' female characters; 'just not very bright'; 'annoying' and 'kind of a moron'; 'a lazy boring writer', 'histrionic', 'most likely autistic'; and 'a slut'.[76] Several of the excerpts discuss the gender politics of what she is doing, with one commenter mockingly reproducing the argument that Calloway is 'a brave feminist writer being courageous enough to write in as obscene a way as men and why the heck shouldn't she', before opining that 'when women are only getting "relevant" in alt lit because of nudity and talking about fucking completely artlessly it is made even harder for women in alt lit to be listened to'; this excerpt ends: 'stop it now marie [sic] you're embarrassing yourself'.[77] The most generous comment (relatively speaking), suggests that while we should 'be horri-fied' by Calloway's choices we should 'also be horrified that it often looks like the only choice', for the 'problem' is actually 'systemic'.[78] The final excerpt (arguably positioned for greatest effect) claims that 'Marie Calloway makes me embarrassed and ashamed to be a female writer in my twenties.'[79] The message, then, is overwhelm-ingly about shame: Calloway should be embarrassed (for her sex life, for her writing, for the dependence of the latter upon the former); Calloway's work makes women writers embarrassed (the shame of it is infectious); as readers we should be ashamed of the culture we inhabit and the 'choices' it offers to young women. Shame is trans-missible (even – especially – to the reader) and writing serves as the conduit of its transmission.

Does including these other – highly critical – viewpoints balance out what Calloway writes, or work to anticipate criticisms she might receive, or does it fatally undermine what she is doing? It makes the book as a whole more, rather than less, incoherent, more muddled in its messages. It implies a dialogue, yet Calloway never comments on or responds to this criticism. One reviewer, Alexandra Molotkow, suggests that this action of '[working] her haters into the book', despite its apparent 'self-indulgence', nevertheless 'serves a purpose. Because so much of the response to Calloway has been processing discomfort – resentment, jealousy, the shame of recognition, good old sexual guilt – and processing that discomfort is central to her writing.'[80] Yet Calloway tends to display rather than 'process' this discomfort, and never gives the sense – as Kraus does – of directing that discomfort outwards, jubilantly transferring it to the reader and to her critics. In fact, the cacophony of critical voices threatens to drown out her own, still emergent voice.

Furthermore, Calloway's use of selfies as the backdrop to this commentary makes the 'criticism' section function as both an extension of her narcissism and an extension of her self-hatred; she appears at once narcissistic and passive; the critical commentary is plastered across her face like cum – similarly debasing (yet pleasurable?), similarly invited (yet coerced?). The original version of 'adrien brody', published online, included a picture of 'Marie' with Brody's cum on her face, and this is a scenario – fantasised and enacted – that recurs repeatedly through her various stories, along with scenarios in which someone pisses on her face or 'facefucks' her, or fantasises about 'making [her] throw up and pushing [her] face in it'.[81] In one of her sex work experiences, the client rubs his penis 'all over' her face, and she thinks: 'I get turned on whenever I watch this happen in porn, but now it's happening to me and I feel sick, though also slightly turned on. *I want to like this more.*'[82]

The inclusion of many close-up 'selfie' photographs of Calloway – photographs in which she is frequently depicted looking directly, nakedly, but always blankly, unemotionally, into the camera – is, however, interesting given the association of shame with the blush, with an averting of the gaze and a turning away of the face. As Charles Darwin noted, in his *Expression of the Emotions in Man and Animals*, in shame:

> We turn away the whole body, more especially the face, which we endeavour in some manner to hide. An ashamed person can hardly endure to meet the gaze of those present, so that he almost invariably casts down his eyes or looks askant.[83]

More recent theorists of shame have reinforced this point, with Tomkins asking:

> Why is shame so close to the experienced self? It is because the self lives in the face, and within the face the self burns brightest in the eyes. Shame turns the attention of the self and others away from other objects to this most visible residence of self, increases its visibility, and thereby generates the torment of self-consciousness.[84]

Elspeth Probyn, meanwhile, titles her 2005 book on shame *Blush: Faces of Shame*. Calloway's refusal to turn away her face, her insistence on presenting the reader with image after image of that face, might then be read as a kind of defiance of the social codes and practices of shaming. However, her blankness and inscrutability (her lack of animation) in these images render them more ambivalent in their intentions and affects, more dissonant in their effects, than such a reading would suggest. For Cooke, in the 'criticism' section of *what purpose,*

> these superimposed reviews highlight how Calloway is perforce a mediated composition rather than identical with the construction of the woman who writes 'I' in *what purpose* or appears in its photographs. If photographs – especially selfies – are deliberate constructions that capture only the surface, these reviews are equally distortive and shallow, Calloway's reframing of them suggests.[85]

And yet, when 'Marie' does look at her own face in the mirror in the course of these stories, the effect is never pleasing to her: 'For ten minutes I tried to see what someone could find attractive about me, but couldn't find anything';[86] 'I caught a glimpse of my face in his vanity mirror and thought I looked trashy and hideous.'[87]

Discontinuous forms: 'The Dumb Cunt's Tale'

Timothy Bewes – whose work I touched upon in the Introduction to this book – raises the question of the extent to which shame can or cannot be written, asking:

> how is it possible to write about shame in a work of literature? Is it possible to speak of a shame that precedes the work, a shame that the work takes for its object, a shame that the writer seems to be attempting to process? Is shame iterable?[88]

In his subsequent book, *The Event of Postcolonial Shame* (2011), he suggests that shame is 'the material embodiment' of 'the tension between the ethical and aesthetic dimensions of literature', representing 'a moment at which the formal possibilities open to the work are incommensurable with, or simply inadequate to, its ethical responsibilities'.[89] Leaving open this question of whether or not shame is 'iterable', I nevertheless now want to consider the related question of whether the writing of shame might produce formal disruptions and disjunctions as a result of this posited 'incommensurability' between the ethical and the aesthetic. In these particular instances – Kraus and Calloway – to what extent are innovative or experimental forms required to explore the complexity of the shame experience or to express the simultaneous sovereignty and subjection of the shamed self?

Trev Lynn Broughton and Linda Anderson see the critical work of the 1980s and 1990s as demonstrating that, 'in autobiography, more vividly and pressingly than elsewhere, gender and genre are reciprocally at stake'.[90] Writing in 1980, Estelle Jelinek famously noted women's attraction to 'discontinuous forms' such as 'diaries, journals, and notebooks' rather than 'autobiographies proper', suggesting that women's autobiographical texts were 'analogous to the fragmentary, interrupted, and formless nature of their lives'.[91] In a later book (first published in 1986) Jelinek again claims a persistent 'pattern' in women's autobiographical writing of the 'episodic and anecdotal, nonchronological and disjunctive'.[92] So stark a suggested contrast on the basis of gender seems to me highly problematic – as Gilmore has noted, it risks 'reifying gender's most negative and least problematized formulations'.[93] All three authors under consideration in this chapter produce narratives marked by incoherence, fragmentariness and discontinuity, but these qualities form part of an experimental practice that, first, has an illustrious, cross-gender history (from Stein and Joyce to Burroughs and Brooke-Rose, and beyond), and second, might be read as critiquing cultural norms of femininity rather than merely enacting them. If narrative discontinuity is a symptom of the authors' femininity, it is so only because of the social imbrication of femininity and shame, and the forms that shame finds to work its way out through writing.

We might consider, then, Kraus's inclusion of theoretical material, her mixing of letters, essay, autobiography and fiction, her switches in tense and perspective, her colloquialisms. Indeed, in the pages of

I Love Dick, Sylvère suggests that Chris is writing 'some new kind of literary form', 'something in between cultural criticism and fiction'.[94] Chris, meanwhile, laments Dick's description of her 'case study' as 'a game':

> By calling it a game you were negating all my feelings. Even if this love for you could never be returned I wanted recognition. [. . .] It's more a project than a game. I meant every word I wrote to you in those letters. But at the same time I started seeing it as a chance to finally learn something about romance, infatuation. [. . .] Don't you think it's possible to do something and simultaneously study it?[95]

Claiming the descriptors 'project' and (elsewhere) 'case study', Chris asserts the seriousness of this enterprise (compared with the non-seriousness of the 'game'), its educative potential, and she ties this directly to her 'recognition' – a quite profound request for status, authority, voice, existence. Joan Hawkins, in her Afterword to the book, chooses to describe *I Love Dick* as 'theoretical fiction'– that is, 'the kind of [book] in which theory becomes an intrinsic part of the "plot"' – thereby emphasising the book's seriousness and its self-conscious innovation.[96] In an interview in *The Believer*, Sheila Heti neatly sums up *I Love Dick*'s style as 'formally both out of control and expertly in control',[97] and this phrase captures the (apparent) spontaneity of style in Kraus's text as well as the political motivations underlying her adoption of an ostensibly 'fragmentary', non-linear style. If, as previously observed, 'Shame is what you feel after letting someone take you someplace past control,' then *I Love Dick*'s controlled simulation of a lack of control both affective and stylistic is well suited to its subject matter.[98]

That 'style' is also marked by a notable degree of self-reflexivity. Thus at one point Kraus avers that, 'fifteen years ago', she was unable to write in the first person:

> I had to find these ciphers for myself because whenever I tried writing in the 1st Person it sounded like some other person, or else the tritest most neurotic parts of myself that I wanted so badly to get beyond. Now I can't stop writing in the 1st Person, it feels like it's the last chance I'll ever have to figure some of this stuff out.[99]

Kraus expresses here both the allure and the anxiety of writing in the first person but also touches on the gendered nature of the judgements attending such writing: 'trite', 'neurotic' – terms implying the non-serious nature of women's first-person narrative and the pathological nature of personal confession. The question of style is, then, a question of who gets to speak, and how, and on what subjects. From the outset, Kraus struggles to reclaim her own narrative from its status as 'reactive', opining, in her first letter to Dick, that:

> Since Sylvère wrote the first letter, I'm thrown into this weird position. Reactive – like Charlotte Stant to Sylvère's Maggie Verver, if we were living in the Henry James novel *The Golden Bowl* – the Dumb Cunt, a factory of emotions evoked by all the men. So the only thing that I can do is tell The Dumb Cunt's Tale. But how?[100]

The 'Dumb Cunt' is, as her name suggests, speechless, passive, unable to utter her 'I' without being labelled 'trite', a receptive, reactive sexual object or organ; but that last question ('But how?') is the crucial one. Kraus and Calloway find themselves in the position of 'The Dumb Cunt' telling a tale (of sexual shame, emotional excess, romantic rejection and victimhood) that is, to some extent, culturally ordained, predetermined, but while Kraus reworks her vulnerability into a position of strength and agency through the innovative revisioning of the 'how', Calloway struggles to escape the passive, reactive role allotted to her. At the close of the 'adrien brody' story, the narrative makes an abrupt shift to the third person (the only time this happens in the book, excepting the inclusion of critical responses from readers) and we are told:

> She writes with a stark and troubling ambivalence. It can be easily misread as apathy, numbness; this is part of what she risks. An elaborate strategy of purification, to blend honesty and revulsion until they are no longer separable, until readers must begin to shut down themselves. She is sure enough of herself to confront and even invite misunderstanding, as though misunderstanding might offer a way forward toward an authenticity beyond the deceptive surfaces of exhibitionism.[101]

This passage acknowledges the element of public display in what Calloway is doing ('exhibitionism') and gives a sense of her stylistic and affective intentions ('a stark and troubling ambivalence'); it concedes the possibility of misreading, but 'apathy' and 'numbness' are nevertheless the principal affects here and the 'authenticity' for which

Calloway strives remains determinedly vague. In various respects, this passage is the most honest, revealing and self-reflexive in *what purpose*, but its presentation in the third person, while distinguishing it from the rest of the narrative, routes her insights through a voice so depersonalised that its authority is difficult to locate. Is this a narrative persona of Calloway's, or simply another example of the incorporation of an external critical viewpoint into the text? The level of detail earlier in the same passage and the wistful tenor of the whole ('She once wished she were in Japan . . .') suggest the former, so one way of reading this is to see Calloway – always alert to the vision of herself as an object for others (a feeling central to the experience of shame)[102] – as using the shift to the third person to illustrate at the level of form her frequent slippage from subject (narrator, agent, observer) to object (passive, objectified, abused).

what purpose also showcases a degree of innovation in its multi-modality, incorporating unattributed excerpts from critical responses to Calloway's writing, screengrabs of social media exchanges, and numerous photographs of 'Marie' herself (selfies), including indistinct, poor-quality images of injuries sustained during sado-masochistic sexual encounters. The writing style evinces both a flattening of emotion and expressiveness (despite, and in tension with, the apparent intimacy of the content) and a colloquial character (using terms like 'OMG', 'whatever', and the repeated 'mew' to signal her sexual and other kinds of compliance; using abbreviations like 'oic', 'idk' and so on); this affects a kind of immediacy or honesty but actually seems highly studied and artificial (this is, however, typical of alt lit writers, including Calloway's hero, Tao Lin, who appears as a character in one of these stories). Sheila Heti is among the writer–reviewers who have lauded *what purpose*'s 'genre muddle and formal complexity',[103] though, distinct from Kraus's experiments with genre, this 'complexity' appears to be symptomatic of Calloway's engagement with and self-construction through social media, rather than springing from a desire to innovate.

The personal and the structural

'Confession', claims Rita Felski, 'poses in exemplary fashion the problem of the relationship between personal experience and political goals within feminism as a whole.'[104] At its most politically productive, Felski suggests, it succeeds in combining the subjective or individual focus of autobiography and 'the feminist concern with the representative and intersubjective elements of women's experience'.[105] Yet Felski also asks:

> Is the act of confession a liberating step for women, which uncovers the political dimensions of personal experience, confronts the contradiction of existing gender roles and inspires an important sense of female identification and solidarity? Or does this kind of writing merely reveal what Christopher Lasch calls 'the banality of pseudo self-awareness,' a narcissistic soul-searching that uncritically reiterates the 'jargon of authenticity' and the ideology of subjectivity-as-truth which feminism should be calling into question?[106]

The texts under discussion here might be read as examples of feminist confession – a genre that Felski traces back to practices of consciousness-raising: Kraus and Angel engage directly with feminist discourse, manifestly seeking to '[uncover] the political dimensions of personal experience'; both appear invested in inspiring 'female identification and solidarity', in their referencing of other/earlier female artists and authors, and in their moments of implied address to the female (and putatively feminist) reader. By contrast, Calloway presents her gender politics more ambivalently, despite that epigraph from Kate Millett, and arguably falls prey to 'the ideology of subjectivity-as-truth' against which Felski cautions.

The confessional text 'makes public that which has been private, typically claiming to avoid filtering mechanisms of objectivity and detachment in its pursuit of the truth of subjective experience' – a non-filtering tendency evident in all three texts – yet this emphasis on the personal can appear naïve and can be politically ineffective.[107] Significantly, Felski argues that 'feminist confession exemplifies the intersection between the autobiographical imperative to communicate the truth of *unique individuality*, and the feminist concern with the *representative and intersubjective* elements of women's experience'.[108] In analysing the Kraus and Calloway texts, I ask how formal innovation might assist in the negotiation between these autobiographical (individualistic) and feminist (collective) 'imperatives', but I also seek to draw attention to the fact that shame, which forms such a large part of the subject matter of these texts, occupies a liminal position at the boundary of the personal and the social, the private and the public, the individual and the collective, the subjective and the intersubjective; to write or speak of shame is, then, always to place oneself at the intersection of these apparently opposed or distinct states. For women, in particular, shame is definitively structural, never 'merely' personal, instead constituting 'a pervasive affective attunement to the social environment', in Bartky's summation: something personally ingrained and socially entrenched.[109] Attending to explorations and representations of female shame (sexual, bodily or otherwise) might then be a productive route to understanding both the 'political dimensions of personal experience' and the reciprocal construction of shame and femininity: that is, the ways in which shame (our cultural understanding/construction of it) helps to maintain and produce gender difference, acting less as a 'guardian of morality'[110] (as the Freudian understanding of shame suggests) and more as a protector of patriarchy.

Interestingly, Kraus's response to the question of whether her work is 'confessional' reveals her unease with the suggestion that that work is merely personal:

> 'Confessional' of what? *Personal* confessions? There's a great line from a book [Semiotext(e)] published by Deleuze: *Life is not personal*. The word 'confessional' is not a good descriptor of my work. We were talking about the New York School poets – they were the ones who pioneered this use of the 'I,' an active 'I' that's turned out onto the world. 'I' in this case isn't the point – *That* would be memoir. The story of 'I.' And mostly I hate that – everything becomes merely a backdrop to the teller's personal development. It's an utterly false, uninteresting view.[111]

Kraus describes the use of the first person in Semiotext(e)'s 'Native Agents' books as employing 'a polemical, not an introspective, I'. Sylvère Lotringer comments on this strategy, 'It's very personal but it's not indulgent. It works and looks outward,' and she elaborates, 'it's like this personal "I" that is constantly bouncing up against the world – that isn't just existing for itself.'[112] Kraus's work has tended to be read as, precisely, 'the story of "I"', but her comments here about 'a polemical, not an introspective "I"' and 'an active "I" that's turned out onto the world' provide some context and justification for what she is doing in *I Love Dick*.

The 'shameful' nature of the subject matter also works to complicate the question of how to read *I Love Dick* – as personal confession, as 'performative philosophy', as social commentary, as emotional outpouring, as postmodern art project, as all of the above[113] – for shame, as I have suggested many times already, is both personal and social, both individual and shared, both covert and spectacular. According to Cooke, 'Kraus's project grounds itself in strong claims for its emotional authenticity and integrity', and 'her emotional credibility is reinforced by the personal and humiliating tenor of her confessions' as she documents, in mortifying detail, scenes and instances of her humiliation.[114] As Cooke argues, 'these factors combine to underwrite the authenticity of her confessions because of the potential shame and public embarrassment to which such intimacies expose her'.[115] Shame, humiliation and embarrassment are, on this reading, routes to 'credibility' and 'authenticity' (note Cooke's use of 'because', implying a causal link between shame and authenticity); they give the text the character of a confession (whatever Kraus's protestations to the contrary), and they seem to give us access to some truth of self, however careful a construction that written 'self' may be. Emotional authenticity is, in *I Love Dick*, always in tension with a more distanced, self-conscious, artful reflection on the political (in the broadest sense) ramifications of Chris's situation.

In her writing and interviews, then, Kraus is also always aware of the gendering of the categories of the personal versus the structural, universal and social, arguing that 'women have been denied all access to the a-personal', and complaining of Simone Weil's reception that

> [a]s a female her 'I' has been pathologized – she can't get fucked, she's manipulative and anorexic, she's ugly and she dresses badly – her 'I' was never read as universal and transparent. That, to me, points towards this great disgust with female-ness. As if a revelatory female self cannot be anything but compromised and murky.[116]

I Love Dick can be read, then (in Kraus's own words), as 'an attempt to analyze the *social* conditions' – including 'this great disgust with female-ness' – 'surrounding my *personal* failure', the two viewed as necessarily inextricable.[117] Throughout the book, Kraus writes often and angrily about her exclusion from certain groups, the way she is treated simply as Sylvère's wife, her own work disregarded. Thus she sets out to find a community of her own, by situating her work within a longer history of women's experimental art practice and, in doing so, she moves her writing beyond the limited trajectory of the 'personal', takes strength from the artistic productions of her forebears and peers, offers some justification for her project, and contributes to that project's generic instability.

One way that Kraus addresses the shame of being too personal is via her engagements with the work and legacy of the feminist artist Hannah Wilke, claiming that,

> while Hannah's tremendous will to turn the things that bothered her into subjects for her art seemed so embarrassing in her life time, at 3 a.m. it dawned on me that Hannah Wilke is a model for everything I hope to do.[118]

'Embarrassment', then, forms the link between Wilke and Kraus, part of a methodology that turns 'the things that [bother you]' into art, projecting the personal outwards. Kraus later writes that she sees Wilke as 'addressing the following question':

> *If women have failed to make 'universal' art because we're trapped within the 'personal,' why not universalize the 'personal' and make it the subject of our art?*
> To ask this question, to be willing to live it through, is still so bold.[119]

As Kraus explains, of her own work: 'I want to make the world more interesting than my problems. Therefore, I have to make my problems social.'[120] The 'embarrassment' of the personal is thus negotiated and redeployed as a way of drawing attention to the structural shame of women (shame as a strategy of social regulation), and the body – so often the source and bearer of shame – becomes the primary site at which the personal and the social meet. In response to a critic who describes Wilke's late work as 'a deeply thrilling venture into narcissism', Kraus writes: 'As if the only possible reason for a woman to publicly reveal herself could be self-therapeutic. As if the point was not to reveal the circumstances of one's own objectification.'[121] In fact, on Amelia Jones's reading, Wilke goes further than simply '[revealing] the circumstances' of her 'objectification', instead 'obsessively [producing] herself as her work through the rhetoric of the pose, reiteratively exaggerating it beyond its veiled patriarchal function of female objectification'; Wilke, writes Jones, succeeds in '[exploring] her body/self as always already not her own', while '[enacting] femininity as, by its very definition in patriarchy, inexorably performed (in process rather than "coherent"), doubly alienated, removed from the lure of potential transcendence'.[122] One way to read the literary experiments of Kraus (in *I Love Dick* and elsewhere in her œuvre) is through these frameworks of corporeal and textual reiteration, exaggeration and performance learned from an earlier innovative practice of feminist body art.[123]

This notion of '[exploring] [one's] body/self as always already not [one's] own' might also be useful in thinking through the question of the 'I' of the autofictional text as something other or more than merely 'personal', and in rebutting the charges of narcissism and self-indulgence laid at the door of autobiographical writing (particularly when that writing is practised by women). As Cooke writes, of her chosen authors in *Contemporary Feminist Life-Writing*:

> [W]hat could be interpreted as a culturally neoliberal over-attention to the self [. . .] is more complex and more politically feminist than such a simple reduction may at first indicate. [. . .] To class women's autobiography as neoliberal or even as narcissistic here because of its attention to the self and the individual misses the gendered dynamics that bedevil our reactions to writers and their work even today.[124]

In a recent article, Yanbing Er reads 'contemporary women's auto-fiction' – her particular examples are Heti's *How Should a Person Be?* (2012) and Jenny Offill's *Dept. of Speculation* (2014) – as 'a literary response to the individualising narrative of a neoliberal and postfeminist sensibility', viewing such work as both 'profoundly influenced by the confessional imperative of earlier feminist autobiographical writing', and as providing 'a counterpoint to a postfeminist subjectivity shaped by a neoliberal logic of self-improvement and individuated ambition'.[125] For Er, it is the self-consciousness of such texts, their reflections on the processes and difficulties of becoming a woman artist, that distinguishes them from the individualistic neoliberal culture from which they might appear to emerge. For Rachel Sykes, meanwhile, writing on the phenomenon of 'oversharing' in contemporary culture, a text such as *I Love Dick* 'can embody a poetics of oversharing that is characterized by an excess of autobio-graphical, sexual, and embodied confessions' while also constituting 'a mode of dissent in contemporary culture'.[126] *I Love Dick*'s 'litany of inappropriately divulged information: sexual, bodily, and mun-dane' is, on this reading, an example of how oversharing can func-tion as 'an experimental literary practice', by pointing up, among other things, 'the performative nature of information sharing' and by '[providing] spaces in which to reflect on the relationship between fame and femininity, the private and the public'.[127]

If Kraus is, as Sykes suggests, '[performing] and [parodying] the act of sharing itself', rather than actually 'sharing', *I Love Dick* is nevertheless reliant on the functioning of shame as spectacle for its affective allure – for the success of that 'performance', if you like. There is also, always, a danger that the attempt to 'universalize the personal' will result, rather, in a projection of the personal outwards, rather than a reading of the personal as (always, already) structural. And if Kraus does manage to 'universalize the personal', then Callo-way can be read – more critically – as personalising the universal; her work is, at best, 'self-therapeutic' (and arguably not even that), and if her writing '[reveals] the circumstances of [her] own objectification', then it does so unwittingly. In an *Observer* interview with Calloway, the interviewer claims that Calloway 'writes to give meaning and permanence to female subjectivity', but the following direct quota-tion hardly seems to bear out that point: 'I feel sad about the idea of events happening and having a big emotional impact on me, and then just passing by and having no significance.'[128] This reads like a comment on the obsessive recording and memorialisation of con-temporary lives and culture – facilitated in large part by the develop-ment of social media, but also by a dogged individualism – and its focus is determinedly solipsistic. The 'events' Calloway writes about are personal occurrences, not public, social or political happenings or shifts; it is not 'female subjectivity' that she is interested in, but only her own subjectivity (which happens to be female). By contrast, Kraus asserts that:

> I've fused my silence and repression with the entire female gender's silence and repression. I think the sheer fact of women talking, being, paradoxical, inexplicable, flip, self-destructive but above all else *public* is the most revolutionary thing in the world.[129]

Calloway might, then, be read more sympathetically as contributing to the overturning of such 'values', however inadvertently, simply by making her feelings public and by refusing a certain kind of 'dignity'.

Yet for both authors this 'suffering in public' stages a kind of vulnerability that risks being read as shameful in various respects:[130] in its recourse to or privileging of the 'personal'; stylistically, in presenting writing as uncrafted, spontaneously expressive; or, from a quite different perspective, as shameful in its confirmation of neurotic femininity. Kraus asks:

> Why is female vulnerability still only acceptable when it's neuroticized and personal; when it feeds back on itself? Why do people still not get it when we handle vulnerability like philosophy, at some remove?[131]

What might it look like to 'handle vulnerability like philosophy'? One clue might lie in comments made by Judith Butler in a recent interview, in which she claims that vulnerability should not be understood as 'pure passivity' or the absence of will, but instead as 'the condition of responsiveness' that might serve to challenge 'the terms by which we are addressed', the forms of recognition that we are or are not accorded.[132] In the case of love, I suggest, that need for recognition – and therefore that vulnerability – is particularly pronounced, that 'condition of responsiveness' particularly heightened. Recall Butler's claim, in *Undoing Gender*, that we 'are undone by each other. And if we're not, we're missing something. If this seems so clearly the case with grief, it is only because it was already the case with desire. One does not always stay intact.'[133] In *I Love Dick*, the recognition being sought by Chris is artistic as well as amatory, and that artistic recognition gradually comes to supplement or even to take the place of romantic recognition – and, in the case of this ultimately unreciprocated love, to compensate for its absence; indeed, in the case of *I Love Dick*, the very refusal of romantic recognition (Dick never answers her letters or acknowledges her feelings) paradoxically becomes a route to Kraus's creative renaissance and critical recognition. As I have argued elsewhere,[134] I read texts such as *I Love Dick*, *Unmastered*, Dodie Bellamy's *the buddhist*, and Maggie Nelson's *Bluets* and *The Argonauts* as making connections between the experiences of romantic injury, vulnerability and, sometimes, shame that they represent and the structural conditions of gendered vulnerability – by which I mean our vulnerability to gender (to practices and processes of gendering), with all that entails, and the particular, changeable, culturally specific, sometimes pernicious vulnerabilities attendant on being identified as a woman. As Butler asserts, 'we are assigned genders, and that assignment is an enormous discursive practice that acts upon us. We are vulnerable to that assignment and subject to it from the start, at the start, against our will.'[135] One way that these texts connect the personal and the structural is via their self-identification as part of a tradition of feminist self-exposure – whether body art or performance or confessional writing – and via their incorporation of other texts, in this way touching on what Butler elsewhere describes as our 'primary vulnerability to [. . .] anonymous others'.[136] In foregrounding a shame that both produces and undoes the self, in using hybrid, experimental forms that refuse coherence and disrupt genre, and in undermining any kind of stable narratorial 'I', such texts *enact* vulnerability as both subject matter and creative method.

If, then, *I Love Dick* comprises Kraus's attempt to 'handle vulnerability like philosophy', it is at least partly successful: via its interweaving of theoretical and essayistic material, in its shifting perspectives and styles, in its pointed self-consciousness, in its careful crafting as 'case study'. The personal, confessional nature of the book is such that distance ('at some remove') is not wholly achieved – indeed, to a large extent the book achieves its effects through a refusal of distance and objectivity – but in the process of (even by means of) this refusal, vulnerability is paradoxically transformed into a kind of agency and dominance. By contrast, Calloway's deployment of vulnerability is, arguably, more 'neuroticized and personal': her presentation of herself as a child or as a 'hurt kitten',[137] her repeated use of 'mew' (for example, in the 'bdsm' story), her self-presentation in photographs (wearing outfits reminiscent of a schoolgirl), and her continual reinforcement of her intellectual inferiority to the men she is sleeping with. In her encounter with 'adrien brody', Calloway tells us, 'Feeling more comfortable now, I tried to make myself vulnerable to him, to gain his affection,' showing how vulnerability remains for her a largely passive affair, to do with the desires of others: a tactic in Marie's seduction of the men that she meets and Calloway's seduction of the reader (in this way it is still, I suppose, a 'resource', however troubling its uses).[138] In the story entitled 'men', Calloway hints at the other possible motivations underpinning this showcasing of her vulnerability, by including an extract from a commentator on her work, who claims that she (Calloway) 'is a spectacle because she has made herself vulnerable', 'there is something fascinating, something profoundly intimate, about directed self-absorption [. . .]. Marie Calloway intentionally lets the raw edge of her damaged youth show.'[139] If the 'intentional' nature of this making-herself-vulnerable contributes to the book's impression of openness and intimacy, then the ambivalent resonances of the confessional female author as 'spectacle' and the shaming nature of some of the responses to Calloway's writing[140] suggest that *what purpose* never succeeds in '[handling] vulnerability like philosophy', as *I Love Dick* arguably does.

Bartky has claimed that 'women's shame is more than merely an effect of subordination but, within the larger universe of patriarchal social relations, a profound mode of disclosure *both of self and situation*'[141] – a sentiment echoed in her later statement, that 'it is in the act of being shamed and in the feeling ashamed that there is disclosed to women who they are and how they are faring within the domains they inhabit'.[142] What I have sought to demonstrate in the course of this chapter are the divergent ways that *I Love Dick* and *what purpose did i serve in your life* narrate individual experiences of personal shame – of an emotional, sexual and romantic nature – as routes to such a 'profound [. . .] disclosure' of 'self and situation', a revelation of 'who they are and how they are faring' in a world in which femininity and shame are utterly imbricated. If life-writing (even of the most self-conscious, autofictional kind) is an attempt (flawed, imprecise, ultimately thwarted) to construct a subject through writing, these narratives might be read as illuminating – in a manner that is never straightforwardly redemptive – the structural connections between shame and female subjectivity, the production and regulation of the latter by and through the former. Bartky concludes that 'shame is profoundly disempowering' – yet this is in large part due to the 'need for secrecy and concealment' that it produces, she writes, which 'isolates the oppressed from one another and in this way works against the emergence of a sense of solidarity'.[143] While Kraus and Calloway may appear to refuse 'secrecy and concealment' in telling their (shameful) stories, producing texts that provide a ground for 'solidarity', this making-public is not in itself a political act, particularly when (as in the case of Calloway), it practises alternative forms of isolation via solipsism or narcissism. This is why Kraus's insistence on a kind of affective and aesthetic solidarity with forebears like Hannah Wilke, Simone Weil and Kathy Acker more productively connects whatever personal shame she may experience (and narrate) to the structural conditions that govern women's daily existence – and thus to the 'larger universe of patriarchal social relations' of which Bartky writes. And it is thus, as Felski argues, that, 'Through the discussion of, and abstraction from, individual experience in relation to a general problematic of sexual politics, feminist confession [. . .] appropriates some of the functions of political discourse.'[144]

Coda: 'You're not really a feminist, are you?'

Writing to Dick, near the end of the book (and the end of their 'relationship'), Kraus asks:

> Why does everybody think that women are debasing themselves when we expose the conditions of our own debasement? Why do women always have to come off clean? [. . .] What hooks me on our story is our different readings of it. You think it's personal and private; my neurosis. [. . .] I think our story is performative philosophy.[145]

The preceding readings show, I hope, that the 'personal and private' can become 'performative philosophy' – due in part, in these instances, to shame's liminal positioning on the border of the private and the public, the subjective and the intersubjective – but there remains a sense in which female authors writing explicitly about sexuality cannot ever 'come off clean'. As Kraus has noted in interview, referencing a Bruce Hainey discussion of Andy Warhol that begins with the line 'I've always liked sucking cock':

> If a straight woman says [this line], people automatically say, Why is she doing this? To debase herself? To grab attention? What really fucks with everyone's heads is when women, gay men, combine graphic first-person sex stuff with quote–unquote objective, analytic cultural thought. There's a deep pity and horror of female sexuality behind this, as if it's this mushy botanical subordinate thing at total variance with the dynamic integrity, the 'masculinity' of analytical thought.[146]

Johanna Fateman notes a related double-bind in her reading of Calloway, asserting that 'She's a heterosexual masochist in the wake of the third wave, one who feels neither the shame nor the empowerment she's supposed to choose between.'[147] Katherine Angel's *Unmastered*, subtitled *A Book On Desire, Most Difficult To Tell*, can be read as a meditation on, among other things, the iniquity of this supposed 'choice'.

Unmastered is much less centrally concerned with experiences of sexual shame and romantic rejection than the Kraus and Calloway books already discussed, yet there are moments when shame surfaces, unexpectedly, in the experience and narration of desire. When Angel confesses that:

I am sometimes afraid of the pleasure that comes from being on top.
I am afraid because it is deeper, rageful, guttural.

I am afraid of becoming a man. All muscle, fur, eruption.

I am afraid of repelling with my desire.[148]

this fear of being unwomanly – 'muscle, fur, eruption' – touches on the 'shame' of defeminisation, but also hints more broadly at the inappropriateness of female desire and female sexual pleasure. This is borne out in two other instances in the book: in the first, Angel recounts sharing a joke with her mother about (the pleasure of) oral sex and notes how they 'erupt in laughter: raucous, unladylike laughter. And then reddening cheeks, averted eyes';[149] in the second, she describes how, as a sixteen-year-old, she is 'caught red-handed, red-faced' when her grandmother sees her flirting with an older boy.[150] In both instances, the blushing body reveals the shame of illicit desire, but these are fugitive instances, shot through with the peculiar awkwardness, the uneasy balance of intimacy and repression, that characterise family relations.

Yet if *Unmastered* is much less about the staging of a scene or scenes of humiliation, it shares with Kraus and Calloway a central concern with the fraught living and narrating of female sexuality 'in the wake of the third wave'. It also, similarly, showcases an innovative approach to genre – being part memoir, part essay, part feminist polemic – and to structure. In an interrupted, discontinuous narrative,

Angel intersperses personal experiences and reflections (interweaving the personal and the political) and excerpts from literature and philosophy (Virginia Woolf, Michel Foucault and Susan Sontag are frequent reference points). The impressionistic, eloquent, sensuous language of the book is occasionally disrupted by a more direct, guttural, vernacular idiom ('Fuck me, oh fuck me').[151] Blank pages and blank spaces on the page contribute to *Unmastered*'s meditative tone, to its sense of stylised fragmentation, and to the realisation, fleetingly entertained, that language might be inadequate to the expression of desire ('I have sounds, but I have fewer words').[152] The numbered sections, some just a few words long, present the discrete thoughts as axioms, though the impression of a logical sequence is always in tension with the book's deployment of intertextuality and non-linearity; the impression of a calm and orderly mind at work is always also in tension with the outbreaks of emotion (and disruptions of/by desire) that similarly mark the text. More profoundly, this very discretion/separation of the different thoughts, feelings and ideas expresses an underlying yet apparently impossible wish to reconcile overlapping but ultimately incommensurable identities (woman, feminist, lover, girlfriend, writer) and desires.

What *Unmastered* adds to the texts already discussed is precisely this more overt reflection on the 'difficulty' of certain desires for the self-aware feminist. These desires are 'difficult to tell', as the subtitle announces, but also necessary to express, according to the argument offered here. Angel cautions against the assumption 'that feminism undoes "problematic" desires', noting that 'we are more than our beliefs. We don't align, neatly, inside ourselves, a stack of equal cards.'[153] The Kraus and Calloway texts illustrate, or at least hint at, this misalignment and its production of an ineluctably riven female subjectivity; Angel makes it the focus of her sexual self-narration. Thus, at an early point in the narrative, when Angel tells her lover how she loves 'his powerful arms around my neck while he came into me from behind; [. . .] feeling the strength of him as he fucked me – yes, as *he* fucked *me*, because – let's not be coy, or disingenuous – that is definitely what was happening', he replies 'You're not really a feminist, are you?'[154] (Her response is to laugh). Immediately after a section that narrates an episode in which he comes over her ('my breasts, my belly, my neck') and she says 'I love this', comes a section that reads simply: 'Dupe. Collaborator.

Victim.'[155] It is left deliberately unclear who voices these accusatory epithets: is this how Angel feels about herself, given these pleasures/desires, or how she fears others will feel about her confession of them? Are the two even separable, given shame's status as simultaneously structural and internal/internalised? What shame there is here, then – and actually this is a book more obviously characterised by joy and excitement, ebullience even – concerns the apparent tensions between a feminist approach to sexuality and the complex demands and manipulations of desire, which might not accord with that political worldview.[156]

Angel writes back to – but still within – a feminism that has hitherto 'contained my desire. [. . .] That tried to rule against my noisy, volatile self; to put a lid on my hunger',[157] and that has 'contained my sexuality, the danger it posed to myself and others, by cloaking it with ambivalence'.[158] In doing so, she seeks to express a sexual self that is 'both powerful and vulnerable',[159] and thus to move beyond the stark oppositions that govern the sexual (and sexual–political) imaginary.[160] These oppositions are encapsulated in the images of Leda and the swan that haunt these pages: when a view of her lover's jutting shoulder blades makes Angel think of a swan's wings, she wonders 'Am I Leda? Is he the swan?'.[161] Later, when, in the midst of desire, they are 'ferocious, and also vulnerable – unmastered', Angel wonders whether she is 'both Leda and the swan' and asks 'Can I be the swan? Must I always be Leda? Must I either take, or be taken?'[162] As before, this choice between shame and empowerment, passivity and agency, is no choice at all. *Unmastered* muses on the inescapability of this cultural baggage, this imagery that crosses from text or image to bedroom, and on the cultural imaginary (what Angel terms 'the symbol that becomes real, the real that becomes symbol. The metaphors we love by') of female sexual submission and the complex pleasures and anxieties it arouses.[163]

In working through the pleasures and anxieties of vulnerability (a kind of openness that facilitates intimacy but that also involves a humbling, a self-humiliation that skirts the borders of shame), Angel goes further than Kraus and Calloway in seeking to explore themes of *male* vulnerability: the idea that sometimes 'he too has to retreat, halt, reground', sometimes 'he too is brought to the brink, the brink of himself' in the midst of the sexual scene;[164] the suggestion that, even 'when he grabs my hair, when he presses my throat, when he holds my hands down, [. . .] I can feel his tenderness, his humility'.[165] For the most part, *Unmastered* is concerned with desire as a kind of hunger ('I am so fucking hungry')[166] that women are not supposed to have, that is even shameful for them, because they are supposed 'to be good' and pleasing to men.[167] And yet, even when Angel writes of the feminine urge – nay, compulsion – to reassure men of their potency (sexual or otherwise), she is alert to the vulnerabilities at work in both participants in this exchange, the precarious forms of collusion and denial, writing:

> You know that deep well of fear that flickers in your eyes? I can see it, I can feel it, and I am telling you that it does not exist. I am pouring myself into that well; I block it up with my sympathy, my empathy, my acute feeling for your anxiety.
>
> I am proof of your masculinity, of your endless potency.[168]

The female body – its sexual availability, its vulnerability – becomes, thus, a stimulus to potency and a 'proof of masculinity', a shoring up against the shame of being less than a man, the shame that might arise from acknowledging that 'deep well of fear'; yet Angel's assertion that 'I can see it' is itself a challenge, a kind of defiance, and a tentative invitation to some alternative understanding of masculinity. What Angel is quick to acknowledge is the female complicity in the system of feminine deferral and reassurance, with sex being just one arena (though arguably the most charged and symbolic) in which this plays out. The complexity comes from the fact that women benefit from this system as well as losing out to it. Thus,

> [i]t is also a way to make you represent something, culturally, that my femininity does not. I want to feel your decisiveness, your force. In lieu, perhaps, of feeling my own. I want to feel your capacity to resist me, your unaccommodatingness. Because otherwise you will not be A Man in the eyes of the world.
>
> Eyes which are, of course, also mine.[169]

What the woman sacrifices in this exchange is 'decisiveness', 'force', but what she gains is 'the king's protection', yet Angel notes how this 'protection' is earned by, in turn, 'protecting the king, by foreclosing the possibility that I don't desire him, by hiding his fear from himself. Inflating him – engorging him – with my facilitating, accommodating desire.'[170]

In this chapter I have considered various narrative instantiations of a female desire that is, by turns, accommodating, resistant, disruptive, voracious, repressed, hungry and vulnerable; a desire that can be shameful (to oneself) and shaming (of others); a desire whose expression, however performative and clever and self-conscious, always carries a taint of shame (Phaidra's legacy living on, it seems). In the next and final chapter, I turn to the question of masculinity and shame, examining the politics and poetics of male shamefulness in various contemporary, male-authored novels and autofictions, and addressing the ways in which the female body – particularly through its cultural status as a locus or repository of shame – works not only as a regulatory tool in the cultural construction of femininity but also as the means by which a man becomes, or remains, A Man.

Notes

1. Euripides, *Grief Lessons: Four Plays*, trans. Anne Carson (New York: New York Review Books, 2006), p. 310.
2. Euripides, *Fragments*, ed. and trans. Christopher Collard and Martin Cropp (Cambridge, MA: Harvard University Press, 2008), p. 479 (Fragment 429).
3. Euripides/Carson, p. 312.
4. Anne Carson, 'Euripides to the Audience', *London Review of Books*, 24: 17 (5 September 2002): 24.
5. See: Emily Gould, *And the Heart Says Whatever* (New York: Simon and Schuster, 2010); Emily Gould, 'Exposed', *The New York Times Magazine*, 25 May 2008. Available at: <http://www.nytimes.com/2008/05/25/magazine/25internet-t.html?pagewanted=all&_r=1&> (last accessed 13 June 2019).
6. Emily Gould, qtd in: Kat Stoeffel, 'Meet Marie Calloway: The New Model for Literary Seductress is Part Feminist, Part "Famewhore" and All Pseudonymous', *New York Observer*, 20 December 2011. Available at: <http://observer.com/2011/12/meet-marie-calloway/#ixzz3BJk03uUZ> (last accessed 13 June 2019).
7. Sandra Bartky, *Femininity and Domination: Studies in the Phenomenology of Domination* (London: Routledge, 1990), p. 84.

8. Bartky, p. 85.
9. Bartky, p. 95.
10. Peter Brooks, *Troubling Confessions: Speaking Guilt in Law and Literature* (Chicago: University of Chicago Press, 2000), p. 6.
11. Emily Gould, 'Our Graffiti', *Emily Magazine*, 29 November 2011. Available at: <http://www.emilymagazine.com/?p=827> (last accessed 13 June 2019).
12. Timothy Bewes, *The Event of Postcolonial Shame* (Princeton: Princeton University Press, 2011), p. 1.
13. Timothy Bewes, 'The Call to Intimacy and the Shame Effect', *differences: A Journal of Feminist Cultural Studies* 22: 1 (2011): 1–16 (5).
14. Bewes, *The Event*, p. 14.
15. Chris Kraus, *I Love Dick* [1997] (Los Angeles: Semiotext(e), 2006), p. 138.
16. Katherine Angel, *Unmastered: A Book On Desire, Most Difficult To Tell* (London: Penguin, 2012), p. 56.
17. Sally Munt, *Queer Attachments: The Cultural Politics of Shame* (Aldershot: Ashgate, 2007), p. 2.
18. Elspeth Probyn, *Blush: Faces of Shame* (Minneapolis: University of Minnesota Press, 2005), p. xvii.
19. Jennifer Cooke, *Contemporary Feminist Life-Writing: The New Audacity* (Cambridge: Cambridge University Press, 2020), 'Introduction: The New Audacity'. Cooke and I were working on this material on Kraus, Calloway and Angel in the same period, and I am immensely grateful to her both for sharing the manuscript of *Contemporary Feminist Life-Writing* with me before its publication and for discussing many of these ideas with me in various conferences and settings (academic or otherwise) with such rigour and generosity.
20. Kraus, p. 211.
21. Sheila Heti, 'Chris Kraus' [interview], *The Believer* (September 2013). Available at: <http://www.believermag.com/issues/201309/?read=interview_kraus> (last accessed 13 June 2019).
22. See, for example, the interview that Kraus gave to Martin Rumsby (available at: <http://www.youtube.com/watch?v=c2DDibS9jnI> (last accessed 13 June 2019)), in which she says: 'everything that I say in the book really happened'. See also the Sheila Heti interview with Kraus in *The Believer* (September 2013), in which Kraus talks about the grounding of her writing in her experience; Heti claims 'the book drew on her real-life experiences, marriage, and letters to a real man', who was, Heti suggests, 'horrified by the publication of this book'.
23. Serge Doubrovsky, *Fils* (Paris: Galilée, 1977), back cover. In the original French, the full quotation reads: 'Fiction, d'évènements et de faits

strictement réels; si l'on veut autofiction, d'avoir confié le langage d'une aventure à l'aventure d'un langage en liberté, hors sagesse et hors syntaxe du roman, traditionnel ou nouveau.'

24. Arnaud Schmitt, 'Making the Case for Self-Narration Against Autofiction', *a/b: Auto/Biography Studies* 25: 1 (2010): 122–37 (126).

25. Armine Kotin Mortimer, 'Autofiction as Allofiction: Doubrovsky's *L'Après-vivre*', *L'Esprit Créateur* 49: 3 (2009): 22–35 (22). Notably, many of the leading contemporary writers of autofiction in France are women authors whose focus often includes matters of gender and sexuality (including sexual violence). See, for example, the work of Christine Angot, Catherine Cusset, Marguerite Duras, Annie Ernaux, Camille Laurens and Catherine Millet.

26. Unlike the other examples given here, Knausgaard is not, of course, writing in English. However, as Chapter 4 will document, his monumental, six-volume autofictional work, *My Struggle* (2009–11), has enjoyed extraordinary success in the English-speaking world.

27. Hywel Dix, 'Introduction: Autofiction in English: The Story so Far', in Dix (ed.), *Autofiction in English* (Basingstoke: Palgrave, 2018), pp. 1–23 (pp. 3, 4, 13).

28. Both quotations are taken from Catherine Cusset, 'The Limits of Autofiction' (2012), a paper presented at a conference, 'Autofiction: Literature in France Today', at New York University in April 2012. The full text is available at: <http://www.catherinecusset.co.uk/wp-content/uploads/2013/02/THE-LIMITS-OF-AUTOFICTION.pdf> (last accessed 13 June 2019).

29. Rita Felski, *Beyond Feminist Aesthetics: Feminist Literature and Social Change* (Cambridge, MA: Harvard University Press, 1989), p. 87. As a corollary, it is worth noting the significant number of publications – again, many by relatively young women authors – detailing experiences of addiction and/or illness: Leslie Jamison's *The Empathy Exams* (2014) and *The Recovering* (2018) spring to mind, as does Amy Liptrot's *The Outrun* (2015) and some of the essays in Dodie Bellamy's *When the Sick Rule the World* (2015). The focus in these texts is (mostly) not romantic or erotic, but they are nevertheless 'confessional', and they are also variously engaged with states and experiences of shame (and shameful embodiment).

30. Brooks, p. 6.

31. Elizabeth Gregory, 'Confessing the Body: Plath, Sexton, Berryman, Lowell, Ginsberg and the Gendered Poetics of the "Real"', in Jo Gill (ed.), *Modern Confessional Writing* (London: Routledge, 2006), pp. 33–49 (p. 35).

32. Brooks, p. 69.

33. Michel Foucault, *History of Sexuality, Vol. 1: The Will to Knowledge* [1976], trans. Robert Hurley (New York: Pantheon Books, 1978), pp. 61–2.
34. Brooks, p. 9.
35. Jo Gill, 'Introduction', in Gill (ed.), *Modern Confessional Writing* (London: Routledge, 2006), pp. 1–10 (p. 6).
36. Leigh Gilmore, *Tainted Witness* (New York: Columbia University Press, 2018), pp. 85, 86.
37. Gilmore, p. 86.
38. A popular take on this subject can be found in Rebecca Solnit's essay 'Men Explain Things to Me', which went viral when it was first published online. In the version published in the collection of the same name, Solnit uses a particular example of a man 'explaining' something to her about which he knows very little and she knows a great deal, to discuss the ways in which women are '[trained] in self-doubt and self-limitation' (p. 4). She also connects this to American politics and foreign policy, to 'those Middle Eastern countries where women's testimony has no legal standing', before using this idea that 'credibility is a basic survival tool' (p. 6) to argue that 'At the heart of the struggle of feminism to give rape, date rape, marital rape, domestic violence, and workplace sexual harassment legal standing as crimes has been the necessity of making women credible and audible' (p. 7) (*Men Explain Things to Me* (London: Granta, 2014)).
39. Gill, p. 4.
40. Brooks, p. 21.
41. Brooks, p. 49.
42. Eileen Myles, 'Foreword', in Chris Kraus, *I Love Dick* [1997] (Los Angeles: Semiotext(e), 2006), pp. 13–15 (p. 13).
43. Giorgio Agamben, *Remnants of Auschwitz*, trans. Daniel Heller-Roazen (New York: Zone Books, 2002), p. 107.
44. Silvan Tomkins, 'Shame-Humiliation and Contempt-Disgust', in Eve Kosofsky Sedgwick and Adam Frank (eds), *Shame and Its Sisters: A Silvan Tomkins Reader* (Durham, NC: Duke University Press, 1995), pp. 133–78 (p. 137).
45. Eve Kosofsky Sedgwick, 'Queer Performativity: Henry James's *The Art of the Novel*', *GLQ* 1: 1 (1993): 1–16 (5).
46. Kraus, p. 170.
47. Kraus, p. 178.
48. Kraus, p. 211.
49. Kraus, p. 202.
50. Marie Calloway, *what purpose did i serve in your life* (New York: Tyrant Books, 2013), pp. 3, 4, 5, 8, 6.

51. Calloway, p. 45.
52. Cooke, Ch. 3.
53. Cooke, Ch. 3.
54. Calloway, p. 67.
55. Calloway, p. 69.
56. Calloway, unpaginated front matter.
57. In a review in *Bookforum*, Johanna Fateman suggests, however, that the epigraph 'is an elegant setup to Calloway's literary experiment. Via Millett we're reminded that avant-garde writers have historically provoked charges of obscenity and ineptitude, and that we're still in want of ruthless counters to men's historical monopoly on what sex is and what it means' (Johanna Fateman, 'Bodies of Work', *Bookforum*, September/October/November 2013. Available at: <http://www.bookforum.com/inprint/020_03/12182> (last accessed 13 June 2019)).
58. Calloway, p. 240.
59. Sedgwick, Queer Performativity', p. 5.
60. J. Halberstam, 'Shame and White Gay Masculinity', *Social Text* 84–5, 23: 3–4 (2005): 219–33 (220).
61. Lisa Carver, 'Marie Calloway on Her New Novel and Being Called "Jailbait"', *Vice Magazine*, 26 June 2013. Available at: <http://www.vice.com/read/marie-calloway> (last accessed 13 June 2019).
62. Stephen Elliott, 'The Rumpus Interview with Marie Calloway', *The Rumpus*, 29 December 2011. Available at: <http://therumpus.net/2011/12/the-rumpus-interview-with-marie-calloway/> (last accessed 13 June 2019).
63. Carver (2013).
64. Myles, p. 15.
65. Anna Watkins Fisher, 'Manic Impositions: The Parasitical Art of Chris Kraus and Sophie Calle', *WSQ: Women's Studies Quarterly* 40: 1–2 (2012): 223–35 (224).
66. Fisher, pp. 223, 225.
67. Fisher, p. 226.
68. Kraus, p. 72.
69. Kraus, p. 81.
70. Fisher, p. 233.
71. Kraus, p. 236.
72. Qtd in Frimer, 'Chris Kraus in conversation with Denise Frimer', *The Brooklyn Rail*, 10 April 2006. Available at: <http://www.brooklynrail.org/2006/04/art/chris-kraus-in-conversation-with-denise-frimer> (last accessed 13 June 2019). My emphasis.
73. Rachel Carroll, 'How Soon Is Now: Constructing the Contemporary/Gendering the Experimental', *Contemporary Women's Writing* 9: 1 (2015): 16–33 (29).

74. Bartky, p. 84.
75. Tomkins, p. 137.
76. Calloway, pp. 141, 142, 146, 149, 150, 151.
77. Calloway, p. 143.
78. Calloway, p. 147.
79. Calloway, p. 152.
80. Alexandra Molotkow, 'Marie Calloway, Degrading Sex, and Books About It', *Hazlitt*, 11 June 2013. Available at: <http://penguinrandomhouse.ca/hazlitt/feature/marie-calloway-degrading-sex-and-books-about-it> (last accessed 13 June 2019).
81. Calloway, p. 58.
82. Calloway, p. 67.
83. Charles Darwin, *The Expression of the Emotions in Man and Animals* (London: John Murray, 1901), p. 340.
84. Tomkins, p. 136.
85. Cooke, Ch. 3.
86. Calloway, p. 7.
87. Calloway, p. 27.
88. Bewes, 'The Call', p. 9.
89. Bewes, *The Event*, p. 1.
90. Trev Lynn Broughton and Linda Anderson, 'Preface', in Broughton and Anderson (eds), *Women's Lives/Women's Times* (Albany: SUNY Press, 1997), pp. xi–xvii (p. xi).
91. Estelle C. Jelinek, 'Introduction: Women's Autobiography and the Male Tradition', in Jelinek (ed.), *Women's Autobiography: Essays in Criticism* (Bloomington: Indiana University Press, 1980), pp. 1–20 (p. 19).
92. Estelle C. Jelinek, *The Tradition of Women's Autobiography* [1986] (Xlibris, 2003), pp. 14–15.
93. Leigh Gilmore, *Autobiographics: A Feminist Theory of Women's Self-Representation* (Ithaca, NY: Cornell University Press, 1994), p. x.
94. Kraus, pp. 258, 43.
95. Kraus, p. 153.
96. Kraus, p. 263.
97. Sheila Heti, 'Chris Kraus' [interview], *The Believer*, September 2013, unpag. Available at: <http://www.believermag.com/issues/201309/?read=interview_kraus> (last accessed 13 June 2019).
98. Kraus, p. 170.
99. Kraus, p. 138.
100. Kraus, pp. 26–7. This Stant–Verver analogy is actually rather odd, as the dynamics of that relationship in James's novel are quite complex: Stant is poor but quite manipulative, Verver is rich but naïve, but Verver ultimately seems to get the upper hand. In what ways, then, is Lotringer Verver?

101. Calloway, p. 139.
102. Cf. Sartre's description – cited in my Introduction – of shame as 'the recognition of the fact that I am indeed that object which the Other is looking at and judging' (Jean-Paul Sartre, *Being and Nothingness* [1943], trans. Hazel E. Barnes (New York: Washington Square Press, 1956), p. 350).
103. Calloway, back cover copy.
104. Felski, pp. 88–9.
105. Felski, p. 93.
106. Felski, p. 86.
107. Felski, pp. 87–8.
108. Felski, p. 93.
109. Bartky, p. 85.
110. Malcolm Pines, 'Shame: What Psychoanalysis Does and Does Not Say' [1987], in Claire Pajaczkowska and Ivan Ward (eds), *Shame and Sexuality: Psychoanalysis and Visual Culture* (London: Routledge, 2008), pp. 93–106 (p. 93).
111. Qtd in Frimer (2006).
112. Anne Balsamo and Henry Schwarz, 'Under the Sign of "Semiotext(e)": The Story According to Sylvère Lotringer and Chris Kraus', *Critique* 37: 3 (1996): 205–20 (214).
113. Kraus, p. 211.
114. Cooke, Ch. 3.
115. Cooke, Ch. 3.
116. Qtd in Frimer (2006). Kraus writes more extensively about Simone Weil in *Aliens and Anorexia* (2000), revering her as, among other things, a 'performative philosopher' (Chris Kraus, *Aliens and Anorexia* (South Pasadena: Semiotext(e), 2000), p. 49).
117. Heti (unpag.). My emphasis.
118. Kraus, *I Love Dick*, p. 172.
119. Kraus, *I Love Dick*, p. 211.
120. Kraus, *I Love Dick*, p. 196.
121. Kraus, *I Love Dick*, pp. 213, 214–15, 215.
122. Amelia Jones, *Body Art/Performing the Subject* (Minneapolis: University of Minnesota Press, 1998), p. 152.
123. In discussions of contemporary women's innovative poetry, there has been some debate about the centrality of the body to that writing, with Jennifer Ashton criticising poetry that 'understands "innovation" as a direct extension and production of women's bodies' (p. 214) and '[insists] on an even more literal connection between the text and the body' (p. 228), and Jennifer Scappettone counter-arguing that this apparent 'return to the body' in fact 'involves no unmediated return to a body proper' (p. 181). See Jennifer Ashton, 'Our Bodies,

Our Poems', *American Literary History* 19: 1 (2007): 211–31, and Jennifer Scappettone, 'Bachelorettes, Even: Strategic Embodiment in Contemporary Experimentalism by Women', *Modern Philology* 105: 1 (2007): 178–84. It is certainly the case that Kraus and Dodie Bellamy – whose engagements with shame, vulnerability and embodiment I have written about elsewhere – look back to feminist body art as a key influence and inspiration, as do Juliana Spahr and Stephanie Young in their 'foulipo' performance piece at the 'Noulipo' conference at CalArts in 2005. See: Kaye Mitchell, 'Vulnerability and Vulgarity: The Uses of Shame in the Work of Dodie Bellamy', in Barry Sheils and Julie Walsh (eds), *Shame and Modern Writing* (London: Routledge, 2018), pp. 165–85, and Juliana Spahr and Stephanie Young, 'Foulipo', in *Drunken Boat* 8. Available at: <https://www.drunkenboat.com/db8/oulipo/feature-oulipo/essays/spahr-young/foulipo.html> (last accessed 13 June 2019).

124. Cooke, 'Introduction: The New Audacity'.

125. Yanbing Er, 'Contemporary Women's Autofiction as Critique of Postfeminist Discourse', *Australian Feminist Studies* 33: 97 (2018): 316–30 (316, 317).

126. Rachel Sykes, '"Who Gets to Speak and Why?" Oversharing in Contemporary North American Women's Writing', *Signs: Journal of Women in Culture and Society* 43: 1 (2017): 151–74 (151).

127. Sykes, p. 165.

128. Stoeffel (2011).

129. Kraus, *I Love Dick*, p. 210.

130. By saying that this is a 'staging of vulnerability', I am in broad agreement with Cooke's description of Kraus, Calloway and Angel as modelling a kind of 'voluntary vulnerability', which should be distinguished from 'victimhood', and with her claim that, for these writers, vulnerability becomes 'a resource' – though I am perhaps more critical of how Calloway uses this particular 'resource'. See Cooke, 'Introduction: The New Audacity'.

131. Kraus, *I Love Dick*, pp. 207–8.

132. Sara Ahmed, 'Interview with Judith Butler', *Sexualities* 19: 4 (2016): 482–92 (485).

133. Judith Butler, *Undoing Gender* (London: Routledge, 2004), p. 30.

134. Kaye Mitchell, 'Feral with Vulnerability', *Angelaki* 23: 1 (2018): 194–8.

135. Ahmed, p. 485.

136. Judith Butler, *Precarious Life* (London: Verso, 2004), p. xiv.

137. Calloway, pp. 5, 6.

138. Calloway, p. 95. See footnote 130 for Cooke's description of vulnerability as a 'resource' in Calloway, Angel and Kraus.

139. Calloway, p. 83.
140. Lisa Carver notes that 'Reviews and comments about Calloway's novel (nearly all mistake the narrator for *her*) are horrendous, and usually start by noting her exploitation of herself by deliberately turning on everyone with such a "jailbait" photo as the cover. [. . .] Notes one commenter, she's "a fame whore, with the accent on the whore." Her "lazy, *Penthouse* Letters style" is "offending to real writers"' (Carver (2013)). The more critical comments tend to derive from blogs and online comments sections, however, while reviews of the book by more reputable websites and magazines such as *Flavorwire*, *Esquire*, *Slate* and *Hazlitt*, even when critical of *what purpose*, tend to give Calloway the benefit of the doubt and to avoid obviously shaming language. Thus, Elizabeth Spiers in *Flavorwire*, for example, suggests that Calloway's alleged narcissism 'is mostly the banal and timeless narcissism of youth' and that such accusations might 'apply to half of the Internet'. See Elizabeth Spiers, 'But Is It Good?: The Problem with Marie Calloway's Affectless Realism', *Flavorwire*, 18 June 2013. Available at: <http://flavorwire.com/398643/but-is-it-good-the-problem-with-marie-calloways-affectless-realism> (last accessed 13 June 2019).
141. Bartky, p. 85. My emphasis.
142. Bartky, p. 93.
143. Bartky, p. 97.
144. Felski, p. 95.
145. Kraus, *I Love Dick*, p. 211.
146. Frimer (2006).
147. Fateman (2013).
148. Angel, p. 116.
149. Angel, p. 121.
150. Angel, p. 190.
151. Angel, p. 29.
152. Angel, p. 42.
153. Angel, p. 215.
154. Angel, p. 9.
155. Angel, pp. 168, 169.
156. For less literary, more popular reflections on these tensions between sexual desire and the desire to be a 'good' feminist, see Jessica Valenti's *Sex Object* (New York: HarperCollins, 2016) and Roxane Gay's *Bad Feminist* (London: HarperCollins, 2014). Valenti writes candidly about her drinking, partying, (relative) promiscuity and infidelity, confessing that 'Doing the right thing has never come easily to me' (p. 125). Gay, meanwhile, declares that 'I am failing as a woman.

I am failing as a feminist. To freely accept the feminist label would not be fair to good feminists. If I am, indeed, a feminist, I am a rather bad one. I am a mess of contradictions. There are many ways in which I am doing feminism wrong, at least according to the way my perceptions of feminism have been warped by being a woman' (p. 314). The things that make Gay feel like a 'bad feminist' include the fact that she (sometimes, at least) wants 'to be taken care of and have someone to come home to', the fact that she wants 'to surrender, completely, in certain aspects of my life' (p. 314); her tastes in 'thuggish rap' music (p. 314), pink (anything pink), reading *Vogue*, her 'fondness for fashion' (p. 315); and, 'Despite what people think based on my opinion writing, I very much like men' (p. 315). She also fakes orgasms, loves babies and so on; through these 'confessions', she expresses a notable anxiety about the projected disapproval of so-called 'good' or 'proper' feminists – 'I feel guilty [about faking orgasms] because the sisterhood would not approve' (p. 316).

157. Angel, p. 186.
158. Angel, p. 188.
159. Ibid.
160. This attempt to tread a line between two unhelpfully polarised positions is also evident in the discussions of pornography and abortion found in *Unmastered*.
161. Angel, p. 68.
162. Angel, pp. 94, 95.
163. Angel, p. 90.
164. Angel, p. 111.
165. Angel, p. 91.
166. Angel, p. 137.
167. Angel, p. 76.
168. Angel, p. 30.
169. Angel, p. 36.
170. Angel, p. 38.

Chapter 4

The Shame of Being a Man: Humiliation and/as Heroism

Introduction

'The shame of being a man – is there any better reason to write?', asks Gilles Deleuze, in an essay entitled simply 'Literature and Life'.[1] (As I have suggested already, the shame of being a *woman* might too often be adduced as a reason *not* to write.) Deleuze's statement sits alongside his assertion that, in writing, 'one becomes-woman, becomes-animal or -vegetable, becomes-molecule, to the point of becoming-imperceptible'.[2] In other words, this is part of an argument about the (necessary) disintegration of authority and dominance – even of identity itself – in the act of writing, where 'man' equals 'a dominant form of expression that claims to impose itself on all matter, whereas woman, animal, or molecule always has a component of flight that escapes its own formalization'.[3] Writing, then, is held to facilitate an escape from the shame of 'being a man' in this quite specific sense.

Steven Connor, in a 2000 paper (later published as a shorter article) on the 'shame of being a man', offers a subtle contestation of Deleuze's point for his own ends, commenting that

> [t]o write is not to free oneself from the shame of being a man, or not, at least, but for sure, if you are this one. Writing might also be a way of meeting with shame, a coming in to male shamefulness. I have surprised myself by wanting to be able to conclude that male shame, or my kind, is less to be regretted than one might at first think.[4]

In doing so, he sets up a discussion of the triangular relation between shame, masculinity and writing, while also positing shame as an affect that is both inextricable from maleness and at least partly desirable: inextricable, thanks to a growing awareness (presumably as a result of feminism) of 'the shamefulness of being a man as such and at all', and hence desirable in the move towards more enlightened gender roles, but also ever-present in the anxiety around 'falling short of being a man'.[5] Both successful and unsuccessful performances of masculinity – whatever the criteria of 'success' might be – therefore have the potential to induce shame. Wayne Koestenbaum, who is less concerned with the role that writing might play in 'meeting with' male shame, nevertheless comes to similar conclusions in his recent book on humiliation,[6] averring that

> 'Masculinity', however questionable a property, and however much women also possess it, is something that can be seen as humiliating (it is humiliating to have a penis, it is humiliating not to have a womb) or as something that can be *taken away* by humiliation (a man who is humiliated has less of a penis than he did before the humiliation occurred).[7]

Koestenbaum's subsequent, numerous, personal examples of frustrated or repudiated desire go some way towards explaining why it might be 'humiliating to have a penis', mitigating the apparent glibness of this claim: its offhand dismissal of female masculinity, its too facile appropriation of a lack traditionally conceived as feminine. Yet for Koestenbaum too, humiliation is no bad thing; indeed, the experience of it may constitute 'a passport to decency and civilization, [. . .] a necessary shedding of hubris', particularly, he implies, as far as men are concerned.[8]

In this chapter, continuing my project of thinking through the complex relations between shame, gender and writing, I take Connor's and Koestenbaum's thoughts as starting points for a discussion of the difficulty of acknowledging or of owning shame, for a man, but also the obstacles to writing masculine shame. Too often, I argue, writing is used not as a way of 'coming in to male shamefulness', but rather to displace or disavow shame in order to shore up precisely the model of masculinity that Connor, for example, eschews as shameful; such attempts at mastery-through-writing are either profoundly un-Deleuzian or, in the light of Deleuze's comments, particularly futile. Philip Roth's *The Dying Animal* (2001) and Martin Amis's *The Pregnant Widow* (2010), which I will consider in due course, are two such instances of novels that seek to displace male shamefulness (particularly sexual shame) on to vulnerable female bodies. By contrast, Karl Ove Knausgaard's *My Struggle II: A Man in Love* (2009/2013) oscillates between the minute, excoriating presentation of male shame as an heroic literary 'struggle' for 'authenticity', and the revelation of a masculine self-consciousness and vulnerability rarely seen in contemporary writing.

In the course of this book I have returned to Sandra Bartky's work on the gendering of shame at various intervals. When Bartky explores this topic in *Femininity and Domination*, she suggests that shame is one of those 'patterns of mood and feeling' that tends 'to characterize women more than men'.[9] As she explains:

> To say that some pattern of feeling in women, say shame, is gender-related is not to claim that it is gender-specific, i.e. that men are never ashamed; it is only to claim that women are more prone to experience the emotion in question and that the feeling itself has a different meaning in relation to their total psychic situation and general social location than has a similar emotion when experienced by men.[10]

Men may feel shame at failing to attain levels of power, influence or success expected of them *as men*, while for women shame may be a kind of generalised condition of being a woman in the world. Shame, then, traditionally signals a loss, lack or failure of masculinity on the part of men, but is part of the condition of – indeed, is constitutive of – femininity; so male and female shame, as Bartky explains here, have different meanings (and effects) psychically and socially. The shame that Bartky characterises as feminine is manifested as 'a pervasive sense of personal inadequacy' and 'a pervasive affective attunement to the social environment'.[11] As we have seen, subsequent critics have echoed Bartky's claim that 'the female socialization process can be viewed as a prolonged immersion in shame',[12] though the gendering of shame (as feminine) actually receives relatively little attention in philosophical, psychoanalytical and queer accounts of it – an oversight that this book seeks to correct.

Koestenbaum echoes the idea of shame as a *loss* or failure of masculinity, thus witnessing a humiliated man 'fills [him] with horror'; but he also feels that the 'maleness' of the humiliated man 'has received a necessary puncture'.[13] Yet if Koestenbaum's reflections on humiliation seem to offer a more radical take on the relation of shame and humiliation to gender, they still betray their grounding in a more conventional account. Humiliation, on his (avowedly subjective and idiosyncratic) reading, equals a 'collapse' of maleness, but not of femaleness – indeed, it is arguably a confirmation of femaleness; Koestenbaum notes that, 'from some points of view, womanliness or femininity is a humiliated quality'.[14] Our understanding of humiliation and shame, then, both proceeds from and confirms, even perpetuates, a binaristic understanding of gender. If we view shame as functioning, in Freudian terms, as a kind of 'watchman' or 'guardian', what it polices is not 'morality' (the Freudian view) so much as patriarchal gender norms.[15] As became clear in the last chapter, the argument underpinning this book goes further than this, suggesting that shame has an active role in the cultural production of gender, not merely a reactive and regulatory role; in other words, I am arguing here that shame is one of the ways, perhaps even the most significant and pervasive way, in which gender is produced in the first place.

If men and women stand in different relations to shame, then it is predictable that they would write it differently. There is, as Connor notes, 'a strong male tradition of attempting to write the weakness of shame' – he mentions Melville, Kafka, Beckett, Genet and Coetzee.[16] However, those attempts to 'write the weakness of shame' are frequently read as engagements with some more abstract, structural and generalised form of shame, thus lifting them out of the realm of the narrowly personal; they are read, that is to say, as interventions of a philosophical and/or moral tenor. For example, while Saul Friedländer does connect Kafka's 'shame and guilt' to the biographical details of his life, finding evidence of homoeroticism in his writings,[17] John Updike reads Kafka's shame as *representative*, '[epitomizing] one aspect of [the] modern mind-set: a sensation of anxiety and shame whose center cannot be located and therefore cannot be placated'.[18] As Brendan Moran explains, Walter Benjamin's take on Kafka similarly views the latter's shame as decidedly impersonal:

> Not strictly shame that one might feel as personal shame (as shame about oneself in relation to other human beings), the gesture [of shame] emerges as *philosophic shame about human history* – about laws or any other measures that indicate a presumption to deal with, somehow overcome, the 'Vorwelt'.[19]

In writing of examples such as Coetzee and Conrad, Timothy Bewes works from the premise that shame 'is not a subjective emotion' and that it 'is not accessible, nor does writing resolve or enable us to "work through" our shame'.[20] Bewes's choice of Coetzee is unsurprising – as he notes, 'the works of few contemporary novelists can be said to be as consistently riven by shame as those of J. M. Coetzee' – but also instructive, because shame for Coetzee becomes, increasingly, a question of 'the disgrace of being alive in these times',[21] a philosophical question of how to inhabit modernity and how to take on the political crimes of the past and present (apartheid, the Holocaust, the War on Terror): questions seemingly divorced from more personal matters of individual identity and gendered shame. And yet, Coetzee has notably used acts of gendered violence (the rapes in *Disgrace* and *Diary of a Bad Year*) as especially resonant examples of shame, shaming and shamelessness. Noting the attacks on female characters in *Diary of a Bad Year* and Salman Rushdie's *Shame*, Bewes concedes that 'For both writers, the question of women's sexual shame is an overdetermined one,' and despite the seeming attempt in *Diary* 'to right the wrong that is done to the woman', 'what we have, indisputably and irreducibly, is a male novelist ventriloquizing a female character'.[22] We could add that, in both novels, the sexual shaming of women (through rape) is used to exemplify some wider social shame or is presented as a paradigmatic case of shame; so female bodies become tropes or signifiers – and what they signify best, most easily, is shame.

In *The Event of Postcolonial Shame*, one of Bewes's inaugural examples – Joseph Conrad's short story *The Return* – bears out this point. In *The Return*, a man returns home to find a letter from his wife of five years telling him that she has left him for someone else; when he discovers she has gone, 'there was nothing but humiliation. Nothing else.'[23] He feels 'a personal sense of undeserved abasement' and thinks, 'If only she had died! Certain words would have been said to him in a sad tone, and he, with proper fortitude, would have made appropriate answers.'[24] He feels himself spied upon by 'emissaries of a distracted mankind' and is 'disgusted with himself, with the loathsome rush of emotion breaking through all the reserves that guarded his manhood';[25] what shame he feels on his own behalf, then, is due to a perceived failure of his 'manhood'. He thinks, at this moment, that:

> Passion is the unpardonable and secret infamy of our hearts, a thing to curse, to hide and to deny; a shameless and forlorn thing that tramples upon the smiling promises, that tears off the placid mask, that strips the body of life. And it had come to him! It had laid its unclean hand upon the spotless draperies of his existence, and he had to face it alone with all the world looking on.[26]

His wife seems to him 'a monster' – 'that abased woman';[27] and her alleged 'depravity'[28] appears to spread out and 'contaminate' all around him. Shame is, again, contagious, transmissible – and women are its vehicle, its host:

> The contamination of her crime spread out, tainted the universe, tainted himself; woke up all the dormant infamies of the world; caused a ghastly kind of clairvoyance in which he could see the towns and fields of the earth, its sacred places, its temples and its houses, peopled by monsters – by monsters of duplicity, lust, and murder. She was a monster – he himself was thinking monstrous thoughts . . . and yet he was like other people.[29]

Bewes comments that 'What is so shameful is not that the husband has lived in a delusion exposed by the betrayal, but that he has been thrust, thereby, into a world of desolate unintelligibility.'[30] Bewes uses this example to argue that 'Shame is an event of incommensurability: a profound disorientation of the subject by the confrontation with an object it cannot comprehend, an object that renders incoherent every form available to the subject.'[31] The shame of Conrad's protagonist is, however, all too coherent and comprehensible. There is no acknowledgement, in Bewes's reading: first, of the deliberate hyperbole and hypocrisy of the man's reaction, which hardly induces the reader to feel sympathy for him;[32] and second, that the social 'shame' produced in this situation is a product of particular, carefully circumscribed and maintained gender politics and relations, and that shame is revealed as something profoundly connected to and associated with female bodies, with the 'impenetrable duplicity' of women – and their illicit, unknowable desires.[33] The man's social shame here is produced by the violation of his 'property':

> He could not help remembering her footsteps, the rustle of her dress, her way of holding her head, her decisive manner of saying 'Alvan,' the quiver of her nostrils when she was annoyed. All that had been so much his property, so intimately and specially his! He raged in a mournful, silent way, as he took stock of his losses. He was like a man counting the cost of an unlucky speculation [. . .].[34]

Were his wife not viewed (by himself and others) as his property, the 'shame' would be different or even non-existent – at the very least, it would not be *his* shame. Furthermore, what is 'unintelligible' or what cannot be 'comprehended' here is that his wife might have desires – desires for more than the social status and security her marriage to him has afforded her – and might act on them.

In addition, while Bewes's rejection of a redemptive or cathartic logic in the writing of shame is admirable, his assertion that the shame one experiences as one writes is a shame 'at the inadequacy of writing' elides the extent to which that shame – and what he also describes as 'the discontinuity of the self, its otherness to itself' in shame – might work differently for writers identifying and identified as female (his examples are all male authors), who might experience 'shame', 'discontinuity' of self and 'otherness' in distinct (and distinctly gendered) ways.[35] Shame's rendering as 'philosophic' and/or 'ethical' in these instances both depersonalises it – in the process degendering it – and renders its presentation heroic, authentic and intellectually admirable.

As Connor notes, women writers have generally sought to '[write] themselves out of shame rather than into it';[36] as I have shown, their efforts to do so have often been read as definitively personal, confessional and embodied. The preceding chapters demonstrate that the tendency to see literary engagements with shame as broadly critical and redemptive, part of a process of *overcoming* or conquering shame, is a common one. The editors of *Scenes of Shame*, for example, set literature up in contrast to traditional psychoanalytical discourse, as providing 'a privileged place of redress, a sphere of expression where emotional life can be explored and refined in ways that are discouraged elsewhere', claiming that 'in art and literature, shame and repression are diminished, and the richness of emotional life [. . .] is investigated in its complexity'.[37] Moreover, that tendency is particularly marked in the case of women writers. It is the 'redemptive' aspect of women's writing on/of shame that is picked up, for example, by J. Brooks Bouson in her readings of Toni Morrison and others, whom she portrays as seeking a 'remedy to shame' and as 'providing a very powerful critique of the cultural narratives that shame women';[38] Erica Johnson and Patricia Moran, meanwhile, identifying shame as 'a marker of female humanity', characterise the representation of shame in women's writing as redemptive, 'defiant' and 'courageous', suggesting that, 'by bringing gendered shame out into the open, by representing it, this volume [*The Female Face of Shame*] will help to counteract shame's mortifying influence in women's lives'.[39] Meanwhile, as I discussed in Chapter 2, when women authors engage with supposedly shameful topics in more ambivalent, less redemptive ways, they are apt to receive censure for doing so. Does this then make it easier for male authors to 'meet with' shame – or does it only give them licence to write about 'shameful' topics? Is an admission of shame even possible without a compromising – rather than, more positively, a transformation – of conventional masculinity? Must it involve a transmutation of shame into guilt (which Connor terms 'the desire to get shame to run along guilt's grooves') or into masochism (and thus into another kind of dominance, through willed subjection)?[40] As Connor asserts, 'male shame [. . .] has a crudely and traditionally heroic aspect [. . .]. It is hard for men to write in shame without attempting to coin glory from it.'[41]

Shame displaced: Amis and Roth

At first glance, recent novels by established, canonical authors such as Ian McEwan, Martin Amis and Philip Roth evince a notable concern with masculine shame, with sexual embarrassment and disappointment, impotence, mortality and the ageing male body – consider, for example, *The Dying Animal* (2001), *On Chesil Beach* (2007), *Exit Ghost* (2007), *The Humbling* (2009) and *The Pregnant Widow*

(2010). However, these apparent interventions into the sphere of masculine shame too often bear out Connor's central point that, from the standpoint of masculinity, shame too easily becomes a form of heroism, a badge of pride. Additionally, the *apparent* confession of shame and vulnerability is, in these novels, too often mitigated by the ultimate displacement of that shame upon female bodies.

Peter Boxall reads Philip Roth's twenty-first-century fiction as exploring what he identifies as a 'conjoined aesthetic and political lateness':

> His recent novels – *The Dying Animal, Everyman, Indignation, Exit Ghost, The Humbling* – have turned obsessively around the experience of exhaustion, the dwindling, failing or expiring of the narrative voice, of the male body, and of the literary talent. For Roth's narrators the experience of entering into the twenty-first century has felt like the entry into a kind of posthumousness, into a life that outlives itself, that persists beyond its own death [. . .].[42]

Boxall's reading picks up on a recurrent set of themes and preoccupations in Roth's post-2000 fiction. However, the 'dwindling, failing or expiring' that recurs in these recent novels is, I would suggest, inseparable from a sense of *shame* at the diminishment of artistic and bodily powers, and inseparable also from Roth's career-long concern with *masculinity*. The 'posthumousness' that is explored, therein, is a kind of afterlife of masculinity and is framed generally as a crisis: what can masculinity be if it is no longer intellectual, creative and physically dominant? To what extent does male ageing produce something like an emasculated (and therefore shameful) state? To what extent is the actual or imminent loss of sexual potency figured as a loss of *masculinity itself*? As Lynne Segal notes:

> Roth is a writer who rarely strays far or for too long from his depictions of the vulnerabilities shadowing the phallic fears and yearnings that trouble and endanger men such as himself as they journey onwards from youth into middle and then old age.[43]

Such vulnerabilities are, indeed, a product of – and utterly inextricable from – those 'phallic fears and yearnings', and seem to be intimately bound up with Roth's experience and representation of masculinity. Segal suggests that, from an early stage in his career, 'Roth's interest in men's power, authority and sexual prowess is always threatened by the frailty of the body servicing them, merging with a pre-occupation with ageing and its humiliations.'[44] If ageing is potentially humiliating for both men and women, in Roth's fictions we find a special kind of 'humbling' – *The Humbling*, of course, is the title of one of his more recent forays into these topics – which is, however, stubbornly resistant to the absolute relinquishment of masculine authority. The 'vulnerabilities', 'frailty' and 'humiliations' with which many of his novels engage are always counteracted by the relative social status, cultural power and narrative authority of the protagonist in each instance; furthermore, the various female bodies that people Roth's recent texts (as objects of desire or disgust – or both) '[emerge] as little more than eroticized assemblages of soft tissue and orifices', as Segal argues, taking on the burden of a shame that his male protagonists can only briefly entertain.[45]

Writing on *Exit Ghost*, Boxall asserts that 'Roth's late artist [the protagonist of *Exit Ghost*], exhausted and impotent, finds in the dwindling of body and of talent a failure also of the capacity to give a voice to the time in which he finds himself cast away'.[46] Yet while this contextualisation forms part of Boxall's highly persuasive arguments concerning shifts in our understanding of temporality, belatedness, 'late style', and history in the twenty-first century, it elides the specifically gendered nature of Roth's engagements with these questions, which are instead presented as supra-personal, disembodied and non-gendered: matters of style and matters of the human condition, rather than scenes of a peculiarly masculine 'impotence', shame and crisis. The 'lateness' with which Boxall concerns himself (derived from Edward W. Said's arguments in *On Late Style*) is the kind that 'does not find reconciliation at the end of a life, or "a sense of resolution", but instead rests on a kind of out-of-jointness, [a] kind of failure of the sense of time'.[47] This is Said's 'artistic lateness not as harmony and resolution but as intransigence, difficulty, and unresolved contradiction', as he seeks to explore 'the experience of late style that involves a nonharmonious, nonserene tension, and above all, a sort of deliberately unproductive productiveness going *against*'.[48] As with the critical responses to Kafka cited previously, the invocation of 'late style' – itself a notably gendered phenomenon[49] – reconceptualises and reframes the presentation of masculine shame and crisis, lending to that presentation an authority that is ultimately redemptive, exculpatory or heroic, however much it resists 'resolution' and 'productiveness'. As will become evident, my reading of Roth and Amis seeks to bring that shame (and its more troubling displacements) back into focus.

In Roth's *The Dying Animal*, the 'vulnerability' of the ageing male professor narrator, David Kepesh, is his vulnerability 'to female beauty'; as a form of weakness it is more indiscipline than powerlessness.[50] Indeed, after informing his largely silent (and never identified) interlocutor of this 'vulnerability', he immediately compares his situation to a Mark Twain story about a man chased by a bull, describing his young female students as his 'meat'.[51] Of Consuela, the twenty-four-year-old student with whom the sixty-two-year-old professor will proceed to have an affair, he says: 'I saw right away that this was going to be my girl.'[52] From the first time they sleep together, Kepesh declares himself 'all weakness and worry from then on' – mainly because of his anxiety that she does not really desire him; later he writes of 'the humiliation and endless uncertainty' of being with her.[53] He worries constantly about younger men luring her away; this is not just a case of sexual jealousy but is bound up with his view of his own ageing body (which, however, is never described). The double bind of his 'vulnerability' and what distinguishes it from any vulnerability that she may feel is evident in statements such as 'I don't feel the authority with her that's necessary for my stability, and yet she comes to me because of that authority'; and 'How do I capture Consuela? The thought is morally humiliating, yet there it is.'[54] His authority is unstable but it is not evanescent; she has no such authority, beyond the 'power' of her body to attract him; and while he may fail to 'capture' her and may feel, consequently, 'humiliated', that humiliation is a product of his sense of entitlement, his possessiveness and her (social and sexual) status as trophy.

Indeed, Kepesh's attraction to Consuela relies on her own apparent dearth of agency and desire; as he notes, 'What could be more erotic in that situation than the seeming absence in the exciting woman of any erotic intention?'[55] Meanwhile, Consuela remains all body, in the descriptions of her. Even after they break up, Kepesh notes 'the trademark Modigliani nude [. . .] that Consuela had chosen to send, so immodestly, through the U.S. mail. A nude whose full breasts, full and canting a bit to the side, might well have been modelled on her own.'[56]

The 'immodesty' is hers here, rather than the artist's – or the recipient's (in his imagined conflation of art object and desired body) – just as the (implied) shamelessness is hers when he possessively imagines her 'unashamedly walking the streets of the world for all to covet and admire'.[57] When Kepesh is playing the piano and talking to her, while she stands next to him, 'when she advances to examine the dial [of the metronome that he is describing], her breasts pitch forward to cover my mouth and to stifle, momentarily, the pedagogy – the pedagogy that with Consuela is my greatest power. My only power.'[58] Her only power, then, is through her body, and he is literally silenced/stifled by her breasts – an image both erotic and anxious, in which Consuela's body evokes the body of a smothering or domineering mother; she, however, remains largely silent (or at least, her words are unrecorded) in *The Dying Animal*.

Segal asserts that, in Roth's writing:

> The desiring male inevitably fears quite as much as he craves the female objects of his desire, seeing their responsiveness as the source of man's sense of power, and also inevitably, sooner or later, their unresponsiveness as his downfall. This is surely why those receiving Roth's protagonists' passion so regularly appear reduced to the fetishized, fresh, firm and juicy 'tits and cunts and legs and lips and mouths and tongues and assholes', which once propelled young Portnoy's masturbatory frenzy.[59]

This reduction of woman to body parts means that, ultimately, any seeming reversal of power is illusory and transitory. When Consuela makes contact with David again a few years later, it is to tell him that she has breast cancer and will have a mastectomy, and to ask him to 'say goodbye' to her breasts (and, by implication, to her desirability).[60] The 'dying animal' of the title, then, is perhaps her rather than him (despite still being young, she 'now knows the wound of age' – a phrase previously used by Kepesh to describe himself),[61] and she becomes before him again a naked, vulnerable body. She arrives at his apartment 'in this bizarrely wretched way' and this seems to kill his desire for her, as 'I knew hers was no longer a sexual life'.[62] How does he know this? While the cancer might alter her relationship with her breasts, at least temporarily, this need not necessarily strip her of her libido; and if her sexual attractiveness to (some) others is diminished, this does not mean that her own desires are thereby quelled. More revealingly, Kepesh asks himself whether, if Consuela came to him in future and asked him to sleep with her, he would be able to do it, and comments: 'In all my years, I've never slept with a woman who has been mutilated in this manner.'[63] Velichka Ivanova argues that 'The prospect of her death renders [Kepesh's] self-defensive misogyny senseless,'[64] but in fact his response to her illness (his continuing lack of attention to her thoughts and opinions,[65] his continuing preoccupation with her body, his desexualising of her, his implied disgust at her 'sick' body) illustrates too starkly the shameless continuation of his misogyny. Even in her fear and sickness, she barely becomes a real and rounded human being in his eyes, and the 'threat' she represents to his solipsism and selfishness is in fact magnified by her illness and by the emotional commitment it seems to require of him: the novel ends with his hitherto silent interlocutor telling him that if he does go to the hospital to be with Consuela, 'you're finished'.[66] If the novel functions formally, ostensibly as a confession (complete with attentive, silent confessor), Kepesh admits little in the way of guilt or shame for his behaviour and its effects on those around him, and despite the obvious intimations of mortality and fear of impotence dotted throughout the text, the shamed bodies here are always female.[67]

Amis's *The Pregnant Widow* opens with the claim that 'This is the story of a sexual trauma', which 'ruined him for twenty-five years'.[68] What is the nature of this ruination, this trauma? Certainly, it involves a kind of sexual shame or, more precisely, a bewilderment, on the part of protagonist Keith Nearing, in the face of the changing rules of sexual engagement. (And if 'rules of engagement' sounds like too combative a phrase, it is deliberately so, for Amis cannot get beyond the view of the relationship between men and women as comprising a 'battle of the sexes'.) On Amis's reading, these changes spell shame for both men and women: men are 'shamed' by feminism (they bear their masculinity, consequently, *as shame*), but women suffer the greater shame for violating the codes of femininity. On male versus female shame, Connor writes that:

> Women are shamed for breaking out, men are ashamed of falling short. Female shame has mostly been regulatory and disciplinary. [. . .] Male shame has traditionally not been the shame of having overstepped the mark, of having exceeded definitions, but the shame of failing to exceed definition as such.[69]

Female shame remains, in *The Pregnant Widow*, 'regulatory and disciplinary'.

While the suggestion from the outset is that it is men – poor, bewildered, traumatised men – who are the primary victims of the social changes of the 1960s and 1970s, and women who are the traumatisers, it is ruined female bodies that bear the shame of the unstable, shifting mores of the sexual revolution.[70] This is evident even in the epigraph that gives the novel its title, Alexander Herzen's assertion (in another context altogether – revolutionary Russian socialism in the nineteenth century) that

> The death of the contemporary forms of social order ought to gladden rather than trouble the soul. Yet what is frightening is that the departing world leaves behind it not an heir, but a pregnant widow. Between the death of one and the birth of the other, much water will flow by, a long night of chaos and desolation will pass.[71]

Setting aside the hyperbolic, inflammatory nature of this language when applied to feminism – 'frightening', 'chaos', 'desolation' – what is notable here is that 'the death of the contemporary forms of social order' equals the death of *man*, and woman is not a person in her own right, but rather a 'widow' and (to appropriate Margaret Atwood's suggestive phrase) 'ambulatory chalice'.[72] She is a transitional figure between past and future, defined as suffering/bereaved and situated only in relation to others (the child is presumably male), her body a vehicle for the future/child/heir but not itself part of that future (and that 'pregnancy' here, implicitly itself a kind of ruination – lending new resonance to Shulamith Firestone's declaration that 'pregnancy is barbaric').[73]

Within the novel itself, it is again female bodies that bear the brunt of shame. Keith's sister's Violet, who has no real voice of her own in the novel but who appears through Keith's memories and letters exchanged with his brother, is notable mainly for her 'extreme sexual delinquency'; she is, we are told, 'the kind of girl who dates football teams'.[74] Ultimately, it is her apparent shamelessness – her alcoholism and her promiscuity – that is presented as killing her: she dies of a heart attack at the age of forty-six. In interviews around the book's publication, Amis reiterated the suggestion that the 'chaos' and 'desolation' of the sexual/feminist revolution had been visited

upon women's bodies, in his acknowledgement that Violet is modelled on his sister Sally Amis, who he described as 'pathologically
promiscuous' and 'one of the most spectacular victims of the revolution'.[75] Sally, he claimed, 'was just harming herself', as were other
women caught up in the 'equalitarian phase' of feminism in 'going
against their natures' by 'behaving like [boys]'.[76] Whether this behaviour invites shame/shaming or merely confirms the already latent and
inescapable shamefulness of femininity is, in *The Pregnant Widow*,
hard to decipher.

Visiting Violet in 'the Church Army Hostel for Young Women',
Keith asks Gloria, 'Why are the girls so silent?', and she replies,
'Because they've been shamed beyond words.'[77] Indeed, Violet loses
any ability or right to speak for herself, becoming simply a shamed/
ruined body, to be 'levered' out from under some unsuitable man
each morning.[78] Her speech is debased, disintegrating, just as her
body is: 'It really is remarkable: to attempt so little in the way of
language – and to bugger *that* up,' thinks Keith, 'Wiv, fanks, elfy: the
explanation for all this would belatedly occur to him.'[79] In his extra-
textual musings about Sally/Violet, Amis comments that

> you would have needed the Taliban to control her. If she'd been
> conditioned by a really strong culture of self-denial, she might have
> made it, although in any kind of shame-and-honour arrangement she
> would already have been killed by her father, her uncle and brother.[80]

Amis, despite his anti-Islamic sentiments within and beyond the
novel, actually sets great store by a 'shame-and-honour' culture and
The Pregnant Widow arguably enacts a secular version of such a
culture in its treatment of its female characters.

When the character of Gloria Beautyman is first introduced, her
arrival at the Italian castle is explained summarily: 'She's in disgrace
and she's being packed off to purdah.'[81] The disgrace is, crucially,
'sexual disgrace', involving drunkenness and infidelity, thanks to
which 'she almost died of shame';[82] when she finally appears, Gloria is
(apparently) meekly compliant with this image of her, appearing in 'a
slightly furry dark-blue one-piece' swimsuit, striking in its 'awkward
modesty', and described by the other girls as 'awful', 'virginal' and
'spinsterish'.[83] The central episode around which the novel pivots, and
the key moment of Keith's sexual 'trauma', involves a pornographic

encounter between Keith and Gloria in the bathroom of the Italian castle where the group of twentysomethings are spending the summer. In this encounter, Gloria is revealed to be fraudulent in her assumed piety and aggressive in her sexuality; she is, she tells him, 'a cock. And we're very rare – girls who are cocks.'[84] Yet this sexual confidence is itself revealed to be fraudulent, in its turn; and whilst Keith's sexual adventuring leaves him ultimately undamaged – he ends the novel happily married and a father several times over, at peace with himself, his history, his ageing, 'his' women – Gloria's promiscuity can only be an expression of a desire for punishment. Witness, for example, this final scene in their subsequent relationship, years after the initial encounter:

> That night they had sex for the first time in nearly a month, and there was a sour caloricity to it, as if they both had fevers and all their bones ached, with savoury breath and savoury sweat. It drew to an end. And with embarrassing copiousness he followed her four-word instruction. Gloria rose and went to the bathroom, and when she returned she was dressed in black.
>
> 'Notre Dame,' she said through her veil. 'Midnight mass.'
>
> He awoke at three in an empty bed with the image of a black shape in the brown Seine, the drifting tresses, the open eyes . . . She was in the other room, kneeling naked on the window seat and looking out at the moonlit square. She turned. Her face was a death mask, encrusted with dried white.
>
> 'I need it to be stronger,' she said. 'Much stronger. It's just not strong enough.'
>
> Gloria wanted a stronger god. One who would strike her down, there and then, for what she wore behind her veil.[85]

As Connor attests, shame 'belongs to the skin'; it is figured 'in blush or blemish or stigma' – 'in my shame I am nothing but face' – and here Gloria bears the mark of sexual shame upon her face.[86] In his invocation of the 'veil', Amis again invokes a 'shame-and-honour culture' in which the female body is both an object of desire (to be endlessly looked upon, scrutinised) and a source of shame (to be hidden away; inviting punishment – that 'stronger god'; inviting destruction). The veil also has racial and religious connotations, of course.

Ayşe Naz Bulamur claims that Amis is 'a writer who is engaged with sexual politics', and reads him as showing 'how women paid the price of the manifestos that separated sex from emotion', asserting that 'his historical analysis of the changing concepts of sex and female roles since the revolution counters the claims of sexism'.[87] However, she gives no details of these 'manifestos' or of Amis's supposed 'historical analysis'; nor does she explain why women would have 'paid the price' and men not. I read the text quite differently, suggesting that, in *The Pregnant Widow*, female shame is disciplinary and systemic. Katha Pollitt claims that the message of the novel is that 'the removal of social constraints [. . .] places women at risk – they are more vulnerable to men's heedless drives and less able to control their own'.[88] Even setting aside that problematically binary understanding of vulnerability on Amis's part, it is evident in the novel that shame belongs to women for their (supposed) lack of control, in a way that it does not belong to men for their (supposed) 'heedless drives'. (Clearly, neither men nor women come off well in this reductive equation, but the male characters are not shamed in the persistent, irrevocable, disciplinary way that the female characters are.) Acknowledging the distinction between the kind of shame that 'is a tonic episode in the life of a subject' and the 'systemic sense of undervaluation' considered by Frantz Fanon (in *Black Skin, White Masks*) and Sandra Bartky (in *Femininity and Domination*), Connor concedes that 'the kind of shame which allows one room to reserve judgement on oneself is not really shame at all'.[89] For Keith, such shame as he experiences can be no more than 'a tonic episode', whilst the shame of Violet and Gloria, respectively, pertains to a 'systemic sense of undervaluation'; fundamentally, Amis refuses to challenge that system or question that undervaluation; he cannot, or will not, face up to the shame of being a man.

Certainly, though, the novel displays some awareness of the fact that, as Connor avers, 'masculinity is a crashed category, the very name of ruin', as Keith reflects on the ignominiousness of his sexual history.[90] He seems to declare his shame and yet, writes Connor, to say 'I am ashamed' is 'self-falsifying': 'The moment that you can say you are ashamed, you break free of shame's suffocating clasp and start puffing the pungent whiff of imposture.'[91] Amis's novel, I argue, performs such an 'imposture' – it gestures towards the 'shame of being a man', whilst producing, at best, what Connor terms 'precautionary guilt' (and, in fact, arguably not even that); it hints at a recognition of masculinity as 'a crashed category', whilst reasserting, regardless, the 'need' to be a man and consigning shame, ultimately, to the sphere of femininity.

Roth's novel – at first glance – appears to tell a different kind of story about the sexual revolution and about the women (a generation younger than the protagonist) pursuing sexual pleasure; such women, epitomised by the promiscuous Janie Wyatt and calling themselves the 'Gutter Girls', are more concerned with pleasure than politics.[92] They are, muses Kepesh, 'the first wave of American girls fully implicated in their own desire. No rhetoric, no ideology, just the playing field of pleasure opening out to the bold.'[93] Yet, even in *The Dying Animal*, there is a dose of retribution meted out to these sexual pioneers, despite the initially admiring and nostalgic way in which they are described. As Kepesh concedes, 'Thirty years later, a Janie Wyatt degenerates into an Amy Fisher, slavishly servicing the auto mechanic all on her own,'[94] comparing Wyatt to a real-life American woman, nicknamed 'the Long Island Lolita', who, aged sixteen, started an affair with a thirty-five-year-old married man and, aged seventeen, in 1992, shot his wife. Fisher was imprisoned for several years, and since her release has worked in pornographic films and reality television, while struggling with alcoholism and addiction problems. Is this implied 'degeneration' of Wyatt into Fisher an indication of what will happen to those individual women who pursued pleasure during the so-called sexual revolution? (Kepesh's estranged, disapproving son, in an angry letter to his father years later, asks, 'Janie Wyatt, where is *she* now? How many failed marriages? How many breakdowns? In what psychiatric hospital has she been a patient for lo these many years?'[95]) Or is the critique here levelled at society, lamenting the degeneration of the sexual ideals promulgated by the 'Gutter Girls', such that now the pursuit of sex is less about pleasure and more about money, celebrity and calculated scandal (as the case of Fisher all too clearly illustrates), any pleasure leeched out of it? Either way, the nomenclature in both novels is telling. Women are 'cocks' or 'Gutter Girls' when they pursue sex for pleasure and self-empowerment; men simply *have* cocks and manage to avoid the gutter, even when their behaviour has been as licentious as possible. In *The Pregnant Widow*, the women who have sought sexual pleasure and excitement most avidly – Gloria, Rita (known disparagingly as 'the Dog') and Violet – end up miserable, childless and lonely – or dead; the more virtuous Scheherazade, meanwhile, who discovers that she cannot be promiscuous, retains her youthful good looks, marries her boyfriend and is a mother several times over, rewarded (even if also gently mocked) for her piety.

In both novels, the narration treads a fine line between desire for and disgust at the female body, figuring it as both source of power and locus of shame. In *The Pregnant Widow*, the day following Gloria's abasement-by-semen, and in the penultimate scene of Keith and Gloria's relationship:

> She was all ice and electricity, all electricity and ice. In a white cotton dress and with narrow white ribbons in her hair, she darkly established herself on the white sofa. [. . .]
>
> Just after one o'clock Gloria stood up suddenly. Her mouth opened and stayed open in disbelief and what seemed to be glee as she looked down at the sudden sarong of scarlet that swathed her hips. And on the sofa behind her, not a shapeless path but a burning orb, like a sunset.[96]

Whatever its surface purity, coolness and restraint/discipline – the white dress and ribbons, her appearance of 'ice' and 'electricity' – Gloria's recalcitrant body betrays its heat and colour (the 'burning orb' of menstrual blood, 'like a sunset'), again marking her. While she does not appear to be shamed by what has happened – expressing 'what seemed to be glee' – this episode of menstruation-as-spectacle foregrounds her unruly femaleness, while also hinting at her racial otherness (both the 'sarong' and the 'burning orb' conjure foreign-ness – the latter perhaps also an act of God, striking her down at last) and the truth of her age (in Gloria's comment – 'that's all finished with' – we can find an allusion to the menopause and to the supposed end of her life of desire and fertility).[97]

The menstruating female body as source of anxiety, shame – and ostensible power – also appears in *The Dying Animal*. One of Consuela's boyfriends when she is sixteen likes to watch her men-struate; Kepesh asks if he can also do this, commenting: 'Men have always been her mirror. They even want to watch her menstruate. She is the female magic men cannot escape.'[98] Figuring the female body as something mystical, 'magic', might seem to imbue it with power but the mythologising impulse keeps that body 'other', denying Consuela more useful and durable powers (of intelligence and articu-lacy) and slyly labelling her as vain; men are 'her mirror' – without them, therefore, she cannot see herself, so this is dependency rather than agency. When Consuela does bleed for him, Kepesh narrates it as follows:

> Then came the night that Consuela pulled out her tampon and stood there in my bathroom, with one knee dipping towards the other and, like Mantegna's Saint Sebastian, bleeding in a trickle down her thighs while I watched. Was it thrilling? Was I delighted? Was I mesmerized? Sure, but again I felt like a boy. I had set out to demand the most from her, and when she shamelessly obliged, I wound up again intimidating myself. There seemed to be nothing to be done – if I wished not to be humbled completely by her exotic matter-of-factness – except to fall to my knees to lick her clean. Which she allowed to happen without comment. Making me into a still smaller boy.[99]

In the image of Consuela as 'Mantegna's Saint Sebastian' we see her once again reduced to an art object, her body aestheticised, idealised and tamed by Kepesh's educated, evaluating gaze; yet the description hints also at her coming martyrdom (whether or not her cancer proves terminal, she is little more than a sacrificial victim in Kepesh's narrative of his own ageing). Consuela is not obviously shamed by her bleeding body; in fact, the description of her while this is taking place is oddly reserved and indifferent – neither abject nor empowered. However, the humiliation (infantilisation, emasculation, intimidation) mimed by Kepesh ('I felt like a boy') implies that this leaking body to which he is submitting is a source or vehicle of *his* degradation, and that that degradation is the more pronounced because of the (despised, feared, feminine) nature of that vehicle. Furthermore, his claim that Consuela 'shamelessly' fulfilled his request implies a critical judgement of her for doing so, as if the revelation of her menstrual blood *should* be shameful. Later, Kepesh's friend George warns him that, with Consuela, 'You'll never be in charge,' claiming that he 'lost the sense of separation essential to your enjoyment', on the night when she took out her tampon and Kepesh got down on his knees:

> I'd say that constituted the abandonment of an independent critical position, Dave. Worship me, she says, worship the mystery of the bleeding goddess, and you do it. You stop at nothing. You lick it. You consume it. You digest it. *She* penetrates *you*. [. . .].[100]

The most shameful, disempowering thing for a man, on this reading, is to be 'penetrated' and to consume the effluvia of the female body; that male shame is, then, derived from or premised upon the more fundamental and inherent shamefulness of the female body itself.

It is worth noting also that, in both novels, the female bodies who are made to bear the shame of the male protagonists' 'crashed' masculinity are also *racially* othered, and thus consigned (simultaneously) to categories of the exotic, the degenerate and the enslaved. In *The Pregnant Widow*, the first (oblique) reference to Gloria and the sexual 'trauma' that Keith will experience at her hands comes immediately after a passage in which he reads about 'the torture cops' in Iraq. The narrative teases:

> He had his wound coming, a different kind of wound, in the castle in Italy. It was the sensory opposite of torture: her pincers of bliss, her lips, her fingertips. And what remained in the aftermath? Her manacles, her branding irons.[101]

Although this may be 'the sensory opposite of torture', Gloria ('her') is still figured as an Iraqi torturer – her racial otherness/foreignness identified as the source of her implied threat and the Iraq torture reference a hyperbolic foreshadowing of the role that she will play in Keith's life and sexual development (indeed, her function within the narrative is as a kind of sexual terrorist who, in blowing his life apart, also destroys her own). Thereafter, Gloria is described as 'being packed off to purdah' in the castle in Italy;[102] she is 'dark' in her colouring, and is mocked for the size of her bottom by the other girls, who give her the racist nickname 'Junglebum';[103] she refuses to sunbathe naked because 'I want to prove I'm a white woman';[104] and when Keith thinks later of Gloria's body, 'he saw something like a desert, he saw a beautiful Sahara, with its slopes and dunes and whorls, its shadows and sandy vapours and tricks of the light, its oases, its mirages', exoticising and othering her even – especially – in his desire for her;[105] in sex, she 'bares her white teeth in what seemed to be savage indignation'.[106] When her hinted-at 'secret', often alluded to ('Her middle, the omphalos, like the smelted convexity at the centre of a shield'),[107] is finally revealed, it combines the double shame of her true age (ten years older than she has claimed) and the fact that she was apparently born 'a Muslim' in Cairo and is, thus, 'a visit from outside history. [. . .] [A] visit from another clock.'[108]

If race is, seemingly, handled more benevolently in *The Dying Animal*, there is nevertheless an insistence on Consuela's Cubanness, which inflects not only how she looks (her 'black, black hair, glossy but ever so slightly coarse' and her 'sleek' pubic hair, 'like Asian hair')[109] and the way she dresses ('carefully, with quiet taste, [. . .] like an attractive secretary in a prestigious legal firm'),[110] but also her manners and way of speaking, her alleged exclusion from the refined (white) cultural world that Kepesh inhabits and she reveres, and the representation of her sexuality as 'Consuela Castillo, superclassically the fertile female of our mammalian species',[111] 'the instinctual girl bursting not just the container of her vanity but the captivity of her cozy Cuban home'.[112] If she is not described in terms of darkness and degeneration, as Gloria is in *The Pregnant Widow*, she is nevertheless exoticised, mythologised – she is 'dressed culturally in the decorous Cuban past, but her permissions flow from her vanity'[113] – and is fetishised for her racial otherness, despite her 'skin of a very white color, skin that, the moment you see it, makes you want to lick it';[114] she is racially other but still appealingly, reassuringly 'white'. Consuela's Cubanness is a major source of her erotic power for Kepesh, but it is also another structural reason (in addition to her gender, age and more limited education) for the ultimate unassailability of his position, however 'vulnerable' his obsession with Consuela may seem to make him.

These examples – *The Dying Animal* and *The Pregnant Widow* – imply an awareness of what Segal has elsewhere (and earlier) described as the 'masculinity in crisis' literature (in sociology, gender studies and so on) of the 1990s, but they can also be read as part of the 'backlash' against feminism that views the feminist attempt to 'reform masculinity' *as* a crisis, rather than a positive development.[115] To this, Segal responds:

> The "masculinity in crisis" literature is problematic insofar as it ignores the central issue: the pay-offs men receive (or hope to receive) from their claims to manhood. For while men everywhere express their anxieties and loss of former privileges, overall they are conceived of and remain the dominant sex.[116]

The 'source' of the crisis is not feminism, but the fact that masculinity 'condenses a certain engagement with power' that is 'largely unrealizable', and thus 'masculinity is always in crisis'.[117] Daniel Lea and Berthold Schoene, in their introduction to *Posting the Male*, suggest that masculinity has, in the contemporary period, 'become visible as a performative gender construct, and a rather frail and fraudulent one to boot', but they 'prefer to speak of masculinity as a gender "in transition" rather than a gender "in crisis"'.[118] Are more nuanced and suggestive literary engagements with masculinity and shame than Roth's and Amis's to be found – with a masculinity 'in transition' (or even, more pertinently, with *the shame of being a man*)?

'The feeling it gave me was one of femininity': Knausgaard's 'struggle' with shame

My final example in this chapter is the Norwegian writer Karl Ove Knausgaard, whose *My Struggle* series of six books (first published between 2009 and 2011 in Norway) has been a literary phenomenon in the Anglo-American world, garnering huge acclaim for its apparent reinvigoration of 'autofictional' writing, for its elaborate, obsessive (sometimes tedious) delivery of the minutiae of a life as well as that life's profundities, but also for its author's engagement with a particular species of masculine shame. In this section I will concentrate on the second volume of *My Struggle*, *A Man in Love* (2009/2014).

Among UK reviewers, Hari Kunzru takes up a familiar theme in claiming that 'The governing emotion of *My Struggle* is shame.'[119] Hermione Hoby avers that 'the most indelible moments tend to involve his own humiliation';[120] and Andrew Anthony writes that 'One aspect of Knausgaard's writing that is distinctly unusual for a modern writer in western Europe is its constant grappling with the question of shame.'[121] The author himself has noted in interview that

> 'When I wrote my first novel [*Out of the World*] my editor wrote the sleeve note and he called it "a monument of male shame". And it had never occurred to me that I was writing about male shame. It was so much a part of me that I didn't see it, didn't recognise it as shame.'[122]

Such a description immediately qualifies 'shame', suggesting the distinctive and unusual character of 'male shame', while the book as 'monument' is attributed a compensatory significance and stature. Toril Moi concurs that 'the experience of shame' is 'the predominant theme' in both *Out of the World* and *My Struggle*,[123] and she reads the latter, the series, as 'Knausgaard's struggle to escape his inauthenticity and become real, a struggle which takes the form of an obsession with the experience of shame'. [124] While conceding the elements of spectacle involved in Knausgaard's project, the likely 'pleasure in exposure', Kunzru also suggests that *My Struggle*

> takes on more than therapeutic importance when one considers the way shame functions as a sort of barrier to authenticity. We do something in private – cheat or steal or tell a lie. If our moral failing is exposed, we feel shame, not because we have transgressed, but because we have been observed in our transgression. Shame is essentially public, and the near-universal desire to avoid it is an effective form of social regulation. So, if your artistic project is to look at yourself without shame [. . .] in order to see yourself authentically, you must pay a social price. [. . .] Seen like this, *My Struggle* becomes an almost political exercise in transparency, a response to the 'always on' culture of cams and surveillance that has destroyed our old expectations of privacy.[125]

We might, however, ask some rather different questions of *My Struggle*, concerning its tacit presentation, through the shame narrative, of a failure of masculinity as a 'moral failing': what kind of 'authenticity' is Knausgaard seeking (or mourning the loss of)? And is the barrier to that 'authenticity' not 'shame', exactly, but rather shame-as-feminisation? (Are women always already inauthentic? Certainly, authenticity, like lateness, seems like a peculiarly male concern.) I will return to Moi's discussion of Knausgaard periodically through this section, but it is worth noting that she does not touch on his relationship with his father as the major source of his shame: Knausgaard may want to 'become real', but he also, more pressingly, wants to become a *real man*, in a way that his father both is and is not, even while labouring to define what a real man might be. Figuring Knausgaard's 'struggle' as a matter of authenticity/ inauthenticity has been central to the eulogising reception of the series in the Anglo-American literary scene, but it has also elided the gendered nature and gendering work of shame in the cultural sphere in which Knausgaard is operating; it implies that there *is* some 'authentic' version of masculinity, when in fact Knausgaard's series of books might be read more interestingly as revealing, precisely, masculinity's in-built conditions of failure (and thus the reason why it is 'always in crisis', as Segal claims), and it ignores the implicit or explicit denigration of femininity in the cultural rhetoric around shame and shaming. In the reading that follows, I concentrate on: the presentation of shame as feminisation – and feminisation as shameful; shame as a structure of painful visibility at odds with the series' own tendency to self-exposure; the difficulties and stylistic peculiarities of writing shame; and the Anglo-American reception of *My Struggle*, which has tended to recast Knausgaard's shame as a form of heroism, thus allowing him, whatever his intentions, to 'coin glory from it'.

Shame and/as feminisation

Lorin Stein, the editor-in-chief of the *Paris Review*, is one of many critics who praise Knausgaard's exploration of masculinity in the pages of *My Struggle*, claiming that 'If there's some kind of masculinity that's particular to our generation, we haven't had a writer who got it down before Karl Ove.'[126] This 'kind of masculinity', it appears, is one that is self-aware, self-critical, highly attuned to various feelings and experiences of shame and humiliation; that very attunement to shame, however, renders masculinity itself precarious and in need of reinforcement.

In interview, Knausgaard has said that 'he formed his views on male identity as a child growing up in the 1970s. He was teased by the other boys for being a "jessie" or gay.'[127] As he explains:

> 'I have all these notions of what it is to be a man. You shouldn't cry for instance [he spends many pages crying or trying to conceal his tears] and you shouldn't talk about feelings. I don't talk about feelings but I write a lot about feelings. Reading, that's feminine, writing, that's feminine. It is insane, it's really insane but it still is in me.'[128]

The first major instance of shame in the first volume of *My Struggle*, *A Death in the Family*, is provoked by Knausgaard's father's response to a news item that the young Karl Ove has asked him to watch, hoping but failing to make a point:

> After the item was over there was the sound of my father's voice, and laughter. The shame that suffused my body was so strong that I was unable to think. My innards seemed to blanch. The force of the sudden shame was the sole feeling from my childhood that could measure in intensity against that of terror, next to sudden fury, of course, and common to all three was the sense that I *myself* was being erased.[129]

Here, the experience of shame is an experience of erasure – the loss of a self not yet established – and in particular it is the father's identity that erases or cancels out the young Karl Ove's; the bodily force of shame also erases or shuts down any intellectual response that the boy might be able to marshal. Particularly through the first three volumes of *My Struggle*, Karl Ove's relationship with his father (and with the memory of his father, following the latter's death) is a decidedly combative, conflicted and contradictory one. It is a relationship defined by fear and shame (the shaming of Karl Ove by his father, but also, later, the shaming of his father via the revelation of the sordid circumstances of his death); it is also, however, a relationship of admiration and imitation to some extent (according to the traditional codes of masculinity). The father–son relationship in *My Struggle* takes masculinity as its primary scene of shame: Karl Ove wants to be a man, but not a man exactly like his father; his father shames him for being weak, unmanly (for crying, for his speech impediment, for failing to do brave things); yet his father is also an embarrassment to him in some situations, for his own failures of masculinity (his skiing style, the way he dives to catch crabs; he is both weaker and more fearsome than other people's fathers).

If writing becomes for Karl Ove a means of overcoming this sense of erasure and of countering his father's voice, it does not thereby vitiate his anxieties about his (inadequate) masculinity or exempt him from feelings of shame. Reflecting on the series as a whole, Siri Hustvedt argues that

> Knausgaard writes a lot about his 'feelings,' and he persists at it even when he is humiliated in the process [. . .]. Such fearless openness is

fascinating in anyone but may be more fascinating in a man because a man who reveals his feelings is at greater risk of being shamed for those revelations. He has farther to fall.[130]

If 'writing about feelings' is both feminine and shameful, it is recuperated, on this reading, by its presentation as 'fearless', as a form of 'risk'; something that might be considered banal or trivial in a novel or autobiography by a female writer becomes 'fascinating'. If men have 'farther to fall', that is only because women are already fallen, and shame is already integral to, and constitutive of, femininity.

In *A Man in Love*, Knausgaard writes frequently of what he sees as the feminisation of men in Norwegian society, but he figures this quite clearly as a symptom of the feminisation of public space and discourse, and as a kind of (personal and social) crisis. Thus children have become 'a sort of accessory', and too much public space is given over to discussing babies, birth and parenthood. And he opines:

> In the midst of this lunacy there was me trundling my child around like one of the many fathers who had evidently put fatherhood before all else. [. . .] [The] sight of these fathers always made me feel a little uncomfortable. I found it hard to take the feminised aspect of their actions, even though I did exactly the same and was as feminised as they were. The slight disdain I felt for men pushing buggies was, to put it mildly, a two-edged sword as for the most part I had one in front of me when I saw them.[131]

The language around fatherhood – in its new, apparently feminised form – is decidedly derogatory, as he describes 'men sinking everywhere into the thralls of softness and intimacy' – the action of 'sinking' implies both passivity and descent, signalling their disempowerment – and he scoffs that 'women may actually have desired these men with thin arms, large waistlines, shaven heads and black designer glasses' who discuss baby things.[132] (In saying this, of course, he implies that women do *not* really desire them, or should not.) Trapped as he feels, in his relationship with his wife Linda, 'I walked around Stockholm's streets, modern and feminised, with a furious nineteenth-century man inside me.'[133] Anger (a proper masculine emotion, by implication) becomes a response to the shameful position he feels compelled to occupy – 'modern and feminised', emasculated, disempowered, undesirable.

The apogee of his experience of fatherhood as humiliating occurs when he takes his small daughter to the 'Rhythm Time' class, with an attractive teacher (who he 'would have liked to bed'): 'My own deep voice sounded like an affliction in the choir of high-pitched women's voices,' he writes; 'I wasn't embarrassed, it wasn't embarrassing sitting there, it was humiliating and degrading.'[134]

> [Sitting] there I was rendered completely harmless, without dignity, impotent, there was no difference between me and her [the teacher], except that she was more attractive, and the levelling, whereby I had forfeited everything that was me, even my size, and that voluntarily, filled me with rage.[135]

His masculinity is itself shameful here (his 'deep voice' like 'an affliction'), but so is his feminisation, most clearly expressed through his literal loss of stature and his symbolic 'impotence'. Again, his response to humiliation is anger: 'Outside on the street I felt like shouting till my lungs burst and smashing something. But I had to make do with putting as many metres between me and this hall of shame in the shortest possible time.'[136] The hyperbolic nature of his response tends towards hysteria (that most feminised of states), but also, in its extremity and disproportion, towards satire. As one critic comments, 'What to most people would be cause for a minor outbreak of sheepishness can lead Knausgaard to suffer agonies of mortification',[137] but the scale and symbolism of such 'agonies' invoke both a religious tradition of martyrdom and a philosophical tradition of existential crisis; either opens up the possibility of a masculine heroising of shame.

Later in the novel, when his friend Geir introduces him to a couple of boxers, Karl Ove thinks, of one of them:

> [E]very time my eyes rested on him it crossed my mind that he could smash me to pulp in seconds without my being able to do anything about it. The feeling it gave me was one of femininity. It was humiliating, but the humiliation was all my own, it could not be seen, nor could it be sensed. Yet it was still there, damn it.[138]

In this way, the association between 'humiliation' and 'femininity' is preserved, even reinforced: feeling feminine is shameful or humiliating, a state of vulnerability (vulnerability to male violence in particular); being humiliated gives him a feeling of femininity; femininity becomes itself here a kind of 'feeling', a set of affects (bodily or otherwise) that may or may not be visible to others, but which are nevertheless ineradicable. For women, shame can arise due to unfeminine behaviour, but also – more fundamentally – due to femininity itself. By contrast, shame for men is nearly always associated with effeminacy and/or a failure of masculinity; masculinity in itself is not shaming (whatever Koestenbaum may claim). *A Man in Love* appears to bear out this point. Nevertheless, Hustvedt maintains that

> Knausgaard's journey into femininity is not parody or transvestism. [. . .] No, Knausgaard's minute descriptions of domestic life, the potato peeling and diaper changing, the hostile feelings he bears toward the children he loves, and his rage at being trapped and suffocated by household responsibilities, belong to nothing so much as the woman's narrative.[139]

(Indeed, one columnist on motherhood for *New York Magazine* describes Knausgaard, approvingly, as 'my favorite mommy blogger'.)[140] Hustvedt does acknowledge, however, the 'contextual problem' of Knausgaard's gender, which means that his work 'would not have had the same critical impact had *My Struggle*'s author been a woman'.[141] She suggests that Knausgaard's longing, in much of the series (and this is particularly the case in *A Man in Love*, I would suggest), is for 'a room of one's own and the freedom to write', and concludes that 'if the thousands of pages of *My Struggle* are testimony to anything, it is that the man did find time to write.'[142]

Shame as visibility

Significantly, Knausgaard notes how, in the transition to being 'modern and feminised', 'the way I was seen changed', and the women that he is 'ogling' no longer return his gaze: 'when I came along with a buggy no women looked at me, it was as if I didn't exist.'[143] What is being erased here is precisely his masculine desirability, and its erasure makes it 'as if I didn't exist'. Yet this shameful sexual invisibility is countered by his sense of being too painfully visible in other respects. In *A Man in Love*, Knausgaard explains how, 'Even when I lived on a tiny island far out into the sea with only three inhabitants I felt I was being watched';[144] in a Stockholm café he feels that 'every glance that came my way penetrated into my inner-most self, jangled about inside me, and every movement I made, even if only flicking through a book, was likewise transmitted outwards to them [the other people in the café], as a sign of my stupidity'.[145] Even though he knows that this feeling (of stupidity) is 'of my own making', the looks of others 'still got inside, into my inner self, they rumbled around inside me'.[146] This hostile gaze of the other, then, despite being his own projection, reveals his true nature, his lack of self-worth; the feeling of being 'penetrated' by the gaze of the other is again a feeling of feminisation. When Linda berates him in the street – for turning up drunk to meet her at the station – 'I walked beside her, burning with shame because people were looking at us';[147] and when he starts crying, 'I turned away, I didn't want her to see, that made the humiliation ten times worse, it wasn't just that I wasn't a person, I wasn't a man either.'[148] His syntax here implies that not being 'a man' is much more profound, much more shameful than not being 'a person'; gender is figured as prior to personhood.

The most extreme example of this painful visibility, in *A Man in Love*, is an incident when he cuts his face with broken glass after Linda tells him she is not interested in him (this is before their relationship begins): The next morning, he wakes and realises what he has done and that he has to face the other people at the writing workshop:

> They would see the ignominy.
>   I couldn't hide it. Everyone would see. I was marked, I had marked myself.
> [. . .]
>   I packed my things in my case, with my face smarting, and inside I was smarting as well, I had never experienced such shame before.
>   I was marked.[149]

When he does see the others, they are shocked and upset – Linda cries – but also speechless: 'I showed myself as I was, and there was silence. How would I survive this?'[150] That sense of self-disgust, of his shame as so deep-rooted, comes out also in what he says, later, to Geir about himself:

'If you have integrity you do the right thing. I have so little integrity, there's always something . . . well, not sick exactly, but something base, fawning, creeping, it oozes out of me. [. . .] I only think about myself, only see myself, ooze out of myself.'[151]

The language here – base, fawning, creeping, oozing – roots his weakness, his inauthenticity, his subservience ('fawning') in his bodily substance, somehow. It is not just his behaviour; it is inseparable from who he is, makes him less than human ('base'). His disgust at himself underlines the feeling of repugnance, a physical recoil at a moral failing. In the light of this, showing himself 'as [he] was' or as he is suggests a quite visceral vulnerability, an exteriorisation of a shameful inner life/ self – yet that is also, paradoxically, the primary motivation for the *My Struggle* series.

When his relationship with Tonje ends, Karl Ove goes to an isolated island for two months; the implication is that he does not want to be seen. Once there, he comes to the realisation, he tells Geir,

that I would have to do everything I could to become a good person. Everything I did should be to that end. But not in the abject, evasive manner that had characterised my behaviour so far, you know, being overcome by shame at the smallest trifle. The indignity of it. No, in the new image I was drawing of myself there was also courage and backbone. Look people straight in the eye, say what I stood for.[152]

Discussing this – and the case of Hauge, who likewise embraced isolation and fought 'his inner struggle' to be a better person – Geir gets to the heart of Karl Ove's feeling of shame (its connection to painful visibility, its foundational role in his character and his writing) when he says:

'The question is whether it was God [. . .]. The feeling of being seen, of being forced to your knees by something that can see you. We just have a different name for it. The superego or shame or whatever. That was why God was a stronger reality for some than others.'[153]

In a postreligious world, it is 'the superego or shame or whatever' that takes the place of God. It matters little, actually, how Knausgaard conceptualises it; the key experience is of this feeling 'of being forced to your knees by something that can see you', a violent humbling or humiliation. Knausgaard hopes, vainly, that becoming 'a good person' and overcoming his shame will allow him to 'look people straight in the eye';[154] but *A Man in Love* exhibits at each turn the ambivalence of the 'shame response' – wishing 'to continue to look and be looked at' while also *not* wishing this.[155] If the writing of *My Struggle* is an attempt to 'look people straight in the eye', what it actually seems to do is compound and make visible his shame through his repeated acts of self-exposure. Hustvedt asserts that, 'when *My Struggle* was published in Norway, it was as if a grown man had stripped naked, walked to the town square, and mounted a bench in order to wail and blubber in full sight of his fellow citizens';[156] to Knausgaard's personal sense of shame is added the particular shame of the writer.

Writing shame

Moi sees shame as the motivating factor in the writing of *My Struggle* and – adopting a familiar critical standpoint on the writing of shame – as something to be overcome through writing:

> [T]here is only one way to escape [shame's] stranglehold: the shameful person must break the other's power to define him by going on the offensive, by expressing himself, by revealing his inner life. If he can find the courage to express himself deeply and fully he will escape the alienating division of shame. There is no other solution: Knausgaard must come into the open.[157]

Despite Knausgaard's own claim that 'Writing is a way of getting rid of shame',[158] and despite the fact that shame is a source of literary inspiration for him, even his main subject matter (as Geir says, 'He's made a career of telling people what a failure he is'),[159] it transpires that it is not so easy for him to 'escape'; his literary success simply produces an additional level of shame. In *A Man in Love*, when Karl Ove is 'forced' to talk or write about his first two books, he finds it 'repugnant', and when audience members congratulate him after a talk, he declares, 'I don't want to meet their eyes, I don't want to see them, I want to escape from the hell.'[160] Later, he berates himself in the most vitriolic terms for accepting praise for his writing:

Oh, I could cut off my head with bitterness and shame that I have allowed myself to be lured, not just once but time after time. If I have learned one thing over these years which seems to me immensely important, particularly in an era such as ours, overflowing with such mediocrity, it is the following:

Don't believe you are anybody.

Do not bloody believe you are somebody.

Because you are not. You're just a smug mediocre little shit.

Do not believe that you're anything special. Do not believe that you're worth anything, because you aren't. You're just a little shit.[161]

This suggests that the writer's relationship to shame is much more complex than the narrative of overcoming permits. The writer is, on some accounts, always already ashamed: unworthy of attention, not up to the task of writing. As I have noted previously, if we accept Probyn's assertion that 'a form of shame always attends the writer' and that this 'is the shame of not being equal to the interest of one's subject',[162] then how much more fraught is this experience when the 'subject' is yourself (and your other subject is writing)? While Koestenbaum suggests that 'writing is abreactive – I release the emotion of humiliation by replaying it',[163] he proceeds to reveal the near-impossibility of that 'release' in his claim that

[t]o avoid humiliation, which is the feared and inevitable outcome of most writing, especially if it knows itself to be writing, I need to speak from a position of wisdom, omniscience, authority. I can't merely pile up the sordid, nude examples. I acquire mastery by stating an argument. Here are its splayed elements.[164]

Knausgaard's method might, in fact, be seen as a form of '[piling] up the sordid, nude examples', while frequently undermining his own 'wisdom, omniscience, authority'. His writing process in *My Struggle* is ostensibly about embracing the shame of (hasty, sometimes clichéd) writing, after years of being too precise and critical; it is also about risking boredom and banality – in the long descriptions of making a cup of tea or smoking a cigarette:

'The critical reading of the texts always resulted in parts being deleted. So that was what I did. My writing became more and more minimalist. In the end, I couldn't write at all. For seven or eight years,

I hardly wrote. But then I had a revelation. What if I did the opposite? What if, when a sentence or a scene was bad, I expanded it, and poured in more and more? After I started to do that, I became free in my writing. Fuck quality, fuck perfection, fuck minimalism. My world isn't minimalist; my world isn't perfect, so why on earth should my writing be?'[165]

Indeed, Hustvedt views Knausgaard's work as a form of 'automatic writing' (though he claims to be unfamiliar with this concept), describing *My Struggle* as 'an uncontrolled text':

In the interview with me, he insisted that he never edited the book, never altered a word once it was written, and I have no reason to doubt him. The work is a raw, uncensored flood of words issuing from a vulnerable, bruised self, a self most of us recognize to one degree or another but choose to protect. It is the novel as an unchecked, autobiographical, often highly emotional outpouring, which nevertheless borrows the conventions of the novel form – explicit description and dialogue, which no human being actually remembers.[166]

These are terms – 'uncontrolled', 'vulnerable', 'unchecked', 'autobiographical', 'highly emotional' – more often used to describe women's writing than men's. Perhaps unsurprisingly, then, and despite the defiance of his 'fuck perfection' attitude, Knausgaard's reflections on his writing and on his success remain ambivalent at best. As Liesl Schillinger notes,

He was ashamed of the writing. 'It's bad,' he still says. 'I wrote it rather blindly, I didn't think it was exceptional. I thought this would be a minor literary book, I thought it would be a step down from my other books, I thought maybe it was boring and uninteresting and really about nothing.'[167]

More significantly, Knausgaard has commented on the 'outpouring' of words that comprises *My Struggle* that: '"I was going to use everything I had, and use it up, so I couldn't use it again, so there would be nothing left to write", [. . .] comparing the impulse to suicide.'[168] And, as James Wood writes, 'he ends the sixth volume of his autobiography [. . .] with the relieved declaration, as if now self-annulled, "I am happy because I am no longer an author."'[169]

The reception of My Struggle

And yet, thanks to the series' reception, Knausgaard not only remains an author, but he becomes, in many respects, *the* author, the paradigmatic literary figure of our age; and his attempts to resist rather than 'acquire mastery' have tended to be thwarted by the reception of the series *as* masterful in various respects. Writes Hoby:

> Knausgaard does indeed seem to have reached a 'writer's writer' status, like that of Marcel Proust, to whom he is most often compared. [. . .] The novelist Rachel Cusk has deemed the series, 'perhaps the most significant literary enterprise of our times'. Plenty of other critics, enthralled to [sic] its radical imperfection, would do away with the 'perhaps'.[170]

Hustvedt asserts that 'The current legacy in the United States and England, if not in France and Germany [where Knausgaard has received less attention], of the writer's tell-all, soul-bearing volumes is not shameful but heroic',[171] but I want to suggest that the shame and the heroism are inextricable, thanks to the peculiar character of masculine shame. The packaging of the books – covers on which his face features prominently – foregrounds his identity as author and subject matter of *My Struggle* and contributes to the view of the romantic, suffering artist; yet the focus on his face – sometimes turned away, sometimes looking directly at the camera – also brings us back to questions of shame, masculinity, self-identity and self-exposure. To reprise Silvan Tomkins's point:

> Why is shame so close to the experienced self? It is because the self lives in the face, and within the face the self burns brightest in the eyes. Shame turns the attention of the self and others away from other objects to this most visible residence of self, increases its visibility, and thereby generates the torment of self-consciousness.[172]

That torment of self-consciousness – a turning inward, a painful solipsism – is, however, complicated by the transmissibility of shame, evidenced by the frequent discussion of the structures of identification and recognition that Knausgaard's writing evokes in readers. Moi claims that *My Struggle* challenges the literary critical 'prohibition on identification'.[173] Evan Hughes writes: 'Speak to Knausgaard's devotees and you will hear a persistent theme: that by writing about himself, Knausgaard has really written about them, that reading *My Struggle* is like opening someone else's diary and finding your own secrets.'[174] Joshua Rothman suggests that readers might find 'that he has written the diary that you would have written, were you a Norwegian man born in 1968', or alternatively you may simply 'discern, in the rhythms and textures of the book, the rhythms and textures of your own life', and he identifies the latter as 'the secret to *My Struggle*'s popularity'.[175] The intense identifications (and dis-identifications) made possible by shame, then, lie at the heart of the series' success. While that success does not help Knausgaard shed his own personal burden of shame – he comments that, 'I think people almost vomit when they hear my name because I'm so often in the news. It's true. Oh, God. I try to keep a low profile in Norway, but it's hard. It's terrible'[176] – it does allow his shameful 'confessions' to achieve the public status of the transcendent and universal. Though he worries, still, that 'The difficult thing for me is that I want basically to be a good man. That's what I want to be. In this project, I wasn't. It is unmoral, in a way,'[177] the reception of the series allows him at least the compensation of being hailed as a great author.

Conclusion

Knausgaard, more keenly than any other writer currently writing, exemplifies what Bewes has described (in a discussion of Coetzee's *The Master of Petersburg*) as 'the intensely private shame of the writer':

> The shame of living always with an eye on the next work; the searing awareness that no means of escaping the shameful, corrosive effect of writing may be found in writing; the knowledge that every attempt to construct justifications for writing within the writing itself will always be dragged down, 'perverted' [. . .] by their appearance in the work; that no ethical reflection on the relationship between writing and shame, no instantiation of shame can erase the shame: quite the opposite.[178]

Perhaps, then, writing offers no compensations for the shame it necessarily involves, even for the celebrated male author. Yet in his reading of Coetzee's *Diary of a Bad Year*, Bewes notes the point in that novel when JC remarks that 'dishonour, the disgrace of being alive in these times' might be in fact 'something punier and more manageable', like depression.[179] And he argues that

> *Diary of a Bad Year* addresses the possibility that shame is a self-serving myth, an alibi that white males erect in order to leave intact the inequality of their relations with others. One of the effects of such a myth would be the relegation of women and other identity formations to the status of things *about which one is ashamed*, and whose subordinate status is perpetuated by the earnest avowal of shame. [. . .] What prevents shame from being yet another register of exculpation, to be placed alongside the myth of the writer's agency and exceptionality?[180]

This reading of Coetzee might help us to a better understanding of the *My Struggle* series – and of the dilemmas of writing masculine shame that I have been considering throughout this chapter. While Knausgaard may demonstrate that 'pervasive sense of personal inadequacy' that Bartky ascribes to female shame, in presenting his shame precisely as feminisation – and feminisation as shameful – that link between shame and the feminine is reinforced rather than challenged and unequal relations are left intact. Indeed, in his belittling of those areas of life and work – domesticity, child-rearing – most closely associated with women, Knausgaard arguably compounds the perception of them as lowly, humiliating. Whatever Knausgaard's intentions, his narrative of shame becomes here, perhaps quite unwittingly, a 'register of exculpation' – excusing his 'bad' writing, his lapses into the banal (stylistically and thematically), and dignified, in its reception, but also in its execution, by the language of authenticity/inauthenticity. This works in parallel with 'the myth of the writer's agency and exceptionality', as evidenced by Knausgaard's elevation to the Proustian, and – whatever his failures of masculinity – he becomes again heroic.

Earlier in this chapter I quoted Steven Connor's claim that 'It is hard for men to write in shame without attempting to coin glory from it.'[181] *My Struggle* (not least in its title) bears this out, not necessarily because Knausgaard is wilfully attempting to 'coin glory' by foregrounding what is shameful about himself, but rather because his attempts to engage with a particular species of masculine shame cannot but be presented and received as an heroic 'struggle' for authenticity, where authenticity too often means 'authentic masculinity', a resistance to feminisation, and the buttressing of a (romantic) conception of authorship that is both hyperbolically feted and doggedly masculine. This is not to be too critical of Knausgaard – in his concern with being a 'good man' he also suggests how the writing of shame and humiliation might become, for men, 'a passport to decency and civilization, [. . .] a necessary shedding of hubris', as Koestenbaum has claimed, even if those states of 'decency and civilization' are never quite reached.[182]

As the preceding readings have demonstrated, however, shame threatens a loss or failure of masculinity, which must then be recouped by some other means. In the case of Roth and Amis, this is achieved via the shaming of bodies identified as female and as racially other or inferior, a punitive gesture that expresses an anxiety about the stigma of both feminisation and shame. This displacement of shame on to these 'othered' bodies (Gloria, Violet, Consuela) relegates them – to use Bewes's phrase – 'to the status of things *about which one is ashamed*, and whose subordinate status is perpetuated by the earnest avowal of shame' on the part of the male protagonists here. While Knausgaard mines anxieties about feminisation and the failures of masculinity, the stories of self that he tells seek to explore rather than disavow the complexities of the shame state and its attendant undoings, illustrating Connor's point that 'to write is not to free oneself from the shame of being a man', but might in fact 'be a way of meeting with shame, a coming in to male shamefulness'.[183] Nevertheless, even in *My Struggle*, we find indications of the challenges of writing male shamefulness: in the subtle aligning of masculinity and authenticity – and its not so subtle alignment in the series' reception. It seems that, ultimately, shame always brings with it some taint of femininity – and femininity carries, likewise, some echo of shame – and that the writing of shame may facilitate its mutation, displacement, expansion or transmission, but never its purgation.

Notes

1. Gilles Deleuze, 'Literature and Life', trans. Daniel W. Smith and Michael A. Greco, *Critical Inquiry* 23: 2 (1997): 225–30 (225).
2. Ibid.
3. Ibid.

4. Steven Connor, 'The Shame of Being a Man' (2000), unpag. Throughout, references are to the longer version of this paper, available at <http://www.stevenconnor.com/shame/> (last accessed 13 June 2019), rather than to the shorter version that appeared in *Textual Practice* (Connor 2000, n.p.).
5. Connor, 'The Shame'.
6. As I discussed in the Introduction, Silvan Tomkins places shame and humiliation together as 'shame-humiliation', arguing that 'the affect that we term shame-humiliation [. . .] is one and the same affect', even though that affect may produce a range of quite diverse experiences (Silvan Tomkins, 'Shame-Humiliation and Contempt-Disgust', in Eve Kosofsky Sedgwick and Adam Frank (eds), *Shame and Its Sisters: A Silvan Tomkins Reader* (Durham, NC: Duke University Press, 1995), pp. 133–78 (p. 133)).
7. Wayne Koestenbaum, *Humiliation* (New York: Picador, 2011), p. 10.
8. Koestenbaum, p. 3. This is one moment at which the etymological differences between 'humiliation' and 'shame' perhaps become clear: while 'humiliation' has some positive connection to 'humbling' and 'humility', to this 'shedding of hubris' that Koestenbaum lauds, it is harder to see the positive resonances of shame, which connects more obviously to debasement and seems less immediately virtuous. Both humiliation and shame are linked in some way to self-improvement, however – both are still tacitly figured as moral emotions that might help to regulate, and make us reflect upon, our behaviour.
9. Sandra Bartky, *Femininity and Domination: Studies in the Phenomenology of Domination* (London: Routledge, 1990), p. 84.
10. Ibid.
11. Bartky, p. 85.
12. J. Brooks Bouson, *Embodied Shame* (Albany: SUNY Press, 2009), p. 2.
13. Koestenbaum, p. 23.
14. Koestenbaum, p. 10.
15. As discussed in Chapter 2, Freud refers to shame and disgust as 'watchmen' in *Five Lectures on Psychoanalysis* (p. 48); Malcolm Pines summarises the Freudian view of shame as the 'guardian of morality' (p. 93). See: Sigmund Freud, *Five Lectures on Psychoanalysis*, trans. and ed. James Strachey (New York: W. W. Norton, 1961); and Malcolm Pines, 'Shame: What Psychoanalysis Does and Does Not Say' [1987], in Claire Pajaczkowska and Ivan Ward (eds), *Shame and Sexuality: Psychoanalysis and Visual Culture* (London: Routledge, 2008), pp. 93–106.
16. Connor, 'The Shame'.
17. Saul Friedländer, *Franz Kafka: The Poet of Shame and Guilt* (New Haven, CT: Yale University Press, 2013).

18. John Updike, 'Foreword', in Franz Kafka, *The Complete Stories*, ed. Nahum N. Glatzer (New York: Schocken Books, 1971), p. ix. Qtd in Friedländer, p. 7.
19. Brendan Moran, 'An Inhumanly Wise Shame', *The European Legacy* 14: 5 (2009): 573–85 (576).
20. Timothy Bewes, *The Event of Postcolonial Shame* (Princeton: Princeton University Press, 2011), p. 23.
21. J. M. Coetzee, *Diary of a Bad Year* (London: Virago, 2007), p. 141.
22. Bewes, *The Event*, p. 149.
23. Joseph Conrad, 'The Return', in *Tales of Unrest* [1898] (New York: Doubleday, Page, 1920), pp. 201–316 (p. 217).
24. Conrad, pp. 219, 220.
25. Conrad, pp. 220, 221.
26. Conrad, p. 222.
27. Conrad, pp. 221, 264.
28. Conrad, p. 226.
29. Conrad, p. 231. Ellipsis in original.
30. Bewes, *The Event*, p. 3.
31. Ibid.
32. Note, for example, when he priggishly informs his wife that, 'a scandal amongst people of our position is disastrous for the morality' (Conrad, p. 279); or when he sees in his wife's disheveled appearance 'that ugliness of truth which can only be kept out of daily life by unremitting care for appearances' (Conrad, p. 284); or when he insists they continue their normal daily routine as if nothing has happened, because 'It seemed to him necessary that deception should begin at home' (Conrad, p. 289).
33. Conrad, p. 294.
34. Conrad, pp. 229–30.
35. Bewes, *The Event*, p. 23.
36. Connor, 'The Shame'.
37. Joseph Adamson and Hilary Clark, 'Introduction: Shame, Affect, and Writing', in Adamson and Clark (eds), *Scenes of Shame: Psychoanalysis, Shame, and Writing* (Albany: SUNY Press, 1999), pp. 1–34 (pp. 6, 15).
38. Bouson, p. 15.
39. Erica L. Johnson and Patricia Moran (eds), *The Female Face of Shame* (Bloomington: Indiana University Press, 2013), pp. 2, 10, 18–19.
40. Connor, 'The Shame'.
41. Connor, 'The Shame'.
42. Peter Boxall, *Twenty-First Century Fiction: A Critical Introduction* (Cambridge: Cambridge University Press, 2013), p. 30.
43. Lynne Segal, 'The Circus of (Male) Ageing: Philip Roth and the Perils of Masculinity', in Stephen Frosh (ed.), *Psychosocial Imaginaries* (Basingstoke: Palgrave, 2015), pp. 87–104 (p. 90).

44. Segal, p. 91.
45. Segal, p. 95. Segal quotes this passage from *Everyman* by way of illustration: 'Only in passing did it occur to him that it might be somewhat delusional at the age of fifty to think that he might find a hole that would substitute for everything else' (Philip Roth, *Everyman* (London: Vintage, 2007), p. 113).
46. Boxall, p. 37.
47. Ibid.
48. Edward W. Said, *On Late Style* (New York: Pantheon Books, 2006), p. 7.
49. The term 'late style' is coined by Adorno in 'Spätstil Beethovens' ('Late Style in Beethoven') (1937), available in translation in the collection *Essays on Music* (Berkeley: University of California Press, 2002), pp. 564–68; and the discussions of 'late style' by Boxall, Said and Michael Spitzer (in *Music as Philosophy: Adorno and Beethoven's Late Style* (Bloomington: Indiana University Press, 2006)) focus overwhelmingly on male authors, musicians and artists (including Beethoven, Beckett, Don DeLillo, Roth, Thomas Mann, Richard Strauss, Jean Genet and C. P. Cavafy). Even Kathleen M. Woodward's 'Late Theory, Late Style', in Anne Wyatt-Brown and Janice Rossen (eds), *Aging and Gender in Literature* (Charlottesville: University of Virginia Press, 1993), pp. 82–101 – which, admittedly, is more about mourning than 'late style' *per se*, though it uses that terminology – focuses on Freud and Barthes. Late style is also ineluctably bound up with (gendered) ideas of artistic greatness and genius: as Said writes, 'I shall focus on great artists and how near the end of their lives their work and thought acquires a new idiom, what I shall be calling a late style' (Said, p. 3).
50. Philip Roth, *The Dying Animal* (London: Jonathan Cape, 2001), p. 2.
51. Ibid.
52. Roth, p. 5.
53. Roth, pp. 23, 104.
54. Roth, pp. 39, 40.
55. Roth, p. 18.
56. Roth, p. 98.
57. Roth, p. 42.
58. Roth, p. 101.
59. Segal, p. 95. Quoting Roth's *Portnoy's Complaint* (1969).
60. Roth, p. 132.
61. Roth, p. 148.
62. Roth, p. 135.
63. Roth, p. 138.
64. Velichka Ivanova, 'My Own Foe from the Other Gender: (Mis)representing Women in *The Dying Animal*', *Philip Roth Studies* 8: 1 (2012): 31–44 (37).

65. Ivanova asserts that 'Kepesh hears her voice at last', but in fact her words are not recorded in any detail and he rather seems scornful at the predictable and banal nature of her response to a potentially terminal illness (p. 38).

66. Roth, p. 156.

67. Carolyn, the woman in her mid-forties with whom Kepesh is also having an affair, is described as 'still beautiful', but 'beneath the pale gray eyes the biggish sockets were now papery and worn', and 'her body took up more space than it used to' (p. 47). Having sex with Carolyn is like 'plowing [. . .] a softly billowing field. Carolyn the undergraduate flower you pollinated, Carolyn at forty-five you farmed' (p. 70). She offers 'straightforward satiation' (p. 71).

68. Martin Amis, *The Pregnant Widow* (London: Vintage, 2010), p. 1.

69. Connor, 'The Shame'.

70. For Amis, the *feminist revolution* and the *sexual revolution* are indistinguishable and isomorphic, as only one critic, Katha Pollitt in *Slate Magazine*, succeeded in pointing out in her review of the novel. See: Katha Pollitt, 'What Was Feminism Really Like in 1970? You Won't Find Out From Martin Amis' Version', *Slate Magazine*, 25 May 2010. Accessible at: <http://www.slate.com/articles/arts/books/2010/05/what_was_feminism_really_like_in_1970.html> (last accessed 13 June 2019).

71. Epigraph, unpag., to *The Pregnant Widow*.

72. See Margaret Atwood, *The Handmaid's Tale* (London: Virago, 1985), p. 136.

73. Shulamith Firestone, *The Dialectic of Sex* (London: Paladin, 1970), p. 188.

74. Amis, pp. 298, 299.

75. Alison Flood, 'Martin Amis says New Novel Will Get Him "In Trouble with the Feminists"', *The Guardian*, 20 November 2009.

76. Mark Lawson, Interview with Martin Amis, *Front Row*, BBC Radio 4, 2 February 2010.

77. Amis, pp. 437–8.

78. Amis, p. 405.

79. Amis, p. 433.

80. Camilla Long, 'Martin Amis and the Sex War', *The Times*, 24 January 2010.

81. Amis, p. 70.

82. Amis, pp. 70, 71.

83. Amis, p. 131.

84. Amis, p. 303.

85. Amis, p. 448.

86. Connor, 'The Shame'.

87. Ayşe Naz Bulamur, 'Scheherazade in the Western Palace: Martin Amis's *The Pregnant Widow*', *Clio* 43: 3 (2014): 1–19 (3, 4).
88. Pollitt (2010).
89. Connor, 'The Shame'.
90. Connor, 'The Shame'.
91. Connor, 'The Shame'.
92. Roth, p. 50.
93. Roth, pp. 50–1.
94. Roth, p. 54.
95. Roth, p. 89.
96. Amis, pp. 448–9.
97. This is despite the fact that (a) fertility and menstruation are not directly connected (one can be infertile but still menstruating); (b) Gloria is only forty-five at this point, so it is rather early for her to be menopausal (more likely she is perimenopausal); (c) increasing numbers of women conceive children in their mid-forties and fertility can persist well beyond this point; and (d) menopause does not and need not signal the death of sexual desire.
98. Roth, p. 46.
99. Roth, p. 71.
100. Roth, p. 99.
101. Amis, p. 63.
102. Amis, p. 70.
103. Amis, pp. 131, 158.
104. Amis, p. 147.
105. Amis, p. 380.
106. Ibid. Compare the moment when, after Kepesh has forcefully pinned Consuela against the headboard of the bed, holding her hair and '[fucking] her mouth', she 'snapped her teeth', a 'forthright, incisive, elemental response' (Roth, pp. 30–1). In both cases, this baring/snapping of teeth indicates something animalistic and primal that, in these particular representations, cannot be separated from questions of gender and race.
107. Amis, p. 347.
108. Amis, p. 456. As a side note: the white mask that Gloria wears thanks to the 'sinister refinement' can be read in at least a couple of ways, as combining her sexual shame – the degradation of not just allowing but instructing a man to come on her face – and her racial shame, the mask of whiteness she wears to conceal her birth identity.
109. Roth, pp. 3, 28.
110. Roth, pp. 2–3.
111. Roth, p. 28.

112. Roth, p. 32.
113. Roth, p. 46.
114. Roth, p. 18.
115. Lynne Segal, 'Back to the Boys? Temptations of the Good Gender Theorist', *Textual Practice* 15: 2 (2001): 231–50 (237).
116. Segal, 'Back to the Boys?', p. 239.
117. Ibid.
118. Daniel Lea and Berthold Schoene, 'Masculinity in Transition: An Introduction', in Lea and Schoene (eds), *Posting the Male* (Amsterdam: Rodopi, 2003), pp. 7–17 (pp. 9, 11).
119. Hari Kunzru, 'Karl Ove Knausgaard: The Latest Literary Sensation', *The Guardian*, 7 March 2014. Available at: <https://www.theguardian.com/books/2014/mar/07/karl-ove-knausgaard-my-struggle-hari-kunzru> (last accessed 13 June 2019).
120. Hermione Hoby, 'Karl Ove Knausgaard: Norway's Proust and a Life Laid Painfully Bare', *The Observer*, 1 March 2014. Available at: https://www.theguardian.com/theobserver/2014/mar/01/karl-ove-knausgaard-norway-proust-profile> (last accessed 13 June 2019).
121. Andrew Anthony, 'Karl Ove Knausgaard: "Writing is a Way of Getting Rid of Shame"', *The Observer*, 1 March 2015. Available at: <https://www.theguardian.com/books/2015/mar/01/karl-ove-knausgaard-interview-shame-dancing-in-the-dark?CMP=twt_gu> (last accessed 13 June 2019).
122. Anthony (2015).
123. Toril Moi, 'Shame and Openness', trans. Toril Moi and Anders Firing Lunde, *Salmagundi* 177 (2013): 205–10 (207).
124. Ibid.
125. Kunzru (2014).
126. Liesl Schillinger, 'Why Karl Ove Knausgaard Can't Stop Writing', *WSJ Magazine*, 4 November 2015. Available at: <http://www.wsj.com/articles/why-karl-ove-knausgaard-cant-stop-writing-1446688727?mod=e2tw> (last accessed 13 June 2019).
127. Anthony (2015).
128. Anthony (2015).
129. Karl Ove Knausgaard, *My Struggle I: A Death in the Family* [2009], trans. Don Bartlett (London: Vintage, 2013), p. 21.
130. Siri Hustvedt, *A Woman Looking at Men Looking at Women: Essays on Art, Sex, and the Mind* (New York: Simon & Schuster, 2016), p. 85.
131. Karl Ove Knausgaard, *My Struggle II: A Man in Love* [2009], trans. Don Bartlett (London: Vintage, 2014), p. 82.
132. Knausgaard, *A Man in Love*, p. 100.
133. Knausgaard, *A Man in Love*, p. 101.

134. Knausgaard, *A Man in Love*, p. 86.

135. Ibid.

136. Knausgaard, *A Man in Love*, p. 88.

137. Anthony (2015).

138. Knausgaard, *A Man in Love*, p. 351.

139. Hustvedt, p. 87.

140. Laura June, 'My Favorite Mommy Blogger, Karl Ove Knausgaard', *The Cut*, 17 June 2016. Available at: <http://nymag.com/thecut/2016/06/karl-ove-knausgaard-mommy-blogger.html> (last accessed 13 June 2019).

141. Hustvedt, p. 87. By contrast, consider the reception of Rachel Cusk's book about motherhood, *A Life's Work: On Becoming a Mother* (2001). Commenting more recently on 'the risks and rewards of self-exposure', Cusk noted the polarised responses to the book, some of which praised her honesty, but many of which questioned her 'conduct as a mother' and described her as a child-hater and a 'self-obsessed bore'. Her reaction upon returning to her children, immediately after seeing the first critical review, is as follows: 'When I laid eyes on my children I was instantly overcome by powerful feelings of guilt and shame. There is always shame in the creation of an object for the public gaze. This time, however, I felt it not as a writer but as a mother. I felt that I had committed a violent act. I felt that I had been abusive and negligent. I felt these things not because of anything I had physically or actually done to them [. . .], but because I had written a book that had malfunctioned, and had allowed our relationship to be publicly impugned' (Rachel Cusk, 'I Was Only Being Honest', *The Guardian*, 21 March 2008. Available at: <https://www.theguardian.com/books/2008/mar/21/biography.women> (last accessed 13 June 2019)).

142. Hustvedt, p. 87.

143. Knausgaard, *A Man in Love*, p. 101.

144. Knausgaard, *A Man in Love*, p. 150.

145. Ibid.

146. Ibid.

147. Knausgaard, *A Man in Love*, p. 300.

148. Knausgaard, *A Man in Love*, p. 301.

149. Knausgaard, *A Man in Love*, p. 223.

150. Ibid.

151. Knausgaard, *A Man in Love*, p. 552.

152. Knausgaard, *A Man in Love*, p. 556. Notice here that being so easily 'overcome by shame' itself produces 'indignity' – his shame is also shameful, self-perpetuating, indicating the spiral nature of this particular affect.

153. Knausgaard, *A Man in Love*, p. 557.
154. Knausgaard, *A Man in Love*, p. 556.
155. Tomkins, p. 137.
156. Hustvedt, p. 94.
157. Moi, p. 208.
158. Anthony (2015).
159. Knausgaard, *A Man in Love*, p. 331.
160. Knausgaard, *A Man in Love*, pp. 538–9.
161. Knausgaard, *A Man in Love*, p. 580.
162. Elspeth Probyn, *Blush: Faces of Shame* (Minneapolis: University of Minnesota Press, 2005), p. xvii.
163. Koestenbaum, p. 7.
164. Ibid.
165. Hoby (2014).
166. Hustvedt, p. 85.
167. Schillinger (2015).
168. Schillinger (2015).
169. James Wood, 'Total Recall: Karl Ove Knausgaard's "My Struggle"', *New Yorker*, 13 August 2012. Available at: <http://www.newyorker.com/magazine/2012/08/13/total-recall> (last accessed 13 June 2019).
170. Hoby (2014).
171. Hustvedt, p. 86.
172. Tomkins, p. 136.
173. Moi, p. 206.
174. Evan Hughes, 'Karl Ove Knausgaard Became a Literary Sensation by Exposing His Every Secret', *New Republic*, 8 April 2014. Available at: <https://newrepublic.com/article/117245/karl-ove-knausgaard-interview-literary-star-struggles-regret> (last accessed 13 June 2019).
175. Joshua Rothman, 'What is the Struggle in "My Struggle"?', *New Yorker*, 28 May 2014.
176. Schillinger (2015).
177. Hughes (2014).
178. Bewes, p. 145.
179. Coetzee, *Diary of a Bad Year*, p. 141.
180. Bewes, pp. 148–9.
181. Connor, 'The Shame'.
182. Koestenbaum, p. 3.
183. Connor, 'The Shame'.

Conclusion: The Shame is (Not) Over

'There is no such thing as a writing devoid of shame,' assert Barry Sheils and Julie Walsh – and I concur.[1] I set out, in *Writing Shame*, to address the complex triangulation of shame, gender and writing in the late twentieth and early twenty-first centuries – to think not only about how shame might be *represented* in contemporary literature, but also about the shame that might lie behind every attempt to put words out into the world in some published form, and the shame that writing itself provokes, puts into play and circulates. Much of the existing scholarship on shame and literature treats the act of writing shame as expressive, as empowered, as liberating, as therapeutic; of course, it can be all of these things. Nevertheless, what interested me above all were those literary engagements with shame that could not be claimed for such heartening messages of redemption, resistance, liberation or overcoming. This is not because I reject those messages or want to dismiss attempts to write oneself out of shame, but rather because it seems to me that shame is not so easily dispensed with, even when individual instances of it appear to have been vanquished. This is not pessimism on my part. As an affect fundamental to the building, maintenance – but also, often, the unravelling – of selfhood and society, shame is so integral to who we are and so pervasive within our culture(s) that it actually provides a useful way of thinking through relationships between the personal and the structural, the psychological and the social; it raises profound philosophical questions about processes of subjectivation and our experiences of self–other relations (including pernicious practices of othering and scapegoating, of course). Furthermore, its operations and effects are so intricate and unpredictable: we can feel shame even in solitude; we can feel shame even when the imagined source of shame is just that – imagined – or when it is distant in time; we can feel shame about feeling ashamed, in a dizzying spiral effect; we can feel shame on behalf of others; so to subject shame to some species of management or mastery seems beside the point. Writing, as I am conceiving it, is not then a way of overcoming shame, but it may be (to borrow Steven Connor's phrase) a way of meeting with it – for readers, critics and theorists, as well as authors.[2]

My starting point, then, was an intuition about the persistence of shame and a curiosity about the challenges it might pose for writers. Despite the striking differences between the texts discussed in the preceding chapters, what they have in common is that all of them (in different ways, to different degrees and certainly with different motivations and effects) recognise that persistence, and therefore seek to inhabit and explore states of shame and to find something generative in them (even if what is generated is simply more shame). There are many other texts that I could have selected as the basis of my analysis, but the examples here facilitate a consideration of interwoven, highly political questions around gender, sexuality, race, embodiment, desire, childhood, confession, self-fashioning, visibility, spectacle and stigmatisation (among other topics). My chosen texts, in their very diversity, also raise questions of genre, form and literariness, taking in scholarly writing (the queer theory of Chapter 1), pulp fiction, literary fiction, and autofiction of a more experimental, hybrid kind. In attempting to theorise shame's movement beyond the page, I have brought into view the formal and generic disruptions incurred in the writing of shame and the interactive, intersubjective functioning of texts as objects in the world with an affective force that draws us to them and interpellates us as reading subjects. I have also attended to the (shameful) anxieties of authorship: think, for example, of the pseudonymous authorship of most pulp fiction (the writers themselves ashamed of their output), of A. M. Homes's disavowal of the 'woman writer' tag, of Calloway's plastering of negative feedback over images of her own face (wearing the shame of her reception), of Knausgaard's positioning (by others) as paradigmatic, Proustian author as a route away from the self-shaming of *My Struggle*.

Most importantly, I have sought to show throughout this book the particular imbrication of shame and femininity. This goes beyond any broadly sociological or empirical claim that, say, women feel shame more often or more acutely than men, or that men and women feel shame for different reasons – though I do believe that to be the case.[3] What the preceding readings indicate is that our very conception of what it is to be a 'woman' (a cultural construction and a state that does not of course imply the possession of a particular kind of body) has shame built into it. To be a 'woman' who fails at 'femininity' (via some perceived impropriety) is to feel shame and be shamed; but even successful performances of femininity involve and invite shame, for femininity is (in a way that masculinity is not) a shamed state to start with. This is most starkly evidenced by the texts I consider in Chapters 3 and 4: in Kraus's invocation (and subversion) of the 'Dumb Cunt, a factory of emotions evoked by all the men';[4] in Calloway's hyperbolic excoriation of herself as 'a stupid worthless whore';[5] in Angel's fear that her desire might expose her as 'Dupe. Collaborator. Victim';[6] and in the way that the ruined female bodies of *The Pregnant Widow* and *The Dying Animal* become ready vehicles for the shame of those novels' male protagonists. Meanwhile, in Knausgaard's 'struggle' with his own identity as parent, partner and writer we see that femininity is shameful even – especially – when it is men who are displaying it. This is women's shame as 'a pervasive affective attunement to the social environment', in Bartky's phrase,[7] and crucially it is 'a perpetual attunement' and must be distinguished from the experience of shame as a 'discrete occurrence' (which might serve some positive purpose as an occasion for 'moral reaffirmation').[8] In analysing these literary texts I have been seeking to reveal this primary, perpetual shame of femininity, rather than concentrating on such 'discrete occurrence[s]' of the kind that might be overcome and might be redemptive in their telling. 'The shame is over', proclaims the title of Anja Meulenbelt's 'political life story' of 1980, a classic of the second wave; but of course it never is.[9]

There is a long history of this association between women and shame – as my discussion of *aidōs* in the Introduction shows – but there is also a historical specificity to our contemporary understanding of, and preoccupation with, shame that owes something to the gender politics of Western societies in recent decades. This preoccupation with shame, the claim that we inhabit a shame culture, is something that I sought to establish in the Introduction – though I suppose it is borne out by the contents of this book as a whole – via Ruth Leys's claim that 'shame (and shamelessness) has displaced guilt as a dominant emotional reference in the West',[10] and via engagements both scholarly accounts of shame (showing an increased scholarly interest in the subject, across disciplines, particularly since the 1990s) and more mainstream discussions and manifestations of shame and shaming (as evidenced by the Jon Ronson and Juliet Jacquet books cited in the Introduction, and as found in realms as seemingly divergent as social media, reality television, popular fiction, misery memoirs and public political discourse). Leys argues that

> the success of current shame theory [. . .] can be explained by its ability to support and reinforce a self-declared postmodernist and posthistoricist commitment to replacing disputes or disagreements about intentions and meanings with an emphasis on who one is, or differences in personal experience.[11]

This is not quite my explanation – I do not think so stark a distinction can be drawn between 'intentions and meanings' and 'who one is' and 'personal experience'. Nevertheless, it is certainly true that contemporary anxieties about the perceived instability of identity and the inaccessibility of any true or authentic history might form part of the context producing our interest in shame. As Eve Sedgwick observes, 'Shame is a bad feeling attaching to what one is: one therefore *is something*, in experiencing shame', so shame might then seem to offer a route to being *something* or even *someone*.[12] It is not coincidental, therefore, that an interest in shame, which is so much a matter of who or what one is, should arise in an era of individualism and identity politics.

It is also not coincidental that this interest in shame should arise in the decades following the emergence of the second-wave feminist movement, the lesbian, gay, bisexual and transgender (LGBT) movement, and the rise of feminist and queer theoretical approaches within the academy. As I have sought to demonstrate in *Writing Shame*, shame is an unavoidable topic within gender and sexuality studies: these are movements motivated, in the first instance, by desires to push back against histories of shaming and pathologisation, movements whose embrace of a pride agenda has, however, faltered in recent years, due to processes of internal critique and fears about assimilation or homonormativity. In turn, as I argued in the Introduction, the relative emancipation of women in many societies in the course of the twentieth century continues to provoke an anti-feminist backlash that often takes the form of shaming: damning women for their 'shamelessness', threatening sexual violence against those deemed shameful, lamenting that 'shame is dead' as a means of asserting moral and actual control over certain kinds of bodies (remember Jill Locke's claim that this lament tends to emerge 'during periods of increased egalitarianism or democratic expansion').[13] Shame's centrality to gender and sexuality studies is also due to the nature of shame itself, for feelings of shame so often concern matters of desire and embodiment; shame is part of the package of vulnerabilities attendant on our avowals of strong feeling, acknowledgements of lack and experiences of (precarious or dysmorphic) physicality.

My use of 'our' and 'we' here is, however, problematic. If shame is as universal and as transmissible as it appears to be, then it might seem to proffer possibilities of contact, solidarity and even, perversely, belonging. Yet my argument in Chapter 1 is really that shame, despite being shared, is not a sound basis for collective action or solidarity. There are various reasons why not. First, to suggest that it is, is to fall prey to another version of the redemption argument, not by overcoming shame but by trying to transform it into something good, and I remain unconvinced that such a thing is possible. (I also think – as I claim in Chapter 1 – that shame might be generative without being, necessarily, productive in some more positive sense.) Second, if shame is 'both peculiarly contagious and peculiarly individuating',[14] as Sedgwick suggests, then contagion (in its unpredictability and uncontrollability) is a poor model of sharing and individuation tends to work against solidarity. Third, to use feeling of any kind as a ground for politics is also potentially problematic. In this claim I am borrowing from Lauren Berlant's assertion that

> the personal is political [. . .] did not mean that there is only the personal, no such thing as the political. It meant to say that feeling is an unreliable measure of justice and fairness, not the most reliable one; and that new vocabularies of pleasure, recognition, and equity must be developed and taught.[15]

There are dangers to a 'feeling politics' that is, in Berlant's formulation, 'beyond ideology, beyond mediation, beyond contestation';[16] feeling should not be presented as an unchallengeable (prelinguistic, pretheoretical, non-ideological) basis of politics, and one can recognise the political nature of the personal without losing sight of the structural conditions in which 'the personal' is formed and lived. Fourth, in relation to shame in particular, and as I aimed to show in my readings of queer theory and lesbian pulp fiction in Chapter 1, to invoke shame as a source of solidarity is to be blind to the privilege that allows some people a greater distance from historical practices of shaming than others. As Nussbaum notes, 'Some people [. . .] are more marked out for shame than others';[17] some are, then, less able to reclaim and ironise it than others. The recuperation of lesbian pulp, as an attempt to 'recycle earlier forms of pain at an ironic distance', is also complicated by that genre's relationship to shame, for shame is not just the (main) subject matter of the novels, it is the primary affect attending the genre: hence pulp's exclusion from the lesbian canon, and hence readers' ambivalent responses to it.[18]

Nevertheless – as the ambivalence of those responses indicates – the pulp fiction discussed in Chapter 1 is associated with pleasure as well as with shame, and its recuperation may even indicate the pleasures *of* shame, its vicarious and not so vicarious appeal for us. The shame–pleasure–spectacle relation set up by my reading of pulp is evident in Chapters 2 and 3, too, in their concern with other forms of sexual shame, the writing of these, and the ambivalent but undeniable pleasures of confession, of humiliation, of vulnerability and of readerly complicity. Notably, every chapter of *Writing Shame* pivots on the idea that the perceived sexual impropriety of women is one of the major sources and sites of shame in our culture; Phaidra casts a long shadow. That impropriety here takes various forms – lesbianism, perverse paedophiliac desires, BDSM, romantic obsession, infidelity, promiscuity, or the writing or 'confession' of any of the above (which comprises a further impropriety); yet, as my reading of Katherine Angel's *Unmastered* suggests, any expression of feminine desire risks the charge of impropriety, even if appropriately heterosexual and consensual, and thus the sexual impropriety of women – that is, the shamefulness of women – is again revealed as foundational, constitutive. Is women's desire then always shadowed by shame?

The most recent text discussed in *Writing Shame* is Marie Calloway's *what purpose did i serve in your life* (2013). Even more recent publications by young female authors reveal a continuing, questing preoccupation with matters of desire, embodiment, sexuality, vulnerability and – by extension – shame. I am thinking here of Carmen Maria Machado's *Her Body and Other Parties* (2017), a collection whose opening story, 'The Husband Stitch', employs an eerie fairy-tale register to tell the story of a girl defined by desire, whose pleasure in wanting cannot go unpunished; other stories in *Her Body* muse on diverse manifestations of desire (often queer desire) in landscapes surreal and dystopian, where the threat of sexual violence still lingers.[19] I am thinking also of Sophie Mackintosh's *The Water Cure* (2018), whose protagonists, three sisters, grow up in an unnamed, isolated location, protected from the supposed hostility of an outside world that would do them damage. Yet again, desire insinuates itself into their lives and again sexual abuse and violence are closer to home than might be imagined: 'the safe place had been contaminated from the start', we are told.[20] Mariana Enriquez's stories, *Things We Lost in the Fire* (2016), find horror in the everyday violence and corruption of contemporary Argentina, highlighting women's vulnerability above all (her protagonists are nearly all young women). In the title story, following a series of attacks on women by boyfriends and husbands in which the victim is set on fire, women start to take matters into their own hands; as one character explains, 'Burnings are the work of men. They have always burned us. Now we are burning ourselves. But we're not going to die; we're going to flaunt our scars.'[21] The deliberate, flaunted ugliness of these burned women becomes, then, a way to shame the men who might hurt them. Han Kang's *The Vegetarian*, first published in South Korea in 2007 and translated into English in 2015 (winning the Man Booker International Prize in 2016), features a protagonist (Yeong-hye) whose protests against a patriarchal culture that seeks violently to control her body and suppress her desires involve a kind of bodily self-abnegation, a desire to become more plant than human; yet there is a sensuality to her actions, alongside their self-destructiveness.[22] What can we conclude from these brief examples? Evidently, desire, sexuality, sexual violence and embodiment remain crucial concerns for contemporary women's writing, cutting across national divides; there is also a notable generic boldness to this writing (in its piecemeal borrowing from dystopian fiction, magic realism, science fiction, fairy tale, gothic fiction and horror) that matches the boldness of its handling of topics contiguous with those considered in *Writing Shame*. Shame itself is not the central strand of these works, but it remains on the edges of all of these considerations of femininity, female desire and women's bodies within patriarchal cultures.

This book is already shamefully long, but there is so much else that could be brought into this wider discussion of gender, shame and writing. Race featured in Chapters 1 and 4 as a problematic intensifier of shame, with brown bodies in the texts under consideration presented as vehicles of both the shame and the desire of white bodies whose privileged whiteness erased itself at each stage; I would like to have thought further about the particular intersections of gender, race and shame in literature, though J. Brooks Bouson covers this topic admirably in her work on Toni Morrison and others.[23] In the light of the recent fiction mentioned above, there would be scope, too, to think further about the notable shame incurred by sexual violence against women; I touch on this in my discussions of the masochistic episodes in Mary Gaitskill's *Two Girls, Fat and Thin* (in Chapter 2) and Calloway's *what purpose* (in Chapter 3), but more detailed attention could be paid specifically to narratives of rape – a subject that Jennifer Cooke addresses with great care and insight in *Contemporary Feminist Life-Writing*.[24] The discussion of shame and gender in *Writing Shame* could also be extended to an analysis of the way that shame is projected upon and attaches to trans and non-binary bodies and identities, particularly trans women, whose stories are only now beginning to be told, in fiction or elsewhere.

I argued above that shame is not well suited to solidarity or collectivity, but it remains, in Leys's words, 'a better affect than guilt to think with' and 'a privileged operator [. . .] for diverse kinds of theoretical–interpretive undertakings'.[25] I have used it here as a tool of analysis to reveal both the workings of literature (its affective intersubjectivity, its adeptness at handling and producing ambivalence and complicity) and the structural (not merely personal, individual) ways in which femininity is constituted in patriarchal societies, but its uses are many and its powers not to be underestimated. In writing shame we do not escape it, but in some instances that writing of shame might help us better understand it and ourselves, and the operations of gender to which we are subject.

Notes

1. Barry Sheils and Julie Walsh, 'Introduction: Shame and Modern Writing', in Sheils and Walsh (eds), *Shame and Modern Writing* (London: Routledge, 2018), pp. 1–32 (p. 1).

2. Steven Connor, 'The Shame of Being a Man' (2000), unpag. Available at: <http://www.stevenconnor.com/shame/> (last accessed 13 June 2019).

3. The studies cited by Jennifer C. Manion also offer some substantiation of this claim. See: 'Girls Blush, Sometimes: Gender, Moral Agency, and the Problem of Shame', *Hypatia* 18: 3 (2003): 21–41.

4. Chris Kraus, *I Love Dick* [1997] (Los Angeles: Semiotext(e), 2006), p. 27.

5. Marie Calloway, *what purpose did i serve in your life* (New York: Tyrant Books, 2013), p. 69.

6. Katherine Angel, *Unmastered: A Book On Desire, Most Difficult To Tell* (London: Penguin, 2012), pp. 168, 169.

7. Sandra Bartky, *Femininity and Domination: Studies in the Phenomenology of Domination* (London: Routledge, 1990), p. 85.

8. Bartky, p. 96.

9. Anja Meulenbelt, *The Shame is Over: A Political Life Story* (London: The Women's Press, 1980).

10. Ruth Leys, *From Guilt to Shame: Auschwitz and After* (Princeton: Princeton University Press, 2007), p. 4.

11. Leys, p. 12.

12. Eve Kosofsky Sedgwick, 'Queer Performativity: Henry James's *The Art of the Novel*', *GLQ* 1: 1 (1993): 1–16 (12).

13. Jill Locke, *Democracy and the Death of Shame: Political Equality and Social Disturbance* (Cambridge: Cambridge University Press, 2016), p. 14.

14. Eve Kosofsky Sedgwick, *Touching Feeling* (Durham, NC: Duke University Press, 2003), p. 36.

15. Lauren Berlant, 'The Subject of True Feeling', in Austin Sarat and Thomas R. Kearns (eds), *Cultural Pluralism, Identity Politics, and the Law* (Ann Arbor: University of Michigan Press, 1999), pp. 49–84 (p. 83).

16. Berlant, p. 58.

17. Martha Nussbaum, *Hiding from Humanity: Disgust, Shame and the Law* (Princeton: Princeton University Press, 2004), p. 174.

18. It is Christopher Nealon who writes of 'the camp pleasure we feel, reading [pulp novels] now, that we can recycle earlier forms of pain at an ironic distance', though he proceeds to clarify that this is not a straightforward 'pleasure', but rather a much more ambivalent relation between text and reader ('Invert-History: The Ambivalence of Lesbian Pulp Fiction', *New Literary History* 31 (2000): 745–64 (745)).

19. Carmen Maria Machado, *Her Body and Other Parties* [2017] (London: Serpent's Tail, 2019).

20. Sophie Mackintosh, *The Water Cure* (London: Hamish Hamilton, 2018), p. 245.

21. Mariana Enriquez, *Things We Lost in the Fire* [2016], trans. Megan McDowell (London: Portobello Books, 2017), p. 193.
22. Han Kang, *The Vegetarian* [2007], trans. Deborah Smith (London: Portobello Books, 2015).
23. See, particularly, *Quiet As It's Kept: Shame, Trauma and Race in the Novels of Toni Morrison* (Albany: SUNY Press, 2000).
24. Jennifer Cooke's forthcoming *Contemporary Feminist Life-Writing: The New Audacity* (Cambridge: Cambridge University Press, 2020) has a chapter on the writing of rape as 'feminist praxis' that is highly interesting in this regard.
25. Leys, p. 124.

Bibliography

Abate, Michelle Ann, 'From Cold War Lesbian Pulp to Contemporary Young Adult Novels: Vin Packer's *Spring Fire*, M. E. Kerr's *Deliver Us from Evie*, and Marijane Meaker's Fight against Fifties Homophobia', *Children's Literature Association Quarterly* 32: 3 (2007): 231–51.

—, *Tomboys: A Literary and Cultural History* (Philadelphia: Temple University Press, 2008).

Adams, Kate, 'Making the World Safe for the Missionary Position: Images of the Lesbian in Post-World War II America', in Karla Jay and Joanne Glasgow (eds), *Lesbian Texts and Contexts* (New York: NYU Press, 1990), pp. 255–74.

—, 'Built out of Books: Lesbian Energy and Feminist Ideology in Alternative Publishing', in Sonya L. Jones (ed.), *Gay and Lesbian Literature since World War II: History and Memory* (New York: Haworth, 1998), pp. 113–41.

Adamson, Joseph, and Hilary Clark (eds), *Scenes of Shame: Psychoanalysis, Shame and Writing* (Albany: SUNY Press, 1999).

Adorno, Theodor W., *Essays on Music*, trans. Susan H. Gillespie (Berkeley: University of California Press, 2002).

Agamben, Giorgio, *Remnants of Auschwitz*, trans. Daniel Heller-Roazen (New York: Zone Books, 1999).

Ahmed, Sara, *The Cultural Politics of Emotion* (Edinburgh: Edinburgh University Press, 2004).

—, *Queer Phenomenology* (Durham, NC: Duke University Press, 2007).

—, 'The Happiness Turn', *New Formations* 63 (Winter 2007/8): 7–14.

—, *The Promise of Happiness* (Durham, NC: Duke University Press, 2010).

—, 'Interview with Judith Butler', *Sexualities* 19: 4 (2016): 482–92.

Aldrich, Ann, *We Walk Alone* [1955] (New York: Feminist Press, 2006).

—, *We, Too, Must Love* [1958] (New York: Feminist Press, 2006).

Allison, Dorothy, 'A Personal History of Lesbian Porn', *New York Native* (24 May–6 June 1982): 22–3.

Amis, Martin, *The Pregnant Widow* (London: Vintage, 2010).

Angel, Katherine, *Unmastered: A Book On Desire, Most Difficult To Tell* (London: Penguin, 2012).

Angelides, Steven, 'Historicizing Affect, Psychoanalyzing History: Pedophilia and the Discourse of Child Sexuality', *Journal of Homosexuality* 46: 1–2 (2003): 79–109.

Anthony, Andrew, 'Karl Ove Knausgaard: "Writing is a Way of Getting Rid of Shame"', *The Observer*, 1 March 2015. Available at: <https://www.theguardian.com/books/2015/mar/01/karl-ove-knausgaard-interview-shame-dancing-in-the-dark?CMP=twt_gu> (last accessed 13 June 2019).

Ashton, Jennifer, 'Our Bodies, Our Poems', *American Literary History* 19: 1 (2007): 211–31.

Atwood, Margaret, *The Handmaid's Tale* (London: Virago, 1985).

Austin, J. L., *How to Do Things with Words* (Oxford: Oxford University Press, 1962).

Balsamo, Anne, and Henry Schwarz, 'Under the Sign of "Semiotext(e)": The Story According to Sylvère Lotringer and Chris Kraus', *Critique* 37: 3 (1996): 205–20.

Bannon, Ann, *Odd Girl Out* [1957] (San Francisco: Cleis Press, 2001).

—, *I Am a Woman* [1959] (San Francisco: Cleis Press, 2002).

—, *Women in the Shadows* [1959] (San Francisco: Cleis Press, 2002).

—, *Journey to a Woman* [1960] (San Francisco: Cleis Press, 2003).

—, *Beebo Brinker* [1962] (San Francisco: Cleis Press, 2001).

Barale, Michele Aina, 'When Jack Blinks: Si(gh)ting Gay Desire in Ann Bannon's *Beebo Brinker*', in Henry Abelove, Michela Aina Barale and David M. Halperin (eds), *The Lesbian and Gay Studies Reader* (London: Routledge, 1993), pp. 604–15.

Barber, Stephen M., and David L. Clark (eds), *Regarding Sedgwick* (New York: Routledge, 2002).

Barnsley, Veronica, 'The Child/The Future', *Feminist Theory* 11: 3 (2010): 323–30.

Bartky, Sandra, *Femininity and Domination: Studies in the Phenomenology of Domination* (London: Routledge, 1990).

Bates, Victoria, '"Misery Loves Company": Sexual Trauma, Psychoanalysis and the Market for Misery', *Journal of Medical Humanities* 33 (2012): 61–81.

Bellamy, Dodie, *the buddhist* (Berkeley: Allone Co. Editions, 2011).

—, *When the Sick Rule the World* (Los Angeles: Semiotext(e), 2015).

Belluscio, Stephen J., *To Be Suddenly White: Literary Realism and Racial Passing* (Columbia: University of Missouri Press, 2006).

Benjamin, Jessica, *The Bonds of Love: Psychoanalysis, Feminism and the Problem of Domination* (London: Virago, 1988).

Benns, Susanna, 'Sappho in Soft Cover: Notes on Lesbian Pulp', in Makeda Silvera (ed.), *Fireworks: The Best of Fireweed* (Toronto: Women's Press, 1986), pp. 60–8.

Berger, John, *Ways of Seeing* (London: Penguin, 1972).

Bergler, Edmund, 'The Myth of a New National Disease: Homosexuality and the Kinsey Report', *Psychiatric Quarterly* 22: 1 (1948): 66–88.

—, *Homosexuality: Disease or Way of Life?* (New York: Hill and Wang, 1956).

Bergman, David, 'The Cultural Work of Sixties Gay Pulp Fiction', in Patricia Juliana Smith (ed.), *The Queer Sixties* (New York: Routledge, 1999), pp. 26–41.

Berlant, Lauren, *The Queen of America Goes to Washington City* (Durham, NC: Duke University Press, 1997).

—, 'The Subject of True Feeling', in Austin Sarat and Thomas R. Kearns (eds), *Cultural Pluralism, Identity Politics, and the Law* (Ann Arbor: University of Michigan Press, 1999), pp. 49–84.

—, 'Two Girls, Fat and Thin', in Stephen M. Barber and David L. Clark (eds), *Regarding Sedgwick* (New York: Routledge, 2002), pp. 71–108.

—, 'Cruel Optimism: On Marx, Loss and the Senses', *New Formations* 63 (2008): 33–51.

—, *The Female Complaint* (Durham, NC: Duke University Press, 2008).

Bewes, Timothy, 'The Call to Intimacy and the Shame Effect', *differences: A Journal of Feminist Cultural Studies* 22: 1 (2011): 1–16.

—, *The Event of Postcolonial Shame* (Princeton: Princeton University Press, 2011).

Biddle, Jennifer, 'Shame', *Australian Feminist Studies* 12: 26 (1997): 227–39.

Blackwood, Evelyn, 'From Butch-Femme to Female Masculinities: Elizabeth Kennedy and LGBT Anthropology', *Feminist Formations* 24: 3 (2012): 92–100.

Blair, Jennifer, 'The Glove of Shame and the Touch of Rebecca Brown's *Gifts of the Body*', *GLQ* 11: 4 (2005): 521–45.

Bonaparte, Marie, 'Passivity, Masochism and Femininity' [1935], in Russell Grigg, Dominique Hecq and Craig Smith (eds), *Female Sexuality* (New York: Other Press, 1999), pp. 266–74.

Bond Stockton, Kathryn, 'Eve's Queer Child', in Stephen M. Barber and David L. Clark (eds), *Regarding Sedgwick* (London: Routledge, 2002), pp. 181–99.

—, *Beautiful Bottom, Beautiful Shame: Where 'Black' Meets 'Queer'* (Durham, NC: Duke University Press, 2006).

—, 'Feeling Like Killing? Queer Temporalities of Murderous Motives among Queer Children', *GLQ* 13: 2–3 (2007): 301–25.

—, *The Queer Child* (Durham, NC: Duke University Press, 2009).

Bouson, J. Brooks, *Quiet As It's Kept: Shame, Trauma and Race in the Novels of Toni Morrison* (Albany: SUNY Press, 2000).

—, *Embodied Shame: Uncovering Female Shame in Contemporary Women's Writings* (Albany: SUNY Press, 2009).

—, *Shame and the Aging Woman: Confronting and Resisting Ageism in Contemporary Women's Writings* (Basingstoke: Palgrave, 2016).

Boxall, Peter, *Twenty-First Century Fiction: A Critical Introduction* (Cambridge: Cambridge University Press, 2013).

Bradley, Marion Zimmer, 'Lesbian Stereotypes in the Commercial Novel', *The Ladder* 8: 12 (September 1964): 14–19.

Bradley, Matt, *Lesbian Lane* (Hollywood: ONSCO Publications, 1963).

Bram, Christopher, 'The Shock of the Old', *Gay and Lesbian Review Worldwide* 10: 2 (2003): 32–3.

Bray, Abigail, 'The Question of Intolerance: "Corporate Paedophilia" and Child Sexual Abuse Moral Panics', *Australian Feminist Studies* 23: 57 (2008): 323–41.

—, 'Governing the Gaze: Child Sexual Abuse Moral Panics and the Post-Feminist Blindspot', *Feminist Media Studies* 9: 2 (2009): 173–91.

Brennan, Teresa, *The Transmission of Affect* (Ithaca, NY: Cornell University Press, 2004).

Brockes, Emma, 'Sheila Heti: "There's a sadness in not wanting the things that give others their life's meaning', *The Guardian*, 25 May 2018. Available at: <https://www.theguardian.com/books/2018/may/25/sheila-heti-motherhood-interview> (last accessed 13 June 2019).

Bronski, Michael, 'Fictions about Pulp', *Gay and Lesbian Review Worldwide* 8: 6 (2001): 18–20.

—, *Pulp Friction: The Golden Age of Gay Male Pulps* (New York: St. Martin's Press, 2003).

Brooks, Peter, *Troubling Confessions: Speaking Guilt in Law and Literature* (Chicago: University of Chicago Press, 2000).

Broughton, Trev Lynn, and Linda Anderson, 'Preface', in Broughton and Anderson (eds), *Women's Lives/Women's Times* (Albany: SUNY Press, 1997), pp. xi–xvii.

Brown, Wendy, *States of Injury: Power and Freedom in Late Modernity* (Princeton: Princeton University Press, 1995).

—, 'Neo-Liberalism and the End of Liberal Democracy', *Theory and Event* 7: 1 (2003): 1–19.

Bruhm, Steven, and Natasha Hurley (eds), *Curiouser: On the Queerness of Children* (Minneapolis: Minnesota University Press, 2004).

Bruns, John, 'Laughter in the Aisles: Affect and Power in Contemporary Theoretical and Cultural Discourse', *Studies in American Humor* 3: 7 (2000): 5–23.

Bulamur, Ayşe Naz, 'Scheherazade in the Western Palace: Martin Amis's *The Pregnant Widow*', *Clio* 43: 3 (2014): 1–19.

Bulhan, Husseen Abdilahi, *Frantz Fanon and the Psychology of Oppression* (New York: Plenum, 1985).

Burman, Erica, *Developments: Child, Image, Nation* (London: Routledge, 2008).

—, and Jackie Stacey, 'The Child and Childhood in Feminist Theory', *Feminist Theory* 11: 3 (2010): 227–40.

Butler, Judith, *Gender Trouble* [1990] (London: Routledge, 1999).

—, *Bodies That Matter* (London: Routledge, 1993).

—, *Precarious Life* (London: Verso, 2004).

—, *Undoing Gender* (London: Routledge, 2004).

Cairns, Douglas L., *Aidōs: The Psychology and Ethics of Honour and Shame in Ancient Greek Literature* (Oxford: Clarendon, 1993).

Califia, Pat, 'A Secret Side of Lesbian Sexuality', in Thomas Weinberg and G. W. Levi Kamel (eds), *S and M: Studies in Sadomasochism* (New York: Prometheus, 1983).

—, *Public Sex: The Culture of Radical Sex* (San Francisco: Cleis Press, 1994).

Calloway, Marie, *what purpose did i serve in your life* (New York: Tyrant Books, 2013).

Caplan, Paula J., *The Myth of Women's Masochism* (New York: E. P. Dutton, 1985).

Caprio, Frank, *Female Homosexuality: A Psychodynamic Study of Lesbianism* (New York: Citadel Press, 1954).

Carroll, Rachel, 'How Soon Is Now: Constructing the Contemporary/ Gendering the Experimental', *Contemporary Women's Writing* 9: 1 (2015): 16–33.

Carson, Anne, 'Euripides to the Audience', *London Review of Books* 24: 17 (5 September 2002): 24.

—, *Grief Lessons* (New York: New York Review Books, 2006).

Carter, Angela, *The Sadeian Woman* (London: Virago, 1979).

Carter, Julian, 'Gay Marriage and Pulp Fiction Homonormativity, Disidentification and Affect in Ann Bannon's Lesbian Novels', *GLQ* 15: 4 (2009): 583–609.

Cartwright, Lisa, *Moral Spectatorship: Technologies of Voice and Affect in Postwar Representations of the Child* (Durham, NC: Duke University Press, 2008).

Carver, Lisa, 'Marie Calloway on Her New Novel and Being Called "Jailbait"', *Vice Magazine*, 26 June 2013. Available at: <http://www.vice.com/read/marie-calloway> (last accessed 13 June 2019).

Case, Sue-Ellen, 'Towards a Butch-Femme Aesthetic', *Discourse* 11: 1 (1988–9): 55–73.

Caselli, Daniela, 'Kindergarten Theory: Childhood, Affect, Critical Thought', *Feminist Theory* 11: 3 (2010): 241–54.

Castañeda, Claudia, *Figurations: Child, Bodies, Worlds* (Durham, NC: Duke University Press, 2002).

Castle, Terry, *The Apparitional Lesbian: Female Homosexuality and Modern Culture* (New York: Columbia University Press, 1993).

Chamarette, Jenny, and Jennifer Higgins (eds), *Guilt and Shame: Essays in French Literature, Thought and Visual Culture* (Oxford: Peter Lang, 2010).

Chauncey, George, 'From Sexual Inversion to Homosexuality: Medicine and the Changing Conceptualization of Female Deviance', *Salmagundi* 58–9 (1983): 114–46.

—, *Gay New York: Gender, Urban Culture, and the Making of the Gay Male World, 1890–1940* (New York: Basic Books, 1994).

Chideckel, Maurice, *Female Sex Perversion: The Sexually Aberrated Woman As She Is* (New York: Eugenics, 1935).

Clough, Patricia, *The Affective Turn: Theorizing the Social* (Durham, NC: Duke University Press, 2008).

Coetzee, J. M., *Diary of a Bad Year* (London: Virago, 2007).

Connor, Steven, 'The Shame of Being a Man' (2000), unpag. Available at: <http://www.stevenconnor.com/shame/> (last accessed 13 June 2019).

Conrad, Joseph, 'The Return', in *Tales of Unrest* [1898] (New York: Doubleday, Page, 1920), pp. 201–316.

Cooke, Jennifer, 'Making a Scene: Towards an Anatomy of Contemporary Literary Intimacies', in Cooke (ed.), *Scenes of Intimacy* (London: Bloomsbury, 2013), pp. 3–21.

—, *Contemporary Feminist Life-Writing: The New Audacity* (Cambridge: Cambridge University Press, 2020).

Corber, Robert, *Homosexuality in Cold War America: Resistance and the Crisis of Masculinity* (Durham, NC: Duke University Press, 1997).

Cory, Donald Webster, *The Homosexual Outlook: A Subjective Approach* (London: Peter Nevill, 1953).

—, *The Lesbian in America* (New York: Citadel Press, 1964).

Crewdson, Gregory, 'Interview with A. M. Homes', *Bomb Magazine* 55 (1996): 38–42.

Crimp, Douglas, 'Mario Montez, For Shame', in Stephen M. Barber and David L. Clark (eds), *Regarding Sedgwick: Essays on Queer Culture and Critical Theory* (London: Routledge, 2002), pp. 57–70.

Cusk, Rachel, *A Life's Work: On Becoming a Mother* (London: Fourth Estate, 2001).

—, 'I Was Only Being Honest', *The Guardian*, 21 March 2008. Available at: <https://www.theguardian.com/books/2008/mar/21/biography.women> (last accessed 13 June 2019).

Cusset, Catherine, 'The Limits of Autofiction' (2012), a paper presented at New York University, April 2012. Available at: <http://www.catherinecusset.co.uk/wp-content/uploads/2013/02/THE-LIMITS-OF-AUTOFICTION.pdf> (last accessed 13 June 2019).

Cvetkovich, Ann, 'In the Archives of Lesbian Feelings: Documentary and Popular Culture', *Camera Obscura* 49, 17: 1 (2002): 106–47.

—, *An Archive of Feelings* (Durham, NC: Duke University Press, 2003).

Darwin, Charles, *The Expression of the Emotions in Man and Animals* (London: John Murray, 1901).

Davis, Kenneth C., *Two-Bit Culture: The Paperbacking of America* (Boston: Houghton Mifflin, 1984).

Davis, Madeline B., and Elizabeth Lapovsky Kennedy, 'Oral History and the Study of Sexuality in the Lesbian Community: Buffalo, New York, 1940–1960', *Feminist Studies* 12 (1986): 7–26.

—, *Boots of Leather, Slippers of Gold: The History of a Lesbian Community* (New York: Routledge, 1993).

Deleuze, Gilles, *Masochism* (New York: Zone Books, 1989).

—, 'Literature and Life', trans. Daniel W. Smith and Michael A. Greco, *Critical Inquiry* 23: 2 (1997): 225–30.

D'Emilio, John, 'Capitalism and Gay Identity', in Ann Snitow, Christine Stansell and Sharon Thompson (eds), *Powers of Desire: The Politics of Sexuality* (New York: Monthly Review Press, 1983), pp. 100–13.

—, *Sexual Politics, Sexual Communities* (Chicago: University of Chicago Press, 1983).

—, and Estelle B. Freedman, *Intimate Matters: A History of Sexuality in America*, 2nd edn (Chicago: University of Chicago Press, 1997).

Derrida, Jacques, 'The Animal That Therefore I Am (More to Follow)', *Critical Inquiry* 28: 2 (2002): 369–418.

Deutsch, Helene, 'The Significance of Masochism in the Mental Life of Women' [1930], in Russell Grigg, Dominique Hecq and Craig Smith (eds), *Female Sexuality* (New York: Other Press, 1999), pp. 183–94.

—, *The Psychology of Women, Vol 1: Girlhood* (London: Research Books, 1946).

Dix, Hywel, 'Introduction: Autofiction in English: The Story so Far', in Dix (ed.), *Autofiction in English* (Basingstoke: Palgrave, 2018), pp. 1–23.

Doan, Laura, 'What's In & Out, Out There? Disciplining the Lesbian', *American Literary History* 6: 3 (1994): 572–82.

—, and Sarah Waters, 'Making Up Lost Time: Contemporary Lesbian Writing and the Invention of History', in David Alderson and Linda Anderson (eds), *Territories of Desire in Queer Culture* (Manchester: Manchester University Press, 2000), pp. 12–28.

Doubrovsky, Serge, *Fils* (Paris: Galilée, 1977).

Duberman, Martin, Martha Vicinus and George Chauncey (eds), *Hidden from History: Reclaiming the Gay and Lesbian Past* (New York: New American Library, 1989).

Duggan, Lisa, *The Twilight of Equality? Neoliberalism, Cultural Politics and the Attack on Democracy* (Boston: Beacon, 2003).

Edelman, Lee, *No Future: Queer Theory and the Death Drive* (Durham, NC: Duke University Press, 2004).

Edwards, Natalie, '"Ecrire pour ne plus avoir honte": Christine Angot's and Annie Ernaux's Shameless Bodies', in Erica L. Johnson and Patricia Moran (eds), *The Female Face of Shame* (Bloomington: Indiana University Press, 2013), pp. 61–73.

Elliott, Mary, 'When Girls Will Be Boys: "Bad" Endings and Subversive Middles in Nineteenth-Century Tomboy Narratives and Twentieth-Century Lesbian Pulp Novels', *Legacy: A Journal of American Women Writers* 15: 1 (1998): 92–7.

Elliott, Stephen, 'The Rumpus Interview with Marie Calloway', *The Rumpus*, 29 December 2011. Available at: <http://therumpus.net/2011/12/the-rumpus-interview-with-marie-calloway/> (last accessed 13 June 2019).

Enriquez, Mariana, *Things We Lost in the Fire* [2016], trans. Megan McDowell (London: Portobello Books, 2017).

Er, Yanbing, 'Contemporary Women's Autofiction as Critique of Postfeminist Discourse', *Australian Feminist Studies* 33: 97 (2018): 316–30.

Euripides, *Hippolytos*, trans. Anne Carson, in *Grief Lessons: Four Plays* (New York: New York Review Books, 2006), p. 189 (l. 368).

—, *Fragments*, ed. and trans. Christopher Collard and Martin Cropp (Cambridge, MA: Harvard University Press, 2008).

Faderman, Lillian, *Surpassing the Love of Men* (New York: William Morrow, 1981).

—, *Odd Girls and Twilight Lovers* (New York: Columbia University Press, 1991).

—, *Chloe Plus Olivia* (London: Penguin, 1994).

Fateman, Johanna, 'Bodies of Work', *Bookforum*, September/October/November 2013. Available at: <http://www.bookforum.com/inprint/020_03/12182> (last accessed 13 June 2019).

Fayard, Nicole, 'Rape, Trauma, and Shame in Samira Bellil's *Dans l'enfer des tournantes*', in Erica L. Johnson and Patricia Moran (eds), *The Female Face of Shame* (Bloomington: Indiana University Press, 2013), pp. 34–47.

Felski, Rita, *Beyond Feminist Aesthetics: Feminist Literature and Social Change* (Cambridge, MA: Harvard University Press, 1989).

—, 'Redescriptions of Female Masochism', *Minnesota Review* 63/4 (2005): 127–39.

Fernie, Ewan, *Shame in Shakespeare* (London: Routledge, 2002).

Firestone, Shulamith, *The Dialectic of Sex* (London: Paladin, 1970).

Fisher, Anna Watkins, 'Manic Impositions: The Parasitical Art of Chris Kraus and Sophie Calle', *WSQ: Women's Studies Quarterly* 40: 1–2 (2012): 223–35.

Fisher, Berenice, 'Guilt and Shame in the Women's Movement: The Radical Ideal of Action and its Meaning for Feminist Intellectuals', *Feminist Studies* 10: 2 (1984): 185–212.

Flood, Alison, 'Martin Amis Says New Novel Will Get Him "In Trouble with the Feminists"', *The Guardian*, 20 November 2009.

Foote, Stephanie, 'Deviant Classics: Pulps and the Making of Lesbian Print Culture', *Signs* 31: 1 (2005): 169–90.

—, 'Afterword: Ann Aldrich and Lesbian Writing in the Fifties', in Ann Aldrich, *We Walk Alone* [1955] (New York: Feminist Press, 2006), pp. 157–83.

—, 'Afterword: Productive Contradictions', in Ann Aldrich, *We, Too, Must Love* (New York: Feminist Press, 2006), pp. 159–85.

Foster, Jeanette H., *Sex Variant Women in Literature: A Historical and Quantitative Survey* (New York: Vantage Press, 1956).

Foucault, Michel, *History of Sexuality, Vol. 1: The Will to Knowledge* [1976], trans. Robert Hurley (New York: Pantheon Books, 1978).

Freccero, Carla, *Queer/Early/Modern* (Durham, NC: Duke University Press, 2006).

Freedman, Estelle B., '"Uncontrolled Desires": The Response to the Sexual Psychopath, 1920–1960', *The Journal of American History* 74: 1 (1987): 83–106.

—, 'The Prison Lesbian: Race, Class, and the Construction of the Aggressive Female Homosexual, 1915–1965', *Feminist Studies* 22: 2 (1996): 397–423.

Freeman, Elizabeth, 'Packing History, Count(er)ing Generations', *New Literary History*, 31: 4 (2000): 727–44.

—, 'Time Binds, or Erotohistoriography', *Social Text* 23: 3–4 (84–5) (2005): 57–68.

—, *Time Binds: Queer Temporalities, Queer Histories* (Durham, NC: Duke University Press, 2010).

Freud, Sigmund, *Five Lectures on Psychoanalysis* [1909], trans. and ed. James Strachey (New York: W. W. Norton, 1961).

—, 'A Child is Being Beaten' [1919], in *On Psychopathology*, trans. James Strachey (Penguin Freud Library, vol. 10) (London: Penguin, 1979), pp. 159–93.

—, 'Beyond the Pleasure Principle' [1920], in *On Metapsychology*, trans. James Strachey (Penguin Freud Library, vol. 11) (London: Penguin, 1984), pp. 269–338.

—, 'The Economic Problem of Masochism' [1924], in *On Metapsychology*, trans. James Strachey (Penguin Freud Library, vol. 11) (London: Penguin, 1984), pp. 409–26.

—, 'Femininity' [1933], in *The Standard Edition of the Complete Psychological Works of Sigmund Freud, Volume XXII (1932–1936): New Introductory Lectures on Psychoanalysis and Other Works*, pp. 1–182.

Friedländer, Saul, *Franz Kafka: The Poet of Shame and Guilt* (New Haven, CT: Yale University Press, 2013).

Frimer, Denise, 'Chris Kraus in Conversation with Denise Frimer', *The Brooklyn Rail*, 10 April 2006. Available at: <http://www.brooklynrail.org/2006/04/art/chris-kraus-in-conversation-with-denise-frimer> (last accessed 13 June 2019).

Gaitskill, Mary, *Bad Behaviour* [1988] (London: Sceptre, 1989).

—, *Two Girls, Fat and Thin* (New York: Simon & Schuster, 1991).

Gallo, Marcia M., *Different Daughters: A History of the Daughters of Bilitis and the Rise of the Lesbian Rights Movement* (New York: Carroll and Graf, 2006).

Gay, Roxane, *Bad Feminist* (London: HarperCollins, 2014).

Gearhart, Suzanne, 'Foucault's Response to Freud: Sado-masochism and the Aestheticization of Power', *Style* 29: 3 (1995): 389–403.

Giardini, Federica, 'Public Affects: Clues Towards a Political Practice of Singularity', *European Journal of Women's Studies* 6: 2 (1999): 149–60.

Gill, Jo (ed.), *Modern Confessional Writing* (London: Routledge, 2006).

Gilmore, Leigh, *Autobiographics: A Feminist Theory of Women's Self-Representation* (Ithaca, NY: Cornell University Press, 1994).

—, *Tainted Witness* (New York: Columbia University Press, 2018).

Gilotta, David, 'The Body in Shame: Philip Roth's Physical Comedy', in Ben Siegel and Jay L. Halio (eds), *Playful and Serious: Philip Roth as a Comic Writer* (Newark: University of Delaware Press, 2010), pp. 92–116.

Ginsberg, Elaine K., 'Introduction: The Politics of Passing', in Ginsberg (ed.), *Passing and the Fictions of Identity* (Durham, NC: Duke University Press, 1996), pp. 1–19.

Glick, Robert A., and Donald I. Meyers, 'Introduction', in Glick and Meyers (eds), *Masochism: Current Psychoanalytic Perspectives* (Hillsdale, NJ: Analytic Press, 1988) pp. 1–25.

Goffman, Erving, *Stigma: Notes on the Management of Spoiled Identity* (London: Penguin, 1963).

Gould, Emily, 'Exposed', *The New York Times Magazine*, 25 May 2008. Available at: <http://www.nytimes.com/2008/05/25/magazine/25internet-t.html?pagewanted=all&_r=1&> (last accessed 13 June 2019).

—, *And the Heart Says Whatever* (New York: Simon and Schuster, 2010).

—, 'Our Graffiti', *Emily Magazine*, 29 November 2011. Available at: <http://www.emilymagazine.com/?p=827> (last accessed 13 June 2019).

Gregory, Elizabeth, 'Confessing the Body: Plath, Sexton, Berryman, Lowell, Ginsberg and the Gendered Poetics of the "Real"', in Jo Gill (ed.), *Modern Confessional Writing* (London: Routledge, 2006), pp. 33–49.

Grier, Barbara [writing as Gene Damon], 'Lesbiana', *The Ladder* 3: 5 (February 1959): 17. Quotation taken from the 1975 Arno Press reprint edition of *The Ladder* (New York).

—, 'Lesbiana', *The Ladder* 4: 7 (April 1960): 18. Quotation taken from the 1975 Arno Press reprint edition of *The Ladder* (New York).

—, 'Lesbiana', *The Ladder* 5: 11 (August 1961): 23. Quotation taken from the 1975 Arno Press reprint edition of *The Ladder* (New York).

Grier, Barbara, *The Lesbian in Literature: A Bibliography* (San Francisco: Daughters of Bilitis, 1967).

—, and Tricia Lootens, 'Ann Bannon: A Writer of Lost Lesbian Fiction Finds Herself and Her Public' [Interview], *Off Our Backs* 13: 11 (December 1983): 12, 15, 20.

Griffin, Gabriele, *Heavenly Love? Lesbian Images in Twentieth-Century Women's Writing* (Manchester: Manchester University Press, 1993).

Guenther, Lisa, 'Resisting Agamben: The Biopolitics of Shame and Humiliation', *Philosophy and Social Criticism* 38: 1 (2012): 59–79.

Gullette, Margaret Morganroth, 'The Exile of Adulthood: Pedophilia in the Midlife Novel', *NOVEL: A Forum on Fiction*, 17: 3 (1984): 215–32.

Hacking, Ian, 'The Making and Molding of Child Abuse', *Critical Inquiry* 17: 2 (1991): 253–88.

Halberstam, J., 'Shame and White Gay Masculinity', *Social Text* 84–5 (2005): 219–33.

Halperin, David M., and Valerie Traub (eds), 'Beyond Gay Pride', in Halperin and Traub (eds), *Gay Shame* (Chicago: University of Chicago Press, 2009), pp. 3–40.

—, *Gay Shame* (Chicago: University of Chicago Press, 2009).

Hamer, Diane, '"I Am a Woman": Ann Bannon and the Writing of Lesbian Identity in the 1950s', in Mark Lilly (ed.), *Lesbian & Gay Writing* (Basingstoke: Macmillan, 1990), pp. 47–75.

—, and Belinda Budge (eds), *The Good, the Bad, and the Gorgeous: Popular Culture's Romance with Lesbianism* (London: Pandora Press, 1994).

Hardie, Melissa Jane, 'Fluff and Granite: Rereading Ayn Rand's Camp Feminist Aesthetics', in Mimi Reisel Gladstein and Chris Matthew Sciabarra (eds), *Feminist Interpretations of Ayn Rand* (University Park: Pennsylvania University Press, 1999), pp. 363–89.

Hatch, James C., 'Disruptive Affects: Shame, Disgust, and Sympathy in *Frankenstein*', *European Romantic Review* 19: 1 (2008): 33–49.

Haug, Frigga, 'Sexual Deregulation or, the Child Abuser as Hero in Neoliberalism', *Feminist Theory* 2: 1 (2001): 55–78.

Heller, Tamar, 'Affliction in Jean Rhys and Simone Weil', in Erica L. Johnson and Patricia Moran (eds), *The Female Face of Shame* (Bloomington: Indiana University Press, 2013), pp. 166–76.

Hemmings, Clare, 'Invoking Affect', *Cultural Studies* 19: 5 (2005): 548–67.

Henke, Suzette A., *Shattered Subjects: Trauma and Testimony in Women's Life-Writing* (New York: St. Martin's Press, 1998).

—, 'A Bloody Shame: Angela Carter's Shameless Postmodern Fairy Tales', in Erica L. Johnson and Patricia Moran (eds), *The Female Face of Shame* (Bloomington: Indiana University Press, 2013), pp. 48–60.

Hennessy, Rosemary, *Profit and Pleasure: Sexual Identities in Late Capitalism* (New York: Routledge, 2000).

Hermes, Joke, 'Sexuality in Lesbian Romance Fiction', *Feminist Review* 42 (1992): 49–66.

Heti, Sheila, 'Chris Kraus' [interview], *The Believer* (September 2013). Available at: <http://www.believermag.com/issues/201309/?read=interview_kraus> (last accessed 13 June 2019).

Hoby, Hermione, 'Karl Ove Knausgaard: Norway's Proust and a Life Laid Painfully Bare', *The Observer*, 1 March 2014. Available at: <https://www.theguardian.com/theobserver/2014/mar/01/karl-ove-knausgaard-norway-proust-profile> (last accessed 13 June 2019).

Holland, Nancy J., 'What Gilles Deleuze Has to Say to Battered Women', *Philosophy and Literature* 17: 1 (1993): 16–25.

Homes, A. M., *Music for Torching* (London: Granta, 1999).

—, *The End of Alice* [1996] (New York: Scribner, 2006).

Horney, Karen, *Feminine Psychology* (New York: Norton, 1967).

Hughes, Evan, 'Karl Ove Knausgaard Became a Literary Sensation by Exposing His Every Secret', *New Republic*, 8 April 2014. Available at: <https://newrepublic.com/article/117245/karl-ove-knausgaard-interview-literary-star-struggles-regret> (last accessed 13 June 2019).

Hustvedt, Siri, *A Woman Looking at Men Looking at Women: Essays on Art, Sex, and the Mind* (New York: Simon & Schuster, 2016).

Hutton, Elaine (ed.), *Beyond Sex and Romance: The Politics of Contemporary Lesbian Fiction* (London: Women's Press, 1998).

Ivanova, Velichka, 'My Own Foe from the Other Gender: (Mis)representing Women in *The Dying Animal*', *Philip Roth Studies* 8: 1 (2012): 31–44.

Ivy, Marilyn, 'Have You Seen Me? Recovering the Inner Child in Late Twentieth-Century America', *Social Text* 37 (1993): 227–52.

Jacquet, Jennifer, *Is Shame Necessary? New Uses for an Old Tool* (London: Allen Lane, 2015).

Jagose, Annamarie, *Inconsequence: Lesbian Representation and the Logic of Sexual Sequence* (Ithaca, NY: Cornell University Press, 2002).

James, Allison, and Alan Prout (eds), *Constructing and Reconstructing Childhood* (London: Falmer Press, 1997).

James, Allison, Chris Jenks and Alan Prout, *Theorizing Childhood* (Cambridge: Polity Press, 1998).

Jamison, Leslie, *The Empathy Exams* (London: Granta, 2014).

—, *The Recovering* (London: Granta, 2018).

Jay, Karla, and Joanne Glasgow (eds), *Lesbian Texts and Contexts* (New York: New York University Press, 1990).

Jelinek, Estelle C., 'Introduction: Women's Autobiography and the Male Tradition', in Jelinek (ed.), *Women's Autobiography: Essays in Criticism* (Bloomington: Indiana University Press, 1980), pp. 1–20.

—, *The Tradition of Women's Autobiography* [1986] (Xlibris, 2003).

Jenks, Chris, *Childhood* (London: Routledge, 2002).

Jennings, Rebecca, *Tomboys and Bachelor Girls: A Lesbian History of Postwar Britain, 1945–1971* (Manchester: Manchester University Press, 2007).

Johnson, David K., *The Lavender Scare: The Cold War Persecution of Gays and Lesbians in the Federal Government* (Chicago: Chicago University Press, 2004).

Johnson, Erica L., and Patricia Moran (eds), *The Female Face of Shame* (Bloomington: Indiana University Press, 2013).

Jones, Amelia, *Body Art/Performing the Subject* (Minneapolis: University of Minnesota Press, 1998).

Jones, Bethan, 'Traces of Shame: Margaret Atwood's Portrayal of Childhood Bullying and its Consequences in *Cat's Eye*', *Critical Survey* 20: 1 (2008): 29–42.

Juhasz, Suzanne, *Reading from the Heart* (New York: Viking, 1994).

—, 'Lesbian Romance Fiction and the Plotting of Desire', *Tulsa Studies in Women's Literature* 17: 1 (1998): 65–82.

June, Laura, 'My Favorite Mommy Blogger, Karl Ove Knausgaard', *The Cut*, 17 June 2016. Available at: <http://nymag.com/thecut/2016/06/karl-ove-knausgaard-mommy-blogger.html> (last accessed 13 June 2019).

Kakutani, Michiko, 'Like Humbert Humbert, Full of Lust and Lies', *The New York Times*, 23 February 1996. Available at: <http://www.nytimes.com/1996/02/23/books/books-of-the-times-like-humbert-humbert-full-of-lust-and-lies.html> (last accessed 13 June 2019).

Kang, Han, *The Vegetarian* [2007], trans. Deborah Smith (London: Portobello Books, 2015).

Kaufman, Gershen, *The Psychology of Shame* (New York: Springer, 1989).

Keller, Yvonne, 'Pulp Politics: Strategies of Vision in Pro-Lesbian Pulp Novels, 1955–65', in Patricia Juliana Smith (ed.), *The Queer Sixties* (New York: Routledge, 1999), pp. 1–25.

—, 'Ab/normal Looking: Voyeurism and Surveillance in Lesbian Pulp Novels and US Cold War Culture', *Feminist Media Studies* 5: 2 (2005): 177–95.

—, '"Was It Right to Love Her Brother's Wife So Passionately?": Lesbian Pulp Novels and U.S. Lesbian Identity, 1950–1965', *American Quarterly* 57: 2 (2005): 385–410.

Kerényi, Karl, *La religione antica nelle sue linee fondamentali*, trans. Delio Cantimori (Bologna: N. Zanchelli, 1940).

Kincaid, James R., *Erotic Innocence: The Culture of Child Molesting* (Durham, NC: Duke University Press, 1998).

Kinsey, Alfred C., *Sexual Behavior in the Human Female* (Philadelphia: W. B. Saunders, 1953).

Kitzinger, Jenny, 'Defending Innocence: Ideologies of Childhood', *Feminist Review* 28 (1988): 77–87.

—, 'Who Are You Kidding? Children, Power, and the Struggle Against Sexual Abuse', in Allison James and Alan Prout (eds), *Constructing and Reconstructing Childhood* (London: Falmer Press, 1997), pp. 165–89.

Knausgaard, Karl Ove, *My Struggle I: A Death in the Family* [2009], trans. Don Bartlett (London: Vintage, 2013).

—, *My Struggle II: A Man in Love* [2009], trans. Don Bartlett (London: Vintage, 2013).

Koestenbaum, Wayne, *Humiliation* (New York: Picador, 2011).

Koski, Fran, and Maida Tilchen, 'Some Pulp Sappho', in Karla Jay and Allen Young (eds), *Lavender Culture* (New York: Harcourt Brace, 1978), pp. 262–74.

Kraus, Chris, *I Love Dick* [1997] (Los Angeles: Semiotext(e), 2006).

—, *Aliens and Anorexia* (South Pasadena: Semiotext(e), 2000).

Krich, Aron M. (ed.), *The Homosexuals: As Seen by Themselves and Thirty Authorities* (New York: Citadel, 1954).

— (ed.) *Women: The Variety and Meaning of their Sexual Experience* (New York: Dell, 1956).

Kunzru, Hari, 'Karl Ove Knausgaard: The Latest Literary Sensation', *The Guardian*, 7 March 2014. Available at: <https://www.theguardian.com/books/2014/mar/07/karl-ove-knausgaard-my-struggle-hari-kunzru> (last accessed 13 June 2019).

Laplanche, Jean, and Jean-Bertrand Pontalis, *The Language of Psychoanalysis* (London: Karnac Books, 1973).

Lasch, Christopher, 'For Shame: Why Americans Should Be Wary of Self-Esteem', *New Republic*, 10 August 1992. Available at: <https://newrepublic.com/article/90898/shame-why-americans-should-be-wary-self-esteem> (last accessed 27 November 2018).

Lawson, Mark, Interview with Martin Amis, *Front Row*, BBC Radio 4, 2 February 2010.

Lea, Daniel, and Berthold Schoene, 'Masculinity in Transition: An Introduction', in Lea and Schoene (eds), *Posting the Male* (Amsterdam: Rodopi, 2003), pp. 7–17.

Lehtinen, Ullaliina, 'How Does One Know What Shame Is? Epistemology, Emotions, and Forms of Life in Juxtaposition', *Hypatia* 13: 1 (1998): 56–77.

Lesnik-Oberstein, Karín (ed.), *Children in Culture* (Basingstoke: Palgrave, 1998).

—, 'Childhood, Queer Theory and Feminism', *Feminist Theory* 11: 3 (2010): 309–21.

— (ed.), *Children in Culture, Revisited* (Basingstoke: Palgrave, 2011).

—, 'Introduction: Voice, Agency and the Child', in Karín Lesnik-Oberstein (ed.), *Children in Culture, Revisited* (Basingstoke: Palgrave, 2011), pp. 1–17.

—, and Stephen Thomson, 'What is Queer Theory Doing with the Child?', *Parallax* 8: 1 (2002): 35–46.

Levi, Primo, *If This is a Man* [1947], trans. Stuart Wolf (London: Orion Press, 1959).

—, *The Drowned and the Saved* [1986] (New York: Simon & Schuster, 1988).

Levinas, Emmanuel, *On Escape* [1935], trans. Bettina Bergo (Stanford: Stanford University Press, 2003).

Lewis, Carolyn Herbst, *Prescription for Heterosexuality: Sexual Citizenship in the Cold War Era* (Chapel Hill: University of North Carolina Press, 2010).

Lewis, Helen Block, *Shame and Guilt in Neurosis* (New York: International Universities Press, 1971).

—, 'The Role of Shame in Depression in Women', in Ruth Formanek and Anita Gurian (eds), *Women and Depression* (New York: Springer, 1987).

— (ed.), *The Role of Shame in Symptom Formation* (Hillsdale, NJ: L. Erlbaum, 1987).

— 'Emotional Rescue', in David M. Halperin and Valerie Traub (eds), *Gay Shame*, (Chicago: University of Chicago Press, 2009), pp. 256–76.

Lewis, Michael, *Shame: The Exposed Self* (New York: Free Press, 1992).

Leys, Ruth, *From Guilt to Shame: Auschwitz and After* (Princeton: Princeton University Press, 2007).

Lilly, Mark (ed.), *Lesbian and Gay Writing: An Anthology of Critical Writing* (Basingstoke: Macmillan, 1990).

Linden, Robin Ruth, Darlene R. Pagano, Diana E. H. Russell and Susan Leigh Star (eds), *Against Sadomasochism: A Radical Feminist Analysis* (East Palo Alto, CA: Frog in the Well, 1982).

Lindo, Karen, 'Interrogating the Place of *Lajja* (Shame) in Contemporary Mauritius', in Erica L. Johnson and Patricia Moran (eds), *The Female Face of Shame* (Bloomington: Indiana University Press, 2013), pp. 212–28.

Liptrot, Amy, *The Outrun* (Edinburgh: Canongate, 2015).

Livesey, Margot, 'Surprise, Surprise', *TLS*, 31 October 1997.

Locke, Jill, *Democracy and the Death of Shame: Political Equality and Social Disturbance* (Cambridge: Cambridge University Press, 2016).

Loewenstein, Andrea, 'Sad Stories: A Reflection on the Fiction of Ann Bannon', *Gay Community News* 7: 43 (24 May 1980).

Loewenstein, Rudolf, 'A Contribution to the Psychoanalytic Theory of Masochism', *Journal of the American Psychoanalytic Association* 5 (1957): 197–234.

Long, Camilla, 'Martin Amis and the Sex War', *The Times*, 24 January 2010.

Lootens, Tricia, 'Ann Bannon: A Lesbian Audience Discovers Its Lost Literature' [Review], *Off Our Backs* 13: 11 (December 1983): 13, 20.

Love, Heather, '"Spoiled Identity": Stephen Gordon's Loneliness and the Difficulties of Queer History', *GLQ* 7: 4 (2001): 487–519.

—, *Feeling Backward: Loss and the Politics of Queer History* (Cambridge, MA: Harvard University Press, 2007).

—, 'Compulsory Happiness and Queer Existence', *New Formations* 63 (Winter 2007/8): 52–64.

—, 'Underdogs: On the Minor in Queer Theory', paper delivered at the Queer Theory Workshop, Columbia University, 8 February 2011.

—, 'Safe', *American Literary History* 25: 1 (2013): 164–75.

Luckhurst, Roger, 'Memory Recovered/Recovered Memory', in Roger Luckhurst and Peter Marks (eds), *Literature and the Contemporary* (Harlow: Longman, 1999), pp. 80–93.

—, *The Trauma Question* (London: Routledge, 2008).

Lynch, Lee, 'Cruising the Libraries', in Karla Jay and Joanne Glasgow (eds), *Lesbian Texts and Contexts* (New York: New York University Press, 1990), pp. 39–48.

Lynd, Helen Merrell, *On Shame and the Search for Identity* (New York: Harcourt, Brace, 1953).

Machado, Carmen Maria, *Her Body and Other Parties* [2017] (London: Serpent's Tail, 2019).

Mackinnon, Jane, 'The Homosexual Woman', *American Journal of Psychiatry* 103: 5 (1947): 661–4.

Mackintosh, Sophie, *The Water Cure* (London: Hamish Hamilton, 2018).

MacLeod, Mary, and Esther Saraga, 'Challenging the Orthodoxy: Towards a Feminist Theory and Practice', *Feminist Review* 28 (1988): 16–55.

Manion, Jennifer C., 'The Moral Relevance of Shame', *American Philosophical Quarterly* 39: 1 (2002): 73–90.

—, 'Girls Blush, Sometimes: Gender, Moral Agency, and the Problem of Shame', *Hypatia* 18: 3 (2003): 21–41.

Marcus, Maria, *A Taste for Pain: Masochism and Female Sexuality* (New York: St. Martin's Press, 1981).

Martin, Della, *Twilight Girl* [1961] (San Francisco: Cleis Press, 2006).

Massumi, Brian, 'The Autonomy of Affect', in Paul Patton (ed.), *Deleuze: A Critical Reader* (Oxford: Blackwell, 1996), pp. 217–39.

—, *Parables for the Virtual: Movement, Affect, Sensation* (Durham, NC: Duke University Press, 2002).

Meeker, Martin, 'A Queer and Contested Medium: The Emergence of Representational Politics in the "Golden Age" of Lesbian Paperbacks, 1955–1963', *Journal of Women's History* 17: 1 (2005): 165–88.

Melosh, Barbara (ed.), *Gender and American History Since 1890* (London: Routledge, 1992).

Mendible, Myra (ed.), *American Shame: Stigma and the Body Politic* (Bloomington: Indiana University Press, 2016).

Merkin, Daphne, 'Random Objects of Desire', *New York Times*, 24 March 1996.

Meulenbelt, Anja, *The Shame is Over: A Political Life Story* (London: The Women's Press, 1980).

Meyer, Moe, 'Introduction: Reclaiming the Discourse of Camp', in Meyer (ed.), *The Politics and Poetics of Camp* (New York: Routledge, 1994), pp. 1–22.

Meyerowitz, Joanne (ed.), *Not June Cleaver: Women and Gender in Postwar America 1945–1960* (Philadelphia: Temple University Press, 1994).

Miller, Susan B., *The Shame Experience* (Hillsdale, NJ: Analytic Press, 1985).

Miller, William Ian, *Humiliation: And Other Essays on Honor, Social Discomfort, and Violence* (Ithaca, NY: Cornell University Press, 1993).

Millett, Kate, *Flying* (New York: Ballantine Books, 1974).

Mills, Catherine, 'Linguistic Survival and Ethicality: Biopolitics, Subjectification, and Testimony in *Remnants of Auschwitz*', in Andrew Norris (ed.), *Politics, Metaphysics, and Death: Essays on Giorgio Agamben's* Homo Sacer (Durham, NC: Duke University Press, 2005), pp. 198–221.

Mitchell, Kaye, 'Gender and Sexuality in Popular Fiction', in David Glover and Scott McCracken (eds), *Cambridge Companion to Popular Fiction* (Cambridge: Cambridge University Press, 2012), pp. 122–40.

—, '"Who Is She?" Identities, Intertextuality and Authority in Non-Fiction Lesbian Pulp of the 1950s', in Heike Bauer and Matt Cook (eds), *Queer 1950s* (Basingstoke: Palgrave, 2012), pp. 150–66.

—, 'Cleaving to the Scene of Shame: Stigmatized Childhoods in *The End of Alice* and *Two Girls, Fat and Thin*', *Contemporary Women's Writing* 7: 3 (2013): 309–27.

—, 'Feral with Vulnerability', *Angelaki* 23: 1 (2018): 194–8.

—, 'Vulnerability and Vulgarity: The Uses of Shame in the Work of Dodie Bellamy', in Barry Sheils and Julie Walsh (eds), *Shame and Modern Writing* (London: Routledge, 2018), pp. 165–85.

Moi, Toril, 'Shame and Openness', trans. Toril Moi and Anders Firing Lunde, *Salmagundi* 177 (2013): 205–10.

Molotkow, Alexandra, 'Marie Calloway, Degrading Sex, and Books About It', *Hazlitt*, 11 June 2013. Available at: <http://penguinrandomhouse.ca/hazlitt/feature/marie-calloway-degrading-sex-and-books-about-it> (last accessed 13 June 2019).

Moon, Jennifer, 'Gay Shame and the Politics of Identity', in David M. Halperin and Valerie Traub (eds), *Gay Shame* (Chicago: Chicago University Press, 2009), pp. 357–68.

Moran, Brendan, 'An Inhumanly Wise Shame', *The European Legacy* 14: 5 (2009): 573–85.

Morgan, Michael L., *On Shame* (New York: Routledge, 2008).

Morrison, Andrew P., 'The Eye Turned Inward: Shame and the Self', in Donald Nathanson (ed.), *The Many Faces of Shame* (New York: Guilford, 1987), pp. 271–91.

Morrison, Blake, *As If* (London: Granta, 1997).

Morse, Benjamin, *The Lesbian: A Frank, Revealing Study of Women Who Turn to Their Own Sex for Love* (Derby, CT: Monarch Books, 1961).

Mortimer, Armine Kotin, 'Autofiction as Allofiction: Doubrovsky's *L'Après-vivre*', *L'Esprit Créateur* 49: 3 (2009): 22–35.

Moynihan, Sinéad, *Passing into the Present: Contemporary American Fiction of Racial and Gender Passing* (Manchester: Manchester University Press, 2010).

Muñoz, José Esteban, 'Thinking Beyond Antirelationality and Antiutopianism in Queer Critique', in 'Forum: Conference Debates', 'The Antisocial Thesis in Queer Theory', *PMLA* 121: 3 (2006): 825–6.

—, *Cruising Utopia* (New York: New York University Press, 2009).

Munt, Sally, 'Shame/Pride Dichotomies in *Queer As Folk*', *Textual Practice* 14: 3 (2000): 531–46.

—, 'The Well of Shame', in Laura Doan and Jay Prosser (eds), *Palatable Poison* (New York: Columbia University Press, 2001), pp. 199–215.

—, *Queer Attachments: The Cultural Politics of Shame* (Aldershot: Ashgate, 2007).

Myles, Eileen, 'Foreword', in Chris Kraus, *I Love Dick* [1997] (Los Angeles: Semiotext(e), 2006), pp. 13–15.

Nabokov, Vladimir, *Lolita* [1955] (London: Penguin, 1980).

Nathanson, Donald L. (ed.), *The Many Faces of Shame* (New York: Guilford Press, 1987).

—, *Shame and Pride: Affect, Sex, and the Birth of the Self* (New York: Norton, 1992).

Nealon, Christopher, 'Invert-History: The Ambivalence of Lesbian Pulp Fiction', *New Literary History* 31 (2000): 745–64.

—, *Foundlings* (Durham, NC: Duke University Press, 2001).

Nestle, Joan, *A Restricted Country* (Ithaca, NY: Firebrand Books, 1987).

Ngai, Sianne, *Ugly Feelings* (Cambridge, MA: Harvard University Press, 2005).

Nussbaum, Emily, 'Mary, Mary, Less Contrary', *New York Magazine*, 2005. Available at: <http://nymag.com/nymetro/arts/books/14988/> (last accessed 13 June 2019).

Nussbaum, Martha, *Hiding from Humanity: Disgust, Shame and the Law* (Princeton: Princeton University Press, 2004).

Ohi, Kevin, *Innocence and Rapture: The Erotic Child in Pater, Wilde, James, and Nabokov* (Basingstoke: Palgrave, 2005).

O'Sullivan, Simon, 'The Aesthetics of Affect: Thinking Art Beyond Representation', *Angelaki* 6: 3 (2001): 125–35.

Packer, Vin, *Spring Fire* [1952] (San Francisco: Cleis Press, 2004).

Pajaczkowska, Claire, and Ivan Ward (eds), *Shame and Sexuality: Psychoanalysis and Visual Culture* (London: Routledge, 2008).

Patnoe, Elizabeth, 'Lolita Misrepresented, Lolita Reclaimed: Disclosing the Doubles', *College Literature* 22: 2 (1995): 81–104.

Peiss, Kathy, and Christina Simmons (eds), *Passion and Power: Sexuality in History* (Philadelphia: Temple University Press, 1989).

Penn, Donna, 'The Meanings of Lesbianism in Postwar America', in Barbara Melosh (ed.), *Gender and American History Since 1890* (London: Routledge, 1992), pp. 106–24.

—, 'The Sexualized Woman: The Lesbian, the Prostitute, and the Containment of Female Sexuality in Postwar America', in Joanne Meyerowitz (ed.), *Not June Cleaver: Women and Gender in Postwar America 1945–1960* (Philadelphia: Temple University Press, 1994), pp. 358–81.

Penney, James, *After Queer Theory: The Limits of Sexual Politics* (London: Pluto Press, 2014).

Percesepe, Gary, 'Ayn Rand and the American Psyche: An Interview with Mary Gaitskill', 14 June 2011. Available at: <http://www.thenervousbreakdown.com/gpercesepe/2011/06/ayn-rand-and-the-american-psyche-an-interview-with-mary-gaitskill/> (last accessed 13 June 2019).

Phillips, Anita, *A Defence of Masochism* (London: Faber and Faber, 1998).

Pines, Malcolm, 'Shame: What Psychoanalysis Does and Does Not Say' [1987], in Claire Pajaczkowska and Ivan Ward (eds), *Shame and Sexuality: Psychoanalysis and Visual Culture* (London: Routledge, 2008), pp. 93–106.

Pollitt, Katha, 'What Was Feminism Really Like in 1970? You Won't Find Out from Martin Amis' Version', *Slate Magazine*, 25 May 2010. Available at: <http://www.slate.com/articles/arts/books/2010/05/what_was_feminism_really_like_in_1970.html> (last accessed 13 June 2019).

Probyn, Elspeth, 'Sporting Bodies: Dynamics of Shame and Pride', *Body and Society* 6: 1 (2000): 13–28.

—, *Blush: Faces of Shame* (Minneapolis: University of Minnesota Press, 2005).

Rabinowitz, Paula, 'Slips of the Tongue: Lesbian Pulp Fiction as How-To-Dress Manuals', in Cristina Giorcelli (ed.), *Abito e identità* (Roma: Ila Palma, 2007), pp. 207–31.

Riley, Denise, 'Lyric Shame', in Barry Sheils and Julie Walsh (eds), *Shame and Modern Writing* (London: Routledge, 2018), pp. 68–72.

Roisman, Hanna M., 'The Veiled Hippolytus and Phaedra', *Hermes* 127 (1999): 397–409.

Ronson, Jon, *So You've Been Publicly Shamed* (London: Picador, 2015).

Roof, Judith, *A Lure of Knowledge: Lesbian Sexuality and Theory* (New York: Columbia University Press, 1991).

—, *Come As You Are: Sexuality and Narrative* (New York: Columbia University Press, 1996).

Rosario, Vernon A., *Homosexuality and Science: A Guide to the Debates* (Santa Barbara: ABC-CLIO, 2002).

Rose, Jacqueline, *The Case of Peter Pan or The Impossibility of Children's Fiction* (Basingstoke: Macmillan, 1984).

—, *On Not Being Able to Sleep* (London: Vintage, 2004).

Roth, Philip, *The Dying Animal* (London: Jonathan Cape, 2001).

—, *Everyman* (London: Vintage, 2007).

Rothman, Joshua, 'What is the Struggle in "My Struggle"?', *New Yorker*, 28 May 2014.

Ryan, Kate Moira, Linda Chapman and Ann Bannon, *The Beebo Brinker Chronicles* (New York: Dramatists Play Service, 2009).

Said, Edward W., *On Late Style* (New York: Pantheon Books, 2006).

Sartre, Jean-Paul, *Being and Nothingness* [1943], trans. Hazel E. Barnes (New York: Washington Square Press, 1956).

Scappettone, Jennifer, 'Bachelorettes, Even: Strategic Embodiment in Contemporary Experimentalism by Women', *Modern Philology* 105: 1 (2007): 178–84.

Schapiro, Barbara, 'Trauma and Sadomasochistic Narrative: Mary Gaitskill's "The Dentist"', *Mosaic* 38: 2 (2005): 37–52.

Scheff, Thomas J., and Suzanne M. Retzinger, *Emotions and Violence: Shame and Rage in Destructive Conflicts* (Lexington: D. C. Heath, 1991).

Schillinger, Liesl, 'Why Karl Ove Knausgaard Can't Stop Writing', *WSJ Magazine*, 4 November 2015. Available at: <http://www.wsj.com/articles/why-karl-ove-knausgaard-cant-stop-writing-1446688727?mod=e2tw> (last accessed 13 June 2019).

Schmitt, Arnaud, 'Making the Case for Self-Narration Against Autofiction', *a/b: Auto/Biography Studies* 25: 1 (2010): 122–37.

Scott, Sara, 'Surviving Selves: Feminism and Contemporary Discourses of Child Sexual Abuse', *Feminist Theory* 2: 3 (2001): 349–61.

Sedgwick, Eve Kosofsky, 'Queer Performativity: Henry James's *The Art of the Novel*', *GLQ* 1: 1 (1993): 1–16.

—, *Tendencies* (London: Routledge, 1994).

—, *Touching Feeling* (Durham, NC: Duke University Press, 2003).

—, *Between Men* [1985] (New York: Columbia University Press, 2015).

— and Adam Frank (eds), *Shame and Its Sisters: A Silvan Tomkins Reader* (Durham, NC: Duke University Press, 1995).

Segal, Lynne, 'Back to the Boys? Temptations of the Good Gender Theorist', *Textual Practice* 15: 2 (2001): 231–50.

—, 'The Circus of (Male) Ageing: Philip Roth and the Perils of Masculinity', in Stephen Frosh (ed.), *Psychosocial Imaginaries* (Basingstoke: Palgrave, 2015), pp. 87–104.

Seigworth, Gregory J., and Melissa Gregg (eds), *The Affect Theory Reader* (Durham, NC: Duke University Press, 2010).

—, 'An Inventory of Shimmers', in Seigworth and Gregg (eds), *The Affect Theory Reader* (Durham, NC: Duke University Press, 2010), pp. 1–25.

Seltzer, Mark, *Serial Killers: Death and Life in America's Wound Culture* (London: Routledge, 1998).

Server, Lee, *Over My Dead Body: The Sensational Age of the American Paperback 1945–1955* (San Francisco: Chronicle Books, 1994).

—, *Encyclopedia of Pulp Fiction Writers* (New York: Facts on File, 2002).

Sharpe, Matthew, 'Interview with Mary Gaitskill', *Bomb Magazine* 107 (2009), unpag. Available at: <https://bombmagazine.org/articles/mary-gaitskill/> (last accessed 5 July 2019).

Sheils, Barry, and Julie Walsh (eds), *Shame and Modern Writing* (London: Routledge, 2018).

Shulman, George, 'On Vulnerability as Judith Butler's Language of Politics: From "Excitable Speech" to "Precarious Life"', *Women's Studies Quarterly* 39: 1/2 (2011): 227–35.

Siegel, Carol, *Male Masochism: Modern Revisions of the Story of Love* (Bloomington: Indiana University Press, 1995).

Silk, Kay, 'Lesbian Novels in the Fifties', *Focus* (August 1973): 4–7.

Silverman, Kaja, 'Masochism and Male Subjectivity', *Camera Obscura* 17 (1988): 33–65.

Sky, Melissa, 'Cover Charge: Selling Sex and Survival in Lesbian Pulp Fiction', in Nicole Matthews and Nickianne Moody (eds), *Judging a Book by its Cover: Fans, Publishers, Designers and the Marketing of Fiction* (Aldershot: Ashgate, 2007), pp. 129–45.

—, *Twilight Tales* (Saarbruck: VDM, 2010).

Smart, Carol, 'A History of Ambivalence and Conflict in the Discursive Construction of the "Child Victim" of Sexual Abuse', *Social and Legal Studies* 8: 3 (1999): 391–409.

Snediker, Michael D., *Queer Optimism: Lyric Personhood and Other Felicitous Persuasions* (Minneapolis: University of Minnesota Press, 2009).

Solnit, Rebecca, *Men Explain Things to Me* (London: Granta, 2014).

Sontag, Susan, *Notes on Camp* [1964] (London: Penguin, 2018).

Spahr, Juliana, and Stephanie Young, 'Foulipo', in *Drunken Boat* 8. Available at: <https://www.drunkenboat.com/db8/oulipo/feature-oulipo/essays/spahr-young/foulipo.html> (last accessed 13 June 2019).

Spiers, Elizabeth, 'But Is It Good?: The Problem With Marie Calloway's Affectless Realism', *Flavorwire*, 18 June 2013. Available at: <http://flavorwire.com/398643/but-is-it-good-the-problem-with-marie-calloways-affectless-realism> (last accessed 13 June 2019).

Spitzer, Mark, *Music as Philosophy: Adorno and Beethoven's Late Style* (Bloomington: Indiana University Press, 2006).

Sprague, W. D., *The Lesbian in Our Society* (New York: Midwood Press, 1962).

Stein, Arlene, *Shameless: Sexual Dissidence in American Culture* (New York: New York University Press, 2006).

Stimpson, Catharine, 'Zero Degree Deviancy: The Lesbian Novel in English', *Critical Inquiry* 8: 2 (1981): 363–79.

Stoeffel, Kat, 'Meet Marie Calloway: The New Model for Literary Seductress is Part Feminist, Part "Famewhore" and All Pseudonymous', *New York Observer*, 20 December 2011. Available at: <http://observer.com/2011/12/meet-marie-calloway/#ixzz3BJk03uUZ> (last accessed 13 June 2019).

Stryker, Susan, *Queer Pulp* (San Francisco: Chronicle Books, 2001).

Sycamore, Mattilda Bernstein, 'Gay Shame: From Queer Autonomous Space to Direct Action Extravaganza', in Sycamore (ed.), *That's Revolting! Queer Strategies for Resisting Assimilation* (Brooklyn: Soft Skull Press, 2004), pp. 268–95.

Sykes, Rachel, '"Who Gets to Speak and Why?" Oversharing in Contemporary North American Women's Writing', *Signs: Journal of Women in Culture and Society* 43: 1 (2017): 151–74.

Tarnopolsky, Christina H., *Prudes, Perverts, and Tyrants: Plato's Gorgias and the Politics of Shame* (Princeton: Princeton University Press, 2010).

Taylor, Gabriele, *Pride, Shame, and Guilt: Emotions of Self-Assessment* (Oxford: Clarendon Press, 1985).

Terry, Jennifer, *An American Obsession: Science, Medicine and Homosexuality in Modern Society* (Chicago: University of Chicago Press, 1999).

Tilchen, Maida, 'Ann Bannon: The Mystery Solved!', *Gay Community News* (8 January 1983): 8–12.

Tomkins, Silvan, *Affect, Imagery, Consciousness – Volume II: The Negative Affects* (New York: Springer, 1963).

—, 'Shame-Humiliation and Contempt-Disgust', in Eve Kosofsky Sedgwick and Adam Frank (eds), *Shame and Its Sisters: A Silvan Tomkins Reader* (Durham, NC: Duke University Press, 1995), pp. 133–78.

Torres, Tereska, *Women's Barracks* [1950] (New York: Feminist Press, 2005).

Updike, John, 'Foreword', in Franz Kafka, *The Complete Stories*, ed. Nahum N. Glatzer (New York: Schocken Books, 1971).

Uszkurat, Carol Ann, 'Mid Twentieth Century Romance: Reception and Redress', in Gabriele Griffin (ed.), *Outwrite: Lesbianism and Popular Culture* (London: Pluto Press, 1993), pp. 26–47.

Valenti, Jessica, *Sex Object* (New York: HarperCollins, 2016).

Valovirta, Elina, 'Reading the Intimacies of Shame in Edwidge Danticat's *Breath, Eyes, Memory*', in Jennifer Cooke (ed.), *Scenes of Intimacy* (London: Bloomsbury, 2013), pp. 37–53.

Vance, Carole S. (ed), *Pleasure and Danger: Exploring Female Sexuality* (London: Routledge, 1984).

Villarejo, Amy, *Lesbian Rule: Cultural Criticism and the Value of Desire* (Durham, NC: Duke University Press, 2003).

Wade, Carlson, *The Troubled Sex* (New York: Beacon Envoy, 1961).

Walters, Suzanna Danuta, 'As Her Hand Crept Slowly Up Her Thigh: Ann Bannon and the Politics of Pulp', *Social Text* 23 (Fall/Winter 1989): 83–101.

Warner, Michael, *The Trouble with Normal: Sex, Politics, and the Ethics of Queer Life* (Cambridge, MA: Harvard University Press, 1999).

Weinstein, Jeff, 'In Praise of Pulp: Bannon's Lusty Lesbians', *Village Voice Literary Supplement* (October 1983): 8–9.

Weir, Angela, and Elizabeth Wilson, 'The Greyhound Bus Station in the Evolution of Lesbian Popular Culture', in Sally Munt (ed.), *New Lesbian Criticism* (New York: Columbia University Press, 1992), pp. 95–113.

Wiegman, Robyn, 'Introduction: Antinormativity's Queer Conventions', *differences* 26: 1 (2015): 1–25.

Williams, Bernard, *Shame and Necessity* (Berkeley: University of California Press, 1993).

Wood, James, 'Total Recall: Karl Ove Knausgaard's "My Struggle"', *New Yorker*, 13 August 2012. Available at: <http://www.newyorker.com/magazine/2012/08/13/total-recall> (last accessed 13 June 2019).

Woodward, Kathleen M., 'Late Theory, Late Style', in Anne Wyatt-Brown and Janice Rossen (eds), *Aging and Gender in Literature* (Charlottesville: University of Virginia Press, 1993), pp. 82–101.

—, 'Traumatic Shame: Toni Morrison, Televisual Culture, and the Cultural Politics of the Emotions', *Cultural Critique* 46 (2000): 210–40.

—, *Statistical Panic: Cultural Politics and Poetics of the Emotions* (Durham, NC: Duke University Press, 2009).

Worley, Jennifer, 'The Mid-Century Pulp Novel and the Imagining of Lesbian Community', in Josh Lukin (ed.), *Invisible Suburbs: Recovering Protest Fiction in the 1950s United States* (Jackson: University Press of Mississippi, 2008), pp. 104–23.

Wurmser, Léon, *The Mask of Shame* (Baltimore: Johns Hopkins University Press, 1981).

—, *The Power of the Inner Judge: Psychodynamic Treatment of the Severe Neuroses* (Northvale, NJ: Jason Aronson, 2000).

Young, Elizabeth, 'Books: Hell in Wonderland', *The Independent*, 1 November 1997.

Yusba, Roberta, 'Twilight Tales: Lesbian Pulps 1950–1960', *On Our Backs* 2: 1 (Summer 1985): 30–2.

—, 'Odd Girls and Strange Sisters: Lesbian Pulp Novels of the '50s', *Out/look* (Spring 1991): 34–7.

Zimet, Jaye, *Strange Sisters: The Art of Lesbian Pulp Fiction 1949–1969* (New York: Penguin Putnam, 1999).

Index

Abate, Michelle Ann, 67–8, 68–9, 70, 75, 78–9, 89n40
Acker, Kathy, 184
activism, 10–11, 66, 90n48
  environmental, 10–11
  feminist, 10
  Gay Shame, 90n48
  queer, 66
Adamson, Joseph, 22, 36n29
Adorno, Theodor, 239n49
Aeschylus, 14
  Prometheus Bound, 14
affect, 133–4, 138, 147n190
  and childhood, 100, 103–4, 135, 138
  in queer theory, 3, 6, 31, 46, 55, 56, 105
Agamben, Giorgio, 4–5, 16–17, 36n26, 44n161, 56, 58, 160
Ahmed, Sara, 138
Aidōs, 14–17, 34, 39n74, 247
Aldrich, Ann, 47, 51–2, 58, 86, 88–9n29, 94n127
  We, Too, Must Love, 88–9n29
  We Walk Alone, 51–2, 58, 94n127
  see also Meaker, Marijane; Packer, Vin, 72
Alice in Wonderland, 109
Allison, Dorothy, 26
Amis, Martin, 17, 33, 201, 206, 209, 211–21, 236, 240n70, 241n97, 241n108, 247
  The Pregnant Widow, 33, 201, 206, 211–21, 241n97, 241n108, 247
Anderson, Linda, 171

Angel, Katherine, 30, 32, 153, 157, 159, 175, 184–9, 196n130, 198n160, 247, 250
  Unmastered, 32, 153, 157, 159, 175, 184–9, 196n130, 198n160, 247, 250
Angelides, Steven, 104
Angot, Christine, 29, 191n25
Antelme, Robert, 44n161
Anthony, Andrew, 221, 223, 224, 226, 230
Aristophanes, 43n158
Armstrong, Louise, 104
  Kiss Daddy Goodnight, 104
Ashton, Jennifer, 195–6n123
Atwood, Margaret, 212
  The Handmaid's Tale, 212
Austin, J. L., 91n52,
authenticity, 33, 173–4, 175, 177, 201, 222–3, 235–6
authorship, 25, 32, 33, 43n151, 137–8, 236, 246
autobiography, 25, 28, 32, 42–3n151, 151, 152, 154, 155–6, 156–7, 171–2, 174–6, 179–80, 225, 232
  by women, 151, 156–7, 171–2, 174–6, 179–80, 225, 232
autofiction, 149–89, 155–6, 179–80, 183, 189, 190–1n23, 191n25, 246

Bannon, Ann, 31, 47, 49, 55, 67, 68, 70–5, 77–82, 84, 87n12, 88n25, 92n94, 94n122
  Beebo Brinker, 71, 94n122

Bannon, Ann (*cont.*)
  I Am A Woman, 94n122
  Odd Girl Out, 94n127
  Women in the Shadows, 31, 67, 68,
    70–5, 77–82, 88n25
Barthes, Roland, 239n49
Bartky, Sandra, 2, 12–13, 19–21, 36n28,
    39n70, 40n99, 137, 151, 167, 176,
    183–4, 201, 215, 235, 247
Beckett, Samuel, 202, 239n49
Beethoven, Ludwig Van, 239n49
Believer, The, 172, 190n22
Bellamy, Dodie, 195–6n123, 157, 181,
    191n29
  the buddhist, 157, 181
  When the Sick Rule the World,
    191n29
Belle de Jour, 156, 157
  *The Further Adventures of a
    London Call Girl*, 156
  *The Intimate Adventures of a
    London Call Girl*, 156
Bellil, Samira, 28
Belluscio, Stephen J., 74–5
Benjamin, Jessica, 127
Benjamin, Walter, 202–3
Benns, Susanna, 47–8
Bentley, Toni, 156
  The Surrender, 156
Berger, John, 19
Berlant, Lauren, 66, 86, 144n123, 249
Bersani, Leo, 57
Bewes, Timothy, 23–4, 25–6, 36n29,
    43n151, 153, 170–1, 203–5,
    234–5, 236
Bouson, J. Brooks, 26–7, 36n29,
    41n112, 97, 99–100, 206, 252
Boxall, Peter, 207, 208, 239n49
Brockes, Emma, 33
Brooke-Rose, Christine, 171
Brookner, Anita, 27
Brooks, Peter, 38n38, 152, 157, 158,
    159–60
Broughton, Trev Lynn, 171
Bruhm, Steven, 107
Bulamur, Ayşe Naz, 214–15

Bulhan, Husseen Abdilahi, 40n99
Burman, Erica, 102–3, 104, 114, 140n23
Burroughs, William, 171
Butler, Judith, 69–70, 81, 91n53,
    181, 182
Byatt, A. S., 27

Cairns, Douglas L., 14–15, 17
Calle, Sophie, 165–6, 167
Calloway, Marie, 30, 32, 34, 150,
    152, 153, 154, 155, 157, 159,
    160, 161–4, 165, 167, 168–70,
    171, 173–4, 175, 180–1, 182–3,
    185, 186, 187, 193n57, 196n130,
    197n140, 246, 247, 250, 252
  *what purpose did i serve in your
    life*, 32, 153, 154, 155, 157, 159,
    160, 161–4, 165, 167, 168–70,
    171, 173–4, 175, 180–1, 182–3,
    185, 186, 187, 193n57, 196n130,
    197n140, 246, 247, 250, 252
camp, 51, 82–4, 85, 89n40, 253n18
Carroll, Rachel, 167
Carson, Anne, ii, 15, 16, 17, 34,
    39n74, 149
Carter, Angela, 28, 135–6
Carver, Lisa, 165, 197n140
Caselli, Daniela, 100
Castañeda, Claudia, 103
Cavafy, C. P., 239n49
Chamarette, Jenny, 37n29
child abuse, 7, 17, 25, 31, 99, 100,
    104–5, 107, 108, 109, 110–11,
    112–13, 114, 115, 116–18, 119,
    120–1, 124–5, 128–9, 131,
    136–7, 251
  explosion of interest in, 104–5
  feminist accounts of, 104–5
  and the figure of the paedophile,
    116–18
  moral panic about, 104–5
childhood, 30, 31, 57, 99, 100–8, 114,
    117, 119–20, 122, 124, 125, 127,
    128–9, 130–1, 135, 136–7, 138,
    144n126
  and affect, 100, 103–4, 135, 138

eroticisation of, 108, 117, 122
and innocence, 101, 108, 124
queer childhood, 57, 105, 107
and sexuality, 122, 124, 125, 128–9
and shame, 100–3, 106–7, 136–7
Christian, Paula, 47, 87n12
Clark, Hilary, 22, 26, 36n29, 41n112
Cleis Press, 67, 92n94
Coetzee, J. M., 24, 25–6, 202, 203, 234–5
   Diary of a Bad Year, 203, 234–5
   Disgrace, 203
   The Master of Petersburg, 234
Colette, 87n15
Collard, Christopher, 43n158
confession, 7, 17, 32, 38n38, 43, 152, 153, 157–60, 167, 173, 174–7, 179–80, 182, 183, 184, 191n29, 205, 207, 211, 234, 246, 250
   as feminist strategy, 174–6, 179, 182, 184, 185
   and oversharing, 160, 179–80
Connor, Steven, 32–3, 199–200, 202, 205, 206, 207, 211, 214, 215, 235, 236, 246
Conrad, Joseph, 17, 203–5, 238n32
   The Return, 203–5, 238n32
Cooke, Jennifer, 153, 163, 170, 177, 179, 190n19, 252, 254n24
Courtman, Nicholas, 40n90
Crewdson, Gregory, 135–6
Crimp, Douglas, 62
Cropp, Martin, 43n158
Cusk, Rachel, 156, 233, 243n141
   A Life's Work, 243n141
Cusset, Catherine, 156, 191n25
Cvetkovich, Ann, 55, 62

Damon, Gene, 87–8n15, 92n97
   see also Grier, Barbara
Danticat, Edwidge, 26
Darwin, Charles, 169
Deleuze, Gilles, 43n151, 176, 199, 201
DeLillo, Don, 239n49
D'Emilio, John, 47

Derrida, Jacques, 91n52
Devi, Ananda, 28
Doan, Laura, 89–90n41
Doubrovsky, Serge, 155, 190–1n23
   Fils, 155, 190–1n23
Douglas, Alfred, 56, 90n46
Duras, Marguerite, 191n25

Edelman, Lee, 57, 91–2n73
Edwards, Natalie, 29
Eliot, George, 22
   Middlemarch, 22
Enriquez, Mariana, 251
   Things We Lost in the Fire, 251
Er, Yanbing, 179–80
Ernaux, Annie, 29, 191n25
Esquire, 197n140
Etzioni, Amitai, 9
Euripides, ii, 14, 15–17, 34, 43n158, 149
   Fragments, 43n158
   Hippolytus, ii, 15–17, 34, 43n158
   Hippolytus Veiled, 34, 43n158, 149
   Iphigenia at Aulis, 14
   Phaidra, ii, 15–17, 34, 149–50, 189, 250

Faderman, Lillian, 46–7
Fanon, Frantz, 40n99, 215
Fateman, Johanna, 185, 193n57
Fayard, Nicole, 28
Felski, Rita, 126–7, 157, 174–5, 184
feminism
   backlash against, the, 220, 248–9
   and body art, 178–9, 182, 196n123
   and child abuse, 104–5
   and confession, 174–6, 179, 182, 184, 185
   and masculinity, 200, 211, 212, 213, 220–1, 240n70
   and masochism, 126
   'parasitical feminism', 166
   and 'problematic' desires, 153, 186–7, 197–8n156
   and shame, 1, 10, 6, 10, 13–14, 20–1, 36n28 248

Fernie, Ewan, 37n29, 41n112
Firestone, Shulamith, 212
Fisher, Anna Watkins, 165–6
Flavorwire, 197n140
Foote, Stephanie, 48, 49, 51–2, 86
Foucault, Michel, 52, 152, 158,
    159, 186
Frank, Adam, 36n23, 37n30
Freud, Sigmund, 2, 5–6, 17–18,
    40n90, 101, 102, 105, 110, 125,
    176, 202, 237n15, 239n49
Friedländer, Saul, 202

Gaitskill, Mary, 30, 31, 34, 98, 99–
    100, 102, 103, 104, 105, 106–7,
    108, 119–35, 136, 138, 144n113,
    145–6n157, 146n169, 146n171,
    147n191, 147n198, 148n215,
    152, 252
    Bad Behaviour, 126
    Two Girls, Fat and Thin, 30, 31,
        99–100, 102, 103, 104, 105,
        106–7, 108, 119–35, 136,
        144n113, 144n123, 145–6n157,
        146n169, 146n171, 147n191,
        147n198, 252
Gay, Roxane, 197–8n156
    Bad Feminist, 197–8n156
Gay Shame activism, 90n48
Genet, Jean, 91n50, 202, 239n49
Gill, Jo, 38n38, 158, 159
Gilmore, Leigh, 159, 171
Ginsberg, Elaine K., 75
Goffman, Erving, 105
Gould, Emily, 150–2, 157
    And the Heart Says Whatever, 157
Gregg, Melissa, 147n190
Gregory, Elizabeth, 157
Grier, Barbara, 87–8n15, 92n97
    see also Damon, Gene
Guenther, Lisa, 44n161
Gullette, Margaret Morganroth, 114

Hacking, Ian, 104
Hainey, Bruce, 184
Halberstam, J., 65–6, 165

Hall, Radclyffe, 47, 87n15
Halperin, David, 29, 56, 63–5, 85
Hamer, Diane, 71, 94n122
Hardie, Melissa, 126, 130, 134,
    144n113
Hawkins, Joan, 172
Hazlitt, 197n140
Heller, Tamar, 28
Henke, Suzette A., 28
Herman, Judith, 104
Herzen, Alexander, 212
Heti, Sheila, 33, 156, 172, 174, 179,
    190n22
    How Should a Person Be?, 179
Highsmith, Patricia, 46
    The Price of Salt/Carol, 46
Hirsch, Gordon, 22
Hoby, Hermione, 221, 233
Holocaust, the, 6, 24, 36n26, 44n161,
    203
Homes, A. M., 30, 31, 34, 98, 99,
    103, 104, 105, 106–7, 107–8,
    108–19, 122–3, 124, 128,
    135–6, 137–8, 142n65, 142n71,
    143n101, 152, 246
    The End of Alice, 30, 31, 98, 99,
        103, 104, 105, 106–7, 107–8,
        108–19, 122–3, 124, 128,
        135–6, 137–8, 142n65, 142n71,
        143n101, 152
    Music for Torching, 138
homosexuality, 31, 46, 48, 50, 51, 52,
    53, 56–66, 68–9, 71–2, 73, 75,
    78–82, 83, 84, 85, 89n41, 105–6,
    138, 248, 250
Hughes, Evan, 234
humiliation, 7, 25, 32, 62, 128, 132,
    134–5, 150–1, 152, 153, 160,
    161–2, 164, 165, 166, 168, 177,
    185, 187, 200, 202, 203, 208,
    209, 218, 221, 223, 226–7,
    228, 230, 231, 236, 237n6,
    237n8, 250
Hurley, Natasha, 107
Hustvedt, Siri, 224–5, 227, 230,
    232, 233

identity politics, 3, 10, 45, 138, 248
Ivanova, Velichka, 211, 24n65

Jacquet, Jennifer, 10–11, 38n58,
    248
Jagose, Annamarie, 89–90n41
James, Allison, 122
James, Henry, 173
Jamison, Leslie, 191n29
    The Empathy Exams, 191n29
    The Recovering, 191n29
Jelinek, Estelle, 171
Jenks, Chris, 122
Johnson, Erica L., 27–8, 97–8, 99,
    100, 206
Jones, Amelia, 178–9
Joyce, James, 171

Kafka, Franz, 24, 202–3, 208
Kahan, Dan K., 9
Kakutani, Michiko, 109, 142n71
Kang, Han, 251
    The Vegetarian, 251
Kaufman, Gershen, 4
Keller, Yvonne, 47, 51, 67
Kerényi, Karl, 16–17
Kincaid, James R., 108, 110, 111, 113,
    116–17, 136
Kitzinger, Jenny, 124
Knausgaard, Karl Ove, 33, 156,
    191n26, 201, 221–36, 246, 247
    *My Struggle I: A Death in the
    Family*, 223–4
    My Struggle II: A Man in Love, 33,
    201, 221–36
    Out of the World, 221
Koestenbaum, Wayne, 200, 202, 227,
    231, 236, 237n8
Kraus, Chris, 30, 32, 34, 152, 153,
    154–5, 156, 157, 159, 160–1,
    164, 165–7, 169, 171–3, 174,
    175, 176–82, 183–4, 185, 186,
    187, 190n22, 195n116, 196n123,
    196n130, 247
    Aliens and Anorexia, 154, 195n116
    Gravity and Grace, 154

I Love Dick, 32, 153, 154–5, 157,
    159, 160–1, 164, 165–7, 169,
    171–3, 174, 175, 176–82,
    183–4, 185, 186, 187, 190n22,
    196n130, 247
    Summer of Hate, 155
    Torpor, 155
Kunzru, Hari, 221, 222

Ladder, The, 72, 87–8n15, 92n97,
    94n122
Laing, Olivia, 156, 157
    Crudo, 157
Laplanche, Jean, 35n4
Larsen, Nella, 81
Lasch, Christopher, 7, 37n35, 175
Laurens, Camille, 156, 191n25
Lea, Daniel, 221
Lee, Abby, 156
    Girl with a One-Track Mind, 156
Lehtinen, Ullaliina, 36n28
Lerner, Ben, 156
Lesbian Herstory Archive, the, 55,
    88n23, 95n166
lesbianism, 46–55, 58, 64, 67–86,
    87–8n15, 88n23, 88–9n29,
    89–90n41, 92n97, 93n106,
    93n115, 93n116, 94n122, 94n127,
    95n166, 99, 248, 250, 253n18
    butch/femme, 50, 68–70, 75, 76, 79,
    88n25, 93n106, 93n115
    passing, 67, 72, 74–5, 84
    sexological theories of, 58–9, 69
    and tomboys, 67–9, 70–1
lesbian pulp fiction, 1, 31, 46–55,
    67–86, 87–8n15, 88n23, 88–9n29,
    92n97, 93n106, 93n115, 93n116,
    94n122, 94n127, 94,n132,
    95n166, 99, 250, 253n18
Lesnik-Oberstein, Karín, 100, 103
Lessing, Doris, 27
Levinas, Emmanuel, 3, 5
Lewis, Helen Block, 18, 40n91
Lewis, Michael, 20, 39n64
Leys, Ruth, 1–3, 6, 7, 13, 14, 19,
    35n5, 36n26, 247, 248, 252

Lin, Tao, 174
Lindo, Karen, 28
Liptrot, Amy, 191n29
  The Outrun, 191n29
Litvak, Joseph, 57
Livesey, Margot, 137, 142n71, 143n101
Locke, Jill, 9–10, 13–14, 36n27,
    38n52, 249
Loewenstein, Andrea, 49, 50, 88n20
Love, Heather, 37n30, 42–3n151, 50,
    53, 56, 62–3, 82–3, 84, 85,
    105, 106
Lowell, Robert, 157
Lynch, Lee, 50
Lynd, Helen Merrell, 6
Luckhurst, Roger, 54, 104–5

McEwan, Ian, 206
  On Chesil Beach, 206
Machado, Carmen Maria, 250–1
  Her Body and Other Parties, 250–1
Mackintosh, Sophie, 251
  The Water Cure, 251
Manion, Jennifer C., 18, 19, 20,
    36n25, 36n28, 39n64, 253n3
Mann, Thomas, 114, 239n49
  Death in Venice, 114
Martin, Della, 31, 55, 67, 68–70, 73,
    74, 75–7, 79, 81, 92n97, 93n106
  Twilight Girl, 31, 67, 68–70, 73, 74,
    75–7, 79, 81, 92n97, 93n106
masculinity, 32–3, 66, 184, 188, 189,
    200–2, 206–8, 209, 211, 215,
    219, 220–1, 222, 223, 224, 226,
    227, 235–6, 247
  and ageing, 206, 207
  in crisis, 209, 215, 219, 220–1, 223
  and lateness, 207, 208
  and sexual potency, 188, 206
  in women, 68, 69, 71, 75, 84
masochism, 25, 98, 125–7, 128–9,
    137, 161–2, 164, 174, 182, 206,
    250, 252
  Mayo, Dallas, 87n12
  Meaker, Marijane, 47
    see also Aldrich, Ann

Meeker, Martin, 52
Meinhof, Ulrike, 155
Melville, Herman, 202
Mendible, Myra, 36n27, 37n35
Merkin, Daphne, 137, 142n71
Meulenbelt, Anja, 247
Meyer, Moe, 83, 84
Millet, Catherine, 156
  The Sexual Life of Catherine M, 156
Millett, Kate, 50, 164, 175, 193n57
misery memoirs, 7, 104–5, 248
Moi, Toril, 222, 230, 233–4
Molotkow, Alexandra, 169
Moon, Jennifer, 62–3
Moran, Brendan, 202–3
Moran, Patricia, 27–8, 97–8, 99,
    100, 206
Morgan, Michael L., 36n26
Morrison, Andrew P., 100, 102
Morrison, Blake, 144n126
Morrison, Toni, 26, 91n50, 97, 206,
    252
Mortimer, Armine Kotin, 156
Moynihan, Sinéad, 67
Muñoz, José, 57
Munro, Alice, 26, 97
Munt, Sally, 14, 37n30, 61, 98, 99, 153
Myles, Eileen, 32, 160, 165

Nabokov, Vladimir, 109–10, 142n64,
    142n65
  Lolita, 109–10, 142n65
Naiad Press, 49
Nathanson, Donald, 36n24
Nealon, Christopher, 46, 49, 51, 52,
    53, 71, 73, 79–80, 82, 88n23,
    93n115, 253n18
Nelson, Maggie, 156
  The Argonauts, 156
  Bluets, 156
Nestle, Joan, 49
New York Magazine, 148n215, 227
New York Times, 109, 137, 142n71
Nussbaum, Emily, 148n215
Nussbaum, Martha, 5, 8–9, 35n5,
    36n25, 250

Offill, Jenny, 179
  Dept. of Speculation, 179
O'Sullivan, Simon, 147n190

Packer, Vin, 72
  Spring Fire, 72
paedophilia *see* child abuse
Paris Review, 223
passing, 31, 67, 70, 72, 73, 74–5,
    78, 84
Patnoe, Elizabeth, 142n65
Pelzer, Dave, 104
  A Child Called 'It', 104
Percesepe, Gary, 144n113
performativity, 57, 74, 83
Phillips, Caryl, 24
Pine, Emilie, 157
  Notes to Self, 157
Pines, Malcolm, 17–18, 101, 121,
    237n15
Plath, Sylvia, 157
Pollitt, Katha, 215, 240n70
Pontalis, Jean-Bertrand, 35n4
poststructuralism, 3, 10, 55
Probyn, Elspeth, 23, 37n30, 42n151,
    61, 85–6, 137, 153, 170, 231
Proust, Marcel, 33, 233, 235, 246
Prout, Alan, 122, 140n23
psychoanalysis, 2, 5–6, 7, 17–18,
    35n4, 40n90, 101, 102, 105, 110,
    125, 176, 202, 237n15, 239n49
  see also Freud, Sigmund

queer theory, 46, 55, 56–66

race, 26, 31, 45, 51, 59, 62, 67,
    74, 75–82, 214, 217, 219–20,
    241n106, 241n108, 246, 252
  and anti-miscegenation laws, 80
  and passing, 31, 67, 70, 72, 73,
    74–5, 78, 84
Rand, Ayn, 126, 143–4n113
rape, 12, 72, 108, 111, 122, 123,
    142n65, 162, 192n38, 203, 252,
    254n24
reality television, 7, 216, 248

Rhys, Jean, 28
Riley, Denise, 25
Roisman, Hanna M., 43n158
Ronson, Jon, 8–9, 12, 248
Rose, Jacqueline, 102
Roth, Philip, 17, 33, 201, 206,
    207–11, 216, 217–19, 220–1,
    236, 239n45, 239n49, 240n65,
    240n67, 241n106, 247
  The Dying Animal, 33, 201, 206,
    207, 209–11, 216, 217–19,
    220–1, 236, 240n65, 240n67,
    241n106, 247
  Everyman, 207, 239n45
  Exit Ghost, 206, 207, 208
  The Humbling, 206, 207
  Indignation, 207
  Portnoy's Complaint, 239n59
Rothman, Joshua, 234
Rush, Florence, 104
Rushdie, Salman, 203
  Shame, 203

Said, Edward W., 208, 239n49
Salem, Randy, 50
Sartre, Jean-Paul, 4, 5, 195n102
Scappettone, Jennifer, 195–6n123
Schapiro, Barbara, 126, 127, 128,
    134–5
Schillinger, Liesl, 232
Schmitt, Arnaud, 155
Schoene, Berthold, 221
Sedgwick, Eve Kosofsky, 3, 4, 6, 30,
    37n30, 57–62, 63, 106–7, 137,
    138, 147n191, 160, 164,
    248, 249
Segal, Lynne, 207–8, 210, 220–1,
    223, 239n45
Seigworth, Gregory J., 147n190
Seltzer, Mark, 7
sexology, 58, 69
Sexton, Anne, 157
shame
  and ageing, 30, 43n151, 114,
    206–8, 209, 214, 218
  and *aidōs*, 14–17, 34, 247

shame (*cont.*)

and authenticity, 33, 173, 175, 177, 201, 222, 229, 235, 236

and childhood, 30, 31, 57, 86, 99, 100–4, 106–7, 125, 136

and confession, 7, 17, 32, 38n38, 43, 152, 153, 157–60, 167, 173, 174–7, 179–80, 182, 183, 184, 191n29, 205, 207, 211, 234, 246, 250

as contagious, 28, 58, 98, 108, 118, 130, 164, 204, 249

death of, the, 9–10, 14

and desire, 1, 15, 16, 23, 30, 31, 34, 51, 62, 77, 83, 98, 105, 108, 112–13, 115, 117, 118, 124, 125, 129, 149–50, 153–4, 161, 167, 185–9, 200, 205, 208, 214, 217, 247, 249, 250, 251, 252

and disgust, 5–6, 29, 31, 80, 98, 109, 111, 114, 115, 122, 123–4, 134, 177, 208, 211, 217, 228–9, 237n15

and embarrassment, 42n151, 150, 152, 177, 178, 206

and embodiment, 1, 12–13, 18, 19, 20, 26, 33, 34, 39n70, 54, 71, 80, 93n115, 100, 101, 105, 115, 118, 120–1, 122, 123, 128, 129, 133, 134, 137, 147n190, 151, 165, 167, 169, 178–9, 185, 188, 189, 191n29, 195–6n123, 206, 207, 208, 209–11, 213, 214, 217–19, 224, 246, 249, 250–1

eroticisation of, 1, 16, 98, 99, 113, 118, 125, 153, 157

and exhibitionism, 6, 25, 102, 111, 160, 173

and the face/blush, 5, 9, 14–15, 16, 23, 44n161, 58, 74, 84, 113, 118, 169–70, 185, 214, 228, 233, 241n108, 246

and feminism, 1, 6, 10, 13, 20–1, 49, 65, 104, 153, 158, 166, 168, 174–5, 178–9, 182, 184, 186–7, 197–8n156, 200, 211, 212–13, 220, 240n70, 248–9

and femininity, 1, 12, 13, 14–22, 27–8, 30, 32, 33, 34, 36n28, 39n70, 40n90, 59–60, 66, 71, 86, 100, 106, 126, 137, 138, 139, 151–2, 157–8, 171, 176, 181, 183, 189, 201–2, 211, 213, 215, 223, 225, 226–7, 236, 246–7, 251, 252

and guilt, 1–3, 6, 7, 10–11, 13, 17–18, 18, 59, 85, 116, 157, 202, 206, 215, 243n141, 247, 252

and homosexuality, 31, 46, 48, 50, 51, 52, 53, 56–66, 68–9, 71–2, 73, 75, 78–82, 83, 84, 85, 89n41, 105–6, 138, 248, 250

and humiliation, 7, 25, 32, 62, 128, 132, 134–5, 150–1, 152, 153, 160, 161–2, 164, 165, 166, 168, 177, 185, 187, 200, 202, 203, 208, 209, 218, 221, 223, 226–7, 228, 230, 231, 236, 237n6, 237n8, 250

and identity, 2–5, 7, 10, 45, 56, 57–60, 61, 63, 74–5, 76, 80, 105–6, 119, 121, 137, 203, 233–4, 248

and identity politics, 3, 10, 45, 138, 248

and interest, 23, 60, 61, 119

and the law, 8–10

and masculinity, 32–3, 66, 184, 188, 189, 200–2, 206–8, 209, 211, 215, 219, 220–1, 222, 223, 224, 226, 227, 235–6, 247

and morality, 2, 6–7, 8, 10, 13, 16, 18, 20, 23, 34, 35n5, 37n35, 60, 85, 102, 121, 135–6, 147n201, 176, 202, 222, 229, 237n8, 237n15, 247, 249

philosophical accounts of, 1, 2, 3–5, 6, 16–17, 35n5, 201, 202–3, 205, 234

and pleasure, 12, 16, 19, 29, 30, 50, 51, 59, 82, 98, 99, 107–8, 110, 116, 117, 123, 136, 138, 150, 152, 159–60, 164, 185, 187, 216, 222, 250, 251, 253n18 and pride, 6, 12–13, 25, 30, 45, 56, 58, 62, 63–5, 85, 90n48, 105, 160, 167, 207, 248

psychoanalytic accounts of, 1, 2, 5–7, 17–18, 22, 40n90, 100–2, 121, 137, 201, 205–6, 237n15

and queer theory, 30–1, 37n30, 45–6, 51, 53, 54–5, 56–66, 85–6, 91n50, 91–2n73, 99, 105–6, 107, 201, 246, 248

and race, 26, 31, 45, 51, 59, 62, 67, 74, 75–82, 214, 217, 219–20, 241n106, 241n108, 246, 252

and the reader, 25, 28, 29, 30, 31–2, 44n161, 48, 49–51, 74, 82, 85, 87–8n15, 88n29, 98, 99, 108–9, 111–12, 116, 118–19, 168, 169, 175, 233–4, 246, 250, 253n18

redemptive accounts of, 1, 7, 22, 26–9, 31, 32, 57, 98–9, 100, 107, 135, 139, 150, 152–3, 158, 183, 205–6, 208–9, 245, 247, 249

and the regulation of behaviour, 1, 5–6, 10, 11, 23, 45, 52, 56, 63, 86, 105, 178, 183, 189, 202, 211–12, 222, 237n8

and sadomasochism, 25, 98, 125–7, 128–9, 137, 164, 174, 206

and selfhood/subjectivity, 1, 2–5, 7, 20, 28, 29, 38n58, 56, 58–60, 64, 83, 105, 127, 153, 180, 183, 245, 252

and sexual propriety, 15–16, 149, 203–5

and the sexual revolution, 212–13, 215, 216–17

and shamelessness, 1, 2, 5, 8, 9, 10, 14, 28, 29, 37n35, 85, 111, 150, 153–4, 158, 160, 203, 204, 210, 211, 212, 218, 247, 249

and (acts of) shaming, 2, 5, 6, 7, 8–13, 28, 29, 30, 31, 58, 98, 101, 114, 151, 154, 170, 183, 189, 197n140, 203, 213, 223, 224, 236, 246, 248–9, 250

and solidarity, 21, 31, 53, 61, 85, 105, 138, 175, 183–4, 249–50, 252

and/as spectacle, 7, 13, 19, 27, 51, 74, 84, 109, 110–11, 117, 119, 150, 151, 154, 158, 164, 167–8, 180, 183, 217, 222, 246, 250

as structural, 1, 10, 18, 21, 27, 30, 32, 33, 54, 60, 66, 73, 86, 99, 139, 151, 174, 176, 177, 178, 180, 181–2, 183–4, 187, 202, 245, 252

transmissibility of, 27, 44n161, 51, 98, 99, 108, 109, 119, 152, 164–5, 168, 204, 233, 249

and trauma, 3, 7, 24, 26, 55, 62, 97, 104–5, 108, 121, 128, 211–12, 213, 219

and visibility/the gaze, 2, 4, 5, 9, 14–15, 19, 31, 48, 50–1, 67, 70, 71–2, 73–4, 79, 80, 83, 84, 111, 118, 121, 125, 129, 150, 169–70, 223, 227–30, 233, 246

and vulnerability, 17, 20, 22, 30, 32, 33, 114, 124, 152, 153, 154, 160, 161, 163, 173, 181–3, 187–8, 189, 196n123, 196n130, 201, 207–8, 209, 215, 226–7, 229, 232, 249, 250

and Western 'shame culture', 1–3, 6–11, 13–14, 65, 152, 247–8

and women's writing, 26–8, 135–9, 184, 202, 205–6, 225, 232, 250–1

and writing, 1, 21, 22–9, 32, 44n161, 50, 51, 98–9, 100, 135–8, 150, 151–2, 153, 157–8, 167, 168, 170–4, 181, 184, 199–201, 202–3, 205–6, 223, 224–5, 230–2, 233, 234–6, 245–6, 250–1

Sharpe, Matthew, 135

Sheils, Barry, 21–2, 25, 28, 29, 37n29, 245

Shute, Jenefer, 97

Slate magazine, 197n140

Smith, Zadie, 138

Snediker, Michael D., 45, 59–60, 61
Solnit, Rebecca, 192n38
Sontag, Susan, 83, 186
Sophocles, 14
Spahr, Juliana, 196n123
Spiers, Elizabeth, 197n140
Spitzer, Michael, 239n49
Stacey, Jackie, 102, 114
Stein, Arlene, 10, 37n35
Stein, Gertrude, 87n15, 171
Stein, Lorin, 223
stigma, 9, 30, 57, 73, 79, 83, 105, 112, 119, 124, 138, 214, 236, 246
  and 'spoiled identity', 105
Stockton, Kathryn Bond, 57, 81–2, 86, 91n50, 107, 122
Strauss, Richard, 239n49
Sykes, Rachel, 179–80

Tarantino, Quentin, 91n50
Tarnopolsky, Christina H., 36n27
Taylor, Gabriele, 19, 36n25
Taylor, Valerie, 50, 87n12
Thek, Paul, 155
Thomson, Stephen, 103
Torres, Tereska, 87n14
  Women's Barracks, 87n14
Tomkins, Silvan, 6, 23, 25, 29, 37n30, 46, 57, 59, 60, 100, 160, 170, 233, 237n6
Townsend, Catherine, 157
  Sleeping Around, 157
Traub, Valerie, 29, 56, 63–5, 85
trauma, 3, 7, 24, 26, 55, 62, 97, 104–5, 108, 121, 128, 211–12, 213, 219
Twain, Mark, 209

Updike, John, 202
Uszkurat, Carol Ann, 49

Valenti, Jessica, 197n156
  Sex Object, 197n156
Vanity Fair, 135
Vice Magazine, 165
Village Voice, 49
Villarejo, Amy, 51, 84
vulnerability, 17, 20, 22, 30, 32, 33, 114, 124, 152, 153, 154, 160, 161, 163, 173, 181–3, 187–8, 189, 196n123, 196n130, 201, 207–8, 209, 215, 226–7, 229, 232, 249, 250

Walsh, Joanna, 156–7
  break.up, 156–7
Walsh, Julie, 21–2, 25, 28, 29, 37n29, 245
Warhol, Andy, 184
Warner, Michael, 30, 45, 62, 85
Waters, Sarah, 89n41
Weil, Simone, 28, 155, 177, 184, 195n116
Weinstein, Jeff, 49
Wiegman, Robyn, 63
Wilde, Oscar, 56
Williams, Bernard, 36n25
Witt, Emily, 157
  Future Sex, 157
Wolf, Naomi, 26
Wood, James, 232
Woodward, Kathleen, 138, 239n49
Woolf, Virginia, 186
Wurmser, Léon, 36n24, 100, 102

Young, Stephanie, 196n123